THE SHOP ON BLOSSOM STREET

Four lives knit together...

There's a little yarn shop on Blossom Street in Seattle. It's owned by Lydia Hoffman, and it represents her dream of a new life free from cancer. A life that offers a chance at love... Lydia teaches knitting to beginners, and the first class is 'How to Make a Baby Blanket'. Jacqueline Donovan wants to knit something for her grandchild, Carol feels her blanket is a message of hope as she makes a final attempt to conceive – and Alix is knitting *her* blanket for a court-ordered community service project. As they knit, the four make unexpected discoveries about themselves ... and each other.

THE SHOP ON
BLOSSOM STREET

The Shop On Blossom Street

by

Debbie Macomber

Magna Large Print Books
Long Preston, North Yorkshire,
BD23 4ND, England.

British Library Cataloguing in Publication Data.

Macomber, Debbie
    The shop on Blossom Street.

    A catalogue record of this book is
    available from the British Library

    ISBN   978-0-7505-3137-5

Magna Large Print is an imprint of Library Magna Books Ltd.

Printed and bound in Great Britain by
T.J. (International) Ltd., Cornwall, PL28 8RW

Dear Reader,

My life is filled with passions, and one of the strongest is knitting. I've had a pair of knitting needles in my hands from the time I was twelve, and intermittently knitted while raising my four children. However, it wasn't until my grandchildren started to arrive that I fell so passionately in love with knitting. This fire was stoked by two wonderful friends, Linda Johnson, who owns Linda's Knit 'n Stitch in Silverdale, Washington, and Laura Early, a lifelong knitter and yarn connoisseur. Laura heads up the knitting and crocheting group at the local senior center, and cajoles and bullies me into one project after another. Both friends have blessed my life.

With *The Shop on Blossom Street* I've been able to combine my love of writing and my love of knitting. The idea for this book has been forming in my mind for the past three or four years. It took that long to find the right characters and the right way in which to tell their stories.

My heartfelt appreciation to Ann Norling for her contribution. She gave me this baby blanket (or lap robe) pattern solely for *The Shop on Blossom Street*. I have knitted the pattern myself, so if you'd like to view the finished product you can check out my Web site at www.debbiemacomber.com.

Several prominent designers have given me quotes about their philosophies of knitting. If you're part of the knitting world, you'll be impressed. If you're not a knitter, you might be compelled to check out your local yarn store and pick up a pair of needles for yourself. You won't be sorry.

Just before *The Shop on Blossom Street* was published in hardcover, I was asked to be a national board member for Warm Up America! If you'd like to be part of this wonderful organization, get in touch with the Warm Up America! Foundation, 2500 Lowell Road, Ranlo, NC 28054. (Or you can call 1-800-662-9999. Visit their Web site at www.WarmUpAmerica.com.) Knitters and crocheters can submit seven-by-nine-inch patches, which will be stitched together to make blankets (or you can submit an entire blanket) for a variety of knitting charities. I'd like to encourage you to get together with friends and knit (or crochet) for charity.

I hope you enjoy *The Shop on Blossom Street*. Lydia, Jacqueline, Carol and Alix are eager to introduce themselves to you. My prayer is that these four women will touch your life in the same way they have mine.

Hearing from my readers is a constant source of joy and encouragement to me. You can reach me either by writing to P.O. Box 1458, Port Orchard, WA 98366 or logging on to my Web site at the address listed above and signing the guest book.

Warmest regards,

Debbie Macomber

To Linda Johnson
for sharing her love of knitting with me.
To Laura Early for taking me under her wing.
And to Lisa, who touched my heart
in her desire for a child.

Baby Blocks
by Ann Norling

Finished Measurements: 33 x 45 inches (crib size)

Materials: 1300 yds worsted weight yarn (600 grams), 2 markers

Gauge: 5 sts = 1" on #8 needle (or size that will give you the gauge)

Needles: 26"-36" circular #8

Glossary: K = knit, P = purl, rep = repeat, st(s) = stitch(es)

Stitch Note: When you see *K3, P3* or a similar stitch group, it means that you repeat whatever is enclosed within the asterisks.

Cast on 171 sts

Border:

Row 1: *K3, P3* across row ending with K3

Row 2: *P3 K3* across row ending with P3

Row 3: RepRow1

Row 4: Rep Row 2

Row 5: *P3 K3* across row ending with P3

Row 6: *K3, P3* across row ending with K3

Row 7: Rep Row 5

Row 8: Rep Row 6

Rows 9-12: Rep Rows 1-4 once more

Body:

Row 13: P3, K3, P3, *K9, P9* across row to last 18 sts, place marker, K9, P3, K3, P3

Row 14: K3, P3, K3, *P9, K9* across row to last 18 sts, place marker, P9, K3, P3, K3

Row 15: Rep Row 13

Row 16: Rep Row 14

Row 17: K3, P3, K3, *K9, P9* across row to last 18 sts, slip marker, K9, K3, P3, K3

Row 18: P3, K3, P3, *P9, K9* across row to last 18 sts, slip marker, P9, P3, K3, P3

Row 19: Rep Row 17

Row 20: Rep Row 18

Row 21-24: Rep Rows 13-16

Row 25: K3, P3, K3, *P9, K9* across row to last 18 sts, slip marker, P9, K3, P3, K3

Row 26: P3, K3, P3, *K9, P9* across row to last 18 sts, slip marker, K9, P3, K3, P3

Row 27: Rep Row 25

Row 28: Rep Row 26

Row 29: P3, K3, P3, *P9, K9* across row to last 18 sts, slip marker, P9, P3, K3, P3

Row 30: K3, P3, K3, *K9, P9* across row to last 18 sts, slip marker, K9, K3, P3, K3

Row 31: Rep Row 29

Row 32: Rep Row 30

Row 33-36: Rep Rows 25-28

Rep Rows 13-36 until piece measures approximately 42' and you have worked Row 36.

Border Repeat:

Rep rows 1-12. Bind off loosely and finish off ends.

CHAPTER 1

The yarn forms the stitches, the knitting forges the friendships, the craft links the generations.'

Karen Alfke, 'Unpattern'
designer and knitting instructor

LYDIA HOFFMAN

The first time I saw the empty store on Blossom Street I thought of my father. It reminded me so much of the bicycle shop he had when I was a kid. Even the large display windows, shaded by a colorful striped awning, were the same. Outside my dad's shop, there were flower boxes full of red blossoms – impatiens – that spilled over beneath the large windows. That was Mom's contribution: impatiens in the spring and summer, chrysanthemums in the fall and shiny green mistletoe at Christmas. I plan to have flowers, too.

Dad's business grew steadily and he moved into increasingly larger premises, but I always loved his first store best.

I must have astounded the rental agent who was showing me the property. She'd barely unlocked the front door when I announced, 'I'll take it.'

She turned to face me, her expression blank as if she wasn't sure she'd heard me correctly. 'Wouldn't you like to see the place? You do realize there's a small apartment above the shop that comes with it, don't you?'

'Yes, you mentioned that earlier.' The apartment worked perfectly for me. My cat, Whiskers, and I were in need of a home.

'You *would* like to see the place before you sign the papers, wouldn't you?' she persisted.

I smiled and nodded. But it wasn't really necessary; instinctively I knew this was the ideal location for my yarn shop. And for me.

The one drawback was that this Seattle neighborhood was undergoing extensive renovations and, because of the construction mess, Blossom Street was closed at one end, with only local traffic allowed. The brick building across the street, which had once been a three-story bank, was being transformed into high-end condos. Several other buildings, including an old warehouse, were also in the process of becoming condos. The architect had somehow managed to maintain the traditional feel of the original places, and that delighted me. Construction would continue for months, but it did mean that my rent was reasonable, at least for now.

I knew the first six months would be difficult. They are for any small business. The constant construction might create more obstacles than there otherwise would have been; nevertheless, I loved the space. It was everything I wanted.

Early Friday morning, a week after viewing the property, I signed my name, Lydia Hoffman, to the two-year lease. I was handed the keys and a copy of the rental agreement. I moved into my new home that very day, as excited as I can remember being about anything. I felt as if I was just starting my life and in more ways than I care to count, I actually was.

I opened A Good Yarn on the last Tuesday in April. I felt a sense of pride and anticipation as I stood in the middle of my store, surveying the colors that surrounded me. I could only imagine what my sister would say when she learned I'd gone through with this. I hadn't asked her advice because I already knew what Margaret's response would be. She isn't – to put it mildly – the encouraging type.

I'd found a carpenter who'd built some cubicles for me, three rows of them, painted a pristine white. Most of the yarn had arrived on Friday and I'd spent the weekend sorting it by weight and color and arranging it neatly in the cubicles. I'd bought a secondhand cash register, refinished the counter and set up racks of knitting supplies. I was ready for business.

This should have been a happy moment for me but instead, I found myself struggling to hold back tears. Dad would've been so pleased if he could have seen what I'd done. He'd been my support and my source of strength, my guiding light. I was so shocked when he died.

You see, I'd always assumed I would die before my father.

Most people find talk of death unsettling, but I've lived with the threat of it for so long, it doesn't have that effect on me. The possibility of death has been my reality for the last fourteen years, and I'm as comfortable talking about it as I am the weather.

My first bout with cancer came the summer I

turned sixteen. I'd gone to pick up my driver's license that day in August. I'd successfully passed both the written and the driving tests. My mother let me drive from the licensing office to the optometrist. It was supposed to be a routine appointment – I was having my eyes examined before the start of my junior year of high school. I had big plans for the day. As soon as I got home from the eye doctor's, Becky and I were going to drive to the beach. It would be the first time I'd taken the car out by myself, and I was looking forward to driving without my mom or dad or my older sister.

I recall being upset that Mom had scheduled the eye appointment right after my driving test. I'd been having some problems with headaches and dizzy spells, and Dad thought I might need reading glasses. The idea of showing up at Lincoln High School wearing glasses bothered me. A lot. I was hoping Mom and Dad would agree to let me wear contact lenses. As it turned out, impaired vision was the least of my worries.

The optometrist, who was a friend of my parents, seemed to spend an inordinate amount of time staring into the corner of my eye with this horribly bright light. He asked a lot of questions about my headaches. That was almost fifteen years ago, but I don't think I'll ever forget the look on his face as he talked to my mother. He was so serious, so somber ... so concerned.

'I want to make Lydia an appointment at the University of Washington. Immediately.'

My mother and I were both stunned. 'All right,' my mother said, glancing from me to Dr. Reid and back again. 'Is there a problem?'

He nodded. 'I don't like what I'm seeing. I think it would be best if Dr. Wilson had a look.'

Well, Dr. Wilson did more than look. He drilled into my skull and removed a malignant brain tumor. I say those words glibly now, but it wasn't a quick or simple procedure. It meant weeks in the hospital and blinding, debilitating headaches. After the surgery, I went through chemotherapy, followed by a series of radiation treatments. There were days when even the dimmest of lights caused such pain it was all I could do not to scream in agony. Days when I measured each breath, struggling to hold on to life because, try as I might, I could feel it slipping away. Still, there were many mornings I woke up and wished I *would* die because I couldn't bear another hour of this. Without my father I'm convinced I would have.

My head was completely shaved and then, once my hair started to grow back, it fell out again. I missed my entire junior year and when I was finally able to return to high school, nothing was the same. Everyone looked at me differently. I didn't attend the Junior-Senior prom because no one asked me. Some girlfriends suggested I tag along with them, but out of false pride I refused. In retrospect it seems a trivial thing to worry about. I wish I'd gone.

The saddest part of this story is that just when I was beginning to believe I could have a normal life – just when I believed all those drugs, all that suffering had served a useful purpose – the tumor grew back.

I'll never forget the day Dr. Wilson told us the cancer had returned. But it's not the expression on his face that I remember. It's the pain in my father's eyes. He, above anyone, understood what I'd endured during the first bout of treatment. My mother doesn't deal well with illness, and Dad was the one who'd held me together emotionally. He knew there was nothing he could do, nothing he could say, that would lessen this second ordeal for me. I was twenty-four at the time and still in college, trying to accumulate enough credits to graduate. I never did get that degree.

I've survived both bouts of cancer, and I'm definitely not the carefree girl I once was. I appreciate and treasure every single day because I know how precious life is. Most people assume I'm younger than thirty but they seem to find me more serious than other women my age. My experience with cancer means I don't take anything, least of all life itself, for granted. I no longer greet each day with careless acceptance. But I've learned there are compensations for my suffering. I know I'd be a completely different person if not for the cancer. My dad claimed I achieved a certain calm wisdom, and I suppose I have. Yet in many ways I'm naive, especially when it comes to men and relationships.

Of all the compensations, the one I'm most grateful for is that while undergoing treatment I learned to knit.

I may have survived cancer twice, but unfortunately my father didn't. My second tumor killed him. That's what my sister Margaret believes.

She's never actually said so, but I know it's what she thinks. The truth is, I suspect she's probably right. It was a heart attack, but he aged so much after that second diagnosis I'm sure it affected his health. I knew that if he could've switched places with me, he would have done it gladly.

He was at my bedside as much as possible. That, in particular, is what Margaret can't seem to forgive or forget – the time and devotion Dad gave me throughout this ordeal. Mom, too, as much as she was emotionally able.

Margaret was married and a mother of two before the second tumor was even discovered. Nevertheless, she seems to assume that she's somehow been cheated because of my cancer. To this day, she acts as if being sick was my *choice,* an option I preferred over a normal life.

It goes without saying that my sister and I have a strained relationship. For Mom's sake, especially now that Dad's gone, I try my best with Margaret. She doesn't make it easy. She can't hide her resentment, no matter how many years it's been.

Margaret was against my opening a yarn shop, but I sincerely doubt she would've encouraged me in any undertaking. I swear, her eyes brightened at the prospect of seeing me fail. According to the statistics, most new businesses do go under – usually within a year – but I still felt I had to give the yarn shop a chance.

I had the funds. The money was actually an inheritance I received from my maternal grandmother who died when I was twelve. Dad invested it wisely and I had a small nest egg. I should have probably saved it for what Mom calls a 'rainy day,' but it's been raining every day since I turned sixteen and I was tired of holding on to it. Deep down, I know Dad would approve.

As I said, I learned to knit while undergoing chemotherapy. Over the years I've become an accomplished knitter. Dad always joked that I had enough yarn to open my own store; recently I decided he was right.

I love to knit. There's a comfort to it that I can't entirely explain. The repetition of weaving the yarn around a needle and then forming a stitch creates a sense of purpose, of achievement, of progress. When your entire world is unraveling, you tend to crave order, and I found it in knitting. In fact, I've even read that knitting can lower stress more effectively than meditation. And I guess for me it was a better approach, because there was something tangible to show for it. Maybe because knitting gave me a sense of action, of *doing* something. I didn't know what tomorrow held, but with a pair of needles in my hands and a ball of yarn in my lap, I was confident I could handle whatever lay ahead. Each stitch was an accomplishment. Some days all I could manage was a single row, but I had the satisfaction of that one small achievement. It made a difference to me. A very big difference.

Over the years I've taught a number of people how to knit. My first students were other cancer patients going through chemotherapy. We met at the Seattle Oncology Center, and before long, I had everyone, men included, knitting cotton washcloths. I think every doctor and nurse in that clinic has enough knit washcloths to last a lifetime! After washcloths, I had my band of beginning knitters move on to a small afghan. Certainly I've had some failures but far more successes. My patience was rewarded when others found the same serenity I did in knitting.

Now I have my own shop and I think the best way to get customers in the door is to offer knitting classes. I'd never sell enough yarn to stay in business if I ran classes in washcloths, so I've chosen a simple baby blanket to start with. The pattern's by one of my favorite designers, Ann Norling, and uses the basic knit and purl stitches.

I don't know what to expect of my new venture, but I'm hopeful. Hope to a person with cancer – or to a person who's had cancer – is more potent than any drug. We live on it, live for it. It's addictive to those of us who've learned to take one day at a time.

I was making a sign advertising my beginners' class when the bell above the door chimed. My first customer had just walked in and I looked up with a smile on my face. The pounding excitement in my heart quickly died when I realized it was Margaret.

'Hi,' I said, doing my best to sound happy to see her. I didn't want my sister showing up on my very first morning and attacking my confidence.

'Mom told me you'd decided to go ahead with this idea of yours.'

I didn't respond.

Frowning, Margaret continued. 'I was in the neighborhood and thought I'd stop by and see the shop.'

I gestured with one arm and hated myself for asking. 'What do you think?' I didn't bother to mention that Blossom Street was decidedly out of her way.

'Why'd you name it A Good Yarn?'

I'd gone over dozens of shop names, some too cute by half, some plain and ordinary. I love the idea that 'spinning a yarn' means telling a story, and sharing stories with people, listening to their experiences, is important to me. Another legacy of the clinic, I suppose. A Good Yarn seems like a warm and welcoming name. But I didn't explain all that to Margaret. 'I wanted my customers to know I sell quality yarn.'

Margaret shrugged as if she'd seen a dozen knitting shops with more impressive names than mine.

'Well,' I said, despite my determination not to ask again. 'What do you think?'

Margaret glanced around a second time, although nothing had changed after her first inspection. 'It's better than I expected.'

I considered this high praise. 'I don't have a large inventory yet, but I'm hoping to build it up over the next year or so. Of course, not all the yarn I've ordered has arrived. And there's more I'm planning to get, some wonderful imports from Ireland and Australia. Everything takes time and money.' In my enthusiasm I'd said more than I intended.

'Are you expecting Mom to help you?' The question was blunt.

I shook my head. 'You don't need to worry. I'm doing this entirely on my own.' So that was the reason for her unannounced visit. Margaret thought I was going to take advantage of our mother. I wouldn't and the question offended me, but I bit back an angry retort.

Margaret glared at me as if she wasn't sure I was telling the truth.

'I cashed in my Microsoft stock,' I confessed.

Margaret's deep brown eyes, so much like my own, nearly doubled in horror at what I'd done. 'You didn't.'

What did my sister think? I had the necessary cash lying around in my bottom drawer? 'I had to.' Given my medical history, no bank would grant me a loan. Although I've been cancer-free for four years now, I'm viewed as a risk in just about every area.

'It's your money, I guess.' The way Margaret said it implied I'd made a terrible decision. 'But I don't think Dad would have approved.'

'He would've been the first one to encourage me.' I should have kept my mouth shut, but I couldn't stop myself.

'You're probably right,' Margaret said with the caustic edge that never failed to appear in our conversations. 'Dad couldn't deny you anything.'

'The money was my inheritance,' I pointed out. I suppose her share is still accruing profit.

My sister walked around the shop, eyeing it critically. Considering Margaret's apparent dislike of me, I don't know why my relationship with her is so important, but it is. Mom's health is fragile and she hasn't adjusted to life without Dad. Soon, I'm afraid, it'll be only Margaret and me. The thought of not having any family at all terrifies me.

I'm so grateful not to know what the future holds. I once asked my father why God wouldn't just let us know what tomorrow would bring. He said that not knowing the future is actually a gift because if we knew, we wouldn't take responsibility for our own lives, our own happiness. As with so much else in life, my dad was right.

'What's your business plan?' Margaret asked.

'I – I'm starting small.'

'What about customers?'

'I've paid for an ad in the Yellow Pages.' I didn't mention that the new phone directory didn't come out for another two months. No need to hand Margaret any ammunition. I'd distributed flyers in the neighborhood, too, but I didn't know how effective that would be. I was counting on word of mouth to generate customer interest and, ultimately, sales. Which was something else I didn't mention.

My older sister snickered. I've always hated that scoffing sound and had to grit my teeth in order to hide my reaction.

'I'm just getting ready to post a sign for my first knitting class.'

'Do you seriously think a handmade sign taped in the window is going to draw people into your store?' Margaret demanded. 'Parking is a nightmare out there and even when the street's open again, you can't expect much traffic through this construction mess.'

'No, but–'

'I wish you well, but–'

'Do you?' I asked, cutting her off. My hands

shook as I walked over to the display window and secured my notice for knitting classes.

'What's that supposed to mean?'

I turned to face my sister who, at five foot six, stood a good three inches taller than me. She outweighed me by about twenty pounds, too. Looking at us now, I wonder if anyone would guess we were related and yet when we were small we resembled each other quite a bit.

'I think you want me to fail,' I said honestly.

'That isn't true! I came this morning because ... because I'm interested in what you're doing.' Her chin went up a notch as if she was daring me to challenge her again. 'How old are you? Twenty-nine, thirty?'

'Thirty.'

'Isn't it time you cut the apron strings?'

That was blatantly unfair. 'I'm trying to do exactly that. I left Mom's house and I moved into the apartment upstairs. I've started my own business, too, and I'd appreciate your support.'

She turned her hands over to display her palms. 'Do you want me to buy yarn from you? Is that what you want? You know I don't knit and have no desire to learn. I much prefer to crochet. And–'

'Just this once,' I said, cutting her off a second time, 'couldn't you think of *one* nice thing to say?' I waited, silently pleading with her to search inside her heart for at least a token word of encouragement.

My request seemed to be an overwhelming task for Margaret. She faltered for several seconds. 'You have a good eye for color,' she finally said.

She gestured toward the display of yarn I'd arranged on the table by the door.

'Thank you,' I said, hoping to sound gracious. I didn't mention that I'd used a color wheel to create the display. Hard as it was for Margaret to offer me praise, I certainly wasn't going to give her an opportunity to withdraw it.

Had we been closer, I would've told her the real reason I'd decided to open a yarn store. This shop was my affirmation of life. I was willing to invest everything I had to make it a success. Like the Viking conqueror who came ashore and burned his ships behind him, I had set my course. Succeed or go under.

As my father might say, I was taking responsibility for a future I couldn't predict.

The bell above the door chimed again. I had a customer! My first *real* customer.

CHAPTER 2

JACQUELINE DONOVAN

The angry exchange of words with her married son had distressed Jacqueline Donovan. She'd honestly tried to keep her negative feelings regarding her daughter-in-law to herself. But when Paul phoned to tell her Tammie Lee was five and a half months pregnant, Jacqueline had lost her temper and said things she shouldn't have. Paul had hung up in mid-rant.

To complicate everything, her husband had phoned soon afterward, asking her to drop off blueprints at the construction site on Blossom Street. The argument with Paul weighing on her mind, she'd confessed what she'd said and now Reese was upset with her, too. Truth be told, she didn't much care what her husband thought, but Paul, her only child – now, that was a different story.

Feeling anxious and depressed, Jacqueline drove down to the job site and wasted twenty minutes finding a parking space. Needless to say, the one she found was quite a distance down the street, across from a seedy-looking video store. Clutching the blueprints, she picked her way through the construction mess, muttering under her breath. Just leave it to Reese to screw up her entire day!

'You brought the drawings?' Her husband of thirty-three years walked out of the trailer to meet her as she neared the site. Jacqueline stepped over steel tubes, trying not to dirty or damage her Ferragamo heels. Her husband's architectural firm, Donovan and Gray, was responsible for this renovation project. Dressed in a Brooks Brothers suit and a hard hat, Reese was still a good-looking man at fifty-nine.

Jacqueline handed him the all-important set of rolled-up prints. It was unusual for Reese to ask anything of her, which suited her perfectly. He set the prints inside the trailer and turned back to face her, standing just outside the door.

'I'm worried about Paul,' she said, doing her best to maintain her composure. Reese gave a tired shrug. He worked long hours and Jacqueline pretended to believe that all the time he spent away from home was business-related. She knew otherwise. So if he was tired, *she* certainly wasn't going to sympathize.

For the sake of Paul and their friends, Jacqueline and Reese managed to put up a good front, but the marriage hadn't been happy for a number of years. Reese had his life and she had hers. They hadn't slept together since Paul left for college twelve years ago. In fact, there was very little they shared except their love for their son.

'So Tammie Lee is pregnant,' her husband said, ignoring her concern.

Jacqueline nodded. 'Obviously Tammie Lee's a breeder, just as I suspected.'

Reese frowned; he disapproved of her natural wariness toward Paul's wife. But they knew practically nothing about her family. What little Jacqueline had unearthed, between the girl's tales of aunts and uncles and God-only-knew how many cousins, had been disheartening to say the least.

The sound of a crane overhead distracted Reese momentarily and when he returned his attention to her he was frowning again. 'You don't seem happy about this.'

'Come on, Reese! How do you *expect* me to feel?'

'Like a woman who's about to be a grandmother for the first time.'

Jacqueline crossed her arms. 'Well, I for one am not thrilled.' Several of her nearest and dearest friends had delighted in their status as new grandmothers, but Jacqueline doubted she'd make this latest adjustment as smoothly as her friends.

'Jacquie, this is our grandchild.'

'I should've known better than to say anything to you,' she said angrily. Jacqueline wouldn't have mentioned it at all if not for the argument with Paul. She'd always been close to her son. He was the reason she'd stayed in this empty shell of a marriage. Her son was everything she'd hoped for: handsome, smart, successful and so much more. He'd gone into banking and was quickly climbing up the corporate ladder – and then, a year ago, he'd done something completely out of character. He'd married the wrong woman.

'You haven't given Tammie Lee a chance,' Reese insisted.

'That is blatantly unfair.' To Jacqueline's horror, her voice shook with emotion. She'd given this awkward relationship with Tammie Lee her best effort. For the life of her, Jacqueline couldn't understand why her sensible son would marry this stranger, this ... this little girl from the swamps, when so many of her friends' daughters were interested in him. Paul called Tammie Lee his southern belle, but all Jacqueline saw was a hillbilly. 'I took her to lunch at the country club and I've never been so mortified in my life. I introduced her to Mary James, and the next thing I know, Tammie Lee's discussing a recipe for pickled pigs' feet or some such with the President of the Women's Association.' It had taken Jacqueline weeks to gather up enough courage to face her friend again.

'Isn't Mary in charge of the cookbook? It makes perfect sense that the two of them would–'

'The last thing I need is for you to criticize me, too,' Jacqueline blurted out. There was no point in trying to explain anything to Reese. They couldn't even have a civil conversation anymore. Besides, this construction dust was ruining her makeup and the wind was playing havoc with her French twist. Reese didn't care, though. Appearances were important, but he had no appreciation of everything she did to maintain herself physically. He didn't have any idea how much work was involved in styling her hair and doing her makeup properly. She was in her midfifties now, and it took a subtle hand to hide age lines.

His voice rose slightly. 'What exactly did you say to Paul?'

Jacqueline squared her shoulders in an attempt to preserve her dignity. 'Just that I wished he'd waited a while before starting his family.'

Her husband offered her his hand to assist her into the construction trailer. 'Come inside.'

Jacqueline ignored his gesture of help and stepped into the trailer. Although Reese routinely visited his work sites, this was the first time she'd been inside one of these trailers. She glanced around and took note of the blueprints, empty coffee cups and general disarray. The place resembled a pigpen.

'You'd better tell me everything.' Reese poured coffee and silently held out a cup. She declined with a shake of her head, afraid the cup hadn't been washed in weeks.

'Why do you assume I said anything more than the fact that I was disappointed?' she asked.

'Because I know you.'

'Well, thank you very much.' Her throat was thickening but she refused to let him see how his rebuke had hurt her. 'To make matters worse, Tammie Lee's nearly six months along. Naturally Paul had a convenient excuse for keeping us out of the picture. He said they didn't want to say anything until they could be sure the pregnancy was safe.'

'And you don't believe him?' Reese crossed his arms and leaned next to the open door.

'Of course I don't. People usually wait three months before they share their *good news,*' she said sarcastically, 'but six? You and I both know he put off telling us because he knew how I'd feel. I've said from the first, and I'll say it again, this marriage is a very big mistake.'

'Now, Jacquie...'

'What else am I to think? Paul goes off on a business trip to New Orleans and meets this girl in a bar.'

'They were both attending the same financial conference, and met for a drink later that evening.'

Why did Reese have to drag up unnecessary details? 'They were together all of three days and the next thing I know he announces that he's married to a girl neither of us has ever met.'

'Now I agree with you there,' Reese conceded. 'I do wish Paul had told us, but it's been almost a year.'

It still upset Jacqueline that her son hadn't had

a large church wedding the way she'd always envisioned. Jacqueline felt it was what Paul was entitled to – what *she* was entitled to. Instead she hadn't even been invited to the wedding.

That wasn't territory she particularly wanted to revisit. Her son's only excuse was that he was in love, knew he wanted Tammie Lee with him for the rest of his life and couldn't bear to be apart from her any longer than necessary. That was the reason he'd given them, but Jacqueline had her suspicions. Paul must've known she wouldn't be pleased – and he must have realized that his in-laws would be an embarrassment. She could only imagine the kind of wedding Tammie Lee's family would hold. The reception dinner would probably consist of collard greens and grits, with deep-fried Hostess Twinkies instead of wedding cake.

'Tammie Lee got pregnant within six months of the wedding.' She didn't hide her contempt.

'Paul's over thirty, Jacqueline.' Reese had that disapproving look in his eyes. She'd always hated it.

'And old enough to know about birth control,' she snapped. Paul had sprung the news on her the same way he had the marriage: over the phone without a moment's warning.

'He told me he wanted a family,' Reese murmured.

'Not this soon, I'll bet,' she burst out. Talking to Reese was impossible. He didn't seem to care that Paul had married beneath him. Her daughter-in-law was nothing like the woman she'd envisioned for their son. Jacqueline had honestly tried to welcome Tammie Lee into the family, but she couldn't bear to be around her for more than a few minutes. All that sweetness and insincere southern charm simply overwhelmed her.

'But Paul's pleased about the baby, isn't he?'

Jacqueline leaned against the table and nodded. 'He's thrilled,' she muttered. 'Or so he says...'

'Then what's the problem?'

'He ... he doesn't seem to think I'm going to make much of a grandmother.'

Reese's eyes narrowed. 'What did you say to him?'

'Oh, Reese,' she said, feeling terrible now. 'I couldn't help it. I told him I thought he'd made a terrible mistake in marrying Tammie Lee and that this pregnancy complicates everything.' She'd assumed that a year or two down the road, Paul would recognize his lapse in judgment and gracefully bow out of the marriage. A child made that a whole lot less likely.

'You didn't actually say that to Paul, did you?' Reese sounded furious and that only made Jacqueline more defensive.

'I realize I should've kept quiet, but really, can you blame me? I'm just getting used to the fact that our only son eloped with a stranger and then he hits me with this pregnancy.'

'It should be happy news.'

'Well, it isn't.'

'It is to our son and Tammie Lee.'

'That's another thing,' she cried. 'Why is it every girl from the south has two names? Why can't we call her Tammie without the Lee?'

'It's her name, Jacqueline.'

'It's ridiculous.'

Reese studied her as if he was really noticing her for the first time. 'Why are you so angry?'

'Because I'm afraid of losing my son.' Paul and her close relationship with him was the only consolation she had in a life that brought her little joy. Now she'd done something stupid and insulted her son.

'Call him back and apologize.'

'I intend to,' she said.

'You could order flowers for Tammie Lee.'

'I will.' But the gesture would be for Paul's sake, not his wife's.

'Why not go to the flower shop on Blossom Street.'

Jacqueline nodded. 'I plan to do something else, too.' She prayed it would be enough. She hoped her son realized she was making an effort to accept his wife.

'What?'

'I saw a sign in the window of that new knitting shop. I'm going to register for a knitting class. The sign says the beginning project is a baby blanket.'

Reese so rarely approved of anything she did that the warmth of his smile moved all the way through her.

'I might not like Tammie Lee, but I will be the best grandmother I can.' Someone had to provide the appropriate influences for Paul's child. Otherwise her grandchild might grow up eating deep-fried pickles. Or going through life as Bubba Donovan...

CHAPTER 3

CAROL GIRARD

Carol Girard had never imagined that getting pregnant could be this difficult. Her mother obviously hadn't had any trouble; Carol and her brother, Rick, were born two years apart.

Before they were married, Doug and Carol had talked about having a family one day. Because of her high-powered job with a national brokerage firm, he wanted to be sure she was as interested in a family as he was. Doug had asked if she'd be willing to put aside her career for a few years in order to have children. The answer had been an unqualified *yes*. Babies were a given with her. She'd always pictured herself as a mother, always saw kids as an important part of her life. Doug would bc a wonderful father and she was deeply, passionately, in love with her husband. She *wanted* to have his children.

Heating her lunch in the microwave, Carol glanced around the kitchen of her sixteenth-floor condo overlooking Puget Sound. She'd quit her job only a month ago and she already felt restless and impatient. She'd left the brokerage firm with the sole intention of allowing her body to relax, to unwind from the demands of her routine. Doug had convinced her that job-related stress was the reason she hadn't conceived, and her obstetrician conceded that it was possible. A barrage of humiliating tests for both her and Doug had revealed that in addition to her age, thirty-seven, she had to contend with something called ASA or antisperm antibodies.

The phone rang and she leapt on it, grabbing the handset before it had a chance to ring twice.

'Hello,' she said cheerfully, eager to talk to anyone, even if it was a sales call.

'Hi, honey. I wondered if you were still at home.'

A momentary panic attacked her. 'Am I supposed to be somewhere?'

Doug chuckled. 'I thought you said you were going for a walk this afternoon.'

That was something recommended by one of the books they'd read. As a result, Carol had decided she should exercise more, and now that she was home during the day she had plenty of opportunity to spend time outside. This was all part of the program they'd discussed and agreed upon before she'd left her job.

'Right. I was just getting ready to head out.' She eyed the microwave and turned her back on her waiting lunch.

'Carol? Are you okay?'

Her husband recognized her mood, her depression and anxiety. Doug had been right to suggest she quit work. They were both frightened, since there was a very real possibility that she might never carry a pregnancy full-term. It didn't help that they had one last shot with in vitro fertilization. The insurance company where Doug worked had its headquarters in Illinois, where state law mandated that company health coverage could pay for three attempts; their first two had failed. IVF was the very end of the technological line, the ultimate procedure the fertility clinic had to offer in the quest for a biological child. July would be their last attempt, and after that they were on their own financially. At the start they'd agreed to limit in vitro to the three attempts. If she wasn't pregnant by then, they'd begin the adoption process. In retrospect, it had been a wise decision. The emotional devastation of the two failures proved she couldn't endure this process indefinitely. Twice a fertilized egg had been implanted and twice she'd miscarried. No couple should repeatedly face this kind of heartache.

Carol and Doug never mentioned that this third IVF attempt was the end of their hopes, but the fact loomed in their minds. It was vitally important that she get pregnant – and stay pregnant – this time.

Carol was willing to give it everything she had. Willing to forsake the job she loved, willing to be poked and prodded and humiliated. She was willing to withstand all the doubts, confront the emotional highs and lows of their attempts at conception, all for the sake of a baby. Doug's baby.

'I love you, sweetheart.'

'I know.' Although she said it flippantly, Carol did know. Doug had been with her through this entire process, through the doctors' visits, the testing, through the tears, the frustration, the anger and the grief. 'One day you'll hold our child in your arms and we'll both know that everything was worth it.' They'd already chosen the names.

Cameron for a boy and Colleen for a girl. She could clearly see their child, could feel the baby in her arms, and see the joy in her husband's eyes.

Carol held on to that dream, and the image of a baby in her arms helped her endure the most difficult aspects of the IVF process.

'What time will you be home?' It had never concerned her before, but now she regulated her life by her husband's comings and goings. His routine shaped her own, and his return from the office was the highlight of her day. Several times each afternoon she checked her watch, calculating how many hours and then minutes until Doug was home.

'Usual time,' he promised.

Her husband of seven years worked as an insurance underwriter. Carol was the one who earned the big bucks in the family. It was her income that had enabled them to make a substantial down payment on the condo. When they got married, her wise and frugal husband had insisted they adjust their lifestyle to live on his income alone. He feared that otherwise they'd come to rely on her salary and defer having a family. They'd waited three years after marrying, not expecting problems, building up their savings. It was a good thing because even with insurance, the cost of infertility treatments was staggering. And now that she wasn't working...

'Have I mentioned how dreadful daytime television is?' she asked.

'Turn off the TV and go for your walk.'

'Yes, sir,' she replied in military fashion.

Doug laughed. 'I'm not that bad, am I?'

'No. It's just that staying home isn't anything like I thought.' Life at home wasn't supposed to be endless hours of boredom, desperately searching for ways to amuse herself until Doug came home. She was used to frequent meetings, adrenaline-fuelled decisions, constant busyness. Being at home alone was a new experience and not one she enjoyed.

'Do you want me to check in with you later?'

'No, I'll be fine. You're right, I do need to get outside and it's a lovely afternoon.' No place on earth was more beautiful than Seattle when the sun was shining. It was a perfect May day and she gazed out at the snow-topped Olympic Mountains in the distance, the blue-green waters of Puget Sound below her.

'See you around five-thirty,' Doug said.

'I'll be here.' Before Carol had left the brokerage firm, it was Doug who'd arrived home first. Doug who started dinner. Doug who had the local news blaring from the television. Carol didn't have any trouble adjusting to this role reversal of a role reversal. Right now, it was one of the few interesting things in her life.

She deposited her lunch in the refrigerator and grabbed an apple on her way out the door. They'd lived in the condo four years, and she still didn't know her neighbors. They were upwardly mobile types just like her and Doug, with both husband and wife working long hours. Only a few had children and the little ones were rushed off to ultra-expensive day-care centers early in the morning.

Carol rode an empty elevator down to the

45

condo foyer and headed out the double glass doors onto the downtown sidewalk. Munching on her apple as she walked swiftly toward the waterfront, she realized that one fear, at any rate, hadn't come to pass.

All the women in the office had given her dire warnings when they learned she was leaving. The word was that stay-at-home wives and mothers battled constantly with their weight. Being in the kitchen and continually around food made it impossible to maintain a slim waistline, according to her former colleagues. That wasn't a problem for Carol. Never in her life had she eaten more healthfully. Diet was all part of her new regime and she'd maintained her size 8 figure without difficulty.

A cool breeze blew off the water as she strolled along her usual route. Then on a whim she headed east, climbing toward Pill Hill, where Virginia Mason Hospital and Swedish Hospital were situated. She was breathing hard as she made it up the steep incline and continued slowly for several blocks, looking around at the unfamiliar neighborhood, until she came to Blossom Street.

A number of buildings were being renovated. The street was blocked off, but the sidewalk was accessible. The work on one side of the street seemed to be completed, with freshly painted storefronts and a green-and-white awning over the florist's shop. Tulips and lilies were arranged in buckets outside the front door.

Despite the clang and racket of construction, Carol ventured down the street. A video store and a depressing brick apartment building sat at the far end of the block and a restaurant called Annie's Café was across the street. The contrast between the old and the new was striking. The unrenovated portion of the street resembled a quaint small town with friendly merchants straight out of a 1960s television series. Granted, some of the buildings were a bit shabby, but they seemed welcoming nonetheless. It was hard to tell that Blossom Street was less than a mile from the heart of downtown Seattle with its high-rises and congested streets.

Next to the florist was another surprise: a yarn store. The shop was new, judging by the computer-lettered 'Grand Opening' sign. A woman, probably close to her own age, sat in a rocking chair inside, her hands busy with a pair of needles. A large ball of lime-green yarn rested on her lap.

Because she had nothing better to do, Carol walked through the door, setting off a pleasant chime. 'Hello,' she said, doing her best to sound cheerful and interested. She wasn't sure what drew her into the shop, since she didn't knit and had never been particularly keen on crafts.

The petite woman greeted her with a shy smile. 'Hello and welcome to A Good Yarn.'

'You're new here, aren't you?'

The proprietor nodded. 'I opened yesterday, and you're my first customer this afternoon.' She laughed softly. 'First customer today,' she corrected.

'What are you knitting?' Carol asked, feeling slightly guilty because she wasn't a customer at all.

'A sweater for my niece.' She reached for her project and held it up for Carol to examine.

The colors, lime-green, orange and turquoise, immediately brought a smile to Carol's face. 'That's so cute.'

'Do you knit?'

The question was inevitable. 'No, but I'd like to learn someday.'

'Then you've come to the right place. I have a beginners' class starting next Friday. If you register for the class you get a twenty-percent discount on your yarn purchases.'

'Sorry. I don't think I'd be any good at knitting.' Carol felt genuinely regretful, but she wasn't the sort of woman who was comfortable doing things with her hands. Calculating compound interest and figuring annuities, investments and mutual funds – that was where her skills lay.

'You won't know if you don't try. I'm Lydia, by the way.'

'Carol.' She offered her hand, and Lydia put down her knitting to clasp it warmly. Lydia was petite and smallboned, her dark hair worn short. Her brown eyes shone with intelligence, and Carol liked her right away.

'I'm starting the class with a simple project,' Lydia continued.

'It would have to be really simple if I were to take up knitting.'

'I thought I'd have everyone work on a baby blanket.'

Carol froze and tears sprang instantly to her eyes. She turned away before Lydia noticed. Under normal circumstances she wasn't a volatile person, but with the hormone shots, her emotions seemed out of control. This was too weird, though, too much of a coincidence.

'Perhaps I will sign up for the class, after all,' she said, fingering a ball of bright yellow yarn.

'That would be wonderful.' Lydia walked over to the counter and brought out a clipboard.

These days, Carol looked everywhere for signs and portents, and she had frequent conversations with God. Without a doubt she knew she'd been sent to this shop. It was His way of letting her know He was about to answer her prayers. When she went in for the fertilization process this third and final time, she would be successful. In the not-too-distant future she was going to need a baby blanket for her child.

CHAPTER 4

ALIX TOWNSEND

Alix Townsend smashed her cigarette butt into the cracked concrete sidewalk with the toe of her knee-high black combat boots. The manager of Blossom Street Video frowned on employees smoking in the break room and rather than put up with his snide comments, she chose to smoke outside. The man was a prick, anyway, constantly complaining about the staff, the economy and life in general.

Lloyd Fund was right about one thing, though

– all this construction was killing business. Alix figured it was only a matter of time before she got her RIF notice, followed by word that her apartment building had been sold. It was inevitable with all the changes taking place in the neighborhood. Either that or she was in for a big rent hike. Thanks a lot, Mr. Mayor.

She burrowed her hands in her black leather jacket and glared down the street at the dust and debris. She wore the leather coat rain or shine, summer or winter. This jacket had cost her big time, and she wasn't taking it off so someone could conveniently walk away with it. Someone like her roommate, the overweight Laurel, although it was doubtful anything Alix owned would fit her. Leaning against the building, knee bent, one foot braced against the wall, she concentrated on the other side of the street.

All the storefronts were newly painted. The new florist shop had already opened, as well as a beauty parlor. Those were a real boon to the neighborhood – as if *she* had use for either one. The shop situated between them remained something of a mystery. A Good Yarn. Either it was a bookstore or a knitting shop. In this neighborhood neither would last long, she suspected. On closer inspection she decided it was a yarn store. The people who lived in her building weren't exactly the type who got off on a ball of yarn.

A knitting shop did bring up an interesting prospect, though. With another five minutes left of her break, Alix crossed the street. She peered through the window and saw a handmade sign offering knitting classes. If she started knitting, it would get the court off her back. Maybe she could do something about those community-service hours Judge Roper had thrown at her.

'Hi,' Alix said, letting her voice boom when she walked in the front door. She liked making an entrance.

'Hello.'

The proprietor was a dainty woman, fragile-looking with large brown eyes and a ready smile.

'You own this shop?' Alix asked, giving the other woman a cool glance. She couldn't be much older than Alix.

'This is my shop.' She rose from her rocking chair. 'How can I help you?'

'I want to know about that knitting class.' Her case worker had once suggested knitting as a means of anger management. Maybe it would work. And if it allowed her to meet her community-service obligations at the same time...

'What can I tell you?'

Slowly Alix walked around the shop, her hands shoved inside her pockets. She'd bet this knitting lady didn't get many customers like her. Recently a notice in the courthouse had caught Alix's attention – all about homemade quilts and blankets for kids who'd suffered domestic violence. 'You ever heard of the Linus Project?' she asked, thinking this yarn lady probably hadn't stepped inside a courtroom in her lifetime.

'Of course.' The woman joined her hands and followed Alix as if she was afraid Alix might try to lift some yarn. 'It's a police-instigated project that involves knitting blankets for children who are the victims of violence.'

51

Alix shrugged it off as if it were merely a passing thought. 'That's what I heard.'

'I'm Lydia, by the way.'

'Alix, spelled A-L-l-X.' She hadn't expected to get on a first-name basis with the woman, but that was all right.

'Hello, Alix, and welcome to A Good Yarn. Are you interested in knitting for the Linus Project?'

'Well...' Her thoughts on the subject had been pretty vague. 'I might be if I knew how to knit,' she finally muttered.

'That's what the classes are for.'

Alix gave a short, humorless laugh. 'I'm sure I wouldn't be any good at knitting.'

'Would you like to learn? It isn't difficult.'

She snorted, making an intentionally derisive sound. The truth was, Alix didn't really know why she was here. Perhaps it was because of something from her childhood, some remembered moment or feeling. Her early years were blocked from her mind. Those court-appointed doctors had said she suffered from childhood amnesia. Whatever. Every now and then a fleeting memory flashed through her mind. Most of the time she didn't know what had really happened and what hadn't. What she did remember was that her parents had fought a great deal. An argument would break out and Alix would hide in her bedroom closet. With the door shut and her eyes closed, she managed to convince herself there was no yelling and no violence. In that closet she had another family, one from an imaginary world where mothers and fathers loved each other and didn't scream or beat each other up. Her imaginary world had a real home where half the refrigerator wasn't filled with beer and there were cookies and milk waiting for her when she got home from school. Through the years, fantasy had played as great a role in Alix's memory as reality did. One thing she recalled in vivid detail was that this fantasy mother who loved her used to knit.

Alix escaped into that closet quite often as a kid....

'I have a beginners' class starting next Friday afternoon if you'd like to join.'

The words shook her from her reverie. Alix grinned. 'You honestly think you could teach someone like me to knit?'

'Of course I do,' Lydia returned without a pause. 'I've taught *lots* of people and there are only two women signed up for the class, so I could give you plenty of attention.'

'I'm left-handed.'

'That's not a problem.'

The lady must be desperate for a sale. Excuses were easy enough to supply and eventually Lydia would give up on her. As for learning to knit, she didn't have money to blow on yarn.

'What about knitting a blanket for the Linus Project, like you mentioned?' Lydia asked.

Alix had walked right into that one.

Lydia kept on talking. 'I've knit several blankets for the Linus Project myself,' she said.

'You have?' So this woman had a heart.

Lydia nodded. 'There are only so many people to knit for, and it's a worthy cause.'

People to knit for... The mother in the closet knit.

She sang songs to Alix and smelled of lavender and flowers. Alix had wanted to be like that mother one day. However, the path she'd followed had led her in a different direction. Perhaps this knitting class was something she could – *should* – do.

'I guess I could try,' she said, jerking one shoulder. If Laurel found out about this, Alix would be the subject of a lot of jokes, but so what? She'd been ridiculed most of her life for one reason or another.

Lydia smiled warmly. 'That's wonderful.'

'If the blanket for the Linus Project doesn't turn out, then it really doesn't matter. It isn't like anyone'll know I was the one who knit it.'

Lydia's smile slowly faded. *'You'll* know, Alix, and that's the important thing.'

'Yes, but ... well, I'm thinking your class could serve a dual purpose.' That sounded good, Alix thought, pleased with herself. 'I could learn to knit, and the time it takes me to finish the blanket will use up some of the hours I owe.'

'You owe someone hours?'

'Judge Roper gave me a hundred hours of community service for a bogus drug bust. I didn't do it! I'm not stupid and he knows it.' Her hands involuntarily clenched. She still felt upset about that charge, because the marijuana had belonged to Laurel. 'Doing drugs is stupid.' She paused, then blurted out, 'My brother's dead because of drugs. I'm not interested in giving up on life just yet.'

Lydia straightened. 'Let me see if I understand you correctly. You'd like to sign up for the knitting class and give the blanket to the Linus Project?'

'Yeah.'

'And the time it takes you to knit this blanket—' she hesitated briefly '—you want to use against your court-ordered community-service hours?'

Alix detected a bit of attitude on Lydia's part, but when it came to attitude, she had plenty of her own to spare. 'Do you have a problem with that?'

Lydia hesitated. 'Not really, as long as you're respectful to me and the other class members.'

'Sure. Fine.' Alix glanced down at her watch. 'I've got to get back to work. If you need me for anything, I'm almost always at the video store.'

'Okay.' All of a sudden Lydia didn't sound as confident as she had before.

The video store was busy when Alix returned, and she hurried behind the counter.

'What took you so long?' Laurel demanded. 'Fund asked where you were and I told him you'd stepped into the ladies' room.'

'Sorry, I went outside for a cigarette.' According to the labor laws, she was entitled to a fifteen-minute break.

'Did you meet any of the construction guys?'

Alix shook her head as she moved over to the cash register. 'Not a one. Four o'clock, and those guys are out of here faster than Seabiscuit.'

'We got to get ourselves a union,' Laurel whispered.

'Benefits.' Alix knew she was back in that dream world again. One day she'd find a job that paid more than minimum wage. It would be nice to have an apartment all to herself and not share it with Laurel. Laurel lived on the edge and was in danger of slipping off entirely. Alix's biggest fear was that when Laurel went, she'd take Alix with her.

CHAPTER 5

'If you can knit, purl and follow instructions, you can make anything.'
>   –Linda Johnson, Linda's Knit 'N' Stitch,
>   Silverdale, Washington

LYDIA HOFFMAN

I was afraid Margaret could be right and A Good Yarn would fail before it even had a chance to get off the ground. So far, only three women had signed up for the knitting class and Alix, the latest one to enroll, looked like a felon. I couldn't imagine how Jacqueline and Carol would react to a classmate who sported a dog collar and wore her hair in purple-tinged spikes. I'd encouraged Alix to join, and then the moment she left the store I wondered if I'd done the right thing. What was I thinking? What *was* I thinking?

The construction noise wasn't quite as disruptive now, which was a relief, but that hadn't brought any more customers into the shop. On a positive note, I hadn't had this much uninterrupted knitting time in months. I should've been counting my blessings, I suppose, but I was too worried about the lack of walk-in traffic.

Every knowledgeable person I've talked to about opening the store suggested I have enough money in the bank to pay for a minimum of six months' expenses. I do, but I hope and pray I'll be able to keep at least part of my inheritance intact. Now that I've actually taken the risk, I feel bombarded with second thoughts and fears.

Margaret always does that to me. I wish I understood my sister. Some days I think she hates me. A part of me recognizes what the problem is: I was the one who got all of Mom and Dad's attention, but I *needed* them. I refuse to believe that my sister would seriously think I was so hungry for attention that I wished the cancer upon myself.

Even more than Margaret resented me, I resented the cancer. I longed to be healthy and normal. I still live my life standing directly under a thundercloud, fearing lightning will strike again. Surely my one and only sibling can appreciate my circumstances and support my efforts to support myself!

On Wednesday morning, I was knitting a pair of socks for display, my concentration focused on shaping the gusset, when the bell above the door chimed. Thrilled at the prospect of a customer – and potential class member – I stood with a welcoming smile.

'Hello, there.' The UPS driver walked into the shop, wheeling his cart stacked five high with large cardboard boxes. 'Since I'm going to be making regular deliveries to the neighborhood, I thought I should introduce myself.' He released the cart and thrust out his hand. 'Brad Goetz.'

'I'm Lydia Hoffman.' We shook hands.

He passed me the computerized clipboard for my signature. 'How's it going?' Brad asked as I signed my name.

'It's only my second week.' I bypassed his question rather than confess how poor business actually was.

'The construction will be finished soon, and customers will flock to your store.' He smiled as he said it and I felt instantly grateful and – shocking as this sounds – attracted, too. I was so starved for encouragement that it was only natural, I suppose, but I was drawn to him like a bird to the sky. I hadn't felt that particular tug in a very long while. Shamelessly, I glanced at his ring finger and saw that he wasn't wearing a wedding band.

This is embarrassing to admit, but my sexual experience is limited to a few groping attempts at lovemaking in the back seat of my college boyfriend's car. Then the cancer returned. Roger was with me for the second brain surgery, but his calls and visits stopped shortly after I started chemotherapy and lost all my hair. Bald women apparently weren't attractive, although he claimed otherwise. I think it had more to do with the fact that he saw me as a losing proposition, a woman who could die at any time. A woman who couldn't repay his emotional investment. Roger was a business student, after all.

Brian had been my high school boyfriend and his reaction was the same as Roger's. He hung around for a while, too, and then drifted away. I didn't really blame either one.

My breakups with Roger and Brian, if you could even call them that, were inevitable. A few short relationships followed after Roger, but no one worth mentioning. After my earlier experiences, I should've realized that most men aren't romantically interested in a two-time cancer patient. Without sounding like a martyr, I understand how they feel. Why get emotionally involved with a woman who's probably going to die? I don't even know if I can have children or if I should. It's a subject I prefer not to think about.

'My grandmother used to knit,' Brad said. 'I hear interest in it's been revived in the last couple of years.'

Longer, although I didn't correct him. Damn, but he was good-looking, especially when he smiled, and he seemed to be doing a lot of that. His eyes were a deep shade of blue, eyes a woman could see a block away. He wasn't overly tall, which was nice. I'm barely five foot three, and when I stand next to someone who's six feet or taller, it's intimidating. Brad was just right and that was the problem. I didn't *want* to notice anything about him, about the boyish, charming way his dark hair fell over his forehead or how the dark-brown uniform stretched across his broad shoulders. But I did notice all those things ... and more.

'What are you knitting?' he asked, gesturing down at my current project. He didn't wait for me to respond. 'Looks like socks.'

'They are.'

'But you're only using two needles. When Grandma knit socks, she had maybe half a dozen.'

'These are circular needles. It's a more modern method,' I explained, holding up the half-completed project for his inspection. He seemed interested and I continued chattering away, giving him far more information than he probably wanted. 'Until only a few years ago, socks were knit using the five-needles method. But now it's possible to knit them on two circular needles, or even one except that it's forty inches long. Notice the yarn, too,' I blathered on. 'I haven't changed colors to make these stripes. The striped pattern is in the yarn itself.'

He touched the strand of yarn and seemed genuinely impressed. 'Have you been knitting long?'

'For almost ten years.'

'You don't look old enough to be out of high school, let alone open a yarn store.'

That was a comment I've heard far too often. I smiled in an offhand manner, but the truth is, I don't consider it a compliment.

'I guess I'd better get back to work,' Brad said when I let the conversation drop. I wouldn't have minded exchanging pleasantries for another few minutes, but I was sure he was on a schedule. So was I, in a manner of speaking. Besides, I never was much good at flirting.

'Before I go, can I help you put these boxes someplace? They're heavier than they look.'

'I'll manage, but thank you.' Distracted as I was by Brad's friendly visit, I'd hardly noticed he was delivering new yarn. One of the delights of opening my own shop was being able to buy yarn at wholesale prices. Unsure of what would interest my clientele, I'd ordered a number of different varieties. My first order was for good solid wool in two dozen colors. Wool is a must, especially with the popularity of felting. That's where the pattern is knit in a bigger size and then shrunk in hot water, which also mats the yarn, creating a consistency like felt. Next came the cotton yarns; they're some of my favorites. The fingering weight yarns have become increasingly popular, too, as well as the imported European sock yarns. The yarns most in demand, I thought, would be the blends of wool and acrylic, so I'd ordered all the basic colors, as well as the colors that were, according to my knitting magazines, this year's trends. Most of my shipments had arrived before I opened my doors but the smaller orders were dribbling in day by day.

'Do you live in the neighborhood?' Brad asked as he tucked the clipboard under his arm and reached for his empty cart.

'I have the apartment above the shop.'

'That's good, because parking around here is a headache.'

As if I didn't already know that. I wondered where he'd left his truck and supposed it must be quite a distance away. Any customers I was bound to attract would need to find parking a block or two down the street, and I worried that many people wouldn't be willing to go to that trouble. The alleyway behind the store was open, but it wasn't the kind of place I wanted to be caught alone, day or night.

'Thank you, Brad,' I said as he opened the door.

He gave a cheery wave and was gone. It seemed for a moment as if all the sunshine had left the room. I recognized that feeling for what it was: regret verging on misery. This wasn't the time or the place, I told myself sternly. If I'm going to wallow in self-pity I want to make sure I've got an Eric Clapton CD playing and a sad movie or two in reserve. Ice cream is always a help, but only if it's a really bad case.

There was nothing stopping me from getting involved in a relationship. Nothing except my own fears. Good grief, I'm thirty years old. Okay, here's the truth. I don't want to risk falling in love when in all likelihood the relationship will end. I've tried several times and as soon as I admit I've had cancer not once, but twice, I can see it in their eyes. I hate that look the most. The wary look that's a mixture of pity and regret, of disappointment and sympathy.

Often the change in attitude is immediate, and I know it won't be long before the relationship that once seemed so promising falls apart and dies. And with it my hopes for what women have always cherished – a husband and children. A family of my own.

I know I sound terribly sorry for myself. I'll admit that I struggle with the subject of men and relationships. Even my girlfriends sometimes act uncomfortable around me. I do my best not to think about it. I have so much for which to be grateful, and for the sake of my sanity, I choose to concentrate on those things.

To put it simply, I don't handle relationships well. That wasn't always the case. BC (before cancer), I'd been popular and outgoing, with lots of friends, boys and girls. All the boys in my life eventually bailed. Actually I'd come to expect that, but I was the one who pushed my female friends away. It was foolish, I know, but I couldn't stand to hear about all the fun they were having. In retrospect I realize I was jealous. I so desperately wanted to be like them, to laugh and stay up all night talking and confiding secrets. To go out on dates. Discover life. Instead, my daily routine consisted of doctors and hospitals and experimental drugs. I've never recaptured what cancer took away from me. The point is, I don't have close friends, and now that I'm thirty, I'm afraid I've lost the knack for making them.

I shoved Brad Goetz out of my mind.

I'd just started to unpack the boxes and sort through my treasure of yarns when I saw a flash of brown uniform in my display window. Despite my earlier determination, I craned my neck, hoping for a glimpse of Brad. I wasn't disappointed as he flung open the door and hurried inside.

'Lydia, are you doing anything after work tonight?'

To my utter astonishment, my mouth went dry. 'Doing anything?' I repeated.

'I know it's last-minute and all, but can I take you to dinner?'

Again I faltered, trapped between the yearning to leap at his invitation and the knowledge that, in the end, I'd be left with nothing but raw feelings and regrets.

'Sorry,' I said, hoping I conveyed just the right tone, 'but I've got plans this evening.' I didn't mention that it was finishing the gusset on the sock, but that was information he didn't need.

'What about tomorrow? My ex has my son for the next two nights and I thought, you know, that we might get together and–'

Before I could give in to temptation, I shook my head. 'Sorry, I can't.'

Brad's smile faded. It probably wasn't often that a woman turned him down. 'See you around, then.'

'Yes,' I whispered as my fingers crushed a bright yellow ball of worsted yarn. 'See you around.'

CHAPTER 6

JACQUELINE DONOVAN

Leaning back in her bubble-filled tub, Jacqueline glanced up from the latest best-selling murder mystery at the sound of the front door opening.

Reese didn't generally arrive home on Tuesdays until long after she'd turned in for the night. For a while, his absence, followed by endless conjecture regarding his whereabouts, had profoundly distressed her. The subject of a mistress wasn't one a wife discussed openly with her husband, so Jacqueline's speculation had run rampant. Years ago, she'd accepted that her husband had another woman. More than one so-called friend had delighted in letting her know that Reese had been seen with some blonde. A careful inspection of their cancelled checks and credit card receipts had confirmed it.

A blonde. Men were so predictable.

Jacqueline had turned her head the other way and pretended all was right in her marriage and her life. That didn't mean this blonde-on-the-side didn't hurt. The pain of Reese's betrayal cut deep, but Jacqueline was mature enough not to dwell on such unpleasantness. Lord knew her husband hadn't come to her bed in years. As far as she was concerned, his mistress was welcome to him.

To be fair, separate bedrooms had been by mutual agreement. Early on in their marriage she'd produced the requisite offspring and following a respectable two-year span they'd tried for another child. But after two late miscarriages and the subsequent depressions, Jacqueline had given up hope.

All too soon Paul was no longer a boy. Almost overnight, it seemed, he was ready for college. When their son moved into a dorm room, Jacqueline had casually suggested Reese take advantage of the extra bedroom. The very next day, he'd moved his things into the other room. She'd been a little chagrined at the promptness of his action, but relieved, too.

Frankly she'd come to look upon sex as an intrusion. All that sweating and heaving and grinding while she did her best to pretend she was interested – it was just plain silly. Oh, the lovemaking had been pleasant and even enjoyable, especially in the beginning and then for a while after Paul. She was sure it would've been different if she'd been able to carry a second pregnancy to term. Jacqueline had wanted a daughter, but that was never to be. With the perspective of the last twenty years, she understood that her lack of interest in sex was due to anxiety or perhaps guilt. Still, it didn't matter now. And she had no intention of visiting the doctors with couches in their offices to find out.

Not having a daughter was one of Jacqueline's lifelong regrets. Reese had told her years ago, when she was feeling particularly depressed, that she'd have her daughter when Paul got married. And that was supposed to be a comfort!

Involuntarily, Jacqueline cringed. Tammie Lee was so far removed from what any daughter of hers would be that it wasn't worth contemplating.

'Jacquie, are you home?' Reese shouted from the hallway leading to their respective bedrooms.

'I'm taking a bath,' she called back, setting the book aside. It was barely after seven; perhaps his interest in the other woman had waned. The scented water and bubbles sloshed as she stood up. On second thought, maybe something was wrong, but she couldn't imagine what. She reached for a thick oversized towel from the heated rack. 'Is everything all right?'

Reese knocked briefly on the bathroom door and, without waiting for her to respond, walked inside. His eyes widened as he took in the sight of her, breathless and rosy from the hot water, with a towel wrapped around her.

'What are you doing here?' she demanded, flustered that he'd walked in on her practically nude. At one time, her body had been sleek and lovely, but the years had taken their toll. Her stomach sagged and her breasts were those of a woman in her fifties. She pulled the towel more securely about her.

'Are you kicking me out of the bathroom, too?'

'I'd appreciate my privacy.'

His eyes seemed to go cold for a moment before a blank look slid into place. 'I'd like to talk to you for a few minutes when you're available.'

'Of course,' she murmured.

Reese backed out of the room and closed the door.

As Jacqueline stepped out of the tub, she realized she was trembling. She rested one hand on the counter to steady herself, and drew in a deep, calming breath while she gathered her wits. She dried off, then slipped into her satin nightgown and matching robe. She cinched it tightly about her waist and paused in an effort to still her pounding heart before seeking out her husband.

Jacqueline found Reese in the kitchen, standing in front of the open refrigerator. He removed a take-out container she'd brought home from lunch two days earlier. She rarely cooked anymore, especially since Martha, their house-keeper, was more than willing to assume the task. Jacqueline had her own commitments and no longer bothered with meal preparation. Reese usually ate alone because he tended to stay late at the office. Or so he said.

'What's wrong?'

He didn't answer. Instead he lifted the lid and

examined what remained of her Caesar salad with shrimp. Apparently it didn't suit him because he closed it again and stuck the container back in the refrigerator. 'Do we have any eggs?'

'I think so,' she said, stepping between him and the refrigerator door. 'Would you like me to make you an omelet?'

'Would you?' He acted surprised that she'd offered.

Irritated, Jacqueline took the egg carton from the door and grabbed a cube of Monterey Jack cheese.

'What are you doing home?' she asked. If she was going to cook for him, the least Reese could do was answer her questions.

He perched on the bar stool and watched as she chose a small frying pan and set it on the burner. 'Do we have any mushrooms?'

'No. Now answer my question.'

Reese sighed laboriously.

'Fine. Don't tell me,' she muttered and turned away. Rummaging in the vegetable bin, she located a useable green pepper, half an onion and a questionable-looking zucchini, which she deftly tossed in the garbage.

'You sent Paul and Tammie Lee a floral bouquet, didn't you?'

'I told you I would,' she said irritably. She wasn't accustomed to explaining her actions to her husband. Since when was she accountable to Reese? And she hated the way he'd been nagging her about their daughter-in-law.

'Did you hear from Paul?'

Jacqueline pinched her lips to hide her displeasure. 'No, but Tammie Lee phoned to thank us for the roses,' she answered with bad grace. Actually Tammie Lee had gushed with appreciation and chattered on as if she'd never seen a dozen roses before.

'Is that all she said?'

'Should she have said more?' she snapped. Jacqueline resented this inquisition, and she wanted him to know it.

Reese glanced away. 'I have no idea. You were the one who spoke to her.'

'She informed me that she's thrilled about being pregnant. According to her, the pregnancy was a surprise.' Jacqueline could hardly wait to hear what her country-club friends said when they learned Tammie Lee was expecting. Everyone knew her feelings toward her daughter-in-law and her hope that Paul would recognize his mistake.

'I think she did it on purpose.' Jacqueline bristled just saying it. Tammie Lee knew exactly what she was doing. This baby was no more an accident than Pearl Harbor had been.

'It's Paul's life.'

'Do we need to keep having the same conversation?' The pan was hot and she cut off a small slice of butter and let it melt before tossing in the chopped vegetables. Taking her frustration out on the eggs, she cracked their shells against the side of the bowl and beat three eggs into a frothy foam.

'Did you sign up for the knitting class?'

Reese was certainly full of questions, and she

concentrated on her task rather than respond. It didn't escape her notice that he was close-mouthed about the details of his own life. She wondered how he'd feel if she started asking *him* questions. Like why he happened to be home at this time of night when he was supposed to be with his mistress. Or why he was suddenly so curious about what Jacqueline was doing. She decided not to answer.

Jacqueline half expected Reese to be angry at her lack of response. Instead he laughed.

'What's so funny?'

'You. I can't imagine you with a pair of knitting needles.'

She decided to let that remark pass. She wouldn't give him the satisfaction of letting him know he'd annoyed her.

'You don't look like any grandma I've ever seen – especially in the bathtub just now, all pink and pretty.'

Again Jacqueline let his comment slide. She poured the beaten eggs on the semi-cooked vegetables and added a heaping handful of grated cheese. With practiced ease she loosened the edges of omelet and flipped it over. When the eggs had cooked the way she knew Reese liked them, she slipped the omelet onto a plate and handed it to her husband.

Reese's eyes lit up appreciatively.

'You never did say why you're home this early.' He'd already refused to answer her once and she wondered if he would again.

'I was hungry,' he said simply and dug into the eggs and cheese.

Whatever had really happened, Reese obviously didn't plan to tell her. She watched him a moment and then said, 'I'm going to bed to read.'

Setting the dirty pan into the kitchen sink for Martha to wash in the morning, she left the kitchen.

Reese didn't say anything until she was halfway out of the room. 'Jacquie.'

'What is it?' she asked in a resigned tone.

'Thanks for making me dinner.'

She sighed audibly and slowly shook her head. 'You're welcome.' With that she walked into her bedroom. She took off the robe and sat on the edge of the queen-size bed piled high with decorative pillows, running her hand over the lacy cover. Turning aside the down comforter, she slid beneath the cool sheets and arranged her pillows so she could sit up and read.

In the distance she heard Reese rinse off his plate and put it in the dishwasher. Soon afterward the television in the den went on; just when she was about to complain, he lowered the volume.

Jacqueline read for about ten minutes – until tears unaccountably blurred her vision. She didn't understand why she was crying. Leaning across the bed to the nightstand, she plucked a tissue from the decorative box.

It was because everything was happening at once, she decided. This untimely pregnancy, and then Paul and their angry exchange the day before, followed by Reese's unexpected arrival tonight. Her life was a shambles. She'd be the laughingstock of her friends, she thought bitterly.

Mrs. Donovan with her white-trash daughter-in-law. Her *pregnant* daughter-in-law, her love-struck fool of a son and her straying husband.

Still, she was determined to prove to Reese and Paul that she'd be a good grandmother if it killed her.

CHAPTER 7

CAROL GIRARD

Carol was in a hopeful mood as she prepared dinner on Thursday evening. Doug was due home any minute and she was full of news. Cutting a chicken breast into bite-size pieces, she poured soy sauce over the uncooked meat to marinate for his favorite stir-fry.

She smiled when the door opened and her husband entered the condo. 'Hi, honey,' he said as he hung up his suit jacket, then joined her in the kitchen. Carol immediately turned into his arms and enthusiastically brought her lips to his. The kiss was long and involved, revealing her eagerness for lovemaking.

'To what do I owe this greeting?' Doug asked, leaning back far enough to take a slow, lingering look at her.

'I had a marvelous day.'

'Tell me what you did,' he said. He loosened his grip on her waist and began to examine the mail, which she'd placed on the kitchen table.

'After you left for work I went for another walk to that yarn store I found on Tuesday. Lydia said it wasn't necessary until our class tomorrow, but I picked out the needles and yarn for the baby blanket. Just wait till I show you the picture! It's so cute!' Carol rushed into the other room and produced a pattern and a ball of off-white yarn. 'Isn't this just perfect?'

Doug stared at the yarn as if he wondered how she could possibly get this excited over something so mundane.

'Don't you see?' she said. 'Doug, we're going to have a baby! I feel so confident. This time everything will be different. Earlier in the week I was thinking I can't endure this agony anymore. Everything's been so hard. But all at once I have hope, real hope. Oh, Doug, Doug, we're going to have a baby.'

She could see that some of her fervor was finally touching him. 'A baby,' she repeated, her voice quavering with emotion. She reached for his free hand and pressed his palm against her flat stomach.

Doug's gaze held hers, desire warming his eyes. He dropped the mail on the floor and wrapped her in his arms. Their kisses were passionate, luxurious. After several minutes of escalating excitement, he drew back slightly and caught her lower lip between his teeth. Familiar with her husband's wants and needs, Carol slowly undulated her hips, stroking his arousal. She murmured words of encouragement, whispered lewd promises for him alone.

Doug moaned softly and kissed her again. 'You

know what you do to me when you talk like this.'

'I know what you do to me,' she countered.

He had her blouse unfastened and half off her shoulders when they stumbled into the living room. Arms entwined, they fell onto the sofa, giggling and eager now to finish what they'd started.

'We've been married too long for this kind of crazy sex,' Doug said as he jerked off his tie and unbuttoned his shirt.

'Are you saying you want to wait until later?'

'No,' he growled.

Carol didn't either. This spontaneity was in stark contrast to the scheduled lovemaking that had become their norm. What had once been impulsive and natural was now as routine, as prosaic, as a doctor's appointment. Their focus was on timing, on the effort to match her ovulation cycle, their purpose to achieve conception. Now, for the first time in years, their lovemaking was liberated – and liberating. Once he'd dispensed with his suit pants and Carol her slacks, she lay back on the sofa and stretched out her arms to welcome her husband.

Doug lowered himself onto her and Carol closed her eyes at the exquisite sensation as his body linked with hers. This was the way lovemaking was supposed to be. She'd nearly forgotten what it was like to feel this urgency. Their purpose was love and hope, and they were drunk on their need for each other.

With Carol's arms around Doug's neck, her fingers delved into his dark hair. She whimpered and arched to meet each thrust and gave herself over to the warmth and the joy of their love-making.

They held each other for a long time afterward, savoring each moment. Neither spoke, afraid, she guessed, to disrupt the peace of this joining of bodies and souls. Their coupling was an affirmation of their deep-rooted love, of their commitment and their unwavering belief that one day they would be parents. Carol was sure. She'd been convinced of it the day she'd walked into the yarn store and learned the project for the beginners' class was a baby blanket. It was a sign.

After a while, Doug lifted his head and kissed her forehead. 'I love you.'

Sated and content, she smiled up at her husband. 'I love you, too. I think little Cameron's going to be very happy with his daddy.'

'Little Colleen, you mean.'

'We could have twins, you know.'

'Good, the more the merrier.'

They continued to gaze at each other until it was too uncomfortable to remain in the same position. After dressing and straightening her blouse, Carol picked up the yarn. Just holding it brought her comfort. She'd knit this baby blanket and with each stitch, each row, her unborn child would feel her love.

The phone rang after dinner while Carol was putting their plates and cutlery into the dishwasher. Doug sat in front of the television, half listening to the news and reading the paper. He lowered the sports pages and saw that Carol had answered the phone in the kitchen.

Caller ID told Carol it was her brother, Rick, a

pilot for Alaska Airlines, calling from his cell phone. He was based in Juneau, Alaska, where his ex-wife, Ellie, lived, too. Rick's schedule often brought him to Seattle, but he rarely had time to see her.

'Hello, big brother,' Carol said, her happiness evident in her voice.

'Carol, you sound wonderful. Are you...?' He hesitated, but Carol knew what he was asking.

'Not yet. Doug and I are working on it, though – all hours of the day and night.' She tossed her husband a saucy look, but he was reading his paper and didn't notice. 'How long are you in town?'

'Tonight and tomorrow this time around. I fly out in the late afternoon. Any chance we can get together? Not necessarily this trip, if that doesn't work for you, but soon.'

Carol immediately checked the calendar. 'I'd love to.' His invitations were few and far between, and she'd make whatever adjustments were necessary to accommodate her brother. 'What about breakfast?'

'You know I'm not much of a morning person.' Carol did remember the trouble her brother had always had getting up for school. 'That's true,' she said.

'What are you doing these days?' he asked conversationally.

'Not much. Doug and I go to the gym three mornings a week and tomorrow afternoon I'm starting a knitting class.'

'Knitting? You?'

'Yes, and if you treat me right, once I learn I'll

knit you a sweater.'

'One of those Irish ones with all the intricate cables?'

'Ah ... I was thinking more along the lines of a simple cardigan with raglan sleeves.'

Her brother chuckled. 'I can't imagine my sister, who managed two-hundred-million dollars' worth of mutual funds, with a pair of knitting needles in her hands.'

'Well, imagine it, because it's happening.' She wondered whether he had something on his mind. 'Any particular reason you want to see me?'

Rick didn't answer right away. 'It's been a while since we talked,' he said. 'I was hoping we'd get a chance to catch up. That's all.'

'That would be great. It doesn't sound as if tomorrow's going to work out. When are you in town next?' She heard pages flipping in the background as Rick checked his work schedule. 'Why don't you come here for dinner?' she suggested.

'I'll be back next week. Does that suit you and Doug?' He gave her the date and Carol wrote it on the wall calendar. With the pencil still in her hand, she paused. While it wasn't unusual for her brother to call, he didn't often pursue the issue of their getting together.

'Is everything okay, Rick?' He'd been divorced for more than a year now and although he spoke about it matter-of-factly, even dismissively, Carol suspected the breakup had caused him a lot of pain. She didn't know the exact reasons Ellie had filed for divorce, but Carol figured it had to do with Rick's career. It couldn't be easy to maintain a relationship with a husband who was away from home so much. At one time Ellie had hinted he was unfaithful, but Carol refused to believe it. Her brother wouldn't cheat on his wife. He just wouldn't.

'Well ... sort of okay, but I don't want to go into it now. There's nothing for you to worry about,' he added, clearing his throat. 'We'll have dinner next week and talk then.'

'I'll look forward to it,' Carol told him. 'Have you seen Mom and Dad lately?' she asked.

'I was in Portland last weekend and they're fit as ever.'

'Great.'

Carol and her brother made polite conversation for a few more minutes. She frowned as she replaced the receiver, curious about Rick's problem, whatever it was.

'That was Rick?' Doug asked from the living room.

'We're having dinner with him next week.'

'We haven't seen him in a while, have we?'

Carol wandered into the other room and sat on the arm of Doug's chair.

He glanced up at her. 'What's wrong?'

She shook her head. 'I wish I knew, but something's going on with my brother.' Resting her arm along the back of the chair, Carol leaned down and kissed the top of Doug's head. 'Promise you'll always love me,' she whispered.

'I already did,' he said and raised his left hand to show her his wedding ring. 'I'm yours, whether you want me or not.'

Carol relaxed against her husband's shoulder. 'I

don't think I've ever loved you more than I do at this moment.'

'Those are words a husband likes to hear,' he said, sliding his arm around her waist and pulling Carol into his lap. She nestled in his arms, grateful to her brother who'd introduced her to Doug, and to her husband for his love. Still, Rick's call bothered her and she couldn't shake the feeling that something was seriously wrong. He might tell her not to worry, but how could she help it?

CHAPTER 8

ALIX TOWNSEND

Alix regretted signing up for the knitting class, but it was too late now. As soon as she'd received her weekly paycheck, she'd returned to A Good Yarn and paid for the class. She'd acted impulsively; it was stupid to throw away good money on a useless knitting class. The more she thought about it, the more annoyed she felt. She'd gotten suckered by some childhood fantasy of the perfect mother. Well, Alix had a mother and she was far from perfect.

'John's here,' Laurel whispered, stepping up behind Alix at the counter. Her roommate had been seeing one of their regular patrons for about six months now, but as far as Alix was concerned, the guy was a sleaze. He might be good-looking and wear suits, but she saw what kind of movies he rented and they all began with X. His favorites were the kinkiest of the lot.

Early on, John had let Alix know he was interested in her, but she didn't encourage him. Laurel, however, had been keen on him from the first and seemed to think the world revolved around him. Laurel was welcome to John Murray, used-car salesman, but Alix wanted to tell her friend she could do better. The problem, Alix suspected, was Laurel's weight. Because she weighed well over two hundred pounds, Laurel seemed to believe no guy would want to be with her. It didn't help that she wore her thin, stringy blond hair long and straight and didn't wash it often. Her entire wardrobe consisted of jeans, T-shirts – most of them with either dumb or offensive slogans – and the occasional blouse. All of Alix's efforts to get her into leather and black pants had failed. Still, no matter how much she weighed or how she dressed, Laurel deserved better treatment than John gave her.

Even if John had been a different kind of guy, Alix wouldn't have been interested. She had her eye on someone else. She'd made a point of being at the counter when he came in recently and learned his name was Jordan Turner. In the looks department, he wasn't anything special. Just a regular guy, clean-cut but with a nice smile and warm brown eyes. His rental history told her he didn't go for kinky stuff the way Laurel's sick puppy did. Jordan didn't watch over-the-top violent movies, either. His last visit, he'd checked out *True Lies* and *Dumb and Dumber,* pretty tame compared to what Lover Boy chose. She'd once known a guy named Jordan Turner, but that was in sixth grade. She'd really liked him. His dad was a minister and she'd gone to church a few times because Jordan had asked her to. So, in a way, her first 'date' had been at a church. Now, that was a laugh!

'Cover for me,' Laurel said from behind her.

'Laurel,' Alix protested, biting off a warning. She hated this because she knew exactly what happened when Laurel and John slipped inside the back office and locked the door.

John watched his sicko sex videos, then returned to the video store all hot and bothered and gave Laurel ten minutes of his time. He left full of promises to take her out, which he had on rare occasions, paying her just enough attention to keep her dangling. The guy was a loser, but if Laurel didn't see that, she wasn't going to listen to anything Alix had to say.

'I won't be long,' her friend promised, giggling as she hurried toward the back of the store, leading John by the hand.

At least it wasn't busy. By nine in the evening, most people who were going to rent movies had already done so. There were only four or five customers browsing among the shelves.

Involved in her thoughts, Alix was surprised when she glanced up to find the very guy who'd been on her mind. Jordan Turner was standing at the counter.

'Sorry,' he said. 'I didn't mean to startle you.'

Caught off guard, Alix needed a moment to control her reaction. She shrugged, then asked in as casual a voice as she could manage, 'Can I help you?'

'Would you please check to see if *The Matrix* is available?'

'Yeah, sure.' Alix turned to the computer keyboard and typed in the movie title. Although no one would guess – she hoped – her heart was hammering wildly. She hadn't expected Jordan on a Thursday night. He almost always came in on Tuesdays.

'I looked on the shelf, but there doesn't seem to be a copy.'

'They're all rented,' Alix told him, staring at the computer screen. 'Would you like me to recommend another movie along the same lines?'

He considered her offer, then shook his head. 'No, thanks.' He put *Catch Me If You Can* on the counter and paid for the rental. Before she could think of anything to delay him, he was gone.

Laurel reappeared at the counter, John in tow. She had a hickey on her neck and her blouse was misbuttoned. Alix glared at John who glared back, and whispered something to Laurel. Alix couldn't hear what he was saying, but she could guess. Laurel shook her head adamantly.

John was out of the store a minute later but not soon enough to suit Alix.

'I'm meeting him after work,' Laurel informed her in a righteous tone. 'He's taking me to dinner.' Her eyes challenged Alix to say anything negative about John now, but Alix wasn't taking the bait.

'He certainly seems to be in a good mood,' she muttered sarcastically.

'He is,' Laurel said. 'He sold a car today and we're going out to celebrate.'

'You might want to fix your blouse before you leave the store.'

'Oh,' Laurel said, looking down. Her fingers immediately went to work righting the last three buttons. 'Thanks.'

Alix shook her head, and lifted a tray of videos to return to the shelf.

'I probably won't come back to the apartment tonight,' Laurel said, 'so don't wait up for me.'

As if Alix would. 'I'm not your mother. Don't worry about it.'

'My mother wouldn't care anyway. She dumped me with my uncle when I was ten. My nasty uncle, if that tells you anything.'

Laurel's home life hadn't been any better than Alix's. They'd met a year earlier when they were both living day to day, mostly in hotel rooms, and not the kind that came with small bottles of shampoo, either. When you're pulling down minimum wage, you can't afford first and last month's rent. It'd taken Laurel and Alix six months to get into their current place. You'd have thought they'd moved into a castle when they found the apartment. Between them they could manage the rent, but with all the neighborhood renovation, Alix was afraid they'd soon be out on the street. Rumor had it the apartment complex had been sold to the same company that bought the old bank.

The apartment was a dump, with sagging floors, a permanently stained bathtub and cracks in the ceiling. But it was the first home Alix had ever considered truly hers. All the furniture was stuff even Goodwill wouldn't take. She and Laurel had collected it piece by piece over the past few months, through word of mouth and a couple of times right off the street.

Neither girl was in contact with her parents. The last Alix had heard, her dad was living somewhere in California but she hadn't seen him in ten years and frankly she didn't feel she was missing much. He hadn't made any effort to find her and she had no desire to seek him out. Her mother was doing time for forging checks. No one knew that, other than Laurel, whom she'd told in a moment of weakness. Alix had sent her mother several letters but when she wrote back, all she wanted was for Alix to send her money – or even worse, get her stuff she shouldn't be asking for.

Alix's only other family was her older brother, but Tom had gotten mixed up with a rough crowd and ended up dead of a drug overdose five years ago. His death had hit her hard. It still did. Tom was all she'd had and then he'd gone and ... given up. When she first heard, she'd been angry; so angry that she'd wanted to kill him for doing this to her. The next thing she knew, she was huddled on the floor, wishing she was eight years old again and could hide in a closet and pretend her world was safe and secure.

Without Tom, she'd faltered, become reckless and got into trouble. It took her a while to find her way, but she had. These days Alix was determined not to make the same mistakes her brother had. She'd looked after herself from the age of sixteen. In her own opinion, she'd done a fairly good job of staying sober and sane. Sure, she'd butted heads with the boys in blue a few times and been assigned a social worker, but she was proud that she'd stayed out of serious trouble – and off welfare.

'You got a call this afternoon,' Laurel informed her just before closing. 'I meant to tell you but it slipped my mind.'

They could afford an apartment but not a phone, so all contacts were made at the video store, which annoyed the manager. 'Who'd be calling me?'

'Someone named Ms. O'Dell.'

The social worker had started coming around after the bogus drug bust. Alix had been caught with Laurel's stash of marijuana. She still hadn't forgiven Laurel for wasting money on it in the first place and, even worse, hiding it in Alix's purse. *She* wasn't the one using, but no one was willing to listen to her protests of innocence, so she'd shut up and accepted the black mark against her record.

'What did she want?' Alix asked, although Mrs. O'Dell was actually returning her call. Before Alix invested all that time, energy and money in knitting the baby blanket, she wanted to be sure the effort would count toward her community-service hours.

'She said it was fine and it might help you with anger management, whatever that means.'

'Oh.' At least the woman hadn't actually mentioned the knitting class, which saved Alix from having to tell Laurel what she'd done.

'Are you going to tell me what this is all about?'

Alix narrowed her lips. 'No.'

'We're roommates, Alix. You can trust me.'

'Sure I can,' she snarled. 'Just like I could trust you to tell the truth to the cops.' She wasn't letting Laurel forget that she'd taken the fall for her.

'All right,' Laurel snapped and held up both hands. 'Have it your way.'

That was exactly what Alix intended.

CHAPTER 9

'We are all knitted together. Knitting keeps me connected to all the women who have made my life so rich.'

–Ann Norling, designer

LYDIA HOFFMAN

Although I'd taught knitting for a number of years, I'd never worked with such an eclectic group as the women in my small beginners' class. They had absolutely nothing in common. The three of them sat stiffly at the table in the back of the store, not exchanging a word.

'Perhaps we should begin by introducing ourselves. Explain why you decided to join this class,' I said and motioned for Jacqueline to start. She was the one I worried about the most. Jacqueline was clearly part of the country-club set, and her initial reaction to Alix had been poorly disguised shock. From the look she cast me, I was afraid she was ready to make an excuse and bolt for the door. I'm not sure what prompted her to stay, but I'm grateful she did.

'Hello,' Jacqueline said in a well-modulated voice, nodding at the other two women who sat across from her. 'My name is Jacqueline Donovan. My husband's architectural firm is responsible for the Blossom Street renovation. I wanted to learn how to knit because I'm about to become a grandmother for the first time.'

Immediately Alix jerked her head up and stared at the older woman. 'Your husband's the one behind this whole mess? You tell him to keep his hands off my apartment, understand?'

'How dare you speak to me in that tone of voice!'

The two women glared at one another. Alix was halfway out of her chair, and I had to admire Jacqueline, who didn't so much as flinch. I quickly turned to Carol. 'Would you mind going next?' I asked and my voice must have betrayed my nervousness.

I'd come to know Carol a little; she'd been in the shop twice already and had bought yarn. I knew why she'd joined the class and hoped we could be friends.

'Yes, hi,' Carol said, sounding as unsettled as I felt.

Alix continued to glare at Jacqueline but the older woman did a masterful job of ignoring her. I should have known something like this would happen, but felt powerless to stop it. Alix and Jacqueline were about as different as any two women could be.

'My name is Carol Girard and my husband and I are hoping for a child. I'm currently undergoing fertility treatments. I'm having an IVF attempt in July. The reason I'm in this class is that I want to knit a blanket for my yet-to-be-conceived baby.'

I could see from Alix's face that she didn't understand the term.

'IVF refers to in vitro fertilization,' Carol explained.

'I read a wonderful article about that in a recent issue of *Newsweek* magazine,' Jacqueline said. 'It's amazing what doctors can do these days.'

'Yes, there are quite a few miracle drugs available now, but thus far Doug and I haven't received our miracle.'

The look of longing on Carol's face was so intense, I yearned to put my hand on her shoulder.

'July is our last chance at the IVF process,' she added. Carol bit down on her lower lip and I wondered if she knew how much of her anxiety she revealed.

'What do they do to you with this in vitro stuff?' Alix asked, leaning forward. She seemed genuinely interested.

'It's a rather long, drawn-out process,' Carol said. 'I'm not sure you want me to take class time to go though it all.'

'Would you mind?' Alix asked, surprising me with her curiosity.

'By all means,' Jacqueline chimed in, but I doubted that her interest was as sincere as Alix's seemed to be.

'Well,' Carol said, clasping her hands on the table, 'it all starts with drugs.'

'Doesn't everything?' Alix laughed at her own joke, but no one else joined in.

'I was on this drug that stimulates the ovaries to produce eggs, and once the eggs appeared, they had to be harvested.'

'Did it hurt?' Jacqueline asked.

'Only slightly, but all I had to do was think about a baby, and any discomfort was worth it. We both want to be parents so badly.'

That much was obvious, and from what I'd seen of Carol I was sure she'd be a wonderful mother.

'After the doctor collected Doug's sperm, my eggs were inseminated to create a number of embryo cultures. These are then transferred to my uterus. We've had two attempts that didn't succeed, and the insurance company will only pay for three and, well, it's just very important that I get pregnant this time.'

'It seems to me you're putting lots of stress on yourself,' Alix said in what I found to be an insightful comment.

'How nerve-racking for you both,' Jacqueline murmured.

'I feel so confident, though.' Carol positively beamed with it. 'I'm not sure why, but for the first time in months I feel really good about all of this. We decided to wait after our last attempt. Mostly because Doug and I needed a while to deal with our disappointment over the second failure. I also felt it was necessary to prepare myself physically and mentally. But it's going to work this time. I just *know* we're going to have our baby.'

'I hope you do,' Alix said. 'People who want children should have them.'

'There's always adoption,' Jacqueline said. 'Have you considered that?'

'We have,' Carol replied. 'It's a viable option, but we don't want to try for adoption until we've done everything possible to have a biological child.'

'From what I understand, there's quite a waiting period,' Jacqueline said and then seemed to regret speaking.

'Yes, I know... Doug and I have talked about that, too. We might have to look into an overseas adoption but we've read that those can be difficult. Anyway, these are all options we're willing to consider if we can't have our own child, but we'll make those decisions when and if the time comes.'

I waited a moment and then gestured to Alix. 'Tell us a little about yourself.'

Alix shrugged. 'My name's Alix Townsend and I work at the video store across the street.'

I hoped she wouldn't mention working on the baby blanket to deduct hours from her court-ordered community service, but I couldn't stop her if she did. Once Jacqueline heard that, I figured she'd probably walk right out of the class. Forgive me for being so mercenary, but Jacqueline would buy far more yarn than Alix ever could.

'I happen to like living in this neighborhood,' Alix said pointedly, 'and I hope I can continue to live here once they're through screwing up the street.' Her eyes narrowed as she stared across the table.

'Don't look at me like that,' Jacqueline muttered. 'I don't have anything to do with it.'

'I thought,' I said, still standing, 'that we could discuss the different weights and types of yarn for our first lesson.' I felt an urgent need to distract Alix, although I was a strong supporter of the Linus Project. 'The pattern I've chosen is one of my favorites. What I like about this particular pattern is that it's challenging enough to keep you interested, but not so difficult as to discourage you. It's done in a four-ply worsted weight yarn and knits up fairly quickly.'

I had a large wicker basket filled with samples of several worsted weight yarns in a variety of colors. 'I know it might sound rather self-serving, but I feel I should mention something here. Always buy high-quality yarn. When you're investing your time and effort in a project, you defeat yourself before you even start if you use bargain basement yarn.'

'I agree one-hundred percent,' Jacqueline said firmly. I'd known she wouldn't have a problem with that.

'What if some people can't afford the high-priced stuff?' Alix demanded.

'Well, yes, that could make things difficult.'

'You said anyone taking the class gets a twenty-percent discount on yarn. Are you sticking to that or have you changed your mind?'

'I'm sticking to it,' I assured her.

'Good, because I don't have a lot of change

jingling around in the bottom of my purse.' She reached for a pretty pink-and-white blend of wool and acrylic. 'This costs how much?'

'Five dollars a skein.'

'For each one?' A horrified look came over her. I nodded.

'How many would I need if I knit the blanket using this?'

I glanced down at the pattern and then calculated the yardage of the worsted against the total amount of yarn required for the project. I grabbed my calculator. 'It looks like five should do nicely. If you only use four you can return the fifth one to me for a full refund.'

Alix stood and reached into her pocket and dragged out a crumpled five-dollar bill. 'I can only buy one this week, but I should be able to pick up the second one next week, if that's all right.'

'It's important to get the same dye lot for each project, so I'll put aside what you need and you can pay me as you go.'

Alix looked pleased. 'That works for me. I suppose the lady married to that fancy architect can buy all the yarn in your shop.'

'My name is Jacqueline and I'd prefer that you use it.'

'I'd like you all to choose your yarn now, if you would,' I said quickly, cutting the two of them off before Alix leaped across the table and attacked Jacqueline. I hated to admit it, but the older woman wasn't the most personable soul. Her attitude, although different, wasn't any better than Alix's.

Jacqueline sat by herself and took up half the table. When Carol arrived, she'd had no choice but to sit next to Alix. It was clear from Jacqueline's manner that she expected to be catered to, not only in this class, but in life.

I couldn't help wondering what I'd gotten myself into with these knitting classes, and frankly I was worried. I'd thought... I'd hoped to make friends with my customers, but this was starting off all wrong.

The class lasted two hours and we barely got through casting on stitches. I chose the knitting on method, which is by far the simplest way to learn but not the preferred method. I didn't want to overwhelm my three students during their first lesson.

I had reason to doubt my teaching abilities by the end of the class. Carol picked up the technique immediately, but Alix was all fingers. Jacqueline didn't take to it quickly, either. When at last it was closing time, my head was pounding with an approaching headache and I felt as if I'd run a marathon.

It didn't help that Margaret phoned just as I was getting ready to close for the day.

'A Good Yarn,' I said, scooping up the receiver, hoping to sound upbeat and eager to be of service.

'It's me,' my sister returned in a crisp business tone. With a voice like that, she should be working for the Internal Revenue Service. 'I thought we should discuss Mother's Day.'

She was right. Opening the store had so completely consumed me that I hadn't remembered.

'Of course, we need to do something special for Mom.' It would be our first Mother's Day without Dad and I realized it was going to be difficult for all of us, but especially for Mom. Despite our differences, Margaret and I did something together every year to honor our mother.

'The girls suggested we take her to lunch on Saturday. We're seeing Matt's mother on Sunday.'

'Excellent idea, but my shop is open on Saturdays.' I knew Saturday was a prime business day and I couldn't afford *not* to be open; I closed the shop on Mondays instead.

My sister hesitated and when she spoke again, she seemed almost gleeful. It didn't take me long to discover why.

'Since you can't get away, the girls and I will see Mom on Saturday and you can have your own time with her on Sunday.' This meant Margaret wouldn't have to share our mother with me. Mom's attention would be on my sister, which was clearly why Margaret had arranged things this way. I didn't understand why everything had to be a competition for her.

'Oh.' I'd hoped we'd all be together.

'You're not working on Sunday, are you?'

My shoulders sagged. 'No, but ... well, if that's what you want.'

'I don't have any choice, do I?' Margaret said in the surly, aggressive tone I have long detested. 'You're the one who can't make lunch on Saturday. I suppose you want me to adjust my schedule to yours, but I won't.'

'I didn't ask you to change anything.'

'Not in so many words, but I could read between the lines. I do have a husband, you know, and he has a mother, too. For once we wanted to spend Mother's Day with her.'

Rather than get into an argument, I kept my voice as unemotional as possible. 'Perhaps we could compromise.'

'How do you mean?'

'I know Mom would love to have lunch on the waterfront. I could meet you there and close the shop for a couple of hours. That way we could all be together and then I'd join her on Sunday, as well.'

I could tell from the lengthy pause that Margaret wasn't happy with that idea. 'You expect me to pick up Mom and drive into Seattle on a Saturday afternoon – because it's more convenient for *you?* We both know how dreadful the traffic is.'

'It's only a suggestion.'

'I'd rather we celebrated Mother's Day separately this year.'

'Fine. Perhaps we should.' I left it at that and made a mental note to call Mom to explain.

'Good. We've got that settled.' I noticed that Margaret didn't ask about my first two weeks of business. Nor did she make any other inquiries or give me an opportunity to ask what was going on in *her* life.

'I have to go,' Margaret said. 'Julia's dancing class starts in fifteen minutes.'

'Give her my love,' I said. My two nieces were a joy to me. I loved them deeply and felt close to both Julia and Hailey. Sensing my feelings, Margaret did her best to keep the girls away from me. But now that they were pre-teens, they had minds of their own. We often chatted and I suspected they didn't let their mother know.

My sister hung up without so much as a goodbye. That was typical behavior for Margaret.

I walked over to the front door and turned over the sign to read Closed. As I did, I saw Brad Goetz coming out of the apartment building where Alix lived. He was in a hurry, half-jogging to his truck. I couldn't see where he'd parked, but I thought I knew the reason for his rush. He was handsome and eligible, and there was every likelihood he had a Friday-night date.

I could've been the one joining him for dinner—only I wasn't. That had been my own choice, a choice I was beginning to regret...

CHAPTER 10

JACQUELINE DONOVAN

In an attempt to hide her nervousness, Jacqueline poured herself a second glass of chardonnay. After the first sip she stepped into the kitchen and brought out the hors d'oeuvre platter for their guests. Martha had put together crackers artfully swirled with herb-mixed cream cheese and decorated with tiny shrimp. Paul had phoned earlier in the week to ask if he and Tammie Lee could stop by the house on Wednesday evening.

They'd spent the Mother's Day weekend in

Louisiana with Tammie Lee's mother, who apparently wasn't feeling well. Jacqueline had made a conscious decision not to take offense.

This was the first time Paul had ever asked permission to visit the family home, and Jacqueline's nerves had been badly frayed ever since his phone call.

'Relax,' Reese said, following her into the kitchen.

'I don't have a good feeling about this,' Jacqueline murmured. She glanced at the clock on the microwave and realized it was a full ten minutes before her son and daughter-in-law were due to arrive. She cringed at the prospect of making small talk with Tammie Lee, and feared that Paul was about to announce he'd accepted a transfer to the New Orleans branch so Tammie Lee could be close to her family.

'Setting up an appointment to come over here isn't like Paul.'

'He was just being thoughtful.' Reese walked around the counter and sat on a stool. 'Isn't knitting supposed to soothe your nerves?'

'That's another thing,' Jacqueline snapped. 'I'm dropping out of that ridiculous class.'

His head flew back at the vehemence of her declaration. 'What's gotten into you?'

'I have my reasons.' She didn't like the look on Reese's face – as if he was disappointed in her. But he wasn't the one confronting that ill-mannered punk rocker or whatever those people called themselves these days. Alix, spelled A-L-l-X, resembled a gang member; the girl frightened her. 'Why should you care what I do?' Jacqueline leaned against the counter across from her husband.

'You seemed excited about it last week,' he said blandly. It was obviously of no consequence to him. 'I thought it was a conciliatory gesture on your part. I assumed you signed up for the classes to show Paul you're planning to be a good grandmother.'

'I am determined to be a *wonderful* grand-mother. For heaven's sake, what chance does a child of Tammie Lee's have? She'll grow up learning how to pickle pigs' feet.' She shivered at the very idea.

'Now, Jacqueline...'

'Actually, I blame you for this.'

'Me?' Reese straightened and for a moment he seemed about to laugh outright. 'You blame me for *what?*'

'For the fact that I'm in this ... this awful knitting class.'

He frowned. 'You'd better tell me what's going on.'

'There's a young woman in the class. I can't imagine why she'd ever want to learn to knit, but it's not important. She's vile, Reese. That's the only word I can think of to describe her. Her hair is the most ludicrous shade of purple and she took an instant dislike to me when she learned that you're responsible for what's happening in the Blossom Street neighborhood.'

Reese reached for his wine. 'Most people there welcome the renovation.'

'Alix lives in the apartment building at the end of the street.' As far as Jacqueline could see, it was a rat-infested dump. If it was slated for demolition, all the better. Alix and her kind would need to look elsewhere for low-rent housing. Girls like that weren't wanted in an upscale neighborhood, which Blossom Street would soon become.

'Ah,' Reese murmured and sipped his wine. 'Now I understand.'

'What's planned for the building?' Jacqueline asked.

'That hasn't been decided.' Reese gently swirled his wine against the sides of the goblet. 'The city is talking to the owner. My idea was to completely remodel the place into condos, but it seems some advocates for low-income housing now have the mayor's ear.'

'That's unfortunate. Those low-rent people will ruin the neighborhood. You might as well kiss all your hard work goodbye.' She hated to sound like a pessimist, but if Alix was any indication of the quality of person living in that building, then the entire street was at risk.

'Maybe you should give the knitting class another try,' Reese suggested, ignoring her outburst.

The truth of it was that Jacqueline *wanted* to continue. She hadn't found the class 'awful' at all; that was an exaggeration for Reese's benefit. Other than the confrontation with Alix, she'd enjoyed the lesson. At one point, Lydia had told them to walk around the shop and choose three balls of yarn in their favorite colors. At the time it'd seemed like a useless exercise. Jacqueline had chosen a silver gloss, a deep purple and a vibrant red. Lydia's next instruction had been to choose wool in the color she disliked most. Jacqueline had gone immediately to a skein of bright yellow, which was the color that appealed to her least. Lydia had talked about contrasting colors and showed how they often complement each other. In fact, the yellow had looked completely different against the purple, and just as Lydia had said, the contrast was surprisingly effective.

She'd discovered that so much of knitting was about choosing the textures and colors, which was something she hadn't considered before. Jacqueline had walked out of the class with the realization that she'd learn far more than the basic knitting stitches. That, however, did little to quell her uneasiness concerning Alix.

'I might decide to attend the second beginners' session later in the summer,' Jacqueline muttered, still unsure of what to do. She'd paid for the entire six-week course and detested the thought of some hoodlum driving her away with intimidation and ill-manners.

The doorbell rang and Jacqueline felt the tension crawl up her spine. While Reese answered the door, she forced a smile and moved into the formal living room, hands clasped in front of her. She waited for Reese to greet Paul and Tammie Lee in the foyer.

'How wonderful to see you both,' Jacqueline purred, extending her arms to Tammie Lee and her son as they entered the room. She briefly hugged her daughter-in-law and grazed Paul's cheek with her lips. Now that she knew Tammie Lee was pregnant, she wondered how she hadn't guessed earlier. Her daughter-in-law was definitely showing – enough to be wearing a maternity top.

Paul and Tammie Lee sat on the sofa, so close their shoulders touched. They held hands, as if to proclaim that nothing would tear them apart.

While Reese poured a glass of wine for Paul, Jacqueline carried in the platter of hors d'oeuvres. Tammie Lee smiled up at Jacqueline.

'I just love shrimp and ever since I've been pregnant I've had the worst craving for them,' she said in a soft twang. 'Just ask Paul. I think he must be thoroughly sick of shrimp, but he never complains.' She gazed lovingly toward her husband as she accepted a small napkin and two crackers.

Paul cast his wife a look of love and pride, and it was all Jacqueline could do to maintain her composure. For the life of her, she couldn't understand what her son saw in this girl.

'What can I get you to drink?' Reese asked Tammie Lee when he brought Paul his wineglass.

'It's so nice of you to ask, but I'm just fine, thank you.' If there was anything for which to be grateful, Jacqueline mused, it was the fact that Tammie Lee seemed to be taking care of herself during the pregnancy. At least she had that much common sense.

Reese and Jacqueline sat across from them in leather chairs, with a polished mahogany end table between them. They so rarely used the formal living room that five years after she'd purchased the chairs they still smelled of new leather.

'I think we should tell them,' Tammie Lee whispered to Paul.

Paul nodded and squeezed her hand. 'Tammie Lee had an ultrasound this afternoon and it seems we're having a baby girl.' He smiled. 'Sometimes they can't be sure, but our technician was quite positive it's a girl.'

'A girl,' Reese repeated and the happiness in his voice was unmistakable. He stood and clapped Paul on the back. 'Did you hear that, Jacquie? We're finally getting our baby girl!'

Jacqueline felt her hands go numb. 'A grand-daughter,' she repeated as the odd tingling sensation spread up her arms. Oh, how she'd once longed for a daughter.

'We haven't chosen any names yet,' Tammie Lee rushed to add in that soft drawl of hers. It always made her sound as if she was talking underwater. 'We only decided this afternoon that we wanted to know the sex of the baby. You're the first people we've told.'

'Your mother and I had always hoped for a little girl,' Reese said, echoing Jacqueline's thoughts.

'That's ... wonderful,' Jacqueline finally managed.

'We decided we should let you know, Mom,' Paul said, directing his attention to her for the first time, 'so you'd know what color yarn to get for the baby blanket.'

'Mrs. Donovan, I declare, when Paul told me you were knitting a blanket for the baby, it just warmed my heart. Y'all have been so kind to me.' She planted both hands over her stomach and sighed.

That twang of Tammie Lee's put Jacqueline's teeth on edge. Some might find it pleasing, but to

Jacqueline it sounded uneducated. Unrefined.

'There's more news,' Paul said, moving toward the edge of the sofa cushion.

'More?' Reese said. 'Don't tell me you're having twins.'

'Nothing like that.' Paul laughed shortly.

Tammie Lee grinned at her husband. 'Twins! I'm so nervous about one baby, I can't even imagine what would happen if we had two.'

Paul turned to share such a gentle look with his wife that Jacqueline glanced away. Any hope she had of her son regretting his marriage died a quick death.

'So what's your other news?' Reese asked.

Paul's face brightened. 'I got word last week that Tammie Lee and I have been accepted into the Seattle Country Club.' The club, to which Jacqueline and Reese belonged, was the most prestigious in the area. New memberships were limited to only a few each year. It went without saying that only the right kind of people were accepted. One of Jacqueline's first thoughts when she was introduced to Tammie Lee was that Paul had ruined his chances of ever joining the country club.

'I'm so pleased,' Jacqueline said, doing her best to smile. Apparently Tammie Lee's lengthy and inappropriate discussions of southern cuisine hadn't been as much of a detriment as she'd assumed.

'I've been asked to work on the cookbook committee,' Tammie Lee gushed as if this was the greatest compliment of her life. 'I can't tell you the number of times someone's asked me to share

103

my mama's, Aunt Thelma's and Aunt Frieda's favorite recipes.'

'Recipes for what?' Jacqueline blurted out the question before she could stop herself.

'Mainly folks want to know about hush puppies. Four or five ladies have already asked me about those.'

'Hush puppies?'

'It's like cornbread, Mother,' Paul supplied.

'I know what they are,' she said between clenched teeth.

'Paul *loves* my hush puppies,' Tammie Lee twanged in her eagerness to continue. 'My mama told me they got their name from hunters who threw leftover ends of the cornbread to their dogs to keep 'em quiet at night.'

'*This* is the recipe you're submitting to the Seattle Country Club Cookbook?' Jacqueline was convinced she'd never be able to show her face in public again.

'Oh, and I asked Mama for Grandma's recipe for Brunswick stew, which is my daddy's all-time favorite. My grandma was raised in Georgia before she married my grandpa and moved to Tennessee. I was almost eighteen before we moved to Louisiana, so I really consider myself a bluegrass girl.'

'Brunswick stew,' Jacqueline said. That at least sounded presentable.

'It's a southern version of chili. Mama always served it when we had a barbecue. Mama has Grandma's original recipe and I'll need to change it a bit. Everyone uses pork or chicken nowadays, instead of possum or squirrel.'

One more word from this woman and Jacqueline was afraid she'd keel over in a dead faint.

'I hope you give them your recipe for deep-fried okra,' Paul said as if he'd never tasted anything so good in his life. 'You wouldn't believe what Tammie Lee does with okra. I swear I've died and gone to heaven.'

Once and only once had Jacqueline sampled the slimy green vegetable. It'd been in some kind of soup dish. Never having seen it before, she'd lifted it from the bowl and been repulsed by the thick slime that had dripped from her spoon. She'd nearly gagged just looking at it and now her son was telling her he enjoyed this disgusting vegetable.

'I have a recipe for pecan pie that's a family favorite and I'd be happy to share that, too.'

'Actually, I think it's because of Tammie Lee's cooking that we got accepted by the country club.'

Jacqueline had to bite her lip to keep from reminding Paul that she'd been volunteering there for years. Her charity projects had been some of the club's most successful fund-raising events. Reese's name carried plenty of weight, too, but apparently their son hadn't taken his parents' longstanding contribution into account. Oh, no, he assumed it was Tammie Lee's method of cooking road kill – squirrel, for heaven's sake! – that had opened the doors.

'You do seem to be full of good news,' Reese said, grinning in a way that conveyed his delight.

'Yes,' Jacqueline agreed, making an effort to

look equally delighted. She was trying, trying hard, but it was difficult.

'I declare I don't know any couple happier than Paul and me,' Tammie Lee drawled. 'I can't believe any man has as much love for a woman as Paul does for me, especially since we found out about the baby.'

'We're thrilled to have you as part of our family,' Reese said.

'I can feel your love,' Tammie Lee said, looking at Reese. 'And I can't thank you enough for welcoming me the way you have.'

Paul's eyes connected with Jacqueline's. He knew her feelings. She might be able to fool Tammie Lee, but her son knew her all too well. Until now, Paul had protected his young wife from her disapproval. At one time, mother and son had shared a special closeness, but since the advent of Tammie Lee, that had virtually disappeared.

In that moment, Jacqueline saw the fierce challenge in her son's gaze. She knew that if she said one word to hurt Tammie Lee, he'd never forgive her.

CHAPTER 11

CAROL GIRARD

Carol placed the bouquet of fresh flowers in the center of the dinner table and stepped back to examine her handiwork. She'd walked down to Pike Place Market early in the afternoon and purchased the white lilies and red astromeria, along with fresh salmon and just-picked baby asparagus spears. She'd arranged the flowers herself, using a porcelain vase that had come with the roses Doug had sent on their last anniversary.

For so many years, all her efforts and energy had gone into her career. When she'd first quit her job she'd faltered, unsure of how to fill her days. She would've been completely lost if not for her online support group. These women had become as close as sisters; they all struggled with the problems of infertility and gave each other information and encouragement. She was heartened to discover that several of the other women had started knitting for relaxation and a sense of accomplishment. Carol shared those goals, but for her knitting was also a symbol of the life she wanted to live, *would* live – as a mother.

Everything had changed for the better the day she'd found the knitting shop on Blossom Street.

After meeting Lydia and the others last week, it was as if a whole world had opened up to her. For the first time she looked upon her condo as more than a place to sleep and occasionally entertain. It was her home and she decided to make it a real one, with small feminine touches that conveyed her love for her husband and soon-to-be child.

Usually when her brother stopped by they went out to eat. This evening, Carol was cooking their meal. Rick had sounded troubled when he'd phoned and she wanted to create a comfortable, intimate atmosphere where they could talk freely. The shopping and flower-arranging had taken up most of the afternoon, but she'd loved every minute of it. Six months ago she would've scoffed at the idea of arranging flowers or spending a morning wandering the aisles at a local farmer's market. Now those small domestic activities were a source of pleasure and satisfaction. Because she was doing them for her family.

Rick called from the lobby and Carol hurried to meet him at the door, hugging her brother hard as soon as he stepped inside.

'Well, well,' Rick said, leaning back, apparently surprised by the warmth of her greeting. 'I didn't expect to be knocked off my feet.'

'Sorry. It's just that it's so good to see you.'

Rick laughed and looked around the condo. 'Where's Doug?'

'He phoned – he's running late. I'm sure he won't be much longer.'

She glanced at her watch as she led Rick into the living room. Doug hadn't shown nearly as much enthusiasm about this dinner with Rick as she had. 'Would you like a beer?' Her brother preferred ale to hard liquor. He only drank when he was twenty-four hours from flying.

'I'd love one.' He sat down where he had an unobstructed view of the waterfront and was quiet for a long moment as he gazed out the window. He accepted the beer and smiled his thanks. 'Can I do anything to help with dinner?'

'Not a thing. Everything's almost ready.'

'You've done all right for yourself, little sister,' he said, sounding almost sad. He tipped back the beer bottle and took a drink.

'So have you,' she told him.

Rick chuckled softly. 'Have I?'

'My goodness, Rick,' she said, trying to lighten his somber mood. 'You're a pilot for a major airline. It's your dream come true.' Her brother had worked his way up through the ranks. For as long as Carol could remember, Rick had talked about being a pilot. From the time he could drive, he started hanging around airports, talking to the pilots, learning what he could.

He smiled as if in agreement. 'I should be happy, then, right?'

'You aren't?' She went into the living room, abandoning the salad she'd set on the counter. The finishing touches could wait. Sitting across from him, she leaned close. 'What's wrong?'

'Sorry, sorry.' He laughed off the question. 'I don't know what came over me. I'm fine. Forget I said anything.'

'I'm not going to forget it. Now, tell me what's on your mind. You didn't come all this way to check out my view for the umpteenth time.'

He shrugged, dismissing her question. 'Actually, I was in a great mood until I saw what you've

109

done with the place.'

'Exactly what have I done?' Carol asked with a smile. 'And why would that ruin your mood?'

Her brother looked around, and, after a few minutes, frowned. 'I don't know *exactly*, but there's a difference.'

He'd noticed. Actually, everything was in the same place it'd been during his last visit. The furniture was all the same, too; outwardly very little had changed. Yet the condo felt transformed. The flowers and polished wood and shining glass were small things, but they expressed her new attitude toward home and what it meant. This was a place of love, a place waiting to welcome a child.

'There *is* a difference,' Carol confirmed, 'but I'm the one who's changed. I'm happy, Rick, genuinely happy.'

The forlorn expression on her brother's face was enough to bring tears to her eyes. 'And you're not,' she said softly.

'No,' he breathed. He leaned forward and braced his arms against his legs, letting the beer dangle between his parted knees. 'Nothing seems right without Ellie.'

Her brother and Ellie had divorced a year ago. He'd never spoken of the breakup before, and his willingness to introduce the subject now was an indication of how miserable he was.

'I'm still in love with her,' he confessed, 'but I screwed up.'

Carol held her breath. Because she loved and respected both her brother and his wife, she'd done her best to stay out of it. The one conversation she'd had with Ellie since the divorce had been awkward and unsettling, and Carol hadn't phoned her since.

Carol wasn't the only one in the dark, either. Even her parents didn't know what had caused the dissolution of Rick's marriage. Whatever it was, he seemed to regret his divorce and want his ex-wife back. 'Have you been in touch with Ellie?' she asked.

Rick nodded. 'She said it'd be better if we went our separate ways. I tried, Carol, I gave it a real effort, but my life isn't any good without her. I had no idea it would be like this.' He briefly tilted his head toward the ceiling and forcefully expelled his breath. 'I hear she's dating again.'

'That must hurt.' Rick and Ellie had been college sweethearts. Carol remembered the first time she'd met the outgoing blonde. She'd instantly liked Rick's girlfriend and had hoped to have her as a sister one day.

'The thought of Ellie with some other man is driving me insane. All I can think about is how stupid I've been. I'd give anything to work this out with her. If it meant quitting my job, I'd do it in a heartbeat.'

'I'm so sorry.' Carol felt at a loss to help him, especially since she still didn't know what had gone wrong.

'Yeah, I am, too.'

'Do you want to explain what happened?'

'Ellie didn't tell you?' he asked, his eyes widening. 'I assumed she had.'

Carol shook her head. 'I called her after you told me she'd filed for divorce, but she said she'd rather not discuss it.' She didn't add that Ellie had been sobbing at the time. Until the end, Carol had hoped the two of them would be able to settle their differences and reunite. After the divorce, though, it seemed Ellie was intent on moving forward with her life.

'I'm away from home so much,' her brother said. 'It gets lonely, you know?'

This was what Ellie had implied but Carol had refused to accept it. Rick would never do such a thing, she'd told herself. He was her older brother, her hero. Still, she had to know. 'You ... didn't have an affair, did you?'

'No,' he said. 'It wasn't like that... But Ellie – well, she can't accept the fact that I'm around beautiful women on the job and away from home. It became a trust issue.'

Carol wouldn't feel entirely comfortable with Doug constantly being around other women, either, but she didn't say so. Her brother didn't need to hear about her own insecurities.

'I don't know why she felt that way,' Rick went on. 'It's Ellie I love.' He wiped his face in a weary gesture. 'I tried to convince her that she's the only woman for me but she wouldn't listen. I can't believe she threw away our marriage because she didn't trust me.'

Carol couldn't believe it, either, but she kept her thoughts to herself. There were two possibilities: Ellie had been jealous and irrational or there was more to Rick's behavior than he was saying.

'I did everything I could to talk Ellie out of the divorce,' he continued. 'Okay, so maybe I was tempted, but hell, what am I supposed to do every night? Sit in my hotel room and watch television?

112

I did go out occasionally. Can you really blame me for that?'

Maybe there *was* some basis for Ellie's distrust. Still, Carol found it practically inconceivable that her brother would cheat on his wife. He was an honorable man but he was a man, and if he had a drink with a flight attendant or a female pilot now and then – was that so bad? Perhaps Ellie had simply overreacted.

'I suppose I should be grateful we delayed having a family,' he mumbled.

Carol agreed; if there was anything to be grateful for, it was that. She hated the thought of children suffering the upheaval of a broken home.

'Ellie wanted kids, but I wasn't ready.'

Carol nodded.

'Any idea what I should do now?' he asked, peering at her as if she could provide him with answers.

She patted his arm gently, not knowing how to respond. Rick could be his own worst enemy. He'd always been a sociable person, the life of the party, a natural daredevil, and she'd loved and admired him as her gallant older brother. It saddened her to see how unhappy he was.

'You need to prove yourself to Ellie.'

'But how?' he cried. 'I'm telling you, Carol, I'm at my wits' end. Ellie claims she doesn't want to see me again.'

'Perhaps you could write to her.'

'Write what?'

'A letter,' she said. 'Better yet, use e-mail. Tell her you're an idiot.'

'I think she already knows that.' For the first

time since they'd started talking, she saw a hint of smile on his face. 'What if she won't answer me?'

'Don't take no for an answer. Let her know you aren't giving up.'

'Should I send her flowers? That kind of thing?'

'Bring her strawberries and fresh fruit from the Pike Place Market.' Fresh fruit was available in Juneau, but it was extremely expensive. 'A whole basket,' Carol suggested. 'As I recall, Ellie loves blueberries.'

'She does?'

'Rick! You should know that. She was your wife.'

'That's the problem,' her brother moaned. 'I didn't pay her near enough attention. I didn't realize how much I loved her until it was too late.'

'Then you're going to make up for lost time.'

He grinned, and it was the same boyish smile she remembered from childhood. 'Your enthusiasm is catching. You really think I can win her back?'

'Yes,' she cried. It felt good to have her brother turn to her, to need her help. Rick had made a mistake and hadn't fought for his marriage, but she'd do everything she could to support him.

CHAPTER 12

ALIX TOWNSEND

Laurel owed Alix, so she had her roommate cover for her the minute Jordan Turner showed up at the video store on Tuesday night. As soon as she saw that he was getting ready to leave, she slipped out front and pretended to be on break. Her hand shook as she lit a cigarette; she leaned against the building and took a deep drag, hoping the nicotine would calm her.

When the door opened and Jordan stepped outside, Alix called to him.

'Hi,' she said.

He looked over his shoulder. 'How's it going?' he asked.

'All right. I didn't see you earlier,' she lied. 'I put aside *The Matrix* for you if you're still interested.'

'Yeah, sure, thanks.'

'I aim to please.' She reached for her cigarettes and silently offered him one.

'No, thanks.'

She should've guessed he was a nonsmoker. She stared at the tip of her lit cigarette. 'I'm trying to cut back. These are the low-nicotine cigarettes, but I swear I'm going to end up with a hernia getting any taste out of this.'

He chuckled at her stupid joke and a warm,

happy feeling came over her.

'I've seen you around the neighborhood,' Jordan said.

'Alix Townsend. Alix, spelled A-L-l-X.' She thrust out her hand, which he shook. 'You're Jordan Turner,' she went on before he had a chance to introduce himself. 'Your driver's license is on file. You live off Fifth Avenue, don't you?' She didn't mind letting him know she was interested. She thought of the boy she'd once known with the same name, but that was years ago, back in grade school. He'd been a decent kid, and she'd had a crush on him, but it felt like something that had happened in another time and another place.

'Yeah, that's me.'

Could it be the same Jordan Turner? She studied him, wondering if it was possible. She took another deep drag of the cigarette in an effort to calm her rattled nerves.

No, this couldn't be the same Jordan Turner, she decided. Still, her memories of him were fleeting and she wasn't absolutely sure. She might have dredged up the courage to ask, except that he continued the conversation.

'I don't work far from here.'

So he stopped in for videos on his way home from work. Lots of people did.

'You can tell a lot about a person from the videos they rent,' she said casually. She tossed the cigarette onto the sidewalk and crushed it with the toe of her combat boot.

'I'll bet you can.'

'Do you want to know what I learned about you?' This was one of her best conversational gambits – character analysis through movie selection – although she didn't have much opportunity to use it.

He grinned, and she was struck by how cute he was when he smiled. Laurel couldn't understand what Alix saw in a guy as average as Jordan. She couldn't explain it to her friend, either. Someone attracted to a guy who rented XXX videos just wouldn't get it.

Jordan leaned against the wall beside her. 'Go ahead and tell me what you've figured out.'

Flustered now, Alix suddenly found it difficult to express herself. She faltered and struggled with what she wanted to say and to her utter humiliation, she couldn't do it. In one final attempt to redeem herself, she gestured weakly with her hands and said. 'They're cool, you know.'

'Cool?' Jordan repeated. 'You mean I pick cool movies?'

'Yeah.' She wanted to crumple onto the sidewalk and disappear.

'Thank you.'

The heat was radiating from her face. 'I've got to get back to work,' she said gruffly and without another word, she practically ran back into the store.

To make matters worse, Laurel was waiting for her. 'How'd it go?' her roommate asked eagerly the instant Alix returned.

Alix glared at her.

Laurel raised both hands. 'That bad, huh?'

A sick feeling attacked Alix's stomach. It was like the nausea she'd experienced as a kid when her parents started to fight. That painful sensation used to corrode her stomach – as if she were somehow responsible for every bad thing that had befallen their lives. Jordan might be the same Jordan Turner she'd once known, but there'd been no time to ask. And she couldn't now, not after she'd run away!

'You okay?' Laurel asked, studying her.

Alix brushed aside the question and marched to the back of the store, where she walked into the employee rest room. The toilet was disgusting. She didn't want to guess how long it'd been since the last cleaning. The blue additive didn't begin to disguise the yellow ring around the inside of the bowl. Funny she'd notice that now.

Standing in front of the sink, Alix stared into the mirror. The voices that came to taunt her were familiar ones. They were the ugly, negative voices that shouted words she tried to ignore. Voices that laughed in her face and said she was a loser. No matter what she did or how hard she tried, she'd never amount to anything. Her life was doomed. This was her lot. She'd never earn more than minimum wage, never be loved, never have a real home with things that normal people took for granted, like a phone and a dishwasher.

Pressing her hands to her face, Alix closed her eyes and felt the dark misery descend. She could feel its oppressive weight settle on her shoulders, shoving her down to a place deep inside. She tried unsuccessfully to shake off the depression, tried to shake off the ugly words that echoed in her mind.

The repulsive names her mother had called her

rang through her head. She could hear a teacher's chastisement and belittling comments next, and the humiliation returned as strong now as it had been twelve years earlier. She wanted to bury all the hurtful words. Instead they reverberated through her mind with such force she nearly slumped to the rest room floor.

A knock sounded at the door, startling her. Alix jerked her head toward the noise.

'Alix, you in there?'

Laurel. Damn. 'What?' she snapped.

'He's back.'

'Who?'

'The guy you were just talking to. I don't know his name.'

Alix bit her lower lip. 'You help him.'

'He asked for you.'

'Why?' she asked, frowning.

'I don't know,' Laurel said irritably. 'Am I supposed to read minds, too?'

'I'll be out in a minute, all right?' Alix straightened, brushing her hands through her hair as she came to grips with this information. She wondered what possible reason Jordan could have for seeking her out.

Because her face was beet-red, she ran cold water over her hands and then brought them to her cheeks, not caring what it did to her makeup.

She didn't know how much time had passed before she finally found the courage to come out and face Jordan.

He was standing at the counter waiting. He smiled as she approached.

'You wanted to see me?' she asked as if he'd

119

interrupted her. She didn't want to give him the impression that she was happy to see him, and in truth, she wasn't. After humiliating herself once, she didn't feel like doing it again. Not this soon, anyway.

'You said you'd put aside *The Matrix* for me?'

Her relief was intense. 'Oh, yeah, I almost forgot. I've got it up front.' She moved past him and behind the counter to the spot where she'd placed the video.

'I appreciate you doing that for me.'

'No problem,' she said, busying herself with the computer screen. She rang up the total and asked for his card. After he'd paid her the rental fee, she set the video in its protective plastic case, then slipped it inside a bag and handed it to him over the counter. 'We've got a special on microwave popcorn this week if you're interested.'

'No, thanks. I bought a case at Costco my last visit. I've got enough popcorn to last me for the next ten years.'

She rested her elbows on the counter, feeling awkward and a bit embarrassed. She had no idea what to say, what to ask. If she mentioned the Jordan Turner from sixth grade, it would sound like a pick-up line. 'Uh, any other movies you want me to put aside for you?' That wasn't exactly a scintillating question but at least it made sense.

He shrugged. 'Can't think of any at the moment, but if I do I'll let you know.'

'Okay.'

With a nod, Jordan left. The glass door closed and as if by magic Laurel appeared. 'What did he want?'

'A movie, what else?'

'How come he only wanted you to help him?'

Alix didn't feel inclined to go into the details. 'How am I supposed to know that?'

'There's no need to get all snappy with me.'

The door chimed and to Alix's astonishment, Jordan stuck his head inside. 'Alix, what time do you get off work?'

She was too shocked to answer immediately. 'Eleven. I close three nights a week.'

'Do you close tomorrow?'

'No. I'm here until nine on Wednesdays.'

'Do you want to meet for coffee then? After work?'

'Ah...' She found it hard to believe he was actually asking her out. Well, sort of out. 'Yeah, I guess,' she said as if it wasn't any big deal.

'Great, I'll see you then.' He waved and was gone.

A bubble of happiness rose up inside her. It demanded every ounce of restraint she possessed not to stamp her feet with joy.

CHAPTER 13

'Knitting – my Amazing Grace.'
–Nancie M. Wiseman, Editor, *Cast On* magazine
and author of *Classic Knitted Vests* and *The Knitter's Book of Finishing Techniques*

LYDIA HOFFMAN

My mother phoned me early in the week to suggest she, Margaret and I go out to the cemetery together on Memorial Day to visit my father's grave. It had only been a few months since we laid Daddy to rest. These were difficult days for Mom as she had yet to find her footing as a widow.

I readily agreed to join her, but I wondered about Margaret's response. She'd managed to manipulate the situation so we didn't see each other on Mother's Day. At every family function, my sister acts prickly and standoffish. It seems she'd prefer to forget we have the same parents. More than once, the thought has passed through my mind that Margaret would rather I was the one who'd died instead of our father. That isn't a pleasant notion to entertain, but given her attitude, I feel it's true. Yet I continue to try. Some perverse part of me refuses to let go. She's my sister. Having been so close to death, I feel that even though we might not like each other, we need each other.

I arrived at my mother's place early Monday afternoon and found Mom sipping tea on the back patio near her garden. She'd dressed in her long black skirt and silk blouse and sat in the wicker chair, enjoying the sunshine.

The roses were trimmed and budding, and the sweet aroma of the lilac bush scented the air. I could see from the linen hankie clutched in her hands that Mom had been weeping.

I moved beside her, wordlessly pressing my hand to her shoulder. She glanced up and managed a teary smile before she laid her hand over mine and gave my fingers a gentle squeeze. 'I still miss him, you know.'

'Me, too,' I whispered, emotion choking my voice.

'Dad would be upset to see us so maudlin. It's such a lovely day and soon I'll have both my daughters with me. How can I possibly be sad?' She reached for the teapot and I realized she'd brought out a second cup, expecting me to join her. Without asking she poured and I sat down beside her.

We chatted a bit. Mom was full of questions about A Good Yarn, my beginning class and the three women who'd signed up. I mentioned Jacqueline, Carol and Alix frequently and talked to her about my other customers, too. Slowly, one by one, I was building my clientele and perhaps just as importantly, I was making friends. My world expanded a little more with each day and I was happy. Whiskers was, too, and has taken to spending time in the shop, often sunning himself in the front window. My cat's become a real conversation starter, and charms my customers no end. He accepts all the attention as his due.

Because of the holiday weekend, my beginners' class decided to skip the previous Friday. Jacqueline and Carol were both going out of town. Alix didn't divulge her plans, but I suspected she didn't have much opportunity to get out of the city.

I was pleased with the progress each woman had made. I'd had a bit of a challenge talking Jacqueline into staying in the class. She'd planned to quit before the third session, but I convinced her to keep at it. I had the feeling she wanted me to change her mind and I'm glad I did. There'd been a couple of rough moments when Alix dropped a stitch during the second class and let loose with a blue streak that nearly put Jacqueline in a coma. Immediately I suggested Alix find an alternative method of expressing her frustration. To my surprise, she apologized and my appreciation for her increased. Alix isn't so bad once you get to know her.

Carol's my star pupil, already half done with the baby blanket, and eyeing other projects. She's been coming by the shop at least twice a week, often staying to chat. Whiskers sat in her lap a couple of times, just to show he approves of my choice of a friend.

Mom loves hearing stories about my customers. We talk nearly every day. She needs that and frankly, so do I. I might be thirty years old but a girl never outgrows her need for her mother.

'Margaret and the girls will be here at one,' Mom said conversationally, but I wasn't fooled. She was giving me fair warning. She set her china cup in the saucer and rested her hands in her lap. My mother possesses a natural grace I envy. Margaret's a great deal like her in that regard.

I'm not sure how to describe my mother. One might well assume she's as fragile as she looks, but that's not the case. She's strong in ways I can only admire. She was a fierce advocate for me in dealing with the doctors and the insurance company during my bouts with cancer. She's loving and generous and constantly tries to meet the needs of others. Her one drawback is in coping with sickness. She couldn't bear to see me – or anyone else – suffer and tended to simply withdraw. Fortunately, Dad was always there for me.

'Are Julia and Hailey coming with Margaret?' I asked. My two nieces are a source of wonder to me. The likelihood of my ever bearing children was slim to none, so my sister's daughters hold an important place in my heart. Margaret seemed to sense this and, for whatever reason, jealously guarded her daughters, keeping them away from me as much as possible.

Julia and Hailey, however, recognized my genuine affection and much to Margaret's consternation, loved me unabashedly. Their undiluted joy at every chance encounter rankled Margaret so much that she did whatever she could to block my access to my nieces.

'Grandma!' Nine-year-old Hailey loped into the backyard, her arms extended. When she saw me, she squealed with delight and after hugging my mother, vaulted into my arms, nearly strangling me in her enthusiasm.

Fourteen-year-old Julia was a bit more restrained, but her eyes revealed her pleasure at seeing me. I stretched out my free arm to her and when she stepped toward me, we clasped hands and I squeezed her fingers. How tall Julia had grown, more woman than child now, and such a beauty. My heart swelled with pride at the sight of her.

'Aunt Lydia, will you teach me how to knit?' Hailey begged, still clinging to me.

I looked over my shoulder just in time to see my sister and brother-in-law come out the back door and onto the patio where I sat with my mother and the girls. From the frown Margaret wore, I could see she'd heard the question. 'I'd love to teach you, but it's up to your mother.'

'We'll talk about it later,' Margaret said sharply. Hailey placed her arm around my shoulders, unwilling to release me.

'Hello, Matt,' I said.

My brother-in-law grinned and winked at me. I remember when Matt and Margaret first started dating. Because she's five years older than me, I viewed seventeen-year-old Matt as mature and sophisticated, a man of the world. They'd married young and my father disapproved, believing Margaret should wait until she'd graduated from college. She did finish her schooling but hasn't used her education in the way Dad wanted. My sister has worked at a number of jobs through the years but she's never found any position that's really suited her. Margaret is currently employed part-time at a travel agency, but she's never discussed her job with me. I do applaud her decision to be home as much as possible for the girls, but I've avoided sharing my thoughts, uncertain of their reception.

After a brief exchange of chitchat and news, we drove out to the cemetery in two cars. Mom had brought a large bouquet of lilacs from her garden, and Julia and Hailey set them in the receptacle at my father's gravesite. A large number of American flags flapped in the wind across the cemetery, reminding us of the men and women who sacrificed their lives for our country.

I've always found cemeteries curious places. As a child, I had an almost ghoulish fascination with tombstones. I especially enjoyed reading the epitaphs on those from the 1800s and early 1900s. While Margaret and my parents paid their respects to my grandparents, I'd invariably wander off. I broke my leg when I was five when a statue of the Virgin Mary fell over on me. I didn't tell Mom and Dad that I'd been climbing on her at the time, hoping to look at her face.

I never really knew my grandparents. One set lived on the East Coast and visited only on rare occasions. My mother's family had come to Seattle at the time of the Great Depression, but her parents had died shortly after I was born. Each Memorial Day we visited their graves and placed flowers by their headstones. I felt little emotion for my long-dead relatives, perhaps a twinge now and then, wishing I remembered them, but that was about it.

Now as I stared down at my father's marker, so fresh and new, a surge of harsh grief came over me. The marble tablet said so little. His name, JAMES HOWARD HOFFMAN, and the dates of his birth and death: May 20, 1940–December 29, 2003.

Birth to death, and all that appeared between those two events was a dash. That silent dash said nothing about his two tours of duty in Vietnam, or his unwavering love for his wife and daughters. That dash couldn't possibly reveal the countless hours he'd spent at my bedside, comforting me, reading to me, doing whatever he could to help me. There are no words to describe the depth of my father's love.

The familiar blinding pain struck me then. One consequence of the tumor that continues to linger is migraine headaches. With the new medicines now available, I can almost always catch them early. The telltale signs are unmistakable. This one, however, had caught me by surprise.

I fumbled in my purse for the pills I carried with me constantly. My mother, aware of my situation, came toward me when she saw me stumble. 'Lydia, what is it?'

I breathed in slowly and deeply. 'I need to get home,' I whispered, closing my eyes to the blinding sunlight.

'Margaret, Matt,' Mom called urgently. She slid her arm around my waist. Within minutes she'd bundled me into the car but instead of having Matt drive me to my own small apartment above the yarn shop, my mother insisted on bringing me to her house.

It wasn't long before I was in bed in the room where I'd spent most of my childhood. The shades were drawn. Mom draped cool washcloths on my forehead and then tiptoed out of the room to allow me to sleep.

I knew that once the medication had been given a chance to work, I'd sleep for a couple of hours. Afterward I'd be fine, but reaching that point – the beginning of relife – was difficult.

Soon after my mother left and the horrible throbbing was at its peak, I heard the bedroom door creak open again. Although I was completely prone and my eyes were closed, I knew it was my sister who'd walked into the room.

'You couldn't do it, could you?' Her words were weighted with bitterness. 'You can't let a day pass without being the center of attention, can you?'

I found it hard to fathom that my sister would seriously believe I'd intentionally bring on a migraine for the sake of a few minutes' attention. If Margaret had ever suffered with one, she'd know differently. But I was in no shape to argue, so I kept silent.

'Someday it's only going to be the two of us, you know.'

I did know and wanted so badly to have a good relationship with my sister. If I hadn't been hounded by pain I would've tried to explain how much I wished things could be different between us.

'If you think I'm going to step in and pick up where Mom and Dad left off, you're sadly mistaken.'

I almost smiled. I couldn't imagine Margaret

doing anything of the kind.

'I refuse to pamper and spoil you. It's time you grew up and became an adult, Lydia. In fact, it's long past time you accepted responsibility for your own life. As far as I'm concerned, you can look for sympathy elsewhere.' Having made her great pronouncement, she stalked out of the room.

The sound of the slammed door reverberated through my head. My lungs froze and my heart skipped a beat. With the cool washcloth over my face, it took me a moment to realize tears had dripped from my eyes.

Now more than ever, I was convinced that a relationship with Margaret was impossible.

CHAPTER 14

JACQUELINE DONOVAN

Jacqueline checked her reflection in the hall mirror and sighed, praying for patience. Paul and Tammie Lee had invited her and Reese to their home for a barbecue. She couldn't refuse; Paul would easily see through any excuse. Trapped, Jacqueline had no choice but to grit her teeth and make the best of it.

'Are you ready?' Reese asked for the third time.

Grumbling under her breath, Jacqueline joined him. He was jingling his car keys and pacing back and forth in front of the kitchen door that led to the garage.

'Can't we get out of this?' she asked, knowing it was impossible.

Reese gave her one of his looks. He had several expressions that spoke as clearly as words, and over the years she'd come to identify them all. This one was the off-center humorless smile that conveyed his displeasure at something she'd said or done.

'What's wrong *this* time?' she asked, fuming. 'Don't tell me you're actually looking forward to this barbecue?' Heaven only knew what Tammie Lee might prepare for their dinner. Grilled possum? Barbecued squirrel?

'Don't you see?' her husband said. 'Paul wants us to get to know Tammie Lee and love her the way he does.'

Jacqueline shook her head in a gesture of denial and frustration. 'It's not going to happen, no matter how many barbecues he insists we attend.'

'The least you can do is give Tammie Lee a chance.'

Jacqueline was beginning to resent Reese's attitude. Her husband was well aware of the importance of marrying the right person. He hadn't chosen her because of her cute smile. Their parents were good friends, and she'd attended all the best schools and so had he. Yes, she'd loved Reese, but there was so much more to finding an appropriate marriage partner than love, which in her opinion was highly overrated, anyway.

She feared Paul was fast becoming like his father, with his brains situated somewhere below his waistline. Only Paul had married the girl. If he held genuine feelings for Tammie Lee, then her son should do as his father had and set her up someplace visiting her once a week. Jacqueline didn't know the extent of her husband's monetary investment in his Tuesday-night woman, but she suspected it was substantial. She hadn't checked his financial records after the first year, preferring not to learn the truth. His absence each Tuesday night told her all she needed to know.

They rode in silence to Paul and Tammie Lee's house, a respectable two-story near Kirkland with a nice view of Lake Washington. Smoke spiraled from the backyard and Jacqueline suspected they'd already put on the meat. Good!

The sooner this family gathering was over the better.

Reese rang the doorbell and together they stood on the steps and waited. Tammie Lee opened the door in bare feet, frayed jean shorts and a maternity top, looking like she'd stepped out of the 1960s television series *Petticoat Junction*.

'I'm so glad you're here,' she drawled, reaching for Jacqueline's hands and practically dragging her into the house.

'Mom. Dad.' Paul was directly behind his wife. He shook hands with his father and briefly hugged Jacqueline.

Jacqueline didn't mean to start the afternoon off on a negative note, but she didn't think it was a good idea for Tammie Lee to be traipsing around the house barefoot. God knows what she could step on or where she might slip.

'I hesitate to mention this, but shouldn't you be

wearing shoes?' She'd asked out of genuine concern for the girl, but Jacqueline could see from the way Paul's mouth thinned that he was annoyed with her.

'I know you're right,' Tammie Lee said, leading everyone through the house and into the freshly mowed backyard. 'Bless his heart, Paul keeps telling me the same thing, but I just can't make myself wear shoes. I kick 'em off the minute I walk in the door. Then last week I made the mistake of walking around the yard in my bare feet and I stepped on a slug.'

Jacqueline cringed.

'I started screaming like the Holy Spirit had come down upon me.'

Paul chuckled. 'I've never run so fast in my life. I thought she'd been attacked by a swarm of bees or something.'

The patio table was already set and Tammie Lee held up two pitchers of iced tea. 'Sweetened or unsweetened?' she asked.

In Jacqueline's view, iced tea should be served only one way and that was unsweetened. Anyone who wanted to add sugar could do so at the time it was served.

'Unsweetened,' she said and took her place at the table.

'I'll have the same,' Reese said.

Tammie Lee poured the tea and handed a glass to Jacqueline, who frowned at the green leaf floating on top. 'There seems to be something in my tea,' she said, picking up her spoon to remove it.

'That's a mint leaf,' Tammie Lee said. 'My

mama wouldn't let me serve iced tea without fresh mint and lemon slices.'

Feeling like a fool, Jacqueline leaned back in her chair, determined not to say another word. *Of course* it was mint – she should've recognized it – but with Tammie Lee one never knew what to expect.

'This is very pleasant. It was nice of you to invite us over,' Reese said.

Jacqueline stared daggers at him. Nothing about this day was pleasant and he damn well knew it.

'Actually it was Tammie Lee's idea,' Paul said, standing in front of the barbecue. To her relief, whatever he was cooking smelled divine. The meat sizzled and Paul coated it liberally with some garlicky kind of sauce.

'Yes,' Tammie Lee said, returning to the patio with a notebook and pen. She pulled out a chair and sat down at the table with Jacqueline and Reese. She opened her notebook to a clean page. 'I wanted to ask you about family traditions,' she said eagerly. 'It's just so important for Paul and me to start some family traditions, and I wanted to include yours as much as possible.'

'Traditions?' Jacqueline repeated as if she'd never heard the word before.

'Yes, you know. Like Derby Day?'

Jacqueline exchanged a quizzical look with her husband.

'The Kentucky Derby,' Tammie Lee explained, glancing from one to the other as if expecting them to smile and nod and exclaim 'of course.'

'My daddy and all my uncles would wear their

134

white suits and Panama hats, and Mama and my aunts would cook for days.'

'We don't feel as strongly about the Kentucky Derby here in Seattle as your family does, sweetheart,' Paul said, joining them at the round patio table. He shared a smile with his father. 'Tell her about Christmas, Mom.'

'Christmas,' Jacqueline repeated. 'What about it?'

'How you used to hang my stockings on the fireplace mantel every Christmas Eve.'

'Yes, but I haven't done that in years.'

'What about football?' Tammie Lee said excitedly. 'Y'all enjoy football here, don't you?' Her drawl had thickened as she grew more enthusiastic.

'Oh, yes.' It was Paul who answered this time. 'Both Dad and I are Husky fans.'

'That's wonderful! We'll do tailgate parties. Mama says tailgate parties are a lot like church. All the women dress up in their Sunday best and cook up a tornado. Then we spend hours praying for a miracle.'

Both Paul and Reese laughed but Jacqueline didn't see the humor in it. 'Why would you pray?'

Tammie Lee grinned. 'So our team would win.'

Jacqueline managed a tight smile.

As it turned out, the barbecue wasn't as bad as Jacqueline had feared. She'd had visions of her daughter-in-law's centerpiece being prepared by a taxidermist, but Tammie Lee had set out a lovely floral arrangement.

All in all, the afternoon was reasonably pleasant – to use Reese's word – despite Jacqueline's dire

135

predictions. Dinner consisted of a delightful guacamole and blue corn chips, grilled brisket and potato salad, which was surprisingly good. The jalapeno cornbread was a bit spicy, but Jacqueline had a small piece. Reese raved about the meal, and Tammie Lee beamed with pleasure at his endless compliments. Now that she'd reduced her work hours, her daughter-in-law had time to lavish on meals to please her husband. As a young married woman, Jacqueline had done the same thing. These days, her interest in cooking was nil.

On the drive home, Reese and Jacqueline were silent. Most of the dinner conversation had revolved around family traditions. Apparently Tammie Lee's family had quite a few, and she happily described each one in lengthy detail, frequently mentioning Aunt Thelma and Aunt Frieda, as well as 'Mama' and 'Daddy.' Jacqueline had begun to wonder if the girl was homesick.

Well, if she was, Tammie Lee could pack her bags and go visit her mama. With his wife out of the house, perhaps Paul would come to his senses.

'We didn't have a lot of traditions with Paul, did we?' Reese said as they pulled out onto the freeway entrance.

'Of course we did,' she countered, although she'd been hard-pressed to think of any over dinner. 'We made gingerbread houses with him every Christmas, remember?'

'Yes, but that was years ago, when he was a kid.'

'And there was always the Easter Egg hunt at the country club.'

'Yes, and Paul and I used to bring you breakfast in bed every Mother's Day.'

136

'That's right,' Jacqueline said, instantly feeling a sense of relief. She hadn't failed completely as a mother. 'Just because we didn't dress up in those dreadful white seersucker suits and Panama hats to watch the Kentucky Derby doesn't mean we didn't have meaningful traditions with our son.'

Reese took his eyes off the road long enough to glance at her. 'Do you remember the year Paul insisted on making you Eggs Benedict?'

'Oh, my goodness, it took Martha months to get the stovetop clean.'

'But you ate every bite. You were such a trouper,' Reese said. 'I don't think I ever loved you more than I did that day.'

Jacqueline's smile faded as she stared out the passenger window. They *had* loved each other, and in their own ways, they still did. All this talk about traditions and family had stirred up the dust of bygone years, swirling a storm of happy memories in her direction. It was all a bit unsettling.

'I'm glad Paul and Tammie Lee want to start traditions with their daughter,' Reese said as they neared the house. 'Aren't you?'

'Yes,' Jacqueline answered softly. She very much wanted that for her grandchild. She imagined a little girl, dark-haired like Paul, her small arms reaching up to Jacqueline. Tammie Lee might not be her first choice of a wife for her son, but Paul seemed happy. Soon he'd make her a grandmother. Yes, there were a few compensations to be found in this marriage.

Whatever the reason, Jacqueline felt better than she had in months. Perhaps Reese was right and she was being too hard on the girl.

CHAPTER 15

CAROL GIRARD

Carol had been in a good mood all week. She and Doug had impulsively gone out for a wonderful Thai dinner last night, she'd had some encouraging conversations with her online group, and her knitting skills were improving daily. She was looking forward to her class the following day, the fourth in the series. In the last three weeks she'd begun to really enjoy knitting and tackled it with the same energy and enthusiasm she brought to everything in her life. Her first blanket had been a bit flawed; it had a few uneven stitches, so she'd donated it to the Linus Project and bought the yarn for a second one. She had much better control of the yarn's tension and was pleased with how this new blanket was turning out.

Carrying in the mail, she set it on the table. An envelope addressed to her was on top and Carol recognized the married name of a college friend who'd moved to California. She tore open the envelope, excited to hear from Christine. It didn't take her long to discover that it wasn't a letter as she'd hoped, but a birth announcement.

In that instant, Carol's good mood spiraled downward. She caught her breath and sank into a kitchen chair as she read the details about Christine's infant born just two weeks earlier on

May 27th. A baby boy, the card said.

Christine was the kind of woman who did everything according to a predetermined schedule. That included marrying the perfect man, getting pregnant exactly when she'd planned to, and then delivering a healthy baby.

Carol swallowed hard. Few people would understand the depression she felt at that moment. Only her online friends could fully appreciate her feelings.

Carol sat staring at the wall as she tried to overcome her sense of inadequacy and frustration. She was genuinely happy for Christine and Bill. Yet at the same time, she wanted to pull her hair out and scream at the heavens – demand to know why *she* wasn't pregnant. Why her body didn't function the way other women's bodies did. These were all questions she'd asked herself dozens of times, questions she'd asked every expert she'd met, and still she had no answers.

Eventually she would have a baby. Carol had to believe that. But it was taking so much longer than she'd ever imagined. The waiting was the most maddening. She had to wait for the medical appointments with the specialists. Then she had to wait for the tests, wait for the treatments and wait again for additional treatments. They weren't pleasant experiences, either. Forget about privacy and modesty. Forget about everything except this compulsion to have a child.

Carol's periods had become far more than a monthly nuisance; it was as if her whole world centered on her menstrual cycle. And when they did start, her heart broke and she struggled with the bitterness of disappointment.

Every month that passed – every period that came – was like an hour chimed off by a grand-father clock. At best she had only twelve oppor-tunities a year to conceive and if she wanted a second child or possibly a third, God only knew how many more years that would take.

Carol knew a lot of her friends thought of her as obsessed and moody. She was. But she was also afraid, so terribly afraid.

Making love with Doug had taken on a routine quality. Sex on schedule. And then the frantic wait, the frequent visits to the bathroom, just to check. Had her period started? And when it did...

This IVF *had* to work, it just had to.

If only someone could give her a definite answer. If only Dr. Ford would tell her and Doug one way or the other whether they could ever have a child. If his diagnosis was negative then they'd learn to deal with it, make adjustments, make other plans.

Instead he allowed them to hope and twice now, they'd plummeted into despair when the IVF failed and she'd miscarried. Twice they'd re-covered, willing to try again, willing to do anything and everything, sacrifice all, for a baby.

Carol rubbed her eyes and stood to put on water for a cup of tea – decaffeinated, of course. She'd begun to avoid so many foods for fear they would hinder conception. Her grocery list read like an inventory list for a health food store. Some experts felt diet was critical; other medical professionals disagreed. Carol wasn't taking any chances. She was going to try anything that might help her stay pregnant.

In so many ways it felt as if her entire life was on hold. She'd left a promising career, went to the best doctors, ate all the right foods, listened to all the motivational tapes and repeated the mantras she'd learned. She had to believe her mind could control her body and that the sheer force of her determination would eventually give her what she wanted most.

Filling the teakettle with water, she set it on the burner and sat down again while she waited for the water to boil. A short handwritten note from Christine caught her eye. Carol hadn't noticed it at the bottom of the birth announcement. Christine's lovely cursive said: 'I haven't heard from you in so long!'

There was a very good reason for that. Carol's friendship with Christine wasn't the only one she'd allowed to lapse. She'd ignored many of her close friends, mainly because the struggle to get pregnant demanded so much energy. Most of the women she knew were already mothers, and her friends with children socialized primarily with other friends who had children.

Carol and Doug had less and less in common with these friends, whose lives seemed to revolve around babies and playgrounds and birthday parties. If that wasn't bad enough, there were often lengthy discussions that excluded them. Conversations about schools or day care, about tantrums and teething problems.

Then there were the so-called friends who dismissed their difficulties, who trivialized her desire for a child. One heartless woman in the office had laughingly suggested Carol was welcome to raise one of her four. Other people wanted to comfort her by saying it wouldn't be long now and modern medicine was so wonderful that within a year's time she was sure to be pregnant. Well, she wasn't, and the most horrible fear of all had taken root. There might never be a baby for her and Doug. She could hardly bear it, but she'd rather face the truth than continue like this.

The kettle whistled and she slowly stood and poured the boiling water into the pot. She couldn't allow such negative thoughts to invade her mind. That only made things worse. She had to believe. She couldn't let a birth announcement do this to her. God had given her a sign. She *had* to believe, push aside all negative thinking. She had faith...

The door opened and Carol whirled around, surprised to realize it was so late. 'Doug! Is it that time already?' She tried to sound cheerful but knew she'd failed.

'You okay?' he asked, studying her.

'Of course.'

He didn't look convinced.

'Did you have a good day?' she asked, returning her attention to the teapot.

'Sure. It was fine.'

Doug immediately zeroed in on the mail. He walked over to the table and discovered Christine and Bill's birth announcement. She watched his face as he read it, and wanted to cry out in pain at the longing she saw in his eyes. After a moment he set it aside as if it were a matter of only the slightest interest. She knew otherwise.

'They had a boy,' she said, fighting to keep the emotion out of her voice.

'So I see.'

It should've been *them,* she wanted to scream. *They* should be the couple mailing out birth announcements. They were good people. They had a strong marriage and they'd be wonderful parents...

The infertility was a constant stress on their marriage. Doug had dealt with as much of the indignity as she had. The semen collection in a bathroom off Dr. Ford's waiting room, the post-coital examinations – all of this was dreadful for him.

People assured her that one day they'd laugh about it. Carol didn't think that was possible.

'I'm almost half done with the second baby blanket. I have another class tomorrow after-noon.'

Her husband nodded and grabbed the news-paper, heading for his favorite chair in the living room.

Carol wanted to shout at him to talk to her. In-stead she bit her tongue and began preparing dinner, a meal she had no appetite for.

CHAPTER 16

ALIX TOWNSEND

Sitting at a window table in Starbucks, Alix concentrated on moving the stitches from one needle to the other and completing the row. No one else in class seemed to have a problem with this basic knitting concept. Carol was already working on her second blanket. Jacqueline was having a few difficulties, but not nearly as many as Alix. No matter how hard she concentrated, Alix would start out with a hundred and seventy-one stitches and by the time she finished the row, there'd be a hundred and eighty or more. Or less, depending on what she'd done wrong.

Lydia reassured her on a regular basis that this was a common problem and explained with limitless patience that Alix wasn't completing the stitch properly. Well, duh! Then she'd show her again. And Alix would make the same stupid mistake. She didn't care; she wasn't giving up until she learned to knit, even if it killed her. She already had thirty bucks invested in this project!

At the end of the row Alix paused, sipped her frappuccino, a rare treat, and counted the stitches. Damn! A hundred and eighty-three! She'd done it again and added stitches where she shouldn't. 'Damn, damn, damn,' she muttered, which was a tame version of what she was thinking. Apparently being around Jacqueline was rubbing off on her. She barely used the F-word anymore.

Shoving the knitting onto her lap, Alix closed her eyes, trying to ignore the frustration. This class was supposed to help her with anger management? That was a joke if she'd ever heard one.

Even more irritating, Laurel was at the apartment with John and had asked Alix to stay away for a couple of hours. She didn't know what was going on with those two, but Alix didn't think it could possibly be good. Things had gotten pretty intense between them recently. John had been making regular appearances at the video store, and Alix hated the way Laurel gushed all over the sleaze. As far as she was concerned, John was bad news.

Once her nerves were calm, Alix carefully unraveled the row, taking out one stitch at a time, which took more effort than it did to complete the frigging row in the first place. Two stitches from the end of the row, she lost her grip on the needle and dropped a stitch. A muttered curse escaped before she could stop herself.

Good thing Jacqueline wasn't there to hear it. She was offended each and every time the knitting got the better of Alix, which unfortunately was often. Still, she *was* improving.

Thus far, Alix had avoided a confrontation with the other woman, but she could feel one brewing. At best Jacqueline tolerated Alix, and Alix felt the same way about her.

Jacqueline had a twisted view of the world, in Alix's opinion. The only things that seemed important to her were pretense and prestige. At each class, she sat and chatted away, putting on airs as if anyone really cared who she saw at social events and club meetings. Most of the time, Alix didn't know who she was talking about, anyway. Jacqueline spent most of the lesson name-dropping or discussing some ritzy party she'd attended. Well, la-dida!

Biting down on her lower lip, Alix managed to pick up the dropped stitch and then just before she could slip it onto the needle, she lost it and the whole thing unraveled another two rows.

She muttered an even more furious curse under her breath and was tempted to ditch the entire project. If she had any sense she'd throw it in the garbage, needles and all, and slam out the door.

Alix felt someone's presence and glanced up to find Jordan Turner standing next to her table. Her mouth went dry and her mind went blank. He was the last person she'd expected to see.

'Looks like you're having a bit of trouble.' He pulled out the chair beside her, turned it around and sat down facing her.

All Alix could do was stare at him with her mouth hanging open. She hadn't seen him in a couple of weeks. After suggesting they have coffee sometime, he'd vanished. Alix had been bummed out ever since. It was the story of her life; the minute she showed interest in a guy he either ended up in jail or skipped town.

'What are you doing here?' she asked, making sure he knew she wasn't pleased to see him.

'Actually, I came in looking for you.' He folded his arms over the top of the chair and leaned toward her.

'Sure you did.' That was the type of line John fed Laurel. Alix wasn't going to fall for it.

'It's the truth. You can talk to Danny. I went into the store and asked him if he knew where I could find you.' Danny worked part-time during the day shift and was reliable. If she asked him about it, he'd be square with her.

Ignoring Jordan, she caught the dropped stitch and finished the row before she raised her eyes. 'Why were you looking for me?'

'I thought I'd buy you a cup of coffee. Are you always this difficult?'

She fixed her gaze on him and refused to blink. 'Not really.'

'So this I-don't-give-a-damn attitude is for my benefit?'

She smiled despite her mood. 'You could say that.'

Her lack of welcome apparently didn't bother him. 'Any particular reason?'

Alix picked up her knitting again. It sounded childish and petty to say she was disappointed because he'd led her to believe he'd be by to take her to coffee. Then ... nothing. Rather than tell him all that, she started knitting again, paying close attention to her stitches, concentrating as she completed the action of slipping it onto the next needle. 'I haven't seen you around lately,' she said casually.

'Are you implying you missed me? I thought a lot about you while I was away, you know.'

She shrugged, looked up and felt a smile lift one side of her mouth. 'I might have.'

He liked hearing that; Alix could tell by the way he shifted in his chair and leaned closer. He watched her for a moment and then asked, 'What are you knitting?'

'A baby blanket for the Linus Project.'

Jordan nodded. 'I've heard of that. There was a notice in the church bulletin about it a couple of months ago.'

Damn, he went to church, too? She really knew how to pick 'em. 'Don't think I'm doing this wonderful deed out of the kindness of my heart,' she said gruffly. 'I'm not putting this much effort into a baby blanket out of civic duty.'

'Then why knit it for the Linus Project?'

She might as well admit the truth, and looked up, wanting to gauge his reaction. 'It's a way to serve the community hours the court assigned me.' If that didn't scare him off, then nothing would. She believed in being honest, and if this clean-cut guy was still interested in her, great. If not, she was better off knowing that now.

'Court-ordered community service? Why?'

'I crossed the law and the law won,' she said, finishing the row and paying less attention to the stitches than she should. 'But it was a bogus rap and the judge knew it. I got community service instead of jail time. Does that shock a good boy like you?'

'No.'

She wasn't sure she believed him but let it slide. 'My mother knits.'

Alix stopped herself just in time from telling him that *her* mother was in prison. Enough honesty for today, she decided; no need to overload him with the truth. His interest flattered her, and she rather liked the fact that he'd sought her out. Glancing up, she was tempted to ask what grade school he'd attended, still wondering if he was the Jordan Turner she'd once known. She only half remembered what that boy had looked like, although she recalled he'd worn glasses. Unlike this Jordan. She might have asked, except that he posed a question instead.

'Are you hungry?' He looked over his shoulder at the display counter in the front. 'They've got great scones if there are any left. Want one?'

'I could eat,' she said which wasn't the most gracious statement she'd ever made.

He got up and walked to the counter. Alix watched him for a moment and tried to calm her pounding heart. She turned back to her knitting and finished the row, then triumphantly counted exactly one hundred and seventy-one stitches. Jordan returned to her table, a coffee cup in one hand, with a plate and scone balanced on top of it. In the other hand he carried a second plate with a scone.

'We're in luck,' he said as he set everything down on the small round table. 'They only had two left.'

She nodded, accepting the scone. 'Thanks.'

Jordan took a sip of his drink. 'Danny didn't actually know where you'd be and I just happened to see you in the window as I walked by.'

She broke the scone in half and was grateful this had been the only table available when she'd arrived an hour earlier. Normally she wouldn't have sat in view of the entire street. it depressed

149

her to see what was happening to the neighborhood, mainly because she sensed it was only a
matter of time before she and Laurel lost the
apartment. If that happened, it wouldn't be long
before she'd be back to sleeping in cheap, rat-
infested hotel rooms every night. Getting another
apartment would mean taking on a second job
and waiting tables for tips in places decent guys
like Jordan didn't frequent.

'Where've you been?' Alix asked, since he
hadn't volunteered the information. He'd said he
was away.

He sipped his coffee, then put it down. 'I was
running a youth retreat at Warm Beach.'

Alix didn't have a clue what that was. 'This
whole time?'

'Not entirely, but the church needed help with
the organization, so I worked in the Stanwood
office for a few weeks.'

'Oh.' This was the second time he'd mentioned
church, and she'd begun to feel a niggling suspicion.

'It's nice to know you missed me,' he murmured.

'I didn't say that,' she said a bit more defen-
sively than she'd intended.

He chuckled.

Alix was relieved to see she hadn't offended
him. 'Well, maybe I missed you a little.'

'I'm glad to hear it.'

'You got any more youth retreats you need to
organize?'

He sighed. 'I don't know. Frankly, I hope not.
When I accepted the job as youth minister, I

expected to spend my time with the teenagers here in the Blossom Street neighborhood.'

Alix felt as if her world had caved in. 'You're ... a preacher?'

'Youth minister,' Jordan corrected. 'I'm currently working at the Free Methodist church in the neighborhood, the one right off Blossom.' His mouth twitched; he seemed to be suppressing laughter.

'What's so funny?' she muttered irritably.

'Nothing. It's just that you made it sound as if being a minister was like being a drug lord. Or worse.'

'It's just that...' Alix was aghast and words failed her – as they always did when she was flustered.

'I'm a youth minister, Alix,' he said and reached for her hand. He smiled then. 'You don't remember me, do you?'

'It is you!' Damn, she'd thought so and wished like crazy that she'd said something first.

'Remember sixth grade at Jackson Elementary? It took me a while to make the connection myself.'

'I thought it might be you... I can't believe it.' Her mind flashed back to grade school and she narrowed her eyes as she studied him. 'We were in the same class, remember?'

'What I remember,' Jordan said, grinning, 'was that you sat next to Jimmy Burkhart.'

Alix remembered Jimmy as though it was yesterday. She'd given him a bloody nose and ended up in the principal's office, and all because Jimmy had been teasing her about wanting to marry Jordan Turner. She and half the other girls in the sixth grade had been agog over the preacher's son – and now, apparently, Jordan had followed in his father's footsteps. He was a minister. Damn, wouldn't you know it?

'I had a valentine for you.'

She stared up at him, overwhelmed by the memory of that fateful year – the year her mother had tried to kill her father.

'I brought it to school and you weren't there and you never came back.'

Alix didn't answer. The night before the sixth-grade Valentine party, her mother shot her father. Both had been drinking heavily and then, inevitably, a fight had broken out. Soon the police had arrived, followed by paramedics. Her mother was led away in handcuffs and because there were no relatives to take them, Alix and her brother had been shuffled off to foster homes. That night was the beginning of the end of Alix's family life, sad as it'd been. Her mother had been sent to prison, and her father, once he was released from the hospital, drifted away, losing contact with his children. Soon she and Tom were wards of the state. With all the turmoil, Alix had never returned to Jackson Elementary.. .and the valentine Jordan claimed to have for her.

'So,' Jordan said, leaning closer. 'I was wondering what you would've said if I'd asked you to be my sixth-grade valentine?'

She nearly laughed aloud. Yeah, sure. The daughter of drunks and the son of a preacher. Somehow, she didn't think this relationship was going to last.

CHAPTER 17

'With a little practice and patience, our hands learn to knit, then our minds are free to enjoy the process.'

–Bev Galeskas, Fiber Trends

LYDIA HOFFMAN

Business was beginning to pick up and I was pleased. I'd sold out of most of my inventory in nearly every yarn weight. I already had my second order into my main supplier. My first beginners' class was about to officially end. I couldn't believe six weeks had gone by so quickly. I was thrilled that after five weeks, my three students claimed they wanted to continue, so I agreed to extend the course. Because each class member was working on a different project now, except Alix, I suggested we turn Friday afternoons into a knitting support group. That way, they could all bring in whatever they wanted to work on, and I'd be there to help them at each stage of development. Despite their differences, these three dissimilar women were becoming friends. I could see it happening. Friends with each other and my friends, too.

As for their skills as knitters, Carol's the most adept and has started a felted hat project.

Alix and Jacqueline still struggle with the basic

stitches, but Alix has limited time to knit and Jacqueline – well, Jacqueline's attitude bothers me. She's obviously not fond of her daughter-in-law, although she's never spoken openly about her. Jacqueline has started eyeing other projects now and is leaning toward the pricier yarns. Alix paid for her yarn a little each week, which made it abundantly clear that this is an extravagance. Still, the group simply wouldn't be the same without her.

Just when I was ready to close on Tuesday afternoon, I saw my sister walking across the street toward the shop. She'd only come here once before, on my first day of business. She'd taken such pride in forecasting financial disaster, but I refuse to allow her to get me down and I braced for a confrontation.

When Margaret entered the store, I knew instantly that something was wrong. She hadn't come to spread doom and gloom or chastise me. Her face was pale and she seemed close to tears.

'Margaret, what is it?' I hurried toward her.

She had trouble speaking and grabbed my hand so hard I almost cried out.

'Come,' I said, steering her to the back of the store where I had the table and chairs set up for my class. 'Sit down. Can I get you a glass of water?'

Margaret shook her head. I've never seen my sister this upset. I couldn't imagine what had caused her distress or driven her to approach me.

'Dr. Abram's office phoned,' she said, looking up at me as if I should be able to figure out the problem from that little bit of information. I didn't know who Dr. Abram was. I wondered if Matt had fallen ill or been involved in some kind of accident. Another possibility loomed and filled me with dread.

'Is this about Mother?' I asked. The thought of something happening to Mom so soon after losing Dad terrified me.

'No,' she cried. 'This is about me. Dr. Abram said my mammogram needs to be retaken.' She grabbed my hand again. 'It seems – it seems I have a lump in my breast.' My sister stared up at me, eyes wide and fearful.

I'll admit I was shaken by this and sat down next to her. The pressure on my hand increased when she realized I understood.

'I'm so afraid,' Margaret whispered.

'This doesn't mean you have cancer.' I tried to sound reassuring, but it was difficult. Margaret was thinking the same thing I was. I'd already been on intimate terms with the big C. Mom and Dad had always worried that they'd passed on a genetic flaw that made us vulnerable to the disease. Two of our grandparents had died of it. When I'd first been diagnosed, Mom had insisted Margaret be thoroughly checked, as well. Everything had seemed all right then – but now...

'When's the second mammogram scheduled?'

'I ... was just there... The technician wouldn't tell me anything. She said Dr. Abram would have the results read. Then he'd like to see me.'

'Oh, Margaret, I'm so sorry. What can I do to help?'

'I ... don't know. I haven't told anyone.'

'Matt?'

She sighed heavily. 'I didn't want to scare him.'

'But he's your husband! He has a right to know.'

'I'll tell him when I have something to report.'

Her voice was cold, and I knew better than to argue. My sister did things her own way and in her own time. Pressuring her wouldn't do any good.

'How did you feel when you found out you had cancer?' Margaret asked.

I had to strain to make out the words. I'd been sixteen during my first illness and I hadn't known what I do now or even what I did the second time. The day I learned the tumor had grown back was the worst of my life. I was well aware of what lay ahead and in some ways death seemed preferable.

I knew what this could mean to my sister, and I couldn't hide my reaction. 'I was frightened, too,' I told her.

Her grip on my hand tightened briefly.

'How long have you been keeping this to yourself?' I asked and gently smoothed the hair away from her face.

'Five days,' she whispered and then added urgently, 'I want you to promise me something.'

'Of course,' I assured her. Margaret had never asked anything of me before and I was willing to comply, no matter what.

'Don't tell Mom.'

I hated keeping secrets from our mother but in this case I agreed with Margaret. It was useless to upset Mom until we had the facts.

'Thank you,' she whispered, clearly relieved.

'Anything, Margaret. You know that.'

Her gaze held mine. 'Would you...' She hesitated. 'I know I shouldn't ask, but would you go to the doctor with me?'

'Of course.' I'd been planning to offer.

She seemed shocked. 'You'd do that?'

I nodded.

'You'd have to close the shop.'

'I won't let you face this alone.'

Her eyes swam with tears and I reached for a box of tissues and handed her one. Then, because I've always regretted that Margaret and I aren't close, I put my arms around her.

'I'll be with you, Margaret.'

'Thank you.' She sobbed against my shoulder for a minute before she regained her composure. Breaking away from me, she blew her nose and sniffled. 'I'll do what I can to get the appointment on a Monday – but if I can't...'

'It doesn't matter what time of day it is or even what day,' I insisted. I intended to help my sister through this, no matter what.

Margaret seemed about to speak when the bell above the door chimed. I wanted to groan at the interruption, but I was in business and my job was to serve my customers. Even at quarter past five...

The friendly whistle told me it was Brad Goetz, my UPS deliveryman. He wheeled in three large boxes and set them next to the cash register. 'How's it goin'?' he asked as he handed me the computerized clipboard, leaning against the counter.

'Really well,' I said and quickly signed my name, eager to push him out the door.

157

'Every time I come by I see women in the shop, especially on Friday afternoons.'

'I've got a class then.'

'That explains it.' He seemed oblivious to my efforts to steer him toward the exit. 'I bet you're pretty beat at the end of the day.'

'Some days,' I agreed.

He grinned then, as if he'd made his point. 'So why don't you relax and have a drink with me?'

This was his second invitation and of all the bad luck, he had to ask me in front of my sister.

'You should go,' Margaret said from the back of the shop.

'Yeah,' Brad said, eagerly leaping on Margaret's encouragement. 'We can stay right here in the neighborhood. There's a nice bar maybe two blocks away. No commitments, just a few minutes to relax and unwind.'

'I appreciate the offer, but I'd better not.' I walked over to the door and all but opened it. He still didn't take the hint.

Brad raised his hands in frustration and glanced in Margaret's direction. 'Is it something I said?'

'No ... no.' I didn't want him to think that.

'Then what is it?'

'It's not you,' Margaret called out. 'It's my sister. She's afraid.'

I wanted to shout at Margaret to kindly keep her trap shut, but I couldn't. I much preferred to tell him the truth in some other way and at some other time, but the choice had been taken away from me. Rejecting him over and over again seemed cruel. Although I didn't want to do it like this, I owed him my honesty.

'I've had cancer,' I said bluntly. 'Not once, but twice, and furthermore I don't have a single guarantee that the tumor won't grow back again and the next time I might not be so fortunate.'

'Cancer?' he repeated and from the shocked look on his face I knew it was the last thing he'd expected me to say.

'The big, ugly scary kind,' I said, unable to hide my sarcasm. 'You don't want to make an emotional investment in me because it might not pay off. That's the problem with cancer.'

'I ... didn't know.'

'Of course you didn't. How could you? I appreciate the offer,' I said again, and I was sincere about that. 'In fact, I'm downright flattered. But I'm saving us both a lot of grief, so please just accept my refusal and leave it at that.' I walked away from him and went to the back of the store where I sank down next to my sister.

Margaret glared at me.

I heard the door close as Brad walked out of the shop. 'Why did you do that?' my sister demanded.

'Do what?'

'Turn him down! What harm would it've done to have a beer with the guy?'

I covered my face with both hands, unwilling to admit that it'd been so long since I'd been on a date, I didn't know how to act around a man.

'He's cute and he's interested.'

'I know,' I whispered.

'You said you started this shop as an affirmation of life.'

I nodded. 'I did–' Margaret didn't allow me to finish.

'Then *live*. Get involved in life, Lydia. You should be thanking your lucky stars a man like that wants to date you. Good grief, what is it with you?'

'I ... I...' I was so disconcerted I couldn't put two words together.

'Live, Lydia,' she said again. 'Get out there and find out what life's all about. And do it before you shrivel up – or die.'

CHAPTER 18

JACQUELINE DONOVAN

Jacqueline had been a member of the birthday club since joining the Seattle Country Club years ago. Once a month, a group of nine friends got together to celebrate their birthdays. If no one had a birthday that particular month, they celebrated anyway.

For June they chose a Mexican restaurant. While the ambience wasn't really up to their usual high standards the food was excellent. After the women had finished a leisurely lunch and several margaritas, four of the waiters came to their table wearing large sombreros. It was time to serenade the birthday girl. One of the waiters had a guitar slung over his shoulder. Another brandished a pair of maracas.

'*Señoritas,* you celebrate a birthday, *si?*'

'*Si,*' Bev Johnson, president of the women's

160

group, told him. 'It's Ginny's birthday.' She pointed across the table at the other woman, who blushed and giggled like a schoolgirl.

The man with the guitar strummed a few chords and strolled over to Ginny. 'Would you like the long version or the short version?' he asked.

Jacqueline loved to see her normally poised and collected friend flustered by the attention. 'By all means the short version.'

All four of the waiters immediately got down on their knees as they sang the traditional birthday song with a definite Mexican flair. The nine women at the table laughed and applauded, Jacqueline included.

She'd needed this outing in order to put Tammie Lee's pregnancy out of her mind. Despite everything, Paul seemed genuinely in love with his wife; Reese, too, was taken with her. That left Jacqueline feeling like the villain of the piece. But even if Tammie Lee wasn't *quite* as manipulative or tasteless as Jacqueline had assumed, she was so obviously wrong for Paul.

After Ginny blew out the candle on her small cake, and passed it around for everyone to taste, the party broke up. Jacqueline was waiting in line to pay the cashier when Bev came to stand beside her.

'I ran into Tammie Lee last week,' the president of the women's club said.

Jacqueline froze. Bev was the most influential member of the association and she could only imagine what her friend thought of Paul's wife. Already Jacqueline could feel the heat creep up

161

her neck. She could think of no way to explain her son's lapse in judgment.

'Haywood said he approved their application to the club.' Haywood was Bev's husband and in charge of admissions.

'Naturally Reese and I were very pleased they were accepted.' It was gratifying to know that her years of volunteer work with the country club were paying dividends.

'We've always liked Paul.'

Jacqueline smiled. Anyone would be impressed with her son. He was charming and intelligent and destined to succeed in life. She had to restrain herself from bragging about his accomplishments.

'I understand Tammie Lee's going to work on the cookbook committee.'

Jacqueline's heart fell. She'd hoped to speak privately to the committee chairwoman and suggest that perhaps Tammie Lee might serve more effectively somewhere else. The thought of her daughter-in-law's recipe for boiled peanuts and cheese grits in the Country Club Cookbook made Jacqueline shudder. What an embarrassment! She couldn't allow that to happen.

'I've been meaning to talk to Louise about that.'

'It's a stroke of genius,' Bev said.

It was Jacqueline's turn to pay her lunch tab, and she set the cash on the counter, breathing far too fast. Surely she'd misunderstood Bev. She stepped aside after collecting her change and waited while the other woman paid.

'A stroke of ... genius?' Jacqueline repeated as

they started out the restaurant door.

'Why, yes. I first met Tammie Lee a few months ago. Haywood and I instantly fell in love with her. She's a breath of fresh air that our women's group badly needs. She's so energetic. Don't you just love that sweet southern accent of hers? I swear I could listen to her speak all day.'

Jacqueline had to bite her tongue to keep from admitting how irritated she was by Tammie Lee's twang.

'It's no wonder Paul fell in love with her. I think Haywood's halfway there himself.'

'Oh.' Jacqueline wasn't sure how to respond.

'The committee puts out a cookbook every two years and it's always the same people and the same recipes. Just how many recipes for Cranberry Mold do we need?'

Jacqueline refrained from mentioning that she'd been the one to submit the gelatin recipe, which had long been a club favorite.

'Tammie Lee had some wonderful ideas, and frankly I'm thinking of asking her to chair the committee. Louise has done it for several years and she's ready to try her hand at something else.'

'I don't know if that's a good idea.' Jacqueline could no longer remain silent. She respected Bev's opinion, but in this case her friend was wrong. Tammie Lee would be an embarrassment to them all.

'I know, of course, that with a baby due in the next few months, I can't ask her to take on any additional responsibility,' Bev said as she neared the parking lot. Her convertible BMW was

163

parked next to Jacqueline's Mercedes. 'I don't want to overwhelm her. Paul would never forgive me, although I think Tammie Lee's a natural.'

'Yes, yes, she's going to have her hands full,' Jacqueline agreed and stood rooted to the spot, too stunned to move while Bev climbed into her car and drove off. Had the entire world gone mad? Jacqueline wondered. Was she the only one who recognized Tammie Lee as the insincere little manipulator she was?

Her thoughts troubled, Jacqueline pulled into the garage at home and was astonished to realize she couldn't remember driving there. One moment she was in the restaurant parking lot and the next she was in her own garage.

Another surprise awaited her when she found Reese in the kitchen. He was dressed in one of his best suits and either he was home early or ready to take his blonde out for the evening. Jacqueline didn't ask. She'd rather not know than have to hear him lie.

She put away her purse and glanced at the mail, paying special attention to the sale flyers. When she'd finished, she walked over to the liquor cabinet and reached for a bottle of gin. 'Want one?'

'I'm driving.'

Jacqueline shrugged. 'I'm not.' The margaritas had long since worn off.

'What's wrong?' he asked.

'What makes you think anything's wrong?'

Reese frowned. 'I've never known you to drink this early in the afternoon.'

'Some occasions call for it.' She turned around

to study this man with whom she'd spent most of her life. She knew him so well – and yet she didn't know him at all.

'Where were you?' he asked.

She couldn't tell if he was genuinely interested or making small talk. Jacqueline found it curious that he was questioning her whereabouts; he'd done that a few times recently but she had no idea why.

'Out with the girls. For our monthly birthday lunch.'

'You might invite Tammie Lee on one of your outings sometime.'

He had to be joking. 'Why would I do that?'

'Because she's your daughter-in-law and it would be one way of welcoming her into the family.'

'I refuse to be a hypocrite. She *isn't* welcome. She's tolerated and frankly even that's becoming difficult.' If one more person sang her daughter-in-law's praises, Jacqueline swore she was going to scream. 'Why does everyone think Tammie Lee's so terrific? I don't get it.'

Reese stared at her for a long moment. 'Have you ever asked yourself why Paul fell in love with her?' His voice was cool and controlled, which usually indicated that he was curbing his anger.

'Of course I understand why Paul married her. He was ruled by hormones instead of common sense.'

'No, he wasn't,' Reese shouted, slapping his palm against the kitchen counter.

Jacqueline nearly leaped out of her skin at her husband's uncharacteristic display of temper.

165

'Tammie Lee is loving and caring and generous. The only person who doesn't see it is you
and only because you're so blinded by your own
agenda for our son you refuse to open your eyes.'

Jacqueline stared at him. 'Are you suggesting
I'm a cold, selfish bitch, Reese?' How dare he
speak that way to her!

It looked as if he meant to leave without any
kind of response, but apparently he changed his
mind. 'Perhaps you should answer that question
yourself,' he said.

Then he walked out, slamming the door behind
him.

CHAPTER 19

'Handknitting is a soothing and comforting
means of creative expression that can result in a
warm, useful and lovingly knitted garment ...
what a bonus.'

—Meg Swansen, Schoolhouse Press

LYDIA HOFFMAN

The three women in my knitting class sat around
the table, eager for the last scheduled lesson.
Before I could start, however, Jacqueline spoke
up.

'I'd like to let everyone know I've decided
against returning for the new session.' She meant
our knitting 'support group,' for which I charged

five dollars a week.

No one made any protest, so I felt I should say something. 'I'm sorry to hear that, Jacqueline.' I was, and my feelings weren't entirely mercenary, although I knew if she stayed, Jacqueline would be inclined to purchase the higher-end yarns.

'I'm not,' Alix said without so much as a second's hesitation.

'I didn't expect anything different from you,' Jacqueline muttered, not hiding her scorn.

Truth be known, I was just as glad not to be stuck refereeing those two, although it did make for an amusing moment now and then. I don't think I've ever seen two women who disliked each other more intensely. I'd believed that their animosity had lessened in the past few weeks, but apparently I'd read the situation completely wrong. Once again, my lack of experience when it came to relationships was showing.

Jacqueline was difficult to know – and to like. I did give her credit, though; she'd made a genuine effort to learn to knit and had nearly completed the baby blanket she was making for her first grandchild.

'I felt I should attend the last class and tell everyone what I'd decided.'

'Like we'd care,' Alix mumbled under her breath.

Standing behind Alix, I placed my hand on her shoulder as a way of asking her to keep her comments to herself. Through the last six weeks, I'd discovered that for all her crusty exterior the girl was actually quite sensitive. Even a hint of criticism was enough to make her withdraw.

'I don't think I could stop knitting now if I wanted to,' Carol said. She was working on a sweater for her brother. The cashmere yarn was the most expensive in the shop and she'd bought it in a creamy gray.

'I'm going to continue, too,' Alix said, glaring across the table at Jacqueline as if to suggest the older woman lacked willpower. 'I'm gonna get this blanket right no matter what it takes.'

I had to admire Alix's determination. She was still rather clumsy in her handling of the yarn and needles, but she refused to give up. I suspect she undid as many rows as she knit in the first few weeks. Thankfully, she'd learned what she was doing wrong and was progressing nicely. Her biggest hindrance was lack of time.

'Are you saying I'm a quitter?' Jacqueline asked, challenging Alix.

'If the fancy shoe fits, then walk in it. It's no biggie, right? You certainly won't be missed by me.'

Jacqueline and Alix's constant bickering wore on my nerves. But before I could react, Carol leaped in.

'I have news,' she said in a blatant effort to change the subject. I was grateful to her.

'Oh, good.' I didn't bother to hide the relief in my voice.

'Monday morning Doug's taking me in for the last IVF attempt.'

Although she presented a cheerful facade, I sensed – and I'm sure the others did, too – a deep-seated fear. I hoped everything would work this time and Carol would carry the pregnancy

full-term. She'd been going in for regular appointments, although she hadn't given us details.
She'd talked briefly to the group about her
fertility problems and a bit more to me privately,
but not much. My heart ached for her.

To my surprise, it was Jacqueline who spoke
first. 'Oh, my dear, I certainly wish you success.
Reese and I only had the one child and we longed
for a second.'

'At this point Doug and I would be ecstatic
with just one.' Her smile trembled.

'I so wished for a daughter.'

'Didn't you mention that your son and his wife
are having a girl?' I seemed to remember that
from an earlier conversation with Jacqueline.

'Yes.'

Jacqueline had been suspiciously quiet about
her son and Tammie Lee lately. It made me
wonder if something had happened that she
preferred not to discuss. With her it was hard to
tell. While Carol and Alix had grown comfortable
with each other, Jacqueline remained emotionally distant. I had the impression that the only
women she allowed into her life were her country
club friends.

Alix kept her head lowered and concentrated on
her knitting. 'I think only people who really want
kids should have them.' She'd said something
similar to this earlier, I recalled. She seemed to
have strong feelings about it. I could only assume
that was because of her own experience.

'I do, too,' Carol agreed. 'What I don't understand is why so many couples who love children
seem to have such difficulty getting pregnant.

When I think back on all the years I put off having a family, I want to weep. I thought I had lots of time, but how was I to know?' A pained look came over her.

'What about you?' Alix asked, glancing in my direction.

I was sure my face went scarlet, although why the subject of children should bother me, I don't know. In response I shook my head.

'What?' Alix demanded. 'You don't want kids?'

'I'm not married.'

'That didn't worry my mother. She was six months pregnant with my brother before she got around to marrying my father. It was the worst mistake of her life, she claims, but that didn't stop her from having me.'

'A child can't be blamed for the circumstances of his or her birth,' Carol said.

'Yeah, well, that's not the way I heard it.' Alix jerked viciously on the ball of yarn. 'It's no big deal. I survived.'

'Surely a lovely young woman like you will marry one day,' Jacqueline said, directing the comment at me.

Jacqueline had a tendency to catch me off guard once in a while. Only moments earlier she'd expressed compassion and understanding for Carol, and her comment about me being lovely – well, that was an unexpected compliment.

'Thank you, but...' I let the rest fade. I'd rather not reveal the details of my life if I can help it.

'But what?' Carol pressed.

'But – well, I don't think I'd make a very good wife.'

'Why not?' Alix again. 'You'd sure as hell be a better wife than *my* mother ever was.'

This conversation was fast becoming uncomfortable. 'Husbands have ... expectations.'

Alix looked up with a puzzled frown. 'What's that supposed to mean?'

I could see the other two were equally curious. 'I've already gone through two bouts of cancer. It's possible that our family has a predisposition to it.'

'Do you have it now?'

'No, thank God, but my older sister had a recent scare.' Thankfully Margaret's second mammogram had been clear. I'd gone to the doctor's office with her and given her the support she needed. Afterward she'd invited me to lunch to celebrate the results.

This was the closest I'd felt to my sister since I was a teenager. Perverse as it sounds, I'm grateful for the alarm that initial mammogram caused. For the first time in years, my sister and I had something in common – fear. And for the first time ever, I was the one who had the greater knowledge ... and the authority of personal experience.

'Why can't you get married?' Alix asked.

I sighed. I really didn't want to get into this. 'There's no guarantee the cancer won't come back,' I said simply.

I discovered all three women staring at me with blank expressions.

'In case you haven't noticed, life doesn't exactly come with guarantees,' Alix said. 'I should know about that.'

'If it did, I'd be a mother by now,' Carol added.

'She's right,' Jacqueline said, gesturing toward Carol.

My sister had been saying the same thing. Our lunch had gone well until she'd mentioned Brad. I hadn't seen the UPS guy for several days and as far as I was concerned, the question of my dating him was a moot point. After two rejections, I doubted he'd ask me out again. Really, why should he? I'd made it plain that I wasn't interested.

'I haven't been on a date in so long, I'm not sure how to act,' I told my friends. It was the truth.

'You just act normal,' Carol said as if that was understood.

'Just be yourself,' Jacqueline threw in. To my astonishment, she drew out her knitting. I'd had the impression earlier that she intended to make her big announcement and leave. I was glad to see her join the others.

'Hey, do you have the hots for some guy?'

Naturally Alix would ask such a question. 'Of course not.' My denial was fast and firm. Once again, the heat in my face reflected my embarrassment.

'You do so,' Carol said, watching me. She laughed softly. 'All right, give. Who is he?'

I shook my head, refusing to answer. 'It's too late.'

'It's never too late.' Jacqueline leaned toward me.

'Tell us the name,' Alix encouraged.

They wouldn't drop the matter and I could

think of nothing to say or do that would take the conversation elsewhere.

'Come on, Lydia,' Alix insisted again. 'Tell us.'

I hesitated, then with a deep sigh told them about Brad. 'He won't ask me out again,' I said when I'd finished.

'Probably not,' Alix agreed. 'What you have to do now is ask *him* out.'

Both Jacqueline and Carol nodded. It seemed Brad had won Margaret to his side and now my entire knitting class, too.

CHAPTER 20

CAROL GIRARD

Sunday night before the IVF procedure, Carol waited until she was sure Doug had fallen asleep. When she heard the heavy, even cadence of his breathing, she slipped out of bed and crept silently into the living room.

She loved the view of Puget Sound at night. From her living room window, she could see the dark, shimmering water. Beyond West Seattle was Vashon Island and the lights of the Kitsap Peninsula.

Sinking into her favorite chair, she dropped her head back and ordered her mind and her body to relax. She couldn't go into this procedure tense; she had to will her body to accept the fertilized eggs, to accept the baby or babies she yearned for.

She didn't understand what was happening to her. If she wanted a child so much, then why did her body reject pregnancy after pregnancy? Nothing added up, nothing made sense, no matter how often she tried to analyze the situation.

Her own body had become her worst enemy, it seemed; her womb had betrayed her in the most fundamental way, by denying her the ability to reproduce. She was fast approaching a time when her age would make it impossible to conceive. Already her egg production had started to fall off.

While outwardly everyone was sympathetic, Carol knew her friends were bored with the subject. She also knew how badly her mother wanted grandchildren. All her mother's friends carried around purseloads of pictures of their grand kids, while her own mother sat by, silent and depressed. Neither Carol nor Rick had given her bragging rights. She said it jokingly, but Carol felt her mother's disappointment as keenly as she felt her own.

To this point, Doug's parents had been supportive and encouraging, but they too were weary of waiting. Thankfully, his younger sister had made them grandparents twice over, but his father was hoping for a grandson to carry on the family name. The pressure wasn't explicit but it was there and Carol nearly suffocated under the weight of it.

Tears filled her eyes. Never in all her life had she wept as much as she had in these last few years. Before long, she had a thick wad of tissues in her hand.

It wasn't as if she hadn't *tried*. She'd submitted

to every therapy available and ingested a pharmacy full of drugs. All those drugs. God only knew what she'd done to her body or what risks she'd taken, but it wouldn't have mattered. Nothing mattered except having a baby. She was willing to swallow anything, inject her stomach with drugs, volunteer for any experimental program, if there was even the slightest possibility it would help her get pregnant—and stay pregnant.

'What are you doing out here?' Doug came into the room wearing striped pajama bottoms and no top; it was how he always slept. He sat down across from her. 'What's the matter? Can't you sleep?'

Afraid that he might hear the tears in her voice, she shook her head.

He didn't say anything and they sat together in silence. After a few minutes, her husband stood up and stretched out his arm to her and pulled her into his embrace.

'You should try to sleep,' he said.

'I know.'

He didn't try to lead her back to bed and she was grateful.

'What about you?' she asked.

'I don't think I can sleep without you.'

She smiled, comforted by the knowledge that she was as much a part of him as he was of her.

A ferry glided toward Vashon Island and Carol forced her attention onto its slow progress from Fauntleroy to Southworth. The terrible tension returned and she had to ask the one question that had hounded her for months. 'What are we going to do if I don't get pregnant this time?' Her words came out a broken whisper. 'Adopt?'

'We'll cross that bridge when we get to it.'

'I can't wait. I need to know now.'

'Why?'

'What if the adoption agencies decide we aren't fit parents? What if we can't get an infant the way we want? What ... what if the IVF fails again? Oh, Doug, I shouldn't think like that and yet I can't stop myself.'

Doug's sigh rumbled from deep within his chest. 'Then don't think like that. If the IVF fails, we'll adopt and if we aren't accepted by the agency, then we won't have children. Other couples have survived and we will, too.'

'No ... we won't.'

'Carol.'

'It might be all right between us for a while, but then one day you'll look at some little boy or girl and–' The lump in her throat made it impossible to continue.

Doug didn't try to deny it. 'Don't say that.'

She gave a helpless shrug.

'What makes you think we won't be able to adopt? Other couples our age adopt. Why can't we?'

'Because we're too late.'

'Too late? Why is it too late?'

'Because the waiting lists are years long. By the time they get to our name, we'll be in our mid-forties.'

'You're erecting roadblocks where there aren't any.'

Carol couldn't respond. Her misery was too great. It was easy for Doug to say she was agonizing over nonexistent problems; it wasn't his body that failed them month after month.

'We're going to have a baby,' Doug said.

'Don't say that,' she cried.

'Carol, stop it. You're getting hysterical.'

'I'm hysterical and frightened and depressed and–'

'Defeated. Why go through with the procedure if you've already decided it isn't going to work?'

'Because I have to know.'

'You want to know that you can't get pregnant?' he asked gently.

Doug thought he was helping but he wasn't. In fact, he was making everything worse. 'Just leave me alone.'

'Carol, for heaven's sake...'

'I don't want you here. I need some time by myself.' It was like this with the drugs, these wild mood swings. They'd been warned; nevertheless, Carol was caught unprepared.

Doug stood up and walked over to the window. Gazing into the moonlit night, he rubbed his hand over his face as though considering his options. 'I don't think I should leave you alone.' He didn't look at her as he spoke.

'Please just go.'

'You need me.'

'Not now... I need to be by myself.'

'Carol...' He turned toward her.

'Please, Doug.'

He hesitated and then reluctantly walked into the bedroom.

As soon as he was gone, Carol wanted him back. She wanted him to take her in his arms and reassure her of his love. She wanted him to tell her he'd love her to the end of time, with or without a child.

Closing her eyes, she fought off the ugly negative voices that harassed her from all sides and tried to think positive thoughts. It was a technique she'd learned from her online support group – creating the image of what you want and seeing it in such clear detail that you begin to accept the possibility ... the reality.

She pictured herself pregnant, her stomach extended, wearing a cheerful maternity top. Doug's hands rested on her tummy and he bent over and kissed her belly. When he straightened, his eyes were full of love and pride. That was the image she held on to, the picture she framed in her mind. She refused to let her doubts defeat her.

At some point during the night, she must have fallen asleep on the sofa. Before dawn, she stirred and climbed back into bed. Pressing her body against Doug's, she cuddled him close and draped her arm across his waist.

When she woke again, Doug was cuddling her. 'Are you awake?' he whispered.

'I am now.' She groaned and rolled onto her back.

'What time did you come to bed?'

'I don't know, I didn't look.'

He nibbled on her ear. 'Do you feel better?'

She managed a soft smile. 'Yes.'

'Good.'

She could hear coffee brewing in the background. 'Is it time to get up already?'

'I'm afraid so.'

She struggled into a sitting position and offered Doug a tired smile.

'Have I told you lately how much I love you?' he asked.

He told her in a thousand different ways. 'Yup,' she said in the middle of a loud yawn.

'This is a very important day, you know,' Doug said, sitting on the edge of the bed.

'I do know,' Carol whispered. This was the day she'd welcome Doug's child into her womb.

CHAPTER 21

ALIX TOWNSEND

Alix stepped outside the video store and lit up a cigarette. She was cutting back, but giving up smoking was difficult. Taking a long drag, she savored the immediate soothing effect and exhaled, tilting her head upward. It was when she started to take a second puff that she noticed Jordan Turner walking down the opposite side of the street. A sense of dread filled her; she didn't want to talk to him.

What was the point? He obviously wasn't interested in her. Oh sure, she amused him, but he saw her as a leftover challenge from the sixth grade – the girl he wanted to save. Another notch in his ministerial belt. Preachers couldn't accept that Alix wasn't looking for salvation. Oh, sure she'd ridden the church bus to Sunday School.

Her parents would've been willing to let her go anywhere if it meant she was out of their hair for an hour or two. She'd done the Jesus thing at ten and eleven, but it hadn't gotten her anywhere. Been there, done that, and been awarded the prize Bible for memorizing scripture.

She'd been on her own since she was sixteen and one of the hardest lessons life had taught her was that the only person she could rely on was herself. It wasn't a lesson she was likely to forget.

Crushing out her half-smoked cigarette, Alix went back inside the store, hoping Jordan would take the hint and leave her alone.

'That was quick,' Laurel muttered as Alix joined her behind the counter.

'I'm going into the back room.'

Laurel frowned. 'Why?'

'If you-know-who comes in, tell him I'm not working tonight.'

'Are you still avoiding Jordan?'

'Just do it,' Alix snapped and hurried to the back of the store before the preacher man caught up with her. It'd been two weeks since they'd bumped into each other at Starbucks and he'd dropped his bomb. The explosion still reverberated in her ears. Jordan was a minister – and she wanted nothing to do with him *or* his God.

No more than a minute later, Laurel appeared, and she didn't look any too pleased. 'He saw you.'

Alix whirled around. 'Then tell him I'm busy.'

'I already tried that.'

This was getting irritating. 'So tell him something else. I don't want to talk to him.'

'You can't hide forever.'

'I'm not hiding,' Alix insisted, which was a pretty weak argument.

'Do what you want,' Laurel said. 'But he told me he was going to wait until you came out.' With that, her roommate and supposed friend returned to the front of the store.

Alix waited an agonizing ten minutes and figured that by then Jordan would've given up on her. No such luck. Arms crossed, he stood by the microwave popcorn display next to the cash register. His eyes narrowed when he saw her.

Rather than try to avoid him anymore, she strolled purposely toward Jordan. 'You don't take a hint, do you?' she asked bluntly.

'Not easily,' he admitted. 'Let's talk.'

'I can't.' She'd already squandered her fifteen-minute break and that was her last of the evening. The video store wasn't doing a robust business, but they were busy enough.

'Meet me after work.'

Alix shrugged. She might as well get this over with. 'All right.'

'Your word is good?'

The challenge in his voice offended her sense of pride. 'Damn straight it is! I'll be at Starbucks ten minutes after closing.'

'Make it Annie's Café.'

'Fine, Annie's.'

'I'll be waiting.'

It could've been Alix's imagination, but she thought she saw Jordan wink at Laurel on his way out the door. She wondered what the hell that was about and then decided it didn't matter. If he

181

was interested in her friend, then fine. She hoped the two of them would be very happy. Jordan was a damn sight better than that slimy used-car salesman.

Only Alix *did* care, and she was in a bitch of a mood for the rest of her shift. By eleven o'clock Laurel was no longer speaking to her and left in a huff. Alix was just as glad to be rid of her.

Exactly ten minutes after closing out the till, locking up the store and making the deposit, Alix walked into Annie's. The café was half a block down from the video store. As a treat every payday, Alix bought herself dinner there. The food was good, plentiful and cheap.

Jordan was in a booth reading the menu when she approached. She scowled at him and said, 'I don't owe you anything.'

'Yeah? And your point is?'

'I don't have to be here.'

He raised his eyebrows. 'True, but I figure you owe me an explanation as to why you ditched me in sixth grade.'

'I didn't ditch you. I ... I got caught up in circumstances beyond my control.'

'All right, but consider it common courtesy to explain what happened.'

He'd obviously been taught etiquette. She, on the other hand, didn't know anything about it.

'Listen,' she said aggressively, 'we can spend the rest of the evening arguing about something that happened in grade school or we can talk. You decide.'

It was all too apparent that Jordan intended to pester her until he got the answers he wanted.

She'd already decided she'd rather not get involved with a minister, but he was making that difficult. Frowning, she slid into the booth across from him.

'What's wrong, Alix?' Jordan asked.

This was an interesting approach but before she could answer, the waitress appeared. Alix knew Jenny, who worked swing shift, and she watched as the older woman glanced between them, not bothering to hide her surprise.

Folding over the top sheet of her pad, Jenny asked, 'What can I get you two?'

Jordan closed the plastic-coated menu. 'I'm thinking about a bacon cheeseburger with the works.' Then he looked at Alix. 'How about you?'

Her mouth watered at the thought of one of Annie's mammoth cheeseburgers. But first she had to find out who was paying for it. 'You buying? Or am I getting my own?'

'I wouldn't ask if I wasn't.'

Alix tucked the menu behind the sugar canister. 'I'll have the same.'

'Two bacon cheeseburgers,' Jordan said. 'And two Cokes.' He gave Alix a questioning smile and she nodded.

Jenny wrote down the order and left.

As soon as the waitress was gone, Jordan rested his hands on the table. 'So,' he began.

Squarely meeting his gaze, Alix sighed heavily. 'So I'm not interested in church,' she said.

'Why not?'

'In case you haven't noticed, I'm not exactly the church-going kind.'

'And what kind is that?'

Alix rolled her eyes. 'Ladies who wear hats and gloves and exchange polite conversation with a few "praise the Lords" thrown in.'

Jordan's head reared back and he snorted with laughter. 'You're describing a garden party, not church. I can tell you haven't attended in a while.'

'I went to Sunday School back in grade school but skipped the church part,' she told him. The truth was, she'd gone a few times but left early, bored by all the preaching. 'Like I said, I'm not interested.'

Jenny brought their Cokes and Jordan waited impatiently before he responded.

'How do you know?' he burst out when she was gone.

'Jordan, I think you're great.' She took a long sip of her drink. 'I remember your dad and he was nice, too.' Jordan's father had come to the house once to talk to her mother, after Alix had been awarded that prize Bible. It was the one and only time he'd stopped by, and she didn't blame him for never visiting again.

'How do you know you're not interested in church unless you try it? Why don't you come one Sunday and see?'

'Listen,' Alix said, trying to be as honest as possible. 'I don't need anyone to save me.'

He frowned. 'So that's what you think?'

'Damn straight.'

'You've certainly got me figured out,' he said, a little sarcastically.

Being rude was natural for her, but she was determined to keep the peace until after she'd eaten the cheeseburger. After all, he *was* paying for it. And she *was* hungry.

'Why is it so important for me to go to church?' she demanded, and then answered for him. 'It's because you want to change me.'

'No,' he argued. 'I want to see you.'

Sure he did!

'I liked you in sixth grade and I like you now. Do I need an excuse?' He leaned across the table, unwilling to break eye contact.

'I'm not your type.'

'Did you decide that on your own, or did someone else make up your mind for you?'

She bristled at his question. 'I make up my own mind.'

She could see he was growing angry. His hand clenched the silverware wrapped in a paper napkin. 'Let me see if I understand you. I was all right to hang with until you found out I'm someone you knew ten or twelve years ago – who just happens to be a minister?'

Alix lowered her eyes and refused to answer.

'You liked me just fine in grade school, and now you don't?'

That bacon cheeseburger had better show up fast, because holding her tongue was damn difficult. Alix bit the inside of her lip.

'The least you can do is answer me.'

'What do you want me to say?' she snapped. 'That it doesn't matter? Well, it does.'

'What changed?'

She opened her mouth and then faltered, unsure of herself. 'You're... You're...' She gestured toward him, making circular motions with her hands. 'You're ... *good.*'

'Good?' Jordan repeated. 'What do you mean by that?'

She folded her arms and searched with growing desperation for Jenny. It never took this long for an order to come up. Her stomach growled and reminded her it'd been mid-afternoon since her latte and she was hungry. As soon as her meal arrived, she could say what she wanted and take her cheeseburger home. Only he was confusing her. All she could think about was how badly she'd wanted to attend that valentine party. She hadn't told him, but she'd had a valentine for him, too.

'You know what I mean,' she challenged.

'No, I don't,' Jordan said, 'so you'd better explain it to me. What the hell makes me good?'

She blinked and realized he was serious. 'God,' she whispered.

His expression went blank. 'God?'

She nodded. 'You're this lily-white guy who grew up with a perfect family. I didn't. You had parents who loved you. I didn't. You–'

'None of that's relevant,' he countered, cutting her off.

'My mother did jail time for shooting my father. Did you know that?'

He nodded slowly. 'There was plenty of talk about it, but all I wanted to know was what had happened to you.'

'Oh.' This was unexpected.

Alix nearly sighed in relief when Jenny appeared with two plates. The cheeseburger was left open and the cheese had melted perfectly. The

French fries glistened and sizzled, fresh from the fryer. Her mouth watered just looking at her meal.

'I asked my dad to find out where you were. He tried, but didn't get anywhere. Apparently you and your brother had already been sent to foster homes in another part of the city,' Jordan said.

Alix reached for the salt shaker but her eyes didn't leave his the whole time she salted her fries. 'You did?'

He nodded and picked up a fry.

Hungry though she was, Alix hadn't touched her food. 'What made you decide to go into the ministry? Like father, like son?'

'That's a story for another night.' He added lettuce and a slice of tomato to his burger and closed it before taking his first bite.

Alix bit into her burger, too. 'Just remember I don't need you to save me,' she said, still chewing.

'I couldn't even if I wanted to.'

She swallowed and drank some more of her Coke. 'Why not?'

'It's not what I do. I leave the salvation up to God. He saves, I just point the way.' He took another fry, dipping it into a small pool of ketchup he'd squirted onto his plate.

She still didn't trust him. 'I don't get it.'

'What's to get?'

'You,' she said. 'Wanting to see me.'

He cast her a strange look. 'Is there some law that says I'm not supposed to be attracted to you? I liked you in sixth grade and I still think you're kinda cute.'

He liked her? He thought she was cute? 'You do?' she asked and was mortified by the slight quiver in her voice.

'I wouldn't say so if I didn't.' He stretched out his hand and stole one of her French fries.

'Hey.' She slapped his hand.

He laughed and gave her his sliced pickle.

They finished eating, talked about movies they'd both seen and then left the café an hour later. 'Are you going to stop avoiding me now?' Jordan asked.

Alix figured she'd play it cool. 'I haven't decided yet.'

'Decide soon, will you?'

'Why?'

'Because I don't know how much longer I can afford to rent movies.'

Alix laughed.

'You coming to church on Sunday?' he asked.

'Probably not.' She didn't see herself sitting next to any church lady with sagging panty hose and a big purse. Jordan might want her to show up, but she didn't think those goody-goody types would take kindly to her purple-tinted hair.

Church was for people who had regular lives and who had goals and dreams. Okay, Alix had dreams, too, but damn little chance of ever seeing them come to life. She wanted to be a chef. Not just a cook, but a real chef in some fancy restaurant. She'd worked in a couple of cafés like Annie's over the years and always liked the kitchen jobs best. The last place she'd worked – before the video store – had closed down, but working there had set the dream in place.

She suspected he was laughing at her. Before she knew what he intended, he pulled her into the shadows of the alley and backed her up against the brick wall.

They stared at each other for a long moment, neither breathing, neither saying anything.

Then his mouth was on hers, and it was all she could do not to crumple at the effect of his kiss. Her head started to spin and her knees actually went weak. The only thing left to do was hold on to him, so she wrapped her arms around Jordan's neck. From there, her senses took her on a roller-coaster ride more exciting than anything Disney had to offer.

'What was that for?' she asked, her voice sounding like something rattling around in a tin can.

When Jordan finally lifted his head, he whispered. 'I figured you owed me that because I had my heart broken in sixth grade.'

Alix moistened her lips. 'Yeah ... well, you weren't the only one.'

CHAPTER 22

'In the hands of a knitter, yarn becomes the medium that binds the heart and soul.'
—Robin Villiers-Furze, The Needleworks Company,
Port Orchard, Washington

LYDIA HOFFMAN

Another Friday had come to an end. The knitting session was one of the best ever, with Alix laughing a lot and Jacqueline more relaxed and tolerant than I'd ever seen her. Carol was at home – doctor's orders. By the time I turned over the closed sign on the shop door and headed upstairs to my apartment, I was exhausted. But this was a good kind of tired. When I first opened A Good Yarn, I'd had plenty of empty hours to work on my own projects.

Not anymore. I had a continuous stream of customers and I was intermittently busy most days. I needed to thank Jacqueline the next time I saw her. She'd spread the word about the store, and two of her affluent friends had recently stopped by. Despite all her threats to quit the class, she showed up each and every Friday. And Jacqueline's country club friends had purchased four hundred dollars' worth of yarn. With big sales like these I didn't need to worry about making the rent payment, which was one of my biggest concerns when I opened my door.

I wasn't actually earning enough to pay myself a real salary yet, but I was managing the rent and after less than three months in business, that excited me. My strategy was to live simply and believe in myself.

When I arrived upstairs, I left the smaller windows in the living room open. A gentle breeze filtered through. Whiskers was all over me, weaving between my feet in an effort to attract my undivided attention. I love my cat and he's excellent company, but there are days I'd like a few moments to myself to unwind. Whiskers's demands come first, however.

I opened a can of his favorite tuna and set it down. He's terribly spoiled, but I can't help it. While Whiskers chowed down on dinner, I sorted through the day's mail and came upon an envelope with a familiar scrawl. Margaret.

I hesitated before I tore it open. Inside were two thank-you notes, one from each of my nieces, thanking me for the sweaters I'd recently knit. It was the first time they'd formally acknowledged my gifts. In the past I'd often suspected Margaret hadn't given them the things I made them.

In retrospect, I probably shouldn't have reacted by phoning my sister. Except that our strained relationship showed recent signs of improvement, and I was feeling encouraged. Before I could change my mind, I punched out her telephone number.

At the first ring, I nearly did change my mind and hang up. But I knew she had Caller ID and would immediately contact me and ask why I'd phoned.

Hailey answered on the second ring.

'I got your thank-you note,' I told her.

'Mom said we should write you, but I would have anyway. It's a cool sweater, Aunt Lydia. I love the colors.'

'I'm glad you like it.' I'd chosen a lime-green yarn and accented the cuffs and button bands with bright orange. It turned out to be really cute, even if I do say so myself.

'Mom's here,' Hailey said and before I could tell her it wasn't necessary to interrupt Margaret, my sister was on the line.

'Is everything all right?' she demanded in that gruff unfriendly tone she holds in reserve for me.

'Of course,' I assured her. 'I got the note from the girls today and I–'

'You only ever phone if something's wrong.'

That was categorically untrue but I didn't want to argue with her. Normally I avoided calling Margaret because the experience was so often unsettling.

'I'm fine, really.' I tried to laugh but it sounded phony.

'Have you seen that handsome UPS driver lately?'

I could feel my face heat up at the mention of Brad. I hadn't phoned her to talk about him. 'He was by the other day.' Instantly I tried to think of something to distract her from the subject of Brad Goetz, and couldn't.

The UPS driver was as friendly as ever but he no longer asked me out. He knew about my cancer now, and that explained it. I was grateful he didn't force me to invent plausible-sounding excuses. But when he'd left after his most recent visit, I'd experienced a twinge of regret. That slight but unmistakable sense of loss stayed with me the rest of the afternoon.

'Did you suggest the two of you get together?' Margaret pressed.

'No. I...' That was all I got out before my sister cut me off.

'Why not?'

' I–'

'You keep telling me this shop of yours is an affirmation of life.'

'Yes, I know, but–'

'Well, why don't you put your money where your mouth is.'

It distressed me that my sister seemed to enjoy harassing me. 'It's my life, Margaret.'

'*Life?*' She said it scornfully. 'What life? All you do is work and knit, which *is* your work. Oh sure, you visit Mom and have a couple of friends, but–'

It was my turn to cut her off. 'I make my own decisions about the men I date.'

Margaret acted as if she hadn't heard me. 'Ask him out for a beer,' she insisted.

'No!'

'Why not?'

I wasn't sure why I was so adamant. 'Because...'

'You're afraid.'

'All right, I'm afraid,' I almost shouted, 'but that doesn't change anything.'

'Get over it.'

'Oh, Margaret, you make everything seem so easy.'

'Ask him out and don't call me again until you do.'

'Are you serious?' I couldn't *believe* she'd say anything like that to me.

'Dead serious.' She disconnected the phone.

I stared at the receiver a full minute before I stepped away. Margaret could be so dictatorial. My own sister refused to speak to me until I contacted a man she'd only seen once, and briefly at that? Well, she could forget it; I wasn't giving in. That decided, I went to find something decent for dinner.

Because I feel diet is so important in maintaining a healthy body, I avoid processed foods as much as possible. On occasion I microwave a frozen entrée, but only rarely. I did that evening, however, because my head was spinning. Margaret had said I should invite Brad out for a drink. Okay, so maybe she had my best interests at heart. Maybe, just maybe she was right, and it was time for me to throw caution to the winds. The women in my knitting class seemed to think so, too. But I had no idea how.

At nine, I phoned her back.

Knowing my sister, I half expected her to slam down the receiver but I didn't give her the chance. 'What do I say?' I asked. 'I've already turned him down twice. Now that he knows I've had cancer, he probably isn't interested. He might tell me no.'

'He might. And I wouldn't blame him.'

'Thanks for the encouragement,' I muttered under my breath and to my surprise Margaret laughed. Generally not even a stand-up comic can get a response out of my sister. She's one of those deadpan women born without a funny bone. I had no idea I was so amusing.

'I mean it,' I said.

'You're actually asking *me* for help?'

'Yes. If you refuse to talk to me until I make a fool of myself over a man, then the least you can do is tell me how to go about it.'

That shut her up, but not for long.

'Tell him you've had a change of heart.'

'Okay.' My voice must have betrayed my lack of confidence.

'Then tell him you think it might be nice for the two of you to have a beer one night if he's still interested. Offer to buy and then leave the ball in his court.'

That sounded reasonable.

'Are you going to do it?' Margaret asked.

I leaned against the wall, fiddling with my hair. 'Yeah,' I said, 'I think I will.'

I sounded brave on Friday night, but by Monday morning it was a different story. It would've been easier if Brad had come with a delivery later in the week, but he didn't. As luck would have it, he showed up Monday afternoon when I wasn't expecting him.

'Hi,' I said. 'I don't usually see you on Mondays.' Now that was a clever remark, I thought with disgust, especially since I'm officially closed on Mondays.

'Not usually,' he said, wheeling the stack of boxes over to the cash register. 'How are you doing?'

'Great.' Instantly my mouth went completely dry.

Brad handed me the computerized clipboard, just the way he always did, so I could sign my name. I looked at it as if I'd never seen it before.

'I need a signature,' he said.

Thankfully I was able to manage that much. I glanced down long enough to finish the task and returned the clipboard. Brad smiled and headed out the door.

'Brad,' I called out.

He looked back.

I came out from behind the counter and walked toward him. My mind whirled with everything Margaret had suggested I say and in my eagerness, the words rushed out, stumbling all over themselves. 'I've had a change of heart, that is, if you're still interested. If you aren't, I understand perfectly, and I'm making a complete idiot of myself, and ... and let's have a beer one night. Oh, and I'll buy. Margaret said I should buy and–'

His eyes widened as he held up one hand. 'Whoa.'

I clamped my mouth shut.

'Now start over at the beginning, only slower this time.'

I was convinced my face was brighter than any fire truck in Seattle. 'I've reconsidered your invitation to meet for a drink after work.'

A smile appeared on his face and I could tell he was pleased. 'I'd enjoy that.'

A warm feeling replaced the chill that had left my teeth chattering. 'Good.'

'How about Friday night after you close the shop?'

I nodded. 'Sure.'

He reached for the cart, whistling on his way back to the truck. A few minutes after he left, I realized I was humming. I had a date!

Hot damn. I had a date. Just wait until Margaret heard about this.

CHAPTER 23

JACQUELINE DONOVAN

Jacqueline had her day all planned. She had a nail appointment at nine, followed by lunch with her friends, then major shopping, a few necessary errands and finally home. Tuesday was her busiest day of the week; she arranged it that way on purpose. Preoccupation was the key to forgetting that her husband would be spending part of the night with another woman.

While she was at the mall, she'd make sure she was justly rewarded for turning the other way, although she still had to grit her teeth every time she thought about it.

Just minutes before she planned to leave for the nail salon, the phone rang. For half a moment, she was tempted to ignore it, but then she saw that it was Reese's cell. Reluctantly she picked up the receiver.

'I need a favor,' her husband said urgently. 'I'm

in a meeting and I forgot my briefcase at the house.'

'Do you want me to drop it off?' It would mean she'd be late for her nail appointment, but Reese wouldn't ask if it wasn't necessary. She intended to spend a good deal of his money that afternoon, so the least she could do was accommodate him.

'Would you, Jacquie? I'd come back for it, but I need it ASAP.'

'I'm on my way.'

He told her where to find it near his desk in the den. Jacqueline went in there and found the briefcase just where he'd said it would be. The den was in Reese's section of the house and she rarely ventured inside. For a moment, she lingered, trailing her fingers over the perfectly aligned books on the mahogany shelves. On rare occasions Reese smoked a cigar and the scent of rich tobacco and leather was more prominent in this room than anywhere else in the house.

A sense of nostalgia filled her and a longing she could hardly explain. She felt a dull ache as she re-membered the love they'd somehow let slip away. The love of their early years... She never allowed herself to acknowledge the isolation they'd forced upon each other. She did now, and the sadness settled over her like a heavy rain-drenched coat.

It was hard to figure out precisely when it'd hap-pened to them or why. His Tuesday-night mistress was a symptom of their alienation, not a cause. They were already drifting apart when *she'd* entered the scene. Slowly, through the years, Jacqueline and Reese had lost that closeness. They were both at fault; Reese was stubborn – but so was she.

Their marriage had eroded to the point that they were roommates more than partners, friends more than lovers. It happened to many couples – she'd heard enough veiled hints and outright confessions from other women to be aware of that. Still, it didn't lessen her feelings of acute loss. Putting aside her thoughts, she reached for the briefcase and hurried to the garage.

Jacqueline phoned the nail salon from her car as she headed directly to Blossom Street. The renovations were going well, although parking was still impossible. Jacqueline suddenly realized Reese hadn't told her where she should leave her car.

She tried calling him, but apparently he'd turned off his cell. Twice around the block turned up nothing. The street wasn't wide enough for her to double park, either. After wasting a precious ten minutes in a fruitless effort to secure a parking space, she pulled into the alley behind A Good Yarn. It wasn't the best area of town in which to leave an expensive car, and Lydia had warned them against using it, but Jacqueline didn't have any choice. The alley was narrow and dark and she shuddered involuntarily as she quickly locked the car.

When she got to the construction site, Reese was nowhere to be seen. However, as soon as she arrived at the trailer, his project manager greeted her. Jacqueline couldn't recall his name, although she was fairly certain Reese had mentioned the young man. It'd been a long time since she'd kept track of his employees' names.

'Thanks,' the youthful-looking man told her. 'I know Reese was pretty upset about forgetting this.'

'It wasn't any problem,' she murmured, stepping over a pile of rebar on her way out.

Grumbling under her breath, she walked across the street and down the block to the alley entrance. Unfortunately the yarn store wouldn't be open for another twenty minutes, or she could've walked through there. As she entered the darkened alley, Jacqueline's anger increased steadily. No wonder her marriage was in trouble. Instead of greeting her personally, Reese had sent his assistant – as if he took for granted that she'd interrupt her entire day on his behalf. Next time he could damn well retrieve his own briefcase.

Disgruntled, Jacqueline was halfway into the alley before an eerie warning sensation crawled up her spine. She stopped and looked suspiciously around. Nothing. She relaxed and mentally chastised herself for being foolish. The sun had yet to clear the tops of the buildings and the area remained cool and shady. She moved forward two more steps and stopped again as the sensation grew stronger, more compelling.

Her imagination was running away with her, Jacqueline decided. She'd watched one too many episodes of *CSI*. Still, her fear persisted, growing more intense by the moment. But she had to get to her car. What alternative did she have? It was either that or stand here all morning.

She was no more than twenty feet from her Mercedes when two men stepped out from the shadows. They loomed in front of her, half-obscured by the darkness. Menacing. She couldn't see their faces clearly but she saw their sneers. They were street people, she thought, unkempt and filthy.

'What do we have here?' one called to the other, who moved quickly to block her exit.

Jacqueline broke into a cold sweat. Instinct told her to run, but she feared her legs were about to collapse. And in her heels, she had little chance of escaping if they decided to chase her.

'Kindly get out of my way,' she demanded and was rather pleased with her bravado.

'Kindly,' the second man, the taller of the two, echoed in a falsetto voice, raising his right arm and dangling his wrist. 'We got ourselves a genuine *lady* here.'

'High society.'

'Lots of money.'

'Now give it up, bitch.'

Jacqueline clutched her purse tighter against her side. 'You wouldn't dare.'

'Never could refuse a dare, could we, Larry?'

'Shut up,' the other man shouted, obviously angry that his friend had said his name. He pulled out a switchblade and brandished it in front of Jacqueline.

Despite her determination to remain calm, she gasped. The blade gleamed in what little light had broken through the alley.

He held out his arm as if he expected her to meekly hand over her purse, and Jacqueline realized this wasn't a request but a command. Any resistance would surely be met with violence.

Although she wasn't aware she'd released it, her

designer bag fell to the asphalt.

'I wouldn't touch that if I were you,' a brusque female voice shouted from behind Jacqueline. 'Aren't you on probation, Ralph? Be a real shame to see your sorry ass back in jail so soon.'

It took Jacqueline a moment to recognize Alix Townsend's voice. Alix, the girl she considered a felon and a crude punk rocker, had risked her own life and come to her rescue.

'Stay out of this,' Larry growled, baring his teeth at the two women.

'Sorry, guys,' Alix said, waltzing forward, 'but this lady happens to be a good friend of mine.'

Jacqueline stayed where she was, incapable of moving. Even her breathing had gone shallow.

Larry looked at the purse. 'You want her for yourself,' he muttered. He clenched the knife tighter and raised it.

A clicking sound followed but the noise didn't immediately register in Jacqueline's mind. Then she understood. Alix carried a switchblade of her own.

'They can have the money.' Jacqueline didn't care; she just wanted both of them out of this mess without getting hurt.

'No, they can't,' Alix yelled as the two men started toward them. 'Get over to the yarn store.'

'No.' Jacqueline didn't know where she found the courage, but she scooped up her purse and swung it wildly at the two men. She'd paid seven hundred dollars for the Gucci bag and it served her well, connecting with a solid crunch against the shorter man's head. Ralph howled with pain.

'What's going on back here?' Lydia shouted

from the rear door of her shop.

'Call 911,' Jacqueline screamed, panic raising her voice.

Alix crouched forward, her arms outstretched with a switchblade firmly gripped in her left hand. The men looked at the two women and at the empty door frame where Lydia had stood only seconds earlier. They glanced at each other and then ran for it, racing past Jacqueline and Alix.

As soon as they were out of sight, Jacqueline started to shake. The trembling began in her hands, and quickly moved down her arms and legs until it seemed that her knees had taken on a life of their own.

'Are you okay?' Alix asked.

Jacqueline shook her head.

'The police are on their way,' Lydia called.

'Larry and Ralph are gone now.' Alix wrapped her arm around Jacqueline's waist and guided her through the back door of Lydia's shop.

The table where they sat for their classes seemed a mile away before Jacqueline reached it and literally fell into a chair.

'I ... I could've been murdered.' She'd seen the look in those men's eyes. God only knew what they would've done to her if Alix hadn't come into the alley when she had.

'Alix,' she gasped. 'You saved my life.' In that moment, Jacqueline wanted to call back every ugly thought she'd ever had regarding the young woman. She didn't care what color Alix dyed her hair. The girl had saved her from a fate she could hardly imagine.

Alix sat down next to her, and Jacqueline soon noticed that she was badly shaken, too. She'd put on a brave front when she confronted the two men, but she'd been terrified.

A siren blared outside and Lydia dashed to the front of the store to wait for the patrolmen. A few minutes later, two police officers entered the shop.

All three women started talking at once. Jacqueline felt she should be the one to explain; she was the one who'd been accosted, after all. She continued speaking, raising her voice in order to be heard above the other two.

'One at a time, ladies,' the first officer said, holding up his hand. He was young and clean-cut and reminded her of her son. Paul would be outraged when he learned she'd nearly been mugged.

The officer started with Jacqueline and when he'd finished, he asked Alix a few questions and finally Lydia. Each woman described the men in slightly different ways, although Alix seemed reluctant to discuss the matter. At first she didn't reveal their names, but if Alix had forgotten, Jacqueline hadn't.

With their descriptions known, plus their first names, it made sense that the two hoodlums would be apprehended shortly. Jacqueline had already decided to press charges. All the while she was speaking, she clutched her Gucci bag with both hands.

'You two know each other?' the patrolman asked, glancing from Jacqueline to Alix.

'Of course,' Jacqueline said. 'We're taking

knitting classes together.'

'Yeah,' Alix muttered, and defiantly tilted her chin in their direction as if daring him to challenge her. 'Jacqueline and I are friends.'

'She saved me from God knows what,' Jacqueline murmured.

The officer shook his head. 'It would've been smarter just to give them your purse.'

Jacqueline knew he was right. All the survival manuals stated that in such a situation, the best course of action was to drop the purse and run.

Once the policemen had left, Jacqueline looked over at Alix who remained seated at the table across from her. 'I don't know how to thank you.'

'You owe me.'

Jacqueline nodded in full agreement. She still wasn't sure what had led Alix into the alley. When questioned by the police she explained that she'd seen Jacqueline go in there and didn't think it was a safe place for her friend to be. So she'd followed her. And Jacqueline would be forever grateful that she had.

Her one concern was that she owed Alix now. She could only speculate what the girl would want as payment.

CHAPTER 24

CAROL GIRARD

The two days following the IVF procedure had been the worst. The specialist had instructed Carol to stay perfectly still for forty-eight hours. The enforced rest got on her nerves after only a few hours, but with every breath she drew, with every solid beat of her heart, she made herself think positive, nurturing thoughts.

She was all too aware that she was at the very end of the road, technologically speaking, for a biological child. She and Doug had decided this was it. They got their three chances through the insurance company and two of them were gone. IVF was expensive, time-consuming, unpredictable and uncertain. Correction, some aspects of the procedure *were* a certainty. Injections, frequent bloodwork and ultrasounds. She'd been poked and prodded so often she barely noticed it anymore.

Carol refused to allow herself to dwell on any of the negatives. This time she'd have her baby. This time at least one of the fertilized eggs implanted in her womb would take hold – and she'd keep the pregnancy. Nine months from now, she'd hold a baby in her arms and experience the joy that had been denied her all these years.

Doug had been wonderful. He'd done everything possible to make her comfortable. Still, Carol recognized the look in his eyes, the longing that went unspoken, and the fear that despite everything, they couldn't, wouldn't, have a child. This wasn't easy for Doug and while he tried to hide it, Carol knew he was worried. So was she.

Thinking positive had grown more difficult by the second day, especially with Doug tiptoeing around her. The argument that flared between them that dreadful evening was neither her fault nor his; it was an explosion of emotion and frustration. Doug had stormed out of the house and didn't return until after midnight. Carol was relieved he hadn't been driving, because she smelled alcohol on his breath when he returned.

They made up the next morning, just as she'd known they would, and Doug had left for work after downing two cups of coffee and refusing breakfast. Now they had to wait, three weeks to be sure of the pregnancy and three months to be confident about it. By then their patience would be even more frayed.

Ten days after the procedure, Lydia phoned. This was the first time she'd called Carol at home and it was good to hear a friendly voice.

'I haven't heard from you and was wondering how you're doing,' Lydia said.

'Great.' The high-pitched burst of enthusiasm betrayed her.

'I mean, how are you *really* feeling?' Lydia murmured.

'Not so great,' Carol admitted. 'Oh, Lydia, this is hard. Right now, it's a waiting game, and both Doug and I are so tense.'

'Let me take you to lunch, and we'll talk.'

Lunch out sounded divine, but she knew Lydia had responsibilities. 'What about the shop?'

'I've already talked to Mom, and she's going to come here for a couple of hours. Would you like to meet on the waterfront? It's such a perfect day for it.'

Carol agreed. The sun was out and Puget Sound was an intense sapphire blue. Nothing would please her more than to get away from the condo for a few hours.

They chose a restaurant, a little hole-in-the-wall place that specialized in fish and chips, scallops and shrimp dishes. By the time Carol arrived, Lydia had already obtained a table on the patio. The breeze off the water had the briny scent of sea air. Seagulls shrieked in their usual exuberant way. The white-topped peaks of the Olympics glowed in the distance and a Washington State ferry was docked at the pier close by. It was everything Carol loved about living in the Pacific Northwest.

'This is an unexpected surprise,' Carol told her as she took the chair across from Lydia.

'It's just so beautiful I couldn't bear to stay inside a minute longer. My mother's been after me to take some time for myself, and today I decided she was right.'

'Does she knit?'

'Only a little – enough to get by. She loves the idea of standing in for me. It gives her an emotional boost to think she's helping, and she is.'

'Thank her for me.'

Lydia smiled. 'Actually, I'm grateful for the

break, too. I needed it. I'm glad you could join me at the last minute.'

Carol had only known Lydia a short while, but she considered the other woman her friend. Not since her college days had she had time to invest in friendships. Lydia had mentioned her eagerness to make new friends, too; they'd arrived at a similar point in their lives but for entirely different reasons. They'd talked frequently and Lydia encouraged Carol's growing love for knitting. It was easy to like Lydia; she was so gentle, so quiet and unassuming. Carol had never once heard Lydia raise her voice or lose her patience. Only when she talked about knitting and yarn did she become animated or excited. Carol was impressed by Lydia's calm manner when she dealt with the outbursts between Alix and Jacqueline. It couldn't be easy having them both in the same class. More than once Carol had to bite her tongue to keep from asking if their behavior wasn't a little juvenile.

Seated under the shade of the overhead umbrella, Carol glanced at the menu. She decided on seafood fettuccini, a longtime favorite. She almost never ordered it in a restaurant because no recipe had ever matched the one her mother had given her. While she hadn't done much cooking until recently, she made a delectable olive-oil-based seafood spaghetti that Doug always raved about.

They discussed knitting and friendship, shared stories of growing up and talked about books they'd both read. The highlight of their lunch was the story of Alix rescuing Jacqueline from muggers in the back alley.

Carol decided to stop at the market on her way home to pick up something for dinner. Her appetite had been nonexistent lately, ever since the procedure, and dinners had been thrown together at the last minute with little forethought or effort. If not for Doug, she would have foregone the meal entirely.

When Carol left the waterfront, she felt a great deal better. Amazing what a little girl-time could do. She bought a small sirloin tip roast at the market and walked back to the condo, feeling refreshed, glorying in the sunshine.

The moment he arrived home, Doug noticed the difference in her mood. He smiled and kissed her, then went into the bedroom to change clothes. When he reappeared, he had on his Mariners baseball jacket and hat.

'You forgot, didn't you?' he said when he saw the look on her face. 'Bill and I have tickets for the game.'

'Of course.' She shrugged off her disappointment. Her afternoon with Lydia had done her a world of good and she wouldn't begrudge her husband a night with his longtime college friend.

Minutes later, he was out the door. It was the first time all week she'd cooked a decent meal, and Doug wouldn't be home to enjoy it. Life seemed to be full of such little ironies.

She wasn't feeling sorry for herself, not really, but her elated mood had definitely sagged by the time her brother phoned. They hadn't talked since his visit the month before.

'Can I come over?' he asked, sounding depressed.

'Of course, but it's just me. Doug's at the Mariners' game with Bill.'

Rick's sigh was audible. 'Actually, that's probably better.'

This was a surprising comment. 'What's up?'

'I'll tell you when I get there.'

Her brother showed up less than half an hour later. Carol hadn't ever seen him look this bad – unshaven, with dark circles under his eyes. He collapsed into a chair and when she offered him a beer, he muttered, 'Do you have anything stronger?'

'Sorry,' she said. 'Just wine.'

'I'll have a beer, then.' He leaned forward and braced his elbow on his knees, letting his forearms dangle.

'Are you going to tell me or do I have to guess?' she asked as she handed him a cold beer.

Rick twisted off the cap and took a deep swig. 'Was I born stupid or did I recently acquire this personality trait?'

'The answer depends on your problem,' she said, sitting across from him. Infuriating though Rick could be, it was difficult to stay angry with him for long. She supposed his easygoing personality was as much of a hindrance as it was an asset. Perhaps everything had come too easily for him.

'Lisa's pregnant,' he said.

Carol stared at him blankly. 'Lisa? Lisa who?'

He rubbed his eyes. 'A flight attendant I've seen a few times.'

'Obviously you've done more than see her,' Carol snapped, unable to hide her anger. This

211

was unbelievable. For a moment she thought it might be a bad joke, but one look told her he was serious. Just a few weeks ago he'd declared his undying love for his ex-wife.

'What about Ellie?' she cried. 'The last time we talked, you were hoping to get back together with her.' Sleeping with some other woman certainly didn't prove his devotion.

'I know... I love Ellie and I want her back.'

'Then what were you doing with Lisa?'

'It just sort of happened,' he mumbled dejectedly.

Carol shook her head, barely able to take in what her brother was telling her. 'You *just sort of* fell into bed together?' Her voice grew more agitated with every word. So this was the reason Ellie didn't trust him. She'd hinted at the truth, but Carol had refused to listen, refused to believe that her big, strong, wonderful brother had clay feet – and a clay heart.

'Say something,' Rick urged.

Carol shook her head again, viewing her brother in an entirely different light. All these years he'd been her hero; now, all of a sudden she saw him for the weak charmer he really was. 'You've certainly made a mess this time.'

'Trust me, little sister, you can't say anything I haven't already said to myself. This ruins everything.'

'And exactly whose fault is that?' she demanded. Unable to stay seated any longer, she jumped to her feet and started pacing the room. 'You're too smart to have unprotected sex, damn it!'

Rick closed his eyes.

'Does Ellie know?'

'No!' He nearly shouted the word. 'I'm not telling her, either, that's for sure.'

'What about Lisa?'

'What about her? She's in shock, too – apparently whatever she used for birth control failed.'

'No kidding.' Carol was furious with her brother and too angry to care what he thought.

She took a few minutes to adjust to the news. She sat down again and placed her hand over her mouth. Her brother hadn't come to her so she could rant at him. He was clearly looking for some sort of direction, although she had no idea what to suggest.

'You're one hundred percent sure the baby is yours?'

He nodded and studied his hands. 'We've been pretty involved lately.'

She swallowed a retort. 'How far along is she?' she asked instead, her voice brisk.

'She just found out. A month, I guess.'

Carol flipped her hair away from her face and tried to concentrate. 'When did she tell you?'

'Yesterday. She phoned me in a panic and, hell, I didn't know what to say. What *could* I say?'

'Do you love her?'

Rick considered her question for a moment, then slowly shook his head. 'I care about her and I like her, but as for loving her, not really. I know I don't want to marry her. Why should I marry her because she forgot to swallow some pill?' Rick's expression was miserable, shocked and angry all at once. 'I love Ellie,' he murmured. 'It's

Ellie I want to be with, it's Ellie I need in my life.'

'Then you should've kept your pants zipped.' Carol didn't mean to be crude, but her brother frustrated her. If he loved Ellie, truly loved her, he should be willing to do whatever it took to win her back. Sleeping with a flight attendant shouldn't even be on that list.

'If you aren't going to marry Lisa, then what?' Carol asked.

'I don't know.'

With her eyes opened, Carol confronted him, daring him to tell her the truth. 'This isn't the first time, is it?'

'First time for what? If you're asking whether I've fathered other kids, you're wrong. I've always been careful, but Lisa said...' He let the rest fade.

'I meant this isn't the first time you cheated on Ellie.' Technically they were divorced, so it couldn't really be considered adultery. 'That's the reason she filed for divorce, isn't it?'

Her brother looked up briefly and nodded.

Rick stayed for an hour, and they talked while dinner went cold. He was still in shock and, frankly, so was she. Rick had always been her idol and in the space of a few minutes he'd tumbled from his pedestal.

She ended up making steak sandwiches and coffee, and Rick left soon afterward for his hotel. He definitely needed sleep, but he and Carol planned to talk again the next day.

Doug returned home an hour later, thrilled that the Mariners had handily defeated the Yankees. Carol told him about the visit from her brother and his devastating news.

'It doesn't surprise me,' her husband told her. They sat side by side on the sofa, Doug's arm around her. 'Rick's always been a ladies' man.'

Carol found it hard to believe her brother could be so morally lacking. It was as if this person she'd grown up with and loved was a stranger. 'You knew and didn't tell me?'

'I couldn't. You always thought he could do no wrong.'

Carol felt sick to her stomach.

'He's been doing it ever since I've known him. Fooling around with one woman while seeing another.' Doug held her close for several seconds. 'The truth is, I'm not overly fond of Rick.'

'Doug! How can you say such a thing?' Rick was the one who'd introduced her to her husband. They'd been college friends and dorm mates. But now that she thought about it, Carol realized Doug had never shown as much enthusiasm for seeing Rick as she did.

'It's true, honey. The only good thing that came out of the friendship was meeting you. I've never liked his ethics.'

Carol let his words sink in. She was seeing her brother realistically for the very first time. He was a selfish little boy who refused to grow up. She wondered how many people had recognized it before her.

Later, as Carol snuggled close to her husband in bed, she couldn't help thinking about life's many injustices.

'Why is it,' she asked in a whisper, 'that women who don't want to get pregnant have such an easy time of it?'

She felt her husband's slight nod of agreement. 'I wish I had an answer, sweetheart, but life just isn't fair.'

'No kidding,' she muttered for the second time that night.

CHAPTER 25

ALIX TOWNSEND

Alix slept late on Friday morning, lying in bed while the last remnants of sleep faded away. She was warm and comfortable and unwilling to move. Keeping her eyes closed, she let her mind linger on the kiss she'd shared with Jordan. Never in all her life had she realized a kiss could be so good.

She'd been kissed plenty, and had lots of other experience, too. Still, no kiss had affected her like that one. The men she knew tended to be rough and sweaty and urgent in their need to dominate. She'd never known such sweet pleasure from a simple kiss. But then, she reminded herself, this could all be tied up with a childhood dream that had been shattered one night in the sixth grade.

Even now, more than a week later, she remembered every nuance of his kiss. His hands had framed her face and his eyes had locked with hers. She'd seen his look of surprise – and uncertainty. They'd parted soon afterward, and it almost seemed to her that they needed to get away from each other in order to assimilate what had happened.

Alix hadn't seen Jordan since, hadn't talked to him, either. She tried not to dwell on that. Unsure what prompted her, on Sunday morning Alix had walked over to the Free Methodist church Jordan had mentioned. She stood across the street and chain-smoked three cigarettes while she watched, people file in.

Jordan was right about one thing: only a few of the older adults wore hats and gloves and dresses. Various families came with youngsters in tow, all carrying Bibles. Alix had only ever owned one Bible and that had been so long ago, she didn't know where it had gone. Staring at the church-goers, she saw that most people wore casual clothes, but that wasn't a strong enough incentive to send her inside.

She'd loitered on the corner, hoping, she guessed, that Jordan would notice her. He obviously hadn't; she didn't see him either.

The music was good, upbeat and lively –not what she remembered at all. Alix had heard church music as a kid and it had sounded like something out of the Middle Ages, but it wasn't that way now. Once she'd even caught herself humming along and quickly stopped.

After about forty minutes, she'd walked away, hands buried deep in her pockets. It wouldn't have hurt to slip into the back pew and take a look, but fear made that impossible. Analyzing her actions now, nearly a week later, Alix wasn't sure what she'd been so afraid of. The possibility of someone talking to her, perhaps.

Rather than brood on last week's disappointment, Alix tossed back the sheets and climbed slowly out of bed. Laurel was sitting in front of the television, an old model with a faded picture tube and tinfoil-wrapped rabbit ears. Her roommate stared intently at a kids' cartoon.

'Morning,' Alix muttered as she wandered into their tiny kitchen.

Laurel ignored her.

'What's your problem?' she asked irritably. They were supposed to be friends, but Laurel rarely spoke to her anymore. She'd been sulking for weeks now.

Laurel shook her head, silently indicating that she didn't want to talk. Alix had no idea what was bothering her, but she assumed it had something to do with that worm of a used-car salesman. He hadn't been around lately. For a while they'd been together constantly and then all of a sudden he was out of the picture. Whatever had happened remained a mystery. Laurel certainly wasn't telling.

'Fine, be in a bad mood.' Alix reached for a banana. 'See if I care.'

Once again Laurel ignored her. Peeling the banana, Alix plopped down on the one stuffed chair in the apartment. Someone had abandoned it in a vacant lot. Alix and Laurel had come upon it and carried it the three blocks back to the apartment. It was pretty ratty, but Alix had found a printed sheet and spread it over the chair. With a few tucks and folds it wasn't half bad. No designers would be asking her to make a guest appearance on their shows, but it worked for now.

Biting into the banana, Alix noticed that the baby blanket she was knitting lay on the floor.

'What the hell happened here?' she demanded. She flew off the chair to rescue her project. The ball of yarn had unwound and ended up near the apartment door.

Laurel wasn't paying her any heed.

Standing directly in front of the television, Alix glared at her roommate. 'I don't know what your problem is, but get over it.'

'Keep your knitting away from me.'

Alix snickered; she couldn't help it. 'What's the matter? Did it chase after you?'

'It was in my way.'

'So you threw it at the door?' Talk about unreasonable!

Laurel didn't answer.

Alix examined the nearly completed blanket, unsure what she'd do if Laurel had caused her to drop stitches or worse, pulled out the needles. Laurel was treading precariously close to a fight. Alix was sick of her roommate's bad moods, sick of her slovenly habits and sick of her mooning over a man who was a loser with a capital L.

'Get a grip, will you?' she snapped on her way back to the bedroom. They shared the one bedroom, which made life all the more difficult. The latest rumors floating around said the apartment building had been sold. Where they'd move next was as unclear as the stitches Alix had yet to master.

'You wouldn't be so cruel if you...' Laurel didn't finish. Instead she buried her face in her hands and burst into tears.

219

Alix felt awful. Sitting next to Laurel, she sighed. 'It's lover boy, isn't it?'

Laurel nodded. 'He said ... he doesn't want to see me anymore.'

Anything Alix could say at that moment would have been wrong. Laurel didn't want to hear what a loser John was. Alix didn't understand why Laurel couldn't see it when everyone else did. Okay, so John had a decent job. Nevertheless, he was a sleaze and nothing would discount that sad truth.

Laurel pulled her feet up and locked her arms around her knees. She'd been overweight when they met but now she seemed to be even bigger than Alix remembered. She'd obviously gained weight since the breakup. Now that Alix thought about it, they'd been going through a lot of groceries lately.

'Eating isn't going to help.' Alix strived to sound sympathetic.

'Are you saying I'm fat?'

'Not fat, exactly.'

'Okay, I'm fat and ugly. You think I don't know that?' Her voice dipped with venom and her greasy blond hair fell forward as she buried her face in her knees. 'And mean.'

'Mean?' Alix asked, her suspicions growing.

Laurel nodded. 'Jordan stopped by the store on Tuesday and asked me to give you a message and I didn't.'

A chill came over Alix. 'What was the message?'

'He ... he wanted to take you roller-skating.'

'When?'

'This afternoon with a bunch of kids from his

church and I didn't tell you... I know I should have, but I didn't want you to have a man when I don't. I'm fat and ugly and no one wants me.'

Laurel stood and reached inside her jeans for a folded-up piece of paper. 'I was supposed to give you this.'

Alix unfolded the flyer and saw that it announced an afternoon skating party at a rink five blocks away. Alix stared at the page and turned it over to find a note Jordan had written her. 'Alix, I'm looking for a partner. You interested?'

The way her heart nearly exploded told her she was. But skating? *Her?* Alix had never put on a pair of skates in her life. When she was five or six, all the kids who lived in the same apartment complex had roller skates. Alix had desperately longed for a pair. But finances were always a problem for her family. There wasn't enough money for beer, cigarettes, drugs and roller skates, too.

'You want to come?' she asked Laurel, well aware of what it felt like to be excluded.

Laurel looked up, then shook her head. 'No. Are you actually doing it?' She didn't hide her astonishment.

Alix shrugged. 'Maybe.'

She took an hour to think it over. Jordan claimed he liked her for herself. She wasn't sure she should believe him; what he remembered was the girl she'd been at eleven, which was a far sight from the woman she was now. Despite her doubts she realized she wanted to trust him, wanted to be with him, the same way she had all those years ago.

Nothing had ever come easy for Alix. Everything had been a struggle. If she was going to have a good life, she had to make it happen herself. That recognition fired her determination to give this relationship a chance.

Alix was waiting outside the skating rink, leaning against the building, when the big yellow church bus pulled up. The doors opened and about a thousand preteens poured out. No one paid much attention to Alix until Jordan walked over to her, wearing the biggest grin she'd ever seen.

'I was hoping you'd show up.'

'I'm not skating.' She wanted that understood. 'I came to watch.' She wasn't willing to play the role of klutz in front of a crowd of teenyboppers.

'You'll be missing out on all the fun.'

She didn't care; no one was strapping her into a pair of skates.

The rink opened and the kids swarmed inside. Alix hung around on the street, smoking a cigarette, then casually wandered into the rink. Already kids were skating on the polished wooden floor, speeding around and around with the music blasting. This wasn't music Alix recognized – but then she realized she did. She'd heard one of the songs while she was standing outside the church last Sunday morning. The rink apparently provided Christian rock.

Alix had to look for Jordan. Then she saw him, surrounded by kids. They followed him wherever he went – as though he were Moses, she thought with a smile. Some of that Bible stuff had definitely stuck. Jordan was busy helping them with their skates and putting on his own. Before he ventured into the rink, he stopped and gazed

222

around. When he saw her, he smiled that lazy, happy grin and she nodded her head in acknowledgement. He winked back, and it felt as if the sun was shining directly on her.

Despite her curiosity, Alix remained in the background, taking everything in. Jordan finally skated into the rink, faltering a bit before he found his balance. Once he did, he began skating smoothly and confidently; she found it a pleasure to watch. A few of the kids skated around him, and some of them were really good, skating backward and doing creative dance-style moves to the music.

When Alix lost sight of Jordan, she moved closer to the railing. Jordan skated past and waved. It didn't take long for the church kids to notice the attention he paid Alix. Several stopped to look at her and chat among themselves. Alix ignored them.

'Is Jordan your friend?' a girl asked. She couldn't be more than thirteen, with perfect dark hair and olive skin. Another girl, a blonde in braces, stood beside her.

Alix nodded.

'He mentioned you,' Blondie said.

Okay, so Alix was curious. 'What did he say?'

The other girl answered. 'Jordan said he'd invited a friend to join him. He said you used to be his valentine.'

Alix shrugged. 'That was a long time ago.'

'He's kinda cute, don't you think?' Blondie said.

Alix shrugged again. Anything she said was sure to get back to Jordan.

'Aren't you going to skate?' the first girl asked.

223

'Maybe later.'

Jordan went around the rink at least a dozen times, then pleaded fatigue and glided over to stand next to Alix. 'I haven't seen you in a while.'

'I've been around.'

'I was beginning to think you wouldn't come.'

She almost hadn't, but she didn't mention the reason.

'You've never skated before, have you?'

'Every kid's skated,' she returned, rather than confess the truth.

An hour later, Alix was wearing a pair of skates. Before she knew it, her two newfound friends had convinced her to give it a try. Once Alix had on the skates, the girls led her into the rink, each holding one of her hands.

'Don't worry we aren't going to let you fall,' the blond girl promised.

The girls gripped her fingers hard enough for Alix to believe it.

She shouldn't have.

Two feet onto the slick wooden floor, Alix started flailing. Not ten seconds later, she was flat on her butt. She didn't have a chance to even think before Jordan came up behind her and tucked his arms under hers, swooping her upright.

'Everyone falls.' Then with his arm around her waist and his free hand holding hers, they made one full circuit of the rink. Kids whizzed past them at speeds that made Alix dizzy. She didn't look. Couldn't look. She needed all her concentration to remain upright.

'This isn't so hard.' She was starting to get the feel of it. Despite herself she laughed. It was as if she were six years old again and Santa had delivered that pair of roller skates, after all.

'Cherie says you're cool.'

Alix didn't care what the little blond girl thought. 'What do you say?' she asked Jordan.

He grinned down at her. 'I think you're pretty cool, too.'

His words were more beautiful than any music she'd ever heard.

CHAPTER 26

'People who say they don't have enough patience to knit are precisely those who could most improve their lives by learning how!'

–Sally Melville,
author of *The Knitting Experience* series

LYDIA HOFFMAN

This has been quite a week. It's unheard of for me to have two social engagements within the same seven-day period. My lunch on Wednesday with Carol did so much good – for both of us. I feel I connected with her and extended a hand of friendship. She responded, and I'm confident we'll stay in touch, whether or not she continues to knit.

The class earlier this afternoon was the best yet. Following the incident in the back alley, Alix and Jacqueline were cordial and just shy of friendly.

Jacqueline relayed the details of the confrontation in minute detail, with Alix leaping in to add comments. Anyone looking at them would think they were longtime friends.

When I asked Jacqueline how her husband had reacted when she told him about the incident, she'd gone suspiciously quiet. I wasn't sure what to make of that, but I have the feeling all is not well between Jacqueline and Reese Donovan.

The class flew by, and then I was seeing Brad for drinks. We were meeting at The Pour House for a beer at six after I'd closed for the day. Despite the drizzle we'd had intermittently since early morning, I was in a great mood.

The Pour House was about two blocks off Blossom, and seemed to be a popular hangout for the after-work crowd. The noise level was high with music blaring from a jukebox, high-spirited laughter and a television above the bar, which had a ball game on. I'm not very interested in sports, but I know lots of men are. Between the noise and the room's darkness, I felt a bit disoriented.

Brad had found a booth near the back, and when he saw me, he stood, waving his arms over his head. I smiled and waved back, then quickly made my way across the room, negotiating tables and chairs.

'I was beginning to think you weren't going to make it,' he said as he slid back into the booth.

'Am I late?' I glanced at my watch, and was surprised to see that it was almost fifteen minutes past six. I shook the rain off my jacket and Brad hung it up for me.

'It's fine, don't worry about it, but I've only got half an hour or so. The day care teacher said she'd keep Cody until seven-fifteen but not a minute longer and it takes me at least twenty minutes to get there.'

'How old is your son?'

'Eight. He keeps telling me he's too old to be in day care, but I'm not letting him stay by himself all day.' Judging by Brad's frown, I guessed this had been a frequent argument over the summer. 'Sometimes I swear that kid's eight going on eighteen.'

I thought of my own two nieces and while I might not be a mother, I understood what he was saying.

'Since we don't have much time,' Brad said, 'I'd rather not waste it talking about me. I want to learn about you.'

I considered myself the least intriguing of subjects. Nevertheless, I was flattered by his curiosity.

'I know there's a lot of interest in knitting, but isn't it risky to open a shop right now?' he asked before I could forestall him with questions of my own. I knew so little about Brad except what my eyes told me. He was as handsome as sin. From bits and pieces of conversation, I also knew he was divorced and apparently had custody of his eight-year-old son, but that was about it.

He certainly wasn't the first person to express concern about my timing. Everyone worried that I was going to become a victim of our weak economy, that I was in over my head. But I'd been treading water since I was sixteen, so opening my own yarn store was no riskier than anything else in my life. Margaret had come right out and declared that I was making a mistake. But if I'd waited until all the conditions were ideal, it would never have happened. After two bouts with cancer, I knew I couldn't wait for life to be perfect. I had to find my own happiness and quit waiting for it to find me.

I saw that he'd already ordered a pitcher of beer, which had just arrived. He paid the waitress and poured us each a glass. 'My dad died just after Christmas,' I said as if that explained everything. 'I was dealing with that loss, and then one day I found myself knitting furiously and remembered a conversation we'd had several years earlier.'

Brad sipped his beer and nodded for me to continue.

My throat got a bit scratchy but I ignored the emotion that filled me at the mention of my father. I don't know if I'll ever grow accustomed to having lost him. I paused for a moment.

'Go on,' Brad encouraged.

'At the time, I figured I was the one who didn't have long to live.'

'You said you had cancer.'

'Twice.' I wanted to be sure he understood. I waited for a reaction from him, but he gave me none.

'Go on,' he said again. 'You were talking about your father.'

I sipped my beer. He'd chosen a dark ale and I liked it. 'I was in the hospital, and it was the night before my second brain surgery. Mom and Dad came to spend the evening with me. Mom was reading, and Dad and I were talking.' I remember that night so well because in my own heart I was convinced I'd be dead before the year was over. Dad was the one who believed in me, who insisted I was going to cheat death a second time.

'He asked me to describe one perfect day,' I told Brad. I knew he was forcing me to acknowledge that I *wanted* to live. The question was his way of drawing me into a future. A future I firmly believed was unavailable to me.

'What did you tell him?' Brad had leaned forward and cupped both hands around his mug.

I closed my eyes for a few seconds. 'That I wanted to wake up in my own bed instead of one in a hospital.'

'Can't blame you there.'

I grinned. Brad made it surprisingly easy to talk about myself. 'Next I wanted to be able to smell flowers and be close to the water and feel sunshine on my face.'

'In the Pacific Northwest?' He smiled as he asked the question and I couldn't help responding with a laugh.

'My perfect day happens in late summer, when we get plenty of sunshine.' This past Wednesday was a good example. 'Now don't distract me.'

'Yes'm.' His eyes fairly twinkled and for a moment I was so mesmerized I had to make myself look away.

'I'd wake to sunshine and the sounds of birds,' I continued, 'and my perfect day would begin with a cup of strong coffee and a warm croissant. I'd take a leisurely stroll along the waterfront.'

'And after that?'

'I'd knit.' I remember how astonished my father had seemed when I told him that. He shouldn't have been. By that time I'd been knitting for years. I remembered how my wanting to knit – seeing it as a perfect part of my perfect day – bothered him. Knitting, in his eyes, was such a solitary activity that I'd soon become a recluse.

'Knitting in your own store?' Brad murmured.

'Sort of.' One of the things I love most about being a knitter is the community of other knitters. Anytime I run into another person (usually a woman but not always) who knits, it's like finding a long-lost friend. The two of us instantly connect. It doesn't matter that only seconds earlier we were strangers, because we immediately share a common bond. I'd talked to other knitters in doctors' offices, in line-ups at the grocery store – anywhere at all. We've exchanged horror stories of misprinted instructions and uncompleted projects. And we all loved to brag about fabulous yarn buys and, of course, discuss our current efforts.

'I wanted to help people discover the same sense of satisfaction and pride that I feel when I finish a project for someone I love.' That was the best way to describe it, I thought.

'How would you end your perfect day?'

'With music and champagne and candlelight,' I said shyly, which was only partially true. I'd told my dad I wanted to end the day dancing.

My father had told me I'd have that perfect day. What neither of us knew was that he wouldn't be there to enjoy it with me.

'What's wrong?' Brad asked, watching me.

I shook my head. 'I was just thinking about how much I miss my father.'

To my surprise, Brad reached across the table and squeezed my hand. 'You've had a rough time of it, haven't you?'

I bristled. I didn't want his sympathy or his pity. What I yearned for more than anything was to be normal. One of my biggest fears was that I could no longer recognize what normal was.

'Cancer is part of who I am, but it isn't everything. I'm in remission today but I can't speak for tomorrow or next week. I was in a holding pattern for most of my twenties but I'm beyond that now. It wasn't just the doctors or the medicine or the surgery that saved me, especially since I'd died emotionally when I learned the cancer had returned.' I took a deep breath. 'My father refused to let me give up, and when I discovered knitting, I felt like I'd found the Holy Grail because it was something I could do by myself. I could do it lying in bed if I had to. It was a way of proving I was more than a victim.'

Brad's eyes grew somber and I think he really heard me.

'Anything else you want to ask me?' I sat up straighter, prepared to back off now.

A grin lifted the corners of his mouth. 'How come it took you so long to say yes to a beer with me?'

'Relationships aren't part of my perfect day,' I teased, although that was far from the truth.

'No, seriously, I want to know.'

Mostly I'd been afraid of rejection, I guess. But

all I said was, 'I'm not sure.'

'Are you willing to go out with me again?' His eyes held mine.

I nodded.

'Good, because I only have a few more minutes and I want us to get to know each other.'

We talked for a little while longer, and I finally had the opportunity to ask *him* some personal questions, mainly about his marriage and his son.

Forty minutes later, I parked in front of Margaret and Matt's house. I realized I've never shown up at my sister's home without an invitation. Come to think of it, I don't think she's ever actually invited me – and yet here I was, so excited I couldn't hold still. I was dying to talk to someone, and since my sister had practically forced me into this, I figured she should be that someone.

I rang the doorbell and then stepped back, half afraid she wouldn't ask me in. it was Hailey who answered. When she saw me, she shrieked with happiness – and left me standing on the porch while she ran to get her mother.

'Lydia.' Margaret burst into the room and stood on the other side of the closed screen door. 'It *is* you.'

'I told you it was,' Hailey said from behind her mother.

My sister unlocked the screen door and held it open for me.

'I don't usually drop by unannounced,' I said, 'but I just had to tell you about my meeting with Brad.'

'Oh, my goodness, that was tonight.' My sister's

232

eyes lit up as she pulled me into the house. Before I could comprehend what was going on, she had me sitting at the kitchen table and was on a stepstool in front of the refrigerator, standing on tiptoe as she removed a liquor bottle from the cabinet above.

'What are you doing?' I asked, almost giddy.

'A night like this calls for homemade margaritas.' She had a bottle in each hand – one of tequila and one of cointreau.

I giggled like a schoolgirl. Hailey dug into the freezer portion of the refrigerator for ice cubes while Margaret found limes, then brought out the blender and special glasses.

In a matter of minutes, my sister had mixed the drinks and dipped the rims of both glasses in salt; she'd also made a virgin drink for Hailey, something involving ginger ale and fruit juice.

'Where are Matt and Julia?' I asked.

'Bonding at a baseball game,' Margaret explained, handing me my glass. 'Now tell all.'

After two beers and now sipping a mixed drink, I wasn't sure where to start. 'I met Brad at The Pour House.' Both my sister and Hailey drew closer. 'He had less than an hour because he had to pick up his son from day care.' If not for that, I had the feeling we could have spent half the night talking.

'He's paying extra time at day care on a Friday night?' Margaret asked.

I nodded.

'You can bet he paid through the nose for that.'

'He didn't say.' I looked from my sister to my niece who hung on every word.

'What did he say?'

'Not much. He asked a lot of questions but he didn't talk much about himself. Mostly he talked about his son.'

Margaret shrugged as if that didn't impress her half as much as his paying extra charges at the day care center. 'What did he have to say about his ex-wife?'

I had to think about that for a moment, which gave me time to take another sip of the margarita. My sister possessed talents I would never have suspected. For one thing, this was the best margarita I'd had in years.

'Mostly he glossed over the divorce. They were too young and she decided she didn't want to be married or responsible for a child. Not once in the entire conversation did Brad say anything negative or derogatory about Cody's mother.'

Margaret smiled. 'I like him, you know.'

So did I, but I was cautious. And nervous.

'You told him about having cancer?' my niece asked.

I nodded. 'I felt it was only fair.'

'Are you going to see him again?' Margaret's gaze was sharp.

'Yes.' I took another sip of my drink. 'One more of these margaritas, and I'd probably be willing to marry him.'

My sister broke into peals of laughter. I can't remember ever seeing Margaret this pleased with me and, silly as it sounds, I basked in her approval.

CHAPTER 27

JACQUELINE DONOVAN

'Is everything all right with you and Reese?'
Tammie Lee asked as she began clearing the
dining room table.

Jacqueline sighed and pretended not to hear the
question. She'd hoped no one had noticed the
tension between her and Reese during tonight's
dinner party. The mayor and two city council
members had been in attendance, along with
their wives and three other couples.

At the last minute, not bothering to check with
Jacqueline, Reese had invited Paul and Tammie
Lee. Having Paul there was, of course, perfect,
but Jacqueline had cringed at the prospect of her
daughter-in-law sharing her unsophisticated
sense of humor with members of the city govern-
ment. Well, there was nothing Jacqueline could
do about it.

Thankfully, the evening had gone surprisingly
well, with only one minor glitch. The mayor had
asked Tammie Lee her opinion of the country
club. Without a pause Tammie Lee said in her
heavy southern twang that it was nothing but
tennis and bridge, dining and whining. After a
second's pause, during which Jacqueline wanted
to slink away and die, the mayor laughed up-
roariously. He said it was the most honest thing

235

anyone had ever said to him. Jacqueline wasn't sure whether he actually meant it or was just being a good guest.

Reese had glared across the dinner table at Jacqueline, as if to tell her how wrong she was about Tammie Lee. And how right *he* was.

The invitation to their son and his wife wasn't the crux of their most recent argument, however. Jacqueline and Reese rarely argued; there was no reason for it. But Reese had exploded when he learned she'd been accosted and nearly mugged by those two creeps. Thank goodness both had been apprehended and arraigned. Despite that, her husband had ranted at her for at least ten minutes, unwilling to listen to reason and all because she'd parked the car in the alley. He had the gall to claim she'd asked to be mugged. And then he'd called her stupid.

Jacqueline was still furious. How dare Reese say such things to her – especially when she'd been doing *him* a favor! Because of him, her entire day had been ruined. She'd missed her nail appointment entirely, was late for lunch and so rattled she hadn't found a thing to buy on her shopping spree.

Other than unavoidable conversation, they hadn't spoken in five very long days. They wouldn't be speaking now except for the dinner party, which had been planned weeks earlier. Canceling at the last minute was not an option, so they'd put their argument behind them and assumed their best behavior. Jacqueline was astonished that Tammie Lee had noticed.

'Did you hear me?' Tammie Lee asked, following Jacqueline into the kitchen with an armload of china.

Anyone else would have gotten the message and dropped the subject. Not Tammie Lee.

'You can put those dishes on the counter,' Jacqueline instructed. 'Really, there's no need for you to help. Martha will be here in the morning.' The housekeeper lived in the small guest house in the back. Now that she was older, she rarely had the energy for serving dinner parties. She wanted to retire but Jacqueline relied on her and so Martha stayed on.

'You don't want to leave these dishes on the table overnight,' Tammie Lee had insisted and she was right. As soon as everyone had left, Jacqueline would put everything in the dish-washer, a task she preferred to do herself.

'It was a lovely party,' her daughter-in-law said.

'Thank you.' Jacqueline bit her tongue to keep from mentioning that one day Tammie Lee would be expected to hold similar parties of her own. She could only hope that when the time came, Tammie Lee would've learned a lesson or two from her. Somehow Jacqueline doubted

'You're such a gracious hostess,' Tammie Lee said, returning with her second load of bone china plates.

'Thank you.' Jacqueline fought the impulse to remind her daughter-in-law that each of those plates cost more than Tammie Lee's entire sum-mer wardrobe. 'Where are Reese and Paul?' she asked curiously. Jacqueline was tired; the party had drained her and she was ready for bed. She wanted Paul and Tammie Lee to go home so she

237

could finish up.

'They're in the den talking.' All the dishes must be in the kitchen now, because Tammie Lee sat down and propped her feet on the opposite chair. She planted her hands on her round belly and rubbed gently. It was more and more obvious now that she was pregnant. Jacqueline hadn't yet forgiven her son and his wife for keeping the news to themselves for nearly six months.

Jacqueline wondered what Reese and Paul were discussing that could possibly take this long. She scraped off the plates and set them inside the dishwasher.

'I hope you didn't mind me showing the mayor the blanket you made for our baby,' Tammie Lee murmured. 'I think it's a perfectly lovely thing to do for your first grandchild.'

Jacqueline scowled but kept her head averted so Tammie Lee couldn't see her reaction. 'No, that was fine.'

'Paul and I are so *thrilled* you knit something for our baby girl.'

Jacqueline nodded rather than respond verbally. She continued to scrape leftovers into the garbage disposal.

When she'd finished, she claimed a chair next to Tammie Lee, first pouring herself a glass of wine. If she was going to be trapped in the kitchen with her daughter-in-law, she needed fortification.

Tammie Lee studied her. 'Did I ever tell you about the time my mama ran over the mailbox with my daddy's tractor?'

Jacqueline swallowed her groan. 'I don't believe I've heard that one,' she said as she swirled the wine around in her goblet.

If Tammie Lee noticed her sarcasm, she chose to ignore it. 'It's the only time I can remember hearing my daddy holler at Mama. My mama went rushing into the house in tears and I went, too, outraged that my daddy would raise his voice to her.'

'Men tend to speak their minds,' Jacqueline said. She sipped her wine and let it linger on her tongue. At fifty dollars a bottle, she was taking the time to appreciate the finer qualities of this merlot.

'Later Mama told me that the only reason Daddy had been hollering was because the tractor might have toppled on her. He didn't care one bit about that mailbox. It was my mama he loved, and she might have been crushed getting that close to the irrigation ditch in the tractor. His yelling was a sign of how much he loved her.'

Jacqueline was sure there was a point to this story, but at the moment it escaped her. She sipped the wine.

'I hope I didn't speak out of turn earlier,' Tammie Lee said softly, her eyes wide.

Jacqueline shrugged carelessly. 'I believe the mayor was ... amused.'

'Not the mayor,' Tammie Lee corrected. 'I meant when I asked if everything was all right between you and Reese.'

'Everything is perfectly fine between my husband and me,' Jacqueline primly informed her. She downed the rest of the merlot – finer qualities be damned – and set the glass on the table.

'Good,' Tammie Lee said, 'because Paul and I

love you so much and our baby's going to need her grandma *and* grandpa.'

Somehow Jacqueline managed a smile. 'So your mother actually ran the tractor over the mail-box?'

'Twice.'

'Twice?' Perhaps it was the wine, but Jacqueline laughed out loud.

'Daddy wasn't any happier about it the second time, either.'

Jacqueline would bet not.

'But my daddy loves Mama the same way Reese loves you.'

Jacqueline stopped laughing. Reese hadn't truly loved her in years. Their marriage was one of convenience and comfort. She didn't complain about his Tuesday night appointments and he didn't mention the balance on their credit cards. They had a mutually agreeable relationship, but whatever real love they'd once shared was dead.

'Tammie Lee.' Paul's voice rang from the dining room.

'In here,' she called, her voice high and animated.

Reese and Paul came into the kitchen, leaving the connecting door between the kitchen and the dining room swinging in their wake.

'You must be exhausted,' Paul said, smiling down on her with such love it was painful to watch. 'Are you ready to head home?'

Tammie Lee nodded and Paul helped her to her feet. Then, to Jacqueline's shock, her daughter-in-law bent down and threw her arms around her neck.

'Thank you,' Tammie Lee whispered, hugging her warmly.

Jacqueline wasn't sure how to respond. She placed her arms carefully around Tammie Lee and hugged back. It'd been so long since anyone had touched her with so much affection that she found herself close to tears.

'You're such a wonderful mother-in-law,' Tammie Lee told her. 'I think I'm the most blessed woman in the world.'

Jacqueline gazed at Reese over Tammie Lee's shoulder. She saw something powerful flickering in his eyes. Could Reese possibly still have feelings for her? Was it the reason he'd been so angry about her parking the car in the alley? That apparently was the point of Tammie Lee's story.

The thought seemed almost inconceivable.

CHAPTER 28

CAROL GIRARD

Carol was the first to show up for knitting class on Friday afternoon. She arrived early in order to look through the pattern book for another project.

'I thought you were knitting your brother a pullover,' Lydia said as Carol leafed through the section of the binder that held men's sweater patterns.

'I was, but I'm too upset with him to knit him

anything.' Carol hadn't spoken to Rick in over a week. That in itself wasn't unusual, but she'd half expected him to keep in touch with her after his confession. This time, his charm wasn't going to be enough to get him out of the mess he'd created. There were no easy answers.

The bell above the door chimed and when Carol glanced up, she nearly did a double-take. Alix walked in – wearing jeans and a T-shirt. It was the first time Carol had seen her without the constant black leather jacket and either black pants or a ridiculously short skirt. Her hair looked ... less punk. Carol opened her mouth to comment but quickly closed it again. Alix didn't like having attention directed at her, even though she blatantly strove to be different. If that wasn't a contradiction in terms, Carol didn't know what was.

'Hi,' Alix said, sauntering up to the table. Her manner seemed self-conscious, and she glared at Lydia and Carol as if defying them to comment on her changed appearance. Then she sat down in one of the chairs and took her knitting out of the plastic video-store bag.

'Hi,' they both responded.

'How's the pregnancy going?' Alix's voice was matter-of-fact; she seemed to consider this a perfectly normal question.

Carol saw that Lydia looked over at them warily. No one else had dared ask Carol about her condition. 'So far, so good,' she said. 'I'm still peeing blue.'

'What?' Alix raised her head.

'The test that tells me I'm registering as positive for a pregnancy,' Carol explained. With the fertilized embryo implanted in her womb, it wasn't getting pregnant that was difficult, it was *staying* pregnant. Twice now she'd lost the baby before the third week. Holding on to the pregnancy this long meant there was hope, but no part of the process was certain. The first three months were the riskiest in any pregnancy. In her online support group, Carol had recently heard from one friend who'd been pregnant for two and a half months only to miscarry. It had been heartbreaking, and every member had felt Susan's loss deeply.

The door opened again and Jacqueline came into the shop, bracelets jangling. She wore a tailored pantsuit Carol considered far too formal for the occasion and carried not only her Gucci purse but a leather tote in which she kept her knitting. The woman did like to make an entrance. It was as if she expected everyone to notice she'd arrived and react accordingly. Actually Carol didn't mind. She'd grown to like all the women in her knitting group.

She and Jacqueline were onto new projects now. The only one who hadn't finished the baby blanket was Alix, and Carol suspected it was because she couldn't afford to buy more yarn.

'I'm starting a new sweater,' Carol said, still leafing through patterns.

'What about the other one?' She knew Alix had especially liked the gray cashmere.

'I'm tired of it.' She glanced at Lydia and shared a conspiratorial smile with her. 'Do you want the yarn?'

Alix's eyes lit up. 'You don't want it?'

'Not really.'

'What about the pattern? Do you need that?'

'Not particularly.'

'Great!' Alix shoved her knitting into the plastic bag and nearly rubbed her hands in glee. 'I'm almost done with the blanket, and I'd like to knit that sweater for a ... friend.'

'Who?' Leave it to Jacqueline to ask.

'A friend, like I said,' Alix muttered defiantly.

'Don't get high and mighty with me,' Jacqueline snapped. 'I was just interested, that's all.'

Jacqueline expressing interest in Alix? A few weeks ago that would've been unimaginable. The change in attitude between them was dramatic and had begun with the near-mugging in the alley. They still sniped at each other but that seemed more out of habit than conviction.

'I didn't know you had a male friend,' Lydia said, smiling at Alix.

'I don't,' Alix said quickly, too quickly to be convincing.

'Then who's the sweater for?'

'Like I said, a friend.'

'Sure,' Jacqueline murmured, grinning. She winked at Alix, whose cheeks immediately blossomed a fetching shade of pink.

'If you must know, it's a guy I met at the video store,' Alix said irritably. Still, Carol had the feeling that Alix wanted to tell them...

'Does he like you?' Jacqueline asked.

Alix shrugged. 'He did when we were in sixth grade – but, well, he's a preacher and I don't exactly see the two of us sailing off into the sunset, if you catch my drift.'

'Why not?' Lydia asked. 'Preachers have lives, too, you know.'

Alix lowered her head and concentrated on her knitting. 'He's a good kisser,' she said in a soft voice.

Predictably, that piqued the group's interest, and a lively discussion broke out.

'Reese was quite a kisser in his day,' Jacqueline volunteered. 'I remember the first time he kissed me. Every cell in my body sprang to life.'

Carol smiled at the dreamy look on Jacqueline's face. 'I thought I'd died and gone to heaven the first time Doug kissed me,' she recalled. She noticed that Lydia was doing busy work around the shop, straightening patterns that were already straight. 'What about you, Lydia?' Carol asked.

Lydia jerked around, almost as if she resented being included in the conversation. Then she sighed. 'I don't think I've ever felt anything more than a ... kiss. It was always pleasant, but nothing earth-shattering happened afterward.'

'It will one day,' Jacqueline assured her.

'Don't you think you're placing a lot of importance on a simple kiss?' Lydia asked. 'Good grief, we've all been kissed, and while it's very nice most of the time, it's not *that* big a deal.'

Jacqueline motioned toward Alix. 'Was it a big deal for you when this preacher kissed you?'

Carol could tell Alix was uncomfortable with the question. The girl tossed her head in a nonchalant movement. 'Yeah, I guess, but I don't think about it, you know?' She looked around, and her expression said she'd thought of little else.

For a moment the room was silent as each woman concentrated on her individual task. Carol wasn't sure what Jacqueline was working on these days. She'd started knitting scarves using an ultra-expensive yarn and then moved on to felting hats and purses. It was hard to keep up with Jacqueline's current projects because she leaped from one to another and seemed to have several in progress at a time. Carol suspected she'd become one of Lydia's best customers.

'Didn't I see you come out of The Pour House last Friday?' Alix suddenly asked Lydia. 'With that UPS driver.'

'Me?' Lydia's cheeks flamed and she raised her hand to her chest. 'Yes ... I was meeting Brad Goetz for a drink.'

Alix let out a low whistle of approval. 'He's hot stuff.'

Lydia seemed to find something that needed attention in her display of knitting books. 'We're going to dinner later in the week.'

'Do I sense a romance developing?' Jacqueline asked in a friendly tone.

'That would be nice,' Carol said. She was amused at how shy Lydia was about men. Brad was the first one she'd mentioned. And this young preacher of Alix's... Carol felt touched that the girl had confided in them.

'Would you like to come up to the condo to get the yarn one day next week?' Carol asked impulsively.

Alix nodded. 'You wouldn't mind?'

'Not at all. Or I can bring it to class, if you'd prefer.'

'I can stop by your place.'

Carol had the feeling the girl didn't get many such invitations. 'Why don't you come for lunch on Monday? Does that work for you?'

'Yeah, sure.' Despite her indifferent-sounding response, Alix couldn't hide her eagerness to accept.

Carol looked around at the others with an affectionate smile. There was Alix, of course, whose defensiveness had diminished so noticeably. And Jacqueline, who no longer tried to impress them with her social connections. Lydia had become less reserved, and her warmth and wit were more in evidence every week.

Odd how these things went, Carol mused as she continued to leaf through the pattern book. A group of mismatched personalities, four women with nothing in common, had come together and over the course of a few months, they'd become real friends.

CHAPTER 29

JACQUELINE DONOVAN

Monday morning following her hair appointment, Jacqueline returned to the house to find that a local florist had delivered a dozen red roses. Martha, the housekeeper, had placed them in the center of the formal living room on a round coffee table.

'Who sent the roses?' she asked, stunned to find them.

Martha shook her head. 'I didn't read the card.'

Jacqueline walked into the living room and examined the red buds, gently taking one in her hand. The roses were perfect, still dewy and just ready to open. Their scent was so lovely, Jacqueline thought they must be antique roses. If so, they would've cost a fortune. She couldn't imagine who'd be sending her roses or why.

She reached for the card but didn't open the small envelope, wanting to linger over the suspense. It wasn't her birthday or her wedding anniversary. Her husband had never had much of a memory for such events, anyway. In fact, Reese hadn't sent her flowers in years. Paul was too much like his father to think of doing such a thing, especially when there was no obvious reason for it.

Unable to guess, she finally tore open the envelope, withdrew the card and read it.

Reese.

Her husband! There was no explanation, no message. Confused, Jacqueline sat down on the sofa, still holding the card. She found Martha staring at her, making no attempt to disguise her curiosity.

'Well?' the housekeeper asked.

'They're from Reese.'

Martha beamed her a broad smile. 'I thought so.'

Despite herself, Jacqueline smiled, too. Maybe her housekeeper knew more about her life than she did.

'Would you like me to start dinner for you this

evening?' Martha asked as she turned toward the kitchen.

Jacqueline shook her head. 'No, I believe I'll cook tonight, Martha.'

The housekeeper didn't so much as blink, but Jacqueline could tell she was surprised. Jacqueline rarely ventured into the kitchen, and hadn't made a complete meal in years. Early in their marriage she'd found a chicken curry dish that Reese had particularly enjoyed. She'd torn the recipe out of a magazine. Jacqueline thought she knew where it was, although it'd been quite a while since she'd gone to the effort of preparing it.

'Martha, do we have any curry spices in the house?'

'I think so. Let me look for you.'

'Is there chicken in the freezer?'

'Should be.'

Jacqueline was only half listening. She moved past the housekeeper and into the kitchen, opening a bottom drawer where she kept her cookbooks. 'Do you remember a recipe I had years ago for chicken curry?'

Martha frowned. 'Can't say I do. Are you going to be making a mess in my kitchen?'

Jacqueline smiled, biting back a retort that would have reminded the other woman whose kitchen this really was. 'Don't worry,' she assured Martha. 'You'll get it back in the morning.'

Martha nodded, but she still looked concerned.

After paging through six cookbooks, Jacqueline found the recipe in the back of Julia Child's *Mastering the Art of French Cooking,* together with a number of other loose recipes she'd collected over the years. Sitting down at the table, she wrote out a grocery list.

By the time Reese walked into the house at six o'clock, the kitchen was redolent with the scent of coconut milk, chicken, curry and yogurt.

'What's this?' Reese asked, loosening his tie. Jacqueline hadn't heard him come in and whirled around, a wooden spoon in her hand. 'Dinner,' she announced cheerfully.

Forgetting herself, she walked over and kissed his cheek. 'The roses are beautiful. Thank you.'

Reese's eyes widened just a little. 'I figured I owed you an apology,' he murmured. 'I came down on you pretty hard about parking in the alley. I shouldn't have said the things I did.'

'You were worried about me. It's a case of me running over the mailbox with the tractor.'

He frowned. 'What?'

Jacqueline laughed and quickly retold Tammie Lee's story. 'That's why her daddy hollered at her mama,' she concluded. 'Twice.'

Reese chuckled and then to Jacqueline's amazement, he kissed her. She was sure he only meant to brush her lips with his, but when their mouths met, something wonderful and exciting took hold of them both.

The wooden spoon clattered to the floor and Jacqueline slid her arms around her husband's neck. Reese's mouth was on hers, as avid as if they were new lovers.

Jacqueline lost all sense of time and didn't know how long they remained locked in each other's arms. When they broke apart they both seemed at a loss as to what to say or do next. This was by far their most passionate kiss in years.

What astonished her most was the zeal with which she'd responded to his kiss. She'd assumed that after years of celibacy, the sexual part of her nature had atrophied. It was a shock to realize just how alive – how sexual – she was capable of feeling.

'I'd better shower,' Reese said as he backed away from her. He seemed to be in a state of shock himself.

Jacqueline didn't trust her voice enough to speak, so she merely nodded. Leaning heavily against the kitchen counter, she closed her eyes.

'Wow,' she whispered to the empty room. Now *that* was something! Once she'd stopped trembling, she retrieved two dinner plates and set them on the dining room table.

When Reese returned from the shower, his hair damp, he'd donned slacks and a golf shirt. Jacqueline had just finished lighting the candles, pleased with her efforts. She could be domestic when called upon and today she'd rediscovered how much she actually enjoyed it.

'Can I do anything?' he asked.

She glanced at him over her shoulder. It was ridiculous to feel shy with her own husband of more than thirty years. She would never have expected this, but she felt as if that kiss was the first one they'd ever shared – as if their intimacy was completely unfamiliar. 'Would you pour the wine?'

'Sure.' He opened the refrigerator and took out a bottle of chilled chardonnay, which he uncorked. After he'd poured them each a glass, he turned on the CD player.

Singing along to the soundtrack of *Les Misérables*, Jacqueline mounded rice on their plates and ladled on generous servings of curry. She carried the plates to the table, where Reese was waiting for her. He stood behind her chair and pulled it out, a courtesy he hadn't bothered with in years.

'It's a long time since you made me chicken curry,' he said when he was seated across from her. 'It smells delicious – thank you.' He reached for his wineglass and raised it. 'Shall I propose a toast?'

'Please.' Happiness settled over her until she was nearly giddy with it. Until now, Jacqueline had lost hope that they might recapture the love in their marriage. She felt light-headed with anticipation as she lifted her wineglass and touched the rim to his.

'To the future,' Reese said.

'The future,' she echoed.

After a sip of wine, Reese picked up his fork. Jacqueline held her breath while he tasted his first bite, anxiously awaiting his reaction.

She knew she'd succeeded when he closed his eyes and murmured a soft sigh of appreciation.

'It's even better than I remember.'

Jacqueline relaxed and took her first taste. The curry was as good as she'd hoped. In retrospect, she wasn't sure why she'd buried the recipe when she knew how much Reese enjoyed her meals – and how much she used to enjoy making them. Years earlier she'd done all their cooking, even for their many social events. More recently, she'd had her parties catered. She'd casually mentioned that in last week's knitting class when they'd started talking about memorable meals. To her surprise, Alix had said she'd like her own catering company one day. Alix of all people! This was a rather unexpected revelation, but it made her wonder. She owed Alix...

'I have a small confession,' Reese said, breaking into her thoughts.

Jacqueline wasn't sure she wanted to hear it, but before she could stop him, he continued.

'You need to thank Tammie Lee for the roses. They were her idea.'

Jacqueline picked up her wine. 'Well, I didn't think you'd come up with that idea on your own.'

'To Tammie Lee,' Reese said, holding up his wineglass.

'To Tammie Lee,' Jacqueline repeated.

The phone rang and she sighed.

'I'll get it.' Reese was out of his chair before she could protest.

For once, just once, she wanted them to have a quiet dinner together. She wished now that she'd taken the phone off the hook.

Whoever was on the line certainly had Reese's attention. His brow furrowed and he frowned and then nodded curtly. Replacing the receiver, he muttered, 'I have to go.'

'Where?' Jacqueline asked before she would stop herself.

'Problems on the job.' He grabbed his car keys and was out the door. 'I'm needed at one of the sites. Not Blossom Street – the Northgate project.

It appears we blew a circuit and the entire block is without electricity.'

Sitting alone at the table, listening as Reese's car engine roared to life, Jacqueline felt numb.

A moment later, she flung her napkin furiously onto her plate and walked over to the sink. She grabbed the counter with both hands, biting down hard on her lower lip.

'He's needed at the site,' she repeated, her voice cracking. She knew exactly who'd phoned and exactly where he'd gone and it wasn't to any job site.

CHAPTER 30

ALIX TOWNSEND

Sunday morning, Alix found herself standing on the same street corner she had for the last few weeks, watching as people filed through the church doors. Ordinary people, some wealthy and some not. People like those in her knitting group. People like Carol Girard and her husband.

Having lunch at Carol's high-rise condo had been an eye-opening experience. Literally! The view was incredible, unlike anything she'd seen before. She might live in Seattle, but she certainly never saw it from this perspective. And Puget Sound was beyond fabulous. Alix felt as if she'd stepped right onto a page in one of those fancy home decorating magazines people left behind at the Laundromat. The condo itself was spacious. The furniture was simple and classic, and there were lots of warm, appealing touches. One thing was for sure. Alix had no intention of returning the invitation. She could just imagine what Carol would think if she saw the inside of *her* apartment. Especially now, since Laurel had taken to being even a bigger slob than usual.

Carol had made a lovely lunch of cold tomato soup – a Spanish recipe, she'd said – and a seafood salad. She'd set the table with beautiful matching dishes, complete with linen napkins. A few weeks ago Alix would have considered details like that pointless, but these days she was taking notice. This was exactly the type of thing she needed to know if she hoped to start her own business one day. Alix had been nervous at first, afraid she might commit some social blunder by using the wrong fork. If Jacqueline had been there, she would've been more worried, but Carol was a normal kind of person. Funny, with all that wealth, she still had her problems.

Everyone had problems, Alix now realized, even if they lived in gorgeous apartments with million-dollar views. Over lunch she and Carol covered a lot of subjects, and after a while, it felt just as if they were in the knitting group at Lydia's shop. Alix had never expected to become friends with these women but that was exactly what had happened. Even with Jacqueline...

All of them encouraged her to pursue the relationship with Jordan.

Following the roller-skating party, Alix had seen him only once. He'd stopped by the video store to tell her he was going out of town. Apparently he was involved in a summer camp program and was driving some kids to eastern Washington. He'd mentioned sending her a postcard, but if he'd mailed one, she hadn't received it. That had been on her mind ever since he'd gone away.

As she stood on the corner across from the Free Methodist church, the music drifted out the open doors. Alix recognized the song, which she'd heard several times before. For some reason she couldn't identify, she boldly marched across the street and up the steps. As she did, she glanced around, half expecting someone to stop her.

She missed Jordan, and if walking into this church was the only way she could feel close to him, then she was doing it. Anyone who questioned her was in for one hell of a fight.

An usher looked in her direction, but she scowled at him with such ferocity that he backed off. She didn't need anyone to tell her where to sit. Slipping into the last pew, she saw that people were standing and singing. She grabbed what she assumed was the hymnal and picked up a Bible instead. She wondered if anyone noticed. As casually as she could, she replaced the Bible and grabbed the red book, opening it to the number posted on a board at the front of the church.

The sanctuary was surprisingly crowded. Alix had no idea so many people actually attended services. Perhaps if her family had prayed together, they might have stayed together. Yeah, right! As a kid she'd done her fair share of praying and a lot of good that had done her. A familiar bitterness welled up inside. These kids were lucky. They had parents who cared about them. By her own choice, Alix was no longer in contact with her mother and hadn't seen her father in years. He hadn't even bothered to show up when Tom died. As she thought of her brother, her hand tightened around the hymnal. All Tom had ever wanted was someone to care about him. They'd both been cheated in that department; their father was more interested in drinking with his friends than he was in his children, and their mother was no better. Little wonder they'd had serious problems of their own, but Alix was determined to have a better life.

She studied the words printed on the page but didn't sing. One of Alix's fears was that she wouldn't know when to stand or sit. That was the advantage of being in the back pew – she simply followed what everyone else was doing.

When the song ended, the congregation sat down and the minister, an older man, stepped up to the podium. Alix figured she'd leave after the sermon, afraid that if she stood up and walked out now, someone might be offended.

The minister preached from the Old Testament and the book of Nehemiah, which Alix had never heard of before. The sermon, about the ruined walls of Jerusalem and how they symbolized people's lives, interested her, although she didn't understand everything he said.

Alix was just getting ready to slip out of the pew when she saw Jordan walk to the front of the church. He was obviously back from summer camp, although he hadn't come by the video store.

She tried to ignore the disappointment and the hurt. Seeing him in church wasn't the only shock she received. Jordan wasn't alone. A blond beauty came with him. The girl eyed Jordan like he was Jesus returning to collect His saints before Armageddon.

The two of them had handheld microphones. The music started, and their voices blended as if they'd been singing together their entire lives. Listening to their performance was more than Alix could bear. In an effort to exit the pew as fast as possible, she nearly stumbled over the feet of the woman next to her. Without looking back, she rushed out the door.

If she'd needed proof that she was deluding herself, this was it. Reeling, she ran into an alley. She closed her eyes and called herself every ugly name she'd ever heard. With her back against the brick wall, she slid down and hung her head.

Naturally Jordan would be singing in church with Miss America. And why not? He was a preacher's kid; he'd been raised in the church. He'd never sat in a jail cell or stood before a judge. His parents had loved him, wanted him. She could just imagine what his daddy would say if he knew Jordan was hanging with *her.*

Alix squatted there, caught in a misery so deep she could barely move.

'Hey, Alix?'

A voice drifted into her awareness, and she glanced up to find Tyrone Houston, better known in the neighborhood as T-Bone, standing above her. He was a gang member and a known drug dealer. The last Alix had heard he was doing time.

Apparently he was out.

'Whatcha doin'?' T-Bone demanded.

'Taking up space. You got a problem with that?' Normally no one flashed attitude to T-Bone and she could be risking her life. For a second, she wasn't sure she cared.

'No problem. You interested in a party?' He gave her the once-over.

In her present frame of mind, Alix was in no mood for company.

'I got the stuff,' he said enticingly.

That meant he had a fresh supply of drugs. Probably meth or cocaine or any of a dozen different substances guaranteed to shut up the voices in her head.

'I could be,' Alix said. She'd been clean a long time – ever since her brother had overdosed – but she hated this dark ugly feeling eating at her gut. If she could swallow something to make her feel good, she wanted it because whatever T-Bone had was better than these awful voices.

The house was a couple of blocks away. Everyone in the area knew that if you needed a hit, T-bone would supply it – for a price, naturally. Alix didn't know his sources, didn't want to know.

When they stepped into the house, the shades were drawn and the room was dark. Five or six guys were lounging around and the air was thick with sweet-smelling smoke. Alix buried her hands in her leather jacket as she slowly surveyed the scene.

In one corner she noticed another girl sitting with a guy. His arm was wrapped around her and he appeared to be out of it, in a drug-induced haze. Alix looked again, harder this time. The girl seemed familiar, but Alix couldn't figure out how she knew her. Working at the video store she saw a lot of people; while she might not remember names, she rarely forgot a face.

This girl hadn't been in the video store, Alix was fairly certain of that. She was young, fourteen, possibly fifteen, and trying to look older. Alix knew the signs because a few years back she'd done the same thing.

Then it came to her. The girl was familiar because Alix had seen her at the roller-skating rink with Jordan. She was a church kid. The girl recognized Alix, too. She averted her gaze.

Anger surged through Alix. This kid didn't belong here with a bunch of druggie losers.

She strolled to the sofa where the girl sat with her stoned boyfriend in a tangle of arms and legs. Alix sat down on the sofa arm and glared at them.

'What are you doing here?' she demanded of the girl.

The teenager glared back at Alix, her eyes full of defiance. 'Same as you.'

The guy she was with rolled his head and pointed at Alix. 'Who's this, Lori?'

Yes, Alix remembered her now. Her name was Lori and she'd come with a couple of friends. Roller skating with church kids one month, doing drugs with criminals and losers the next. Quite a contrast.

Lori stared up at Alix, her face hard and her eyes cold. 'This,' she said, sneering, 'is no one.'

'That's where you're wrong,' Alix said as she

came to her feet. 'Sorry, we have to go now.' She grabbed Lori by the arm. The girl protested but let Alix pull her up.

'What are you doing?' she cried.

'Getting you outta here.'

'Like shit you are.'

'You don't belong here any more than I do.'

'Baby?' Her boyfriend was so out of it he didn't protest, which was good. T-Bone, however, wasn't pleased. He blocked the door, his arms crossed over his massive chest as he focused narrowed eyes on Alix. Fear shivered down her spine. T-Bone could slit her throat if he perceived that she was hurting his business. He wouldn't hesitate, either.

'She's a church kid,' Alix said, meeting his gaze. 'You keep her here and you're gonna have a pack of little ol' ladies marching outside your door, carrying signs and bringing the heat.'

T-Bone's gaze shifted from Alix to Lori, who squirmed under his scrutiny.

'You want trouble, it's up to you.' Alix raised both arms in a hands-off gesture.

'Get out,' he said to Alix, 'and take her with you.'

Alix seized Lori's upper arm and dragged her out of the house.

Once outside, Lori jerked her arm free. 'What the hell do you think you're doing?' she screamed.

'What am *I* doing?' Alix repeated, laughing. 'What I'm doing, little girl, is saving your sorry ass.'

'I don't need anyone to save me.'

Those words were almost identical to what

she'd said when Jordan announced he was a youth minister. But they weren't true for Lori – and maybe not for Alix, either. Lori had no idea what kind of danger she'd so blithely stepped into. She didn't appreciate the risk Alix had taken by pulling her out, either. Alix's knees shook when she realized what she'd done in standing up to T-Bone. It was time to make herself scarce.

'Go home,' Alix said.

Lori rolled her eyes and headed back into the house, only to be stopped at the door. Alix didn't hear what was said but apparently Lori got the message and came scurrying out a moment later. She hurried down the street without a backward look.

With no place else to go, Alix returned to her apartment. Laurel was gone. In her unhappiness her roommate was eating everything in sight – and leaving the mess for Alix to clean up. She wondered if Laurel still fit into her jeans. She must've gained twenty pounds since her breakup with John. If Laurel wasn't at work, scarfing potato chips on the sly, or at home, sitting in front of the television with her face in a bowl of ice cream, Alix didn't know where she could be. But for once she was grateful to be alone.

Picking up her knitting, she heaved a sigh when she saw what she was doing and threw it down in disgust. Carol had given her the gray yarn and the pattern, as well as the work she'd already done. Alix had painstakingly continued the project, knitting a sweater for Jordan. Yeah, right, like he cared. Like anyone did.

Lying on the sofa, Alix stared at the ceiling for an

hour before she was scheduled to work. The video store did good business on Sunday afternoons and she was kept busy, especially when Laurel didn't bother to make an appearance, even though her name was on the schedule to work with Alix.

An hour into her shift, Jordan walked into the store. Alix's heart reacted instantly and that infuriated her. As effectively as she could, she ignored him.

'Alix,' he said.

'You're back.' She made sure he knew it wasn't any big thing to her.

'Is something wrong?'

She shrugged and handed two videos to the customer at the register, offering him a wide smile. When she turned her attention to Jordan, the smile was gone. 'Should there be?'

He frowned. 'I was hoping we could get together tonight.'

She considered his invitation. Part of her was shrieking with excitement and another part, the part that insisted she get over him, was saying something else.

'Who's Miss America?' she asked coldly.

'What?' Jordan said, blinking in confusion.

'You sang with her this morning.'

His eyes widened. 'You were in church?'

'Long enough to see you and Miss America smiling at each other. You seem to be very good friends.'

'We are.'

'I'll just bet.'

'Can I get some help here?' the next customer at the counter asked.

Alix reached for his videos and typed in the codes before taking his money. She gave him his change and smiled sweetly in his direction. Once again she returned her attention to Jordan, making sure there was no evidence of pleasure at seeing him.

Jordan frowned. 'You're jealous of Pastor Sutton's seventeen-year-old daughter?'

The girl was only seventeen? From the back of the church it was hard to tell. Still...

'I don't have time to put up with petty jealousy. If you want to be angry with me, then fine. But I've got better things to do.'

Alix was about to answer when he whirled around and left the store.

CHAPTER 31

'If you can count the number of projects you have going, you need to begin another, so you have a varied range of complexity, from the very simple 'mindless' ones to those that demand undivided attention.'

–Laura Early, lifetime knitter

LYDIA HOFFMAN

I've spent so much time in doctors' offices that over the years I've come to dread even the most routine appointments. It's almost always the same. I sit in an uncomfortable chair in a waiting room full of strangers and we all avoid looking at one another. Generally, I bring my knitting or I flip through magazines that are months if not years old.

The one advantage of being in Dr. Wilson's office is that after all this time the staff have become practically as familiar as family, especially Peggy, Dr. Wilson's nurse.

Peggy was working for Dr. Wilson when I came in for my first appointment, nearly fifteen years ago. I remember when she was pregnant, not once but twice. I vividly recall wondering if I'd be alive to see her second baby. The thing with cancer is that you learn to take nothing for granted. Not one day, not one season, not even a minute. At sixteen I wanted to make it to seventeen so I could attend the Junior-Senior Prom. I survived, but no one asked me to the prom.

'Lydia.' Peggy stood in the doorway holding my chart, which must weigh twenty pounds. My medical history was filled with details, of symptoms and procedures, as well as documentation of the different medications I'd taken.

When I got up, it seemed that every eye in the waiting room was on me. If I'd been the type of person to grandstand, I would've leaped to my feet and announced I was a two-time winner in the lottery of life. Having a more subdued nature, however, I calmly stuffed my knitting into my quilted bag and followed Peggy.

'How are you doing?' Peggy asked after she'd weighed me and made a notation on the chart.

'Great.' I stepped off the scale and sighed with relief to note that my weight was within a couple of pounds of my last visit. Peggy led me to the cubicle at the far end of the hallway, where she thrust a disposable thermometer under my tongue and reached for my wrist. She stared at her watch and quickly made a second notation on my chart. 'Good strong heartbeat,' she said, sounding pleased.

I should hope so; my insurance company had paid plenty for the privilege of having that heartbeat. I would've told her as much but talking wasn't an option at the moment.

Peggy was pumping the blood-pressure cuff, which she'd wrapped around my upper arm. It grew uncomfortably tight before she released it. When she'd finished listening, she nodded. 'Very good.'

At last she removed the thermometer. 'You're feeling well?'

'I feel fabulous.'

Peggy smiled. 'There's a sparkle in your eyes. You've met someone, haven't you?'

'Oh, hardly.' I brushed aside her insight, but found I really did want to tell her about Brad. I didn't, because there wasn't that much to tell. Not yet, anyway. We'd met for drinks twice, talked on the phone two or three times a week, sometimes for an hour or more. He came by the shop at least once during the course of a week and occasionally – no, more than occasionally – we kissed.

Brad and I were only beginning to know each other. We weren't serious, weren't even close to being serious. Brad was deeply involved in his son's life and I was deeply involved in my business. We were friends in the same way I was friends with Carol Girard. Okay, maybe not *exactly* the same way, but nevertheless friends. For now, that was comfortable for me and apparently for him, too.

'*Have* you met someone?' Peggy asked again.

I nodded hesitantly.

I thought she was ready to burst into applause. 'I always knew you would,' she said with a smile of delight.

'Oh, honestly, Peggy, I'm thirty years old.'

'And your point is?'

It was embarrassing to be this transparent, especially at my age, but that's another aspect of having had cancer as a teenager. My social maturity seemed stuck where it was the day I got my driver's license. Social development is delayed for those of us who are detoured by the fight for life. I don't want to sound like I'm feeling sorry for myself because I'm not; this is a simple fact that needs to be taken into account in relationships.

I knew the routine visits well enough to know that the next part was to stretch out my arm for Peggy to extract vial after vial of my blood. I once teased her that I should be paid for the amount she collected. Not one vial but four, two large and two small.

I barely blinked as the needle pricked my skin. In the beginning, though, I used to get dizzy with fear at the sight of a needle. Once I nearly fainted, but that was years ago. Compared to some of the procedures I've endured, having my blood drawn is kid's play.

Peggy paused to exchange a full tube for an

empty one and glanced up.

'I don't think I've ever seen you look happier.'

'I am happy,' I assured her. My new happiness had come about for several reasons. Opening my shop played a big role in how I felt and so, of course, did meeting Brad. A Good Yarn was my affirmation of life and allowing myself to get involved with Brad was an additional act of faith.

'I'm so pleased for you.' Peggy repeated the process with the tubes and then wrote my name on each one. 'I'll give you a call in a couple of days.'

I nodded.

She walked out to the front with me and got someone else's file.

My spirits were high as I strolled out of the doctor's office. It was a glorious August afternoon and while the store was closed on Mondays, I could think of nowhere else I'd rather be. I truly loved my shop. It gave me pleasure just to be there with all the yarn around me. There's something completely satisfying about standing in the middle of a store that only a few months earlier was little more than a dream.

I had on a sleeveless summer dress made of seersucker with a pretty white eyelet collar. The dress was a favorite of mine, and yes, I'll admit it, I hoped that if I ventured into my shop I might accidentally-on-purpose run into Brad. He made deliveries in the neighborhood on Mondays and he always knocked on my door if he saw I was there.

Listening to the radio, I kept an eye on the windows in case he happened to drive past. Blossom Street was open to traffic now and this had dramatically increased business. Lots of people came to the neighborhood just to see the changes. The stores along both sides of the street had put out their welcome mats.

The construction directly across from me appeared to be nearly finished, although there seemed to be plenty of men in hard hats still parading around. I wasn't sure when everything was officially scheduled to be completed, but I knew it wouldn't be much longer.

Just as I'd hoped, Brad's dark-brown delivery truck came into view. It was all I could do not to stand like a mannequin in the window. It was even harder to resist the urge to jump up and down and wave my arms. I did neither, but I was definitely tempted. I was in just that silly, quirky frame of mind.

I saw my man-in-brown leap out of his truck with a couple of packages for the floral shop next door. I didn't know if he'd seen me or not until he came out with a single long-stemmed red rose. I waved despite my resolve not to and he winked at me.

Unlocking the front door, I let him into the shop. 'For me?' I asked.

'It'll cost ya,' Brad teased.

'Name your price?'

'A kiss,' he said, grinning boyishly. 'Maybe two.'

I know it sounds ridiculous, but I blushed. He took me by the hand and led me behind a tall shelf filled with worsted yarn. At least there we had a bit of privacy.

'How'd the doctor's visit go?'

'I didn't even see him. It was for routine blood tests.'

'Are you nervous?'

I shook my head. Maybe I should've been, but the cancer had left me alone for a long time now and after a certain period you can't help growing a little confident. More than that, I felt too good to be sick again and showed none of the symptoms I had in the past other than an occasional migraine. Besides, for the first time in years, I was truly hopeful for the future.

'I'm free on Saturday night.' Brad was looking down at me, his eyes so intense and provocative it was nearly impossible to breathe.

'That's nice.'

'How about if I take you to dinner and a movie?'

I smiled and nodded.

'Anyplace you want to eat, as long as it isn't McDonald's.'

I smiled again. Cody was a big fan of their cheeseburgers, and Brad was thoroughly tired of fast food.

'You got it. Anyplace but McDonald's.'

Then, with such ease I was barely aware of what he was doing, Brad brought me into his arms and kissed me. The earth didn't move, the sky didn't fall, but I swear I felt that kiss from the top of my head to the tips of my toes. If a man could make me feel all that with a simple kiss, I could only imagine what it would be like if – when – we made love. I closed my eyes, wanting to hold on to this wonderful feeling as long as I could.

'You smell so good,' he whispered, nuzzling my neck.

'It's my perfume.' I let my head fall back and he spread small kisses along my throat. I was practically purring like Whiskers, my cat, when he lies on the windowsill, basking in the afternoon sun.

'I don't care what it is, just promise to wear the same one on Saturday night, okay?'

'Okay,' I whispered, and he kissed me again. Neither of us wanted to stop, but he was still on the clock and we knew it had to end. When he released me I felt his reluctance as keenly as my own. A girl could get mighty accustomed to Brad's kind of kisses.

'I'll pick you up at seven on Saturday evening, all right?'

'Perfect,' I told him.

In that moment, 'perfect' was how I'd describe my life.

CHAPTER 32

CAROL GIRARD

The critical first three weeks following embryo transfer had passed and so far so good. Carol was a full five weeks pregnant now and felt every aspect of this pregnancy in a way few women ever would.

After talking to her mother in Oregon for twenty minutes, she hung up the receiver and fixed herself a healthy lunch of cottage cheese and fresh fruit. Carol had never been fond of cottage cheese, and this was her way of announcing to the universe that she was willing to suffer for the sake of her baby. No sacrifice was too great. When her child was born, she wanted to know she'd done everything possible to give him or her a good start in life.

Smiling, Carol scooped cottage cheese onto a plate, then added sliced pineapple. She'd heard from one of the women in her online support group that a substance in pineapple was believed to improve the chances of an embryo attaching to the uterus.

The phone rang as the fork was halfway to her mouth. She lowered it and reached for the receiver.

It was Doug. Normally he was too busy to phone from work, but he'd made a habit of calling her at least once a day since the last IVF.

'I just spoke with Mom,' she told him.

'What's new with her?'

'She and Dad want to buy us a crib.'

'Did you tell her we already have one?'

'I didn't have the heart.' Three weeks after the procedure, Carol had gotten a Bon-Macy's flyer advertising baby furniture. That night she'd dragged Doug to the department store and, giddy with excitement, they'd purchased everything they could possibly need for a nursery.

'So we're going to have two cribs?'

'I could be having twins.'

Doug chuckled and it was the unrestrained laugh she'd fallen in love with all those years ago.

He so rarely laughed like that anymore, and she knew beyond a doubt that her pregnancy explained his joy.

'Besides, I was thinking that if we can't use the crib, maybe she could give it to Rick.' She hated to put an end to her husband's fun-loving mood, but her brother would be presenting their parents with another grandchild a few weeks before Carol was due to deliver.

'Have you heard from him lately?' Doug asked.

'Not a word.'

'I take it he hasn't mentioned anything to your parents?'

'Not that I can tell, but I don't dare ask about it, either.'

'You're right – it's not your place.'

She sank back into her chair. 'I hope Rick does the proper thing and marries this woman.'

Doug hesitated. 'From what you told me, he's already decided against that.'

'But there's a *baby* involved.'

'I know that, but I also know Rick.'

Carol sighed. She wondered what her parents would say when they heard about the situation. Her mother was waiting impatiently for grand-children. She'd be thrilled whether Rick was married to the woman or not, but she'd prefer it if Rick gave the child his name.

'I'm having cottage cheese for lunch,' she told Doug. He'd appreciate her sacrifice.

'I hope the baby likes it,' Doug teased.

'I hope so, too.'

They chatted for a few more minutes and then Carol went back to her sacrificial lunch.

She lost the baby later that afternoon.

Just when the dream had started to become a reality... Just when she'd given herself permission to believe... Just when she was so sure everything had gone according to plan.

At four in the afternoon the spotting started. The instant she saw the blood, she thought she'd faint. Severe cramping followed and there was no longer any doubt. She'd miscarried.

'No,' she whispered, clenching her fists at her sides. 'Please no ... please, oh please.' Her throat was thick with tears. She sat on the end of her bed and covered her eyes.

The routine should be standard by now. After phoning the doctor's office, she collected her purse. She didn't call Doug, couldn't ruin the rest of his day. She'd give him the afternoon before she shattered his life with the news that there would be no baby for them.

When Dr. Ford examined her, he confirmed what she already knew. Her body had rejected the fetus. The baby was dead, expelled from her womb. Dr. Ford was sympathetic and concerned. After she'd dressed, he gently squeezed her arm.

'I'm sorry.'

Emotionless, Carol stared straight ahead.

'Would you like one of my staff to phone Doug for you?'

She shook her head.

'Is there anyone you'd like me to call?'

His words sounded slurred to Carol as her mind struggled to comprehend each one. She was drowning in a sea of pain. Functioning normally was impossible just then.

'I want my mother,' she whispered. Her body had rejected three pregnancies now, and there wouldn't be another chance. This was the end for her and Doug. It was over.

'Can I have someone phone her?'

She looked up at him, wondering who he meant, and realized he was asking about her mother. Carol shook her head. 'She lives in Oregon.'

Dr. Ford said a bit more, offered his condolences and after a few minutes left her. Carol slipped off the examination table, dressed and went out the door. She didn't know where she was going, didn't care. She started walking – a slow, shambling walk, without purpose – and before long found herself on the waterfront near the Seattle Aquarium. Tourists crowded the sidewalk and she felt like a boulder in a stream, disrupting the flow of traffic as men, women and children darted around her.

When she was finally too tired to move, she sat down on a bench. The tears came then. Hoarse, painful sobs from the depths of her soul. She'd failed again. Disappointed her husband, disappointed her parents and everyone who'd believed in her.

Her cell phone rang and why she should be so angry with it, Carol didn't know. Without checking to see who might be calling her, she grabbed it from her purse and threw it into the street. She felt a sense of grim satisfaction as a city bus passed by and drove directly over it. All that was left was a flattened piece of plastic with wires protruding.

'Is everything all right, miss?' a young police officer stepped up to ask her.

'No,' she said, her face streaked with tears and her eyes dull with pain. 'Nothing is right.' She understood then that someone must have seen her and thought she needed help. Unfortunately, there wasn't anything the policeman or anyone else could do for her.

'Should I call someone?'

'No, thank you.'

'You're sure?'

She stood, needing to escape. 'I appreciate your concern, but you can't help me. No one can.' If she didn't leave now, she might end up in Emergency or even the Psych ward. Escape became key, so she started walking again. Walking and walking and walking.

It was dark when she discovered she was miles from home. Doug must be frantic by now but she couldn't face him yet, couldn't watch the look in his eyes when he learned there wasn't a baby anymore.

An hour later, Carol took a taxi home.

When she walked in the door, Doug nearly flew across the room. 'Where the hell were you?'

'I lost the baby.'

He didn't seem to be listening. 'Why didn't you answer the phone?'

'Didn't you hear me?' she sobbed, her shoulders shaking uncontrollably. 'I lost the baby.'

'I know,' Doug whispered and wrapped her in his arms.

Carol was weeping again, unable to stop. The tears came from deep inside her, sobs that wrenched her soul. This was an agony that could be understood only by those who'd experienced such a loss. It felt as if her beating heart had been ripped from her chest, as if she would never again know joy or happiness or anything good. Her future stretched before her, bleak and without hope.

'I so badly wanted to have our child,' she sobbed into her husband's arms.

Doug held her tightly in his embrace, his head against her shoulder. Then she realized he was weeping, too. They clung to each other, neither able to offer anything to the other. Empty, bereaved, in agony.

'I'm so sorry,' she choked out. 'So sorry.'

'I know ... I know.'

'I love you.'

He nodded.

'I tried so hard...' She couldn't think of anything she might have done differently, any effort she hadn't made.

'I'll always love you,' Doug assured her.

Exhausted, Carol showered and went to bed and with Doug's arms around her, she fell into a deep sleep.

At three, she woke with pain heavy upon her chest and remembered there was no longer a child growing in her womb. The tears came fresh, stinging her eyes.

Slipping out of bed, she walked into the nursery and stood in the middle of the darkened room. She curled her fingers around the end of the crib and bit her lower lip hard to hold back the sobs.

It was then that she noticed the wall. She squinted, certain she was seeing things. Flicking on the light switch, she looked again. Her knees went weak and she sagged to the floor as she stared at the place where her husband's fist had gone through the wall.

CHAPTER 33

JACQUELINE DONOVAN

Friday afternoon Jacqueline arrived at A Good Yarn, her usual five minutes after starting time. Being 'fashionably late' was a habit she'd picked up long ago and seemed unable to break. To her surprise, Carol was missing. Alix was slouched down in her chair with a morose look on her face.

'Where's Carol?' she asked Lydia, who stood at the end of the table, knitting needles in hand. Lydia carried her yarn and needles around with her, so her hands were constantly busy.

'Carol decided to stay home this afternoon,' Lydia explained. 'I'm afraid she had bad news. She lost the baby.'

Jacqueline had feared as much. 'I'm so sorry.'

'She's taking a few days to regroup, but I hope she'll be back.'

Jacqueline nodded; she felt terrible for Carol. The other woman's desire for a child was so strong it verged on desperation. Jacqueline was worried about her and hoped Carol could, somehow, rebound from the loss. She recalled her own bitter disappointment over her inability to give birth to a second child, but at least she'd been able to have Paul. The likelihood that Carol and Doug would get a baby through adoption was slim. Jacqueline sighed. This was a sad turn of events, and there wasn't a thing any of them could do.

'I'm afraid we might lose Carol,' Lydia said.

'Why? What do you mean?' Alix asked, anxiety in her voice.

'She didn't say anything, but I think she might be returning to work. The only reason she quit was for the baby, and she told me a couple of weeks ago that the brokerage firm would like her to come back.'

Alix looked, if anything, even more dejected.

Jacqueline wondered what was bothering her so much. Worry about Carol was obviously part of it, but Jacqueline sensed that something else was wrong.

'How are you, Alix?' Jacqueline murmured, reaching inside her bag for her knitting. She was working on a scarf for her son. It was a lovely worsted wool, the same brown shade as a pony Paul had loved as a child. Jacqueline wondered if her son would remember Brownie and make the connection.

'Hi,' Alix murmured, keeping her head lowered.

Jacqueline looked to Lydia, who shrugged, indicating she didn't know what was wrong, either. The shop grew quiet, the silence broken only by traffic noises from outside.

Alix glanced up, and Jacqueline saw that she was no longer working on the man's sweater she'd taken over from Carol. In fact, she was knitting something entirely different.

'What's your problem?' Jacqueline asked bluntly.

'That's my business.' Alix's eyes flared to life as if she'd welcome a verbal confrontation.

'Man trouble if I've ever seen it,' Jacqueline announced to Lydia, who grinned slightly and nodded in agreement.

Alix's mouth thinned but she didn't take the bait.

'My guess is it involves that minister you're dating.'

'We weren't dating... We were just friends.'

'Past tense?' Lydia pried gently. 'You aren't seeing him anymore?'

'I haven't seen him in a while. He's got more than one friend, if you know what I mean.'

'You saw him with someone else,' Jacqueline guessed.

Alix's head was so low her chin sank into her chest when she nodded.

'Someone pretty,' she mumbled. 'And blond.' The girl in church.

'Naturally,' Jacqueline added. She'd always imagined that Reese's mistress was blond, and regarded with suspicion any blonde who came near him. Not that she cared, she told herself, but Jacqueline had to admit she occasionally wondered what the woman looked like. At the same time, she *didn't* want to know. In fact, she usually tried not to think about her at all.

Jacqueline's marriage, what was left of it, had been strained since the night Reese had walked out on their dinner. She hadn't forgiven him; more than that, she'd avoided him.

Reese hadn't made any effort to bridge the gap,

either. Apparently, finding his roses stuffed in the garbage the next morning had been message enough.

The three of them sat knitting together in silence. Lydia had to put her own knitting aside twice to help customers, and that left Jacqueline alone with Alix.

Jacqueline wasn't sure what prompted the idea, but once it took hold in her mind, it refused to leave.

'I owe you a favor,' she announced with some fanfare.

'For what?'

Jacqueline was astonished that Alix had forgotten. 'Dear girl, you might very well have saved my life.'

A hint of a smile came and then quickly vanished. Alix shrugged as if her stepping into the alley that day and standing up to those hoodlums was just a routine incident. An ordinary, everyday event.

'It's time I repaid your kindness,' she said decisively.

Alix was plainly curious. 'How?'

'I think,' Jacqueline said with flair, 'that we'll go for a complete makeover. My treat, naturally.'

'A what?'

'A beauty treatment.'

Alix frowned. 'What good's that going to do?'

'It might get you noticed by a certain young man.'

'What kind of beauty treatment?' Alix tried to disguise her interest, but she didn't fool Jacqueline.

'We'd start with your hair.' Jacqueline examined the purple-tinted ends with a critical eye and resisted the urge to cringe. That dreadful color had to go. Motioning with her hand, she offered a few suggestions. 'Get it cut and styled. Perhaps dye it a different color.'

'Only if I like it,' the girl said warily.

'Of course!'

'Any color I want?'

'Within reason.'

Alix made a careless movement with her shoulders. 'I suppose that would be all right.' She acted as if she was doing Jacqueline a favor. Two months ago Jacqueline would have taken offense at that but now she knew it was simply posturing.

'I'd like to take you to my fashion consultant and–'

Alix was shaking her head even before Jacqueline had finished the sentence. 'I don't need any advice on how to dress.'

'Whatever you say, but I do think we should get you a couple of new outfits.'

Still Alix hesitated, but then she gave a half-hearted nod. 'Your treat?'

'Of course.'

'I guess it's okay. When do you want to do this?' She asked as if her social calendar was full.

'Soon.' Jacqueline set aside her knitting and retrieved her cell phone. 'I'll call Desiree right now. She's the best hairdresser in town. It sometimes takes weeks to get an appointment.'

'Okay.' Alix couldn't hide her eagerness now. She sat up straight, nibbling on her lower lip.

'I need an appointment with Desiree ASAP,'

Jacqueline said, hoping the receptionist caught the hint of urgency in her voice. Desiree was a top beautician and the prices she charged were enough to perm Jacqueline's hair *without* chemicals. Still, she was worth every penny because of the miracles she performed. All the women at the country club went to her, and if they didn't, they wanted to.

Jacqueline waited impatiently while the receptionist put her on hold. It seemed forever before she returned. 'Desiree says she'll stay late this evening if you can be here by four-thirty.'

'Four-thirty?' She glanced at Alix, who nodded. 'We'll be there,' Jacqueline crowed triumphantly. She turned off the cell and placed it inside her purse. She felt certain that Alix didn't realize her good fortune. Jacqueline had to book her haircuts a month in advance.

Lydia was back, and although she hadn't heard a lot of the conversation, she seemed to understand what was happening and nodded in approval. Jacqueline was on a mission now, confident that with a change in wardrobe and a decent haircut she could turn Alix into an attractive young woman. A thrill of excitement went through her. This was going to be *fun*.

As soon as the knitting session was over, Jacqueline took Alix to Nordstrom for a new outfit. She purchased her own designer clothes at the Seattle-based department store, where one particular sales clerk had been in charge of Jacqueline's wardrobe for years.

Victoria took one look at Alix and immediately went to work. Jacqueline accompanied the girl into the dressing room and was shocked at her lack of proper intimate apparel. She insisted on new bras and panties first, and none of those ridiculous and indecent thongs, either.

Alix made a fuss, but it didn't last long. Still, while Jacqueline might have won *that* battle, Alix was the undisputed victor when it came to the war. She refused to even try on the St. John knitted suit or anything else Victoria delivered.

Considering the limited time available today, Jacqueline had to be content with buying Alix good-quality underwear. Before she was through, she swore she'd get her into something tasteful.

Unfortunately, the trip to the hairdresser didn't go much better. Desiree gasped at Alix's purple-tinged hair and started swearing in French. Even after years of high school and college French classes, Jacqueline couldn't understand what the woman said. But judging by the tone of her remarks, it was preferable not to attempt a translation.

Jacqueline sat in the waiting area and sipped coffee while a verbal skirmish occurred in the background. Fortunately, most of the shop's elite clientele had already departed; otherwise, their ears would've been assaulted by the ongoing exchange between Alix and Desiree.

Ninety minutes after they arrived, Alix flew to the front of the salon as if she'd just been released from prison. Jacqueline hardly recognized her. Gone was the tar-black hair with the eggplant-purple highlights. Instead, Alix's hair was a soft shade of brown with a reddish tinge that was similar to the yarn she'd chosen for Paul's scarf.

'Alix,' she said, coming to her feet. Once again, Desiree had performed a miracle. Not only had she colored Alix's hair but she'd styled it in a froth of curls.

'I *hate* it,' the girl cried as she ran her fingers through her hair, disarranging it. 'This isn't me.'

'No, my dear,' Jacqueline said patiently, 'this is a new you.'

For a moment it seemed Alix was about to burst into tears. 'I look like ... like one of the Brady Bunch,' she moaned.

'You look lovely.'

'Greg,' she cried. 'I look like Greg from the Brady Bunch.'

'You're being silly,' Jacqueline said sharply.

'I'm not! Everyone's going to laugh at me.'

The girl was making absolutely no sense. 'I'm sure you're wrong.'

'I know you meant well, but this just isn't me... It just isn't me.'

Without a word of gratitude, Alix stormed out of the salon, leaving Jacqueline speechless.

'Where did you ever meet such a girl?' Desiree asked, shaking her head.

'It's a long story,' Jacqueline murmured, discouraged now. She'd wanted to do something nice for Alix, something kind to show her appreciation, and she'd failed.

When she got back to the house, she discovered Reese in the kitchen getting a beer from the fridge.

'Are you okay?' he asked as she hurried past him to her own area of the house.

Jacqueline was surprised at his question. They

hadn't spoken, other than to exchange basic household information, for days now. Another time she might have pretended not to hear, but tonight she was hurt and confused, and couldn't hide it.

She didn't know how her good intentions toward Alix could have gone so badly awry. Sitting down at the kitchen table, she accepted the glass of wine Reese brought her and launched into an explanation of her adventure with Alix.

'I just don't know what I did wrong!' Jacqueline said hopelessly.

'How old is Alix?' Reese asked.

Jacqueline wasn't sure. 'Early twenties, I suppose.'

'You were trying to make her into another you, Jacquie.'

'I most certainly was not,' she cried, angry that Reese was so ready to find fault with her. She should've known better than to confide in him.

Then, at once, she realized he was right. She'd taken Alix to *her* salesclerk and *her* hairdresser. She met his gaze and slowly nodded. 'Perhaps I was.'

'Next time, ask Tammie Lee to give you a few suggestions.'

'Tammie Lee,' Jacqueline repeated and automatically shook her head. 'She couldn't do any better than me.'

'Maybe not, but she's closer to Alix's age and might have a few ideas.'

'I suppose I could ask her,' she said. Her daughter-in-law might not do better, but she certainly wouldn't do any worse than Jacqueline had.

CHAPTER 34

'Knitting goes with us, it calms us.'
    –Morgan Hicks, Sweaters by Design

LYDIA HOFFMAN

When I didn't hear from Dr. Wilson's office by the end of the week, I didn't think anything of it. Generally Peggy calls patients with their test results while the office is officially closed for lunch. From experience, I knew that if I needed a prescription refilled, I needed to contact Dr. Wilson's office before eleven.

When I opened the shop on Tuesday morning, it occurred to me fleetingly that I hadn't heard back from Peggy. Of course, she might have tried to reach me on Monday, but with the shop closed she would've gotten the answering machine. I realized I hadn't given her my new phone number and the only way she had of getting hold of me was through the shop. I checked as soon as I'd flipped the sign from CLOSED to OPEN, but found no messages.

I thought of it later and meant to phone the office myself, but was interrupted in the most pleasant manner possible. Brad stopped in on what he termed his coffee break.

My heart continued to do leaps of joy whenever he walked into the shop. We'd gone out to dinner twice in the last week and were together for much of Sunday afternoon. Cody spent the weekend with his mother who was often away on business, and this was a rare treat for us, even though I really enjoy Cody. He's a lively little boy with a quirky sense of humor. He asked me to knit him a sweater with a dinosaur on the front, and I said I would.

'Hi there, handsome,' I said as Brad let himself into the shop. He dazzled me with one of his smiles.

'Have you got coffee made?' he asked when it seemed I was capable of doing nothing but staring at him in wide-eyed adoration.

'Not yet,' I said. 'I barely got here.'

'I'll put on a pot.' He headed for the back room, where we'd escaped any number of times for a private moment.

We both knew his coffee-making ploy was just an excuse for the two of us to be alone. I followed him on the pretense of helping, but the instant I walked past the floral curtain that served as a door, Brad placed his arms around my waist and pulled me close.

'I had a wonderful weekend,' he whispered with his hands locked at the small of my back.

'I did, too.' We'd gone for a canoe ride on Lake Washington and halfway across he'd brought out a guitar and attempted to serenade me. It was truly romantic and quite possibly the sweetest thing any man had ever done for me. 'Just promise you'll never sing to me again.'

'You don't like my baritone?' He jutted out his lower lip in an exaggerated pout.

'No,' I said. 'That's not it. I love your singing, but I'm in serious danger of falling in love with you.' That wasn't what I'd intended to say, but it seemed my heart had its own purpose.

'That's what I want, Lydia.' He brought me closer still and kissed me with such energy and need that I was afraid I might collapse at his feet. We'd explored the attraction between us quite a bit over the weekend. I recognized that we'd reached a decision point in the relationship. It would be easy for this attraction to slip into the physical. Before that happened, though, I needed to be absolutely sure we shared the same values and life goals.

Margaret had warned me – and my mother had spoken her piece, too – about the importance of taking the relationship slow. I knew they were both right, but I felt so *good* in Brad's arms.

'I want to be with you more and more,' Brad said. 'You're the first thing I think of when I wake in the morning and the last thing on my mind at night.'

He was in my thoughts day and night, too, and to be honest, it frightened me. Twice before, I'd been in promising relationships. The first time I'd been too young to really understand what I'd lost when Brian and I broke up after I was diagnosed with a brain tumor.

It was a different story with Roger, who broke my heart. I wanted to die when he walked out on me and in retrospect, I see that was exactly what I assumed would happen. Time is a great healer, as the old saying has it, and I understand now, almost six years later, why Roger left when he did. He loved me. I truly believe that. Because he loved me, he couldn't bear to watch me die. He reacted the only way he knew how – by running away.

I heard that he got married just four months after we broke up. I tried not to think about him, but every now and then I felt a twinge of sadness. I didn't want any regrets with me and Brad, no matter where the relationship took us.

'You're very quiet.' He tenderly brushed the hair from my forehead as he looked down at me.

'We need to go slow,' I said. I'd told him about Brian and Roger, and just about everything else in my life there was to tell. He'd already known the basic facts, the outline of my emotional history, but I'd filled in the details when we were in the canoe. I'd leaned against him and gazed out over the beautiful green water of Lake Washington as we drifted. Brad had his arms around me. I found it easier to talk about my lost loves when I wasn't facing him.

In turn, Brad described his marriage, and said he felt he'd failed Janice, his ex-wife. That was something I couldn't understand, although I understood the impulse to assume blame. It's part of the same impulse that makes us believe we're responsible for everything that happens in a relationship or a family. But I've learned we can't control other people's feelings...

'What about dinner Friday night?' he asked now. He kissed me before I could respond.

The phone rang and I sighed with annoyance. 'Hold that thought,' I whispered, easing myself out of his arms.

I hurried to the phone and grabbed it just before the answering machine kicked in. 'A Good Yarn,' I said, hoping my voice didn't betray what I'd been doing a moment or so earlier.

'Lydia, this is Peggy from Dr. Wilson's office.'

'Oh, hi, Peggy,' I said, glad to have finally heard from her. 'I was wondering when you'd contact me.'

'I meant to call on Friday.'

'That's fine. I was busy all day.'

She hesitated and perhaps I should've caught it then, but I didn't.

'I should have phoned,' Peggy said.

By now I'd detected reluctance in her voice.

'Bad news?' If it was, I didn't want her to delay it a second longer. She'd given me the weekend as a gift and instinctively I realized that without her having to put it into words.

'I tried to call yesterday,' she murmured, 'but then I remembered your shop's closed on Mondays, isn't it?'

'You didn't leave a message.' The reason was obvious now. The news she had to give me couldn't be left on an answering machine.

'No,' she said, her voice uneasy.

'What is it?' I asked, steeling myself for the worst.

'Oh, Lydia, I'm so sorry. Dr. Wilson looked over your bloodwork and he's scheduled a series of X-rays for you. He'd also like to see you in his office at your earliest convenience.'

'All right.' It went without saying that the cancer was back. Another tumor was forming in my brain even as Peggy spoke. It was growing back and nothing would stop it this time, no surgery, no drugs, nothing. Had I been alone, I would have insisted Peggy tell me the worst of it then and there. But I couldn't do that with Brad in hearing distance.

'Can I make you an appointment with the radiologist for tomorrow morning at eight?'

'Fine,' I mumbled.

'Dr. Wilson will want you to bring the X-rays for an appointment here at nine.'

'Okay.' I was numb. I'd been given this reprieve of six years and I felt cheated not to have more. I wanted *so many* more.

Twice now, my father had been my strength, but this time he was gone and I was alone. Mom was incapable and Margaret would be furious when she heard this. I couldn't help believing that my sister would find some way to blame me for the return of my tumor. She'd say my need for sympathy had encouraged its growth. I almost groaned as I imagined her reaction.

'Bad news?' Brad asked when I replaced the receiver.

I hadn't noticed he was no longer in the back room. The coffee had obviously finished brewing because he held a mug in his hand.

'No,' I lied. 'But unfortunately I won't be able to make dinner on Friday.'

'Everything's all right, isn't it?'

'Of course.' How I managed to smile I'll never know, but I did, gazing up at him with a look worthy of an acting award.

Brad left soon afterward and if he suspected anything was wrong, he didn't let on. I'd give it an hour or two, then phone him on his cell and make sure he understood that our relationship was over. I knew I was taking the coward's way out, but I didn't want to argue about it or discuss the details with him. I didn't want to hold out false hope or have it held out to me. Experience is the best teacher. I would make it easy on Brad and save him the trouble later.

Just when I'd begun to feel that I had a real chance at life, it was being snatched away from me – again. I knew this routine, having lived it. The tests come back with questionable results. A consultation is followed by even more tests, extensive ones that require an overnight stay in the hospital.

Then the prognosis is delivered by a grim-faced Dr. Wilson, who would squeeze my hand before he left the hospital room.

I'd always wondered what that little gesture was supposed to mean. At first I thought Dr. Wilson was telling me to be brave. To fight the good fight, to give this battle my all. Now I know differently. He was telling me how sorry he was. He's only human, and there's only so much he can do.

As soon as I could, I'd break all ties with Brad. Someday he'd understand and while he might not thank me now, I knew he would later.

CHAPTER 35

CAROL GIRARD

It'd been a week since Carol's miscarriage. Doug slept soundly beside her, but she was wide awake. Staring at the digital display on the clock radio, she saw that it was 3:27 a.m. Knowing it would be impossible to fall back asleep, she stole quietly out of bed. Walking blindly in the dark, she made her way into the silent living room.

All her lost dreams, all her and Doug's abandoned plans for the future, fell upon her like a collapsing building. There would be no baby. She wouldn't cuddle an infant in her arms or know the joy of nursing her own baby at her breast.

An entire seven days had passed since the miscarriage and, other than that first dreadful night, Carol hadn't stepped foot inside the baby's nursery. She couldn't; it was just too painful. The door had remained closed, and she was sure Doug hadn't gone in there, either.

Over dinner last evening, he'd suggested they call the department store and arrange to have the baby furniture returned. They had no reason to keep it, and while she knew her husband was only being practical, it felt as if he'd plunged a knife straight through her heart.

This couldn't be happening. Not to them. They were so much in love and they were good people.

Everyone who knew them said they'd make wonderful parents.

Carol had hoped this gut-wrenching agony would lessen with time. It'd only been a week, but the ache, the emptiness inside her, hadn't even begun to dissipate. If anything, it'd grown worse. The only solace she'd found had been with her online support friends. They understood and had wept with her.

Leaning her head back and closing her eyes, Carol clamped her arms around her middle and started to rock in grief and pain and loss.

It wasn't right. It just wasn't right. Rick, her irresponsible, reckless, immature brother, was able to father children he didn't want with a woman he didn't love. Where was the fairness in that? Where was the justice? That poor baby... Neither parent seemed to care.

Carol's eyes flew open. A tingling sensation ran up and down her arms. Rick! Carol bolted off the sofa and hurried back into the bedroom. Intent on waking her husband, she leaped onto the bed.

'Doug, wake up!' she cried, kneeling over him.

Her husband ignored her and rolled onto his side.

'Doug!' she shouted, giddy with relief and joy. Hope could be a powerful drug and at the moment she was infused with it. 'Doug, I have to talk to you.' She shook him urgently.

'Carol,' her husband protested, peering at the clock with one eye, 'it's the middle of the night!'

'I know ... I know.' On her knees, she bent over him and kissed his neck. 'You have to wake up.'

'Why?' he groaned.

'Because I have something very important to tell you.'

With reluctance marking every movement, Doug rolled onto his back and rubbed his face. He blinked and stared up at her, then frowned. 'Is there a reason you're smiling?'

She nodded, and leaning forward again, she hugged her husband.

'What happened?' Doug asked.

'I was sitting in the living room just now.' She stretched out her arm, her gestures wild with energy. 'I was feeling so awful and thinking how unfair life is. I was so sure we'd have a baby and we didn't and ... and then I realized something and I had to wake you.'

Doug struggled into a sitting position so they were eye to eye.

'There's going to be another baby for us,' she whispered.

'Hold on.' Doug shook his head. 'You lost me.' He frowned as he studied her. 'Are you talking about adoption?'

This was a familiar subject and with so few infants available, they knew their chances weren't good. 'Not just any baby. I'm talking about adopting Rick's baby.'

'Your brother?'

She laughed. 'Do you know any other Rick?'

'No, but he isn't the one who's pregnant.'

'I know, Lisa is. Or was it Kim? I don't remember and really it doesn't matter. Don't you see? God meant for that baby to be ours.'

Doug wasn't following her plan or if he was, he didn't feel nearly as enthusiastic. He held her gaze and said gently, 'Sweetheart, you're not thinking straight.'

'I am,' Carol insisted. 'It makes perfect sense. Can't you see? My brother has fathered a child he doesn't want. He told me he has no intention of marrying the mother. This pregnancy was a shock to Lisa, too – or Kim. Whoever she is. She certainly wasn't anticipating a child as a result of their affair. Rick told me himself she was using birth control.'

'Yes, but–'

'I know it all sounds very sudden, but I honestly feel this baby was no accident. This is *our* baby.'

Doug's sigh echoed through the bedroom. 'Honey...'

'The baby's related to me. It won't be like adopting a stranger's child.'

'And you think Rick will agree to this?' Clearly Doug had his doubts.

'Agree?' she repeated, laughing again. 'I think he'd leap at the chance to escape child support payments. Furthermore, I want to assure him that neither one of us will ever tell Ellie that this baby is his biological child. We'd give him our word on that, wouldn't we?'

'Yes, sure.'

'If he ever gets back together with Ellie, he can rest assured that our lips are sealed.'

'What about the baby's mother?' he asked. 'She has some say in this.'

'I've been thinking about that,' Carol said. 'She's going to have to take several weeks off work and we should be willing to compensate her for any lost wages.'

Doug lifted his shoulders in a halfhearted shrug. 'I suppose we could make that offer.'

'I could go back to work to help pay for whatever she wants.'

'That isn't a good idea.'

'Why not?' Carol protested. Already he was objecting to her plans and it was crucial that he feel as certain about all of this as she did.

'You can't go back to work for just a few months and then quit again. If you do return to the brokerage, it has to be with the understanding that you only intend to work a set amount of time.'

He was right, but that didn't thwart her hopes – or her plans. 'I'm willing to do whatever it takes to make this adoption work. Just promise you'll support me.'

'Honey, you know I will.'

'This baby is ours. I can feel it in my heart.' Needing to convince him, she lifted his hand and held it.

Doug closed his eyes and she couldn't tell what he was thinking. He was afraid – she was, too – but the certainty that this was how things were meant to be overshadowed her fears.

'You're afraid we're setting ourselves up for disappointment, aren't you?'

Doug nodded. 'I hate to see you put yourself through this. What if it's another dead end?'

'I'm the one who should be worrying about that, don't you think?' Despite Doug's concern, she was convinced her brother would like the idea.

'Should I call Rick, or do you want to do it?' Doug asked.

Joyfully, Carol tossed her arms around her husband's neck. 'I'll phone him first thing in the morning and explain everything.' She still hadn't heard from Rick, not since that evening he'd told her about the pregnancy. By now, he would have received from her parents the devastating report of the miscarriage. Carol realized he purposely hadn't called or written her. He wouldn't know what to say and it was easier to ignore her pain. Her brother tended to take the route of least resistance, which was something she hadn't learned about him until recently.

'Can I go back to sleep now?' Doug asked and without waiting for a response, he slid down and pulled the sheet and comforter up to his ears.

Carol felt herself slip from her alert, energetic state into sudden tiredness. She got under the covers, too, burying her head in the pillow. Doug was on his side and she cuddled against him spoon-fashion, draping her arm over his waist.

Tired though she was, her head swam with thoughts of this child and what the adoption would bring to their lives. The old proverb was right: God never closes a door without opening a window. That window was wide open. She'd just had to stand in front of it for a few moments to feel the winds of change. She finally understood what should have been obvious all along.

CHAPTER 36

ALIX TOWNSEND

Alix dumped her dirty T-shirts into the washing machine, added soap and inserted quarters into the proper slots. She had enough shirts from rock bands and concerts to last her a full two weeks. With the old-lady underwear Jacqueline had insisted on buying her, Alix now had the same number of panties as she did T-shirts.

To save money, Alix and Laurel combined their dirty clothes and took turns hauling the bags down to the Laundromat. It was Alix's turn to deal with the laundry and she hated it, which was one reason she went there early Monday morning. She'd feel like a success if one day she was rich enough to afford her own washer and dryer.

Sitting on the hard plastic chair, she reached for a magazine. The date on the issue of *People* was Christmas a year ago and Alix set it aside once she realized she'd read it on her previous visit. In fact, she'd read everything the Laundromat had to offer.

Crossing her arms, she stretched out her legs and closed her eyes. She smiled as she thought about Jacqueline. Her friend meant well, but there was no way in hell Alix was going to try on a knit dress. One look at the price tag and she'd nearly passed out. That dress and sweater combination cost over a thousand bucks. A thousand bucks for a dress? That was crazy!

Her experience at the hairdresser's had been even worse. The French woman with the heavy accent refused to listen to anything Alix said. She had her own ideas of what needed to be done and simply dismissed Alix's instructions. By the time Desiree, or whatever her name was, had finished, Alix was ready to scream. To be fair, her hair did look fairly decent – if she'd wanted to resemble that Brady Bunch guy. Alix had needed a week to get it styled the way she liked it after Desiree had snipped off so much with those fancy scissors.

Alix didn't mean to sound unappreciative; Jacqueline had wanted to do something nice for her, and Alix was grateful, especially since her friend was footing the bill. But Jacqueline's efforts had backfired. She just didn't understand Alix's taste, and Alix wasn't letting the other woman get that close to her again.

On a brighter note, Carol was back at A Good Yarn this past Friday and – surprisingly – in a great mood. Everyone had been worried about her after the news of her miscarriage. Alix wasn't sure what, if anything, to say. She wanted Carol to know she was sorry, but at the same time she didn't want to bring up a painful subject in case Carol wasn't ready to talk about it. Jacqueline and Lydia obviously felt the same way.

Then Carol had arrived for class as cheerful as ever, and Alix was stunned. Everyone was. Carol seemed convinced that she and Doug would be able to adopt a baby. Alix was full of questions, but when the others didn't ask anything, she took

301

the hint and didn't either. Carol hadn't provided any details, so they all pretended everything was fine. Alix worried that Carol was in denial or caught up in some kind of wish-fulfillment fantasy. She tried to be encouraging, but frankly she was concerned.

Carol wasn't the only one in the group Alix was concerned about. Something was definitely wrong with Lydia. She just wasn't herself, acting subdued and withdrawn, walking around in a fog. Jacqueline had noticed it, too. At first Alix assumed Lydia was on the outs with the delivery guy she'd been so keen on all summer. That could be it, but she was doubtful. When questioned, Lydia claimed everything was fine, but Alix didn't need a psychic to see that things were definitely off kilter.

And Laurel... Laurel was even worse than before. Having a roommate was a mistake, but they were stuck with each other. For the past three months Laurel had been irritable and short-tempered. Thinking she was being helpful, Alix gave her a tabloid with big headlines about a miracle diet. Laurel had hurled it back at Alix, hitting her in the face. Alix had avoided her roommate ever since. It was easier now that Laurel wasn't working at the video store. She'd quit the week before and taken a job at a day care center as an assistant, which meant she was basically a baby-sitter and a cleaner, wiping up spilled juice and putting away Lego blocks. She hadn't taken courses or anything. But Laurel didn't seem to like that job any better.

The washing machine buzzed, and Alix got up

from the chair and dumped the clean clothes into the plastic basket. She was ready to bring the load to the dryer, but when she turned around she nearly bumped into Jordan Turner.

She hadn't seen Jordan since their disagreement, and after making a fool of herself she didn't expect a second chance with him. The only reason she'd let Jacqueline give her a fashion makeover was in the hopes that Jordan would notice the difference, that it might give him an excuse to talk to her. She should've known what to expect. Everything she'd ever done to improve her life had ended in this same predictable way.

'Hi-i,' she stammered.

'I thought that was you.' He studied her hair. 'I like the new style. Nice color.'

'You do?' Alix couldn't make her heart stop hammering like one of those staple guns the construction guys used. 'This is my natural color. Well, almost, from what I remember.' Until Jordan's comment, she'd always viewed her hair as mousy brown. He made her feel beautiful, and special.

'I guess we should talk,' he said.

She shrugged, too nervous to speak.

'Have you got a minute?'

'I guess.' She deliberately walked over to the huge wall dryer and dumped her load inside. After adding the coins, she waited a moment to be sure the dryer had started to tumble before joining him.

He sat at the table used to fold clothes. It was early in the day and the Laundromat wasn't busy yet. By ten it would fill up. Alix preferred to avoid

303

the more crowded times, when kids ran around out of control and people squabbled over whose turn it was for the dryers.

She lowered her head, struggling to find the words to apologize.

'I heard what you did,' Jordan said.

Alix frowned as she tried to figure out what he meant.

'Lori told me you got her out of a drug house.'

'Oh.' Alix had nearly forgotten that. 'Yeah, well, she wanted out but didn't want to admit it.'

'Lori's a troubled kid.'

'Who isn't?' She didn't mean to sound flippant, but it was an honest response. All teenagers seemed to go through a period when they were convinced the world was out to get them. The only defense available was to lash back. Her own rebellion had led her down several dark paths, and in retrospect, she wished there'd been someone in her life who would've taken *her* out of a drug house.

'Lori asked me to tell you she's grateful for what you did.'

That wasn't the way Alix remembered it

'I'm grateful, too,' Jordan said.

She nodded dismissively. 'I knew Lori didn't belong in that house with those men.'

'Neither did you,' Jordan said, holding her gaze.

'I know that.'

Jordan refused to release her eyes. 'Are drugs a problem?'

That made her angry, and she would have snapped back a retort, but she swallowed her outrage. It was a fair question, since she'd voluntarily walked into a drug house. 'Not anymore. I've used in the past, but these days I don't.'

He nodded, taking her word for it.

'I suppose I should apologize,' she said in as offhand a manner as she could. 'You're right, I was jealous.' Seeing Jordan standing in the church with that perfect all American girl had nearly tripped her up. She had no right to feel the things she did, but that didn't seem to matter. In her heart she viewed Jordan as hers. The red-hot suspicions that burned through her were too consuming to ignore, so she'd reverted to a time and place she'd sworn never to visit again.

It wasn't Lori who should be grateful, but Alix. The girl's danger had brought her back.

'Apology accepted.' Jordan grinned at her.

Alix felt as if her heart was melting. She smiled back.

'Friends?'

'Friends,' she agreed, happy and a bit melancholy at the same time. Did this mean she couldn't be more than his friend?

Jordan reached across the table and squeezed her fingers. 'I've missed you.'

For a few seconds, she could hardly catch her breath. He'd missed her! 'I'm knitting you a sweater,' she whispered.

'You are?'

Alix cursed the day she'd inherited this pattern from Carol. It'd been causing her problems from the moment she'd started. For a while she'd stopped working on it, but she'd begun again, hoping to feel close to Jordan. She'd also supposed it might give her an excuse to contact him.

She'd finished the baby blanket and showed it to her social worker; now all she had to do was deliver it to the appropriate agency.

'You shouldn't be jealous, you know.'

Alix slid her gaze to his.

'There's no one else.'

She swallowed tightly. 'Oh.'

His fingers tightened around hers. 'Do you remember the day you brought cupcakes to class for your birthday?'

Alix wasn't likely to forget. Her mother wasn't much of a homemaker so Alix had made them herself. From scratch, too, not from a mix.

'I baked those.' She was surprised that he'd remembered.

'You gave me two.'

She dropped her eyes. 'Yeah, I know. If I had a decent oven I'd bake you a whole batch right now.'

'Do you like to bake?'

Alix nodded. It was her dream to attend a cooking school and be the kind of chef who prepared fancy dinners at places like the ones Jacqueline and her husband frequented. Or maybe one day she'd have her own catering business. She didn't talk about this often. Over the years she'd worked in a few restaurants and she loved the craziness in the kitchen. She'd tried to get on at Annie's but the video store had offered her a job first.

'Do you have plans for Saturday night?' Jordan's thumb stroked the back of her hand.

'Not really.'

'Would you like to go to dinner with me?'

'Annie's Café?' A meal there was as close to

restaurant dining as she got.

'Not this time. How about a real three-course dinner at a fish and steak house?'

That sounded like a dress-and-panty-hose place. But the thought of turning him down didn't so much as enter her mind. Maybe, just maybe, Jacqueline would be willing to give her a second chance at a fashion makeover.

It wouldn't hurt to ask.

CHAPTER 37

'In knitting, as in everything else, you learn as much from your mistakes as you do from your successes.'

–Pam Allen, Editor, Interweave Press

LYDIA HOFFMAN

I suppose it sounds melodramatic to say I felt my life was over. Still, that's exactly what I believed as I lay in the hospital bed with the sterile scents of rubbing alcohol and antiseptic wafting around me. I've always detested the smell of hospitals. For someone who's spent as much time in them as I have, you might think I would've grown accustomed to it by now. I haven't, though. The X-rays revealed what I'd feared most. Another tumor had formed. If there was anything to be grateful for, it was that this one was accessible through my sinus cavity, without the necessity of drilling into my skull.

The tumor was gone now and the biopsy had been completed. Unfortunately the results were inconclusive, and a tissue sample had been sent out for a second opinion. With my medical history no one was willing to take chances.

Margaret's bouquet of carnations sat on the table at my bedside and cheered me. It was the first time my sister had ever sent me flowers. Our relationship was changing, but even her gesture of support wasn't enough to get me through this.

In my heart I knew what was coming and I couldn't bear it. Not again. Everything within me wanted to scream how unfair this was. Like a little girl, I wanted to jump up and down and throw a temper tantrum.

Dad's not here to help me anymore, and the sense of abandonment I experienced was overwhelming. Irrational as it might seem, I was furious with my father for dying. I'm so angry. Angry with Dad. Angry with God. Angry at the world.

Having spent most of two days drugged for the surgery, I now found the escape of sleep unavailable. Every time I closed my eyes, all I saw was Brad's face. All I heard was his voice. What kept coming to mind was the last confrontation we had, that day on the phone, when I told him I didn't want to see him again. I made it as plain as I could that I was not interested in continuing our relationship.

He didn't understand, of course, that I was doing him a favor and seemed bent on arguing, trying to change my mind. I regret the things I said, but I couldn't tell him the truth, so I'd led him to believe my interests lay elsewhere.

I knew Margaret strongly disapproved of my breaking up with Brad. However, I told her this is my life and I make my own decisions. That shut her up, but I could tell she was furious I can deal with her displeasure, though. I have dealt with it nearly all of our lives.

I don't think she's blamed me for the return of the cancer. I've tried to be grateful for that one small bit of compassion on my sister's part. When I told her the news, she grew very solemn and told me how sorry she was.

As if my thoughts had conjured her up, Margaret stood in the doorway to my room. 'I see the flowers arrived,' she said, looking ill-at-ease. She glanced around warily, as if she half expected an orderly to grab her, throw her on a gurney and wheel her off for experimental surgery.

'The flowers are very nice,' I told her. 'It was a thoughtful thing to do.'

'So,' she said, tentatively stepping closer to the bed. 'How did the tests go?'

I shrugged because there wasn't anything to say. 'About the same as last time.'

Margaret's eyebrows rose in sympathy. 'That bad?'

I made a genuine effort to smile, but the best I could manage was a grimace.

'Mom wanted to come...'

I nodded. My mother didn't know the reason I'd been admitted, and I wanted to keep it that way. On reflection, if there's anything positive about my father's death, it's that he went quickly.

Mom wouldn't have been able to cope with a long illness.

I suspect Margaret's a lot like our mother, and her willingness to visit me now revealed how much our relationship had evolved over the past few months.

Once she figured it was safe to relax, Margaret pulled the visitor's chair to the side of my bed.

'I'm glad you came,' I told her, 'because there are a few things I want to discuss.'

It was as if she hadn't heard me. 'I don't think now is a good time...'

'Please.' The tone of my voice seemed to reach her, even if my words didn't.

Resigned, Margaret sighed heavily. 'All right, what is it?'

'I've been thinking about what will happen to A Good Yarn.'

Margaret's expression was painful. 'I've given that some thought myself. You know I don't knit, but I'd be willing to step in and–'

'I wouldn't ask you to do that.' Asking my sister to take over my business hadn't occurred to me.

'It's a possibility. Mom and I could trade days.'

Her generosity touched me deeply, and for the first time since I'd entered the hospital, I felt tears clogging my throat and filling my eyes. 'I can't believe you'd be willing to do that.'

Margaret stared at me in surprise. 'You're my sister. I'd do anything I could to help you, including...' She hesitated, drew in a deep breath and looked over her shoulder. 'We can talk about this later, all right? Nothing's for sure, so why don't we cross that bridge once we get to it.'

'But—'

'You have another visitor.'

I imagined one of my nieces had come with her and looked expectantly toward the door. I'd wanted to settle the future of my yarn shop immediately, but it made sense to wait until Dr. Wilson delivered his verdict. I hadn't believed I'd survive the second bout of cancer, and I had no illusions about the third. The fight had gone out of me and I was willing to accept my fate.

The awful truth, what I could never say aloud to Margaret or my mother, is that I preferred death over treatment. I felt I couldn't do this again, couldn't endure the agony of chemotherapy. I was an adult and capable of making my own decision. Well, I'd made it. I'd decided to refuse treatment and let the cancer take its course. The only person I could discuss this with was Dr. Wilson, and I wouldn't see him until he'd had a chance to analyze the test results.

'Give me a moment,' Margaret said. She rose from the chair and disappeared into the hallway outside my room.

I was in for a shock when she returned. The visitor she brought in with her wasn't Julie or Hailey, but Brad. Everything inside me wanted to scream at him to leave and for Margaret to go with him. I couldn't stand it. One look at the tender concern on Brad's face, and I reacted like a juvenile, covering my face with both hands. Then, to my horror, I unceremoniously burst into tears.

I felt Brad's arms come around my shoulders. 'You could have told me, you know.'

I dropped my hands and refused to look at him or speak. My fury was focused on my meddling sister. 'How could you?' I shouted at her. 'How could you?'

'How could *you?*' she shouted right back. It was as though the room had developed an echo.

Brad interrupted our shouting match. He spoke in a strong, determined voice. 'If you'd told me what was wrong we could have talked it out, Lydia.'

'Go away.' I turned to look him straight in the face, although my heart was breaking.

He shook his head. 'Sorry, that isn't going to happen.'

'You don't have any choice.'

'I'm not letting you drive me away.'

'Don't you get it?' I cried, and nearly choked on the words. 'There's no future with me.'

Eyes soft, he reached for my hand. 'But there's today and tomorrow and the next day.'

I tilted my chin toward the ceiling. I didn't understand why everyone had to make this so difficult.

'Lydia,' Margaret said. 'Would you stop feeling so damned sorry for yourself and get a grip?'

I didn't expect anything different from my sister. She wasn't the one who'd gone through this nightmare. She wasn't the one who'd suffered weeks of chemotherapy and radiation treatments. My sister acted as though my cancer was a minor inconvenience. As though I should just get over it and deal with life.

'I can't tell you what the future holds,' Brad said, his gaze earnest, 'but I can tell you that whatever happens, I intend to be here, for you and with you.'

I'd heard that before, too. Same words, different year. But after two days of being poked and prodded, I was in no state of mind for an argument. 'Please, just leave... I can't deal with this now.'

Margaret and Brad exchanged glances. They didn't seem to believe me. Nor did they care what I wanted or needed, because they utterly ignored my request. They gave me no option, so I slammed my hand on the bell to call the nurse.

'What do you need?' A tinny voice rang through the intercom.

'Peace,' I cried. 'I need peace and quiet and these people refuse to leave.'

Margaret pinched her lips together and slowly shook her head. And from the grim frown on Brad's face, it would take the Seventh Cavalry – or one annoyed nurse – to make him vacate my room. I slid down in the bed and rolled over, offering him my back.

'We haven't finished our discussion,' he said.

I didn't answer him. As far as I was concerned, I'd already told him everything I intended to. Nothing he said was going to change my mind.

I heard footsteps enter the room.

'We were just leaving,' Margaret told the nurse.

I forced myself not to roll over and watch my sister and Brad walk out.

Perhaps I had a bigger problem than cancer. I'd just thrown out the only two people in the world who'd come to offer me their love and support.

CHAPTER 38

CAROL GIRARD

Carol and Doug arrived at the fondue restaurant in the Seattle University district before Rick. They were already seated and had each ordered a glass of chardonnay while they waited for her brother and possibly Lisa.

It had taken Carol several days to reach him. Their conversation had been short. She'd invited Rick to dinner and asked him to bring Lisa, too, if she was available. After setting the date and time, he'd promised to see if Lisa could come.

'Do you think she'll be with him?' Carol asked, clutching her husband's arm. This night could be one of the most important in their married life.

Before Doug had an opportunity to answer, Carol saw the hostess leading her brother to the table. He was alone, but perhaps that was for the best. After talking the matter over, she and Doug had decided her brother could present their idea to Lisa. She might have found it awkward to discuss such a private matter with complete strangers.

Carol had intended to spend the evening socializing with Rick – or the couple if Lisa showed up – and then afterward invite them to the apartment, where they'd make their suggestion. Doug would do the talking, they'd agreed, and that would give

Carol a chance to gauge Rick's feelings.

'Here you are,' Rick said. He kissed Carol's cheek before taking a seat across from them. His eyes avoided hers. 'Mom told me about the miscarriage. I'm so sorry.'

'Thank you.'

Their drinks came then, providing a distraction. Rick ordered a double whiskey. 'I'm not flying until tomorrow night,' he explained.

'How's everything in your life?' Doug asked as soon as the waitress had taken their dinner order.

'Hunky dory,' Rick said flippantly.

Carol reached for her husband's hand beneath the table. 'How's Lisa?'

'Fine, I guess. I haven't talked to her in a week or so.'

So he hadn't bothered to extend the dinner invitation, after all. Well, she supposed it didn't matter.

'You certainly seem to be in good spirits.' Rick directed the comment at Carol. 'I expected you to be all depressed. Mom said you'd taken the miscarriage really hard.'

She grimaced. 'I did, but life goes on.'

His drink arrived and Rick raised the ice-filled tumbler. 'To life,' he said. Carol and Doug raised their glasses in response but didn't echo his words.

'Actually, you and Lisa have a great deal to do with the improvement in my mood,' Carol ventured. Doug cast her a warning glance. She knew he was right. This wasn't the time to bring up the reason for their dinner invitation.

'Me?' Her brother looked surprised.

Thankfully their server arrived with the first

315

course of their meal, saving Carol from answering. The waitress lit the fondue burner and set a bowl filled with a hot cheese mixture on top. She added a variety of items to dip, including bread, sliced vegetables and fresh apples and pears.

Carol's appetite had increased over the last week, but since the miscarriage she'd lost enough weight that many of her clothes no longer fit properly. For that evening out, she'd been forced to change her outfit three times. Everything in her closet hung on her like a tent.

'We're thinking of adoption,' Carol announced. She simply couldn't resist saying something, despite Doug's caution.

Rick nodded as if he approved. 'Good idea.'

'We thought so,' Carol murmured and rubbed her leg against Doug's. Rick was so dense he hadn't picked up on what should've been obvious.

'I talked to Ellie last week,' her brother said.

'How did it go?'

'She was cordial but I could tell that beneath all the politeness, she was pleased to hear from me. I asked her out to dinner next week.'

'Is she going?'

Rick shook his head. 'I should've waited until I was back in Juneau. It's much harder to turn me down in person.'

'What's happening with Lisa?' Carol asked, hoping for information about the pregnant flight attendant.

'We decided to go our separate ways. We were never much of an item.'

Carol's heart fell. 'But you do intend to keep seeing her, don't you?'

Her brother looked up, holding a piece of bread dripping with cheese over the fondue pot. 'Oh, sure, that's unavoidable with the two of us working the same flights. She's a sweetheart and what happened is unfortunate. I have to say she's handled it well.'

Carol sighed with relief. 'You know, sometimes what seems like an accident isn't one at all.'

'I guess.' Rick reached for another piece of bread. 'Damn, this is good. Did either of you notice what kind of cheese this is?'

'Can't say that I did,' Doug said.

Carol noticed a sharpness in her husband's voice and glanced over to find him frowning. She wanted to ask what was wrong, but couldn't. Now that the subject of Lisa had been introduced, Carol couldn't bear to wait another moment.

'I'm sure you know how dreadful it was when I miscarried,' she said, studying her brother intently.

Rick sipped his drink, and then speared a slice of pear. 'That was really bummer news.'

'One night last week, just before dawn, I was sitting in the dark thinking about all of this. I felt like a complete failure.'

'How so?'

'I'd failed myself. I'd failed Doug. You and I both know what a wonderful father he'd be. And I knew how disappointed Mom and Dad would be. They're really looking forward to becoming grandparents. I felt as if my whole world had collapsed.'

Rick glanced at her. 'Why would you feel like that?'

It would take too long to explain. 'A woman feels those kinds of emotions when she can't carry a pregnancy to term.'

Rick's gaze slid to Doug and he winked. 'Women. Can't live with 'em, can't understand 'em, but they sure as hell make life interesting, don't they?'

Doug didn't bother to respond.

'The reason I bring this up now–'

'Carol.' Doug placed his hand over hers. 'Let's enjoy our dinner.'

She nodded, but nearly had to bite her tongue to keep from prodding her brother with more questions about Lisa. Without the double whiskey – in fact, Rick was now on his second – he might have picked up on what she was trying to say.

The meal seemed to take forever. Any other night, Carol would have savored this time with her two favorite men in the world. Following the appetizer of cheese was the main course with shrimp and lobster cooked in a bubbling white wine sauce. When dessert finally arrived, strawberries and pound cake dipped in rich chocolate, Carol was so tense she couldn't wait another minute.

'Would you like to come to our house for a nightcap?' Doug asked.

Rick glanced at his watch. 'I'd better not.'

'But it's important,' Carol blurted out. 'Doug and I need to talk to you.'

Rick gave her a surprised look. 'About what?'

Carol refused to let the evening end without broaching the subject of the adoption. 'Doug and

318

I want to ask about you and Lisa.'

Rick's forehead creased in a frown. 'I thought I told you we split up.'

'Yes, I know, but this doesn't have anything to do with you as a couple. Doug and I–' she paused and looked at her husband briefly before returning her gaze to Rick '–we want to ask about the baby.'

'What baby?' Her brother seemed genuinely puzzled.

Carol leaned closer to him. 'Lisa's pregnant, right?'

'Was pregnant, you mean.'

Carol felt as if the chair had been yanked out from under her. 'She miscarried?'

Rick shook his head. 'She and I talked about this, you know. We both agreed there wasn't any other option. Neither of us had planned on this pregnancy.'

'Yes, but–'

'All I could think was what Ellie would say if she found out, and then there's eighteen bloody years of child support. A kid isn't a responsibility I take lightly.'

'She had an abortion.' Carol felt needles of pain move up and down her arms.

'Like I said, Lisa and I discussed it. It's her body, and the choice was hers.'

'But you told her you didn't want the baby!'

'Damn straight. I don't need that kind of complication in my life.'

'But Doug and I wanted to adopt the baby!'

'Honey.' Doug's gentle voice broke through the fog of dismay and disbelief. 'It isn't going to

319

happen. Let go of it.'

After the first jolt of shock she felt nothing. No anger, no outrage, no disappointment. Nothing. They might have been discussing the weather for all the emotion she experienced.

'I'm sorry,' Rick said, 'but even if we'd known that, I don't think we would've made any other choice.'

'Come on, honey, I think it's time we left.' Doug helped her to her feet and if she wasn't revealing any distress, he was.

'You were making a big assumption, weren't you?' Rick demanded. 'This is my life. It isn't up to me to solve your problems for you.'

'Right,' Doug said. 'This is our problem.'

Rick downed the last of his drink. 'No need to get upset about it. These things happen.'

'Right.' Doug's arm came around Carol.

'Thanks for dinner, you two. We'll have to get together again soon.' Rick continued to sit at the table, staring blankly into space.

CHAPTER 39

ALIX TOWNSEND

Jacqueline picked up Alix outside her apartment building promptly at ten on Saturday morning. During the knitting session on Friday afternoon, Alix had casually mentioned her dinner date with Jordan in a fancy restaurant. Jacqueline had leaped upon it, eager for another opportunity to prove herself.

'I know what I did wrong,' Jacqueline insisted. 'Give me a second chance and you won't be sorry.'

Alix hoped that was true. When Jacqueline's Mercedes pulled up to the curb, Alix stepped forward and opened the passenger door. 'You're sure about this?'

'Positive. Now get in, we're on a schedule.'

Three months ago if anyone had told Alix she'd be friends with this society broad, Alix would have laughed outright. She and Jacqueline still sniped at each other, but now it was mostly for show. They had a reputation to live up to, and Alix wasn't going to let it slide. Apparently Jacqueline shared her feelings.

Alix sat in the car and waited, wondering why Jacqueline hadn't pulled onto the street.

'Seat belt,' the older woman said sternly.

Grumbling under her breath, Alix reached for the seat belt and clicked it in place.

'What?' Jacqueline snapped.

'Don't be so prissy.'

'I'm not. By the way, we're going to my daughter-in-law's house.'

'Tammie Lee's?' This was a switch. Alix had noticed a softening in Jacqueline not only toward her, but her daughter-in-law too. When Alix had first signed up for the knitting classes, Jacqueline had nothing good to say about the woman who'd married her precious son. That seemed to have changed, at least a little.

'Tammie Lee's young and trendy. That's the

321

look you're after, isn't it?'

'It's better than having you dress me like Barbara Bush.'

To Alix's surprise, Jacqueline laughed. 'Don't put down our former First Ladies. I changed the spelling of my name in the fifth grade because of Jacqueline Kennedy.'

'My mother says she spelled my name with an I on purpose,' Alix confessed, 'but I don't think it was for any good reason. The fact is, she was probably drunk when she made out the birth certificate and accidentally misspelled it.' Alix didn't know if that was true or not, but it was certainly possible.

They chatted on the ride to Tammie Lee's, mostly about which fork to use first in a fancy restaurant and other rules of etiquette Jacqueline felt it was essential Alix know. They also discussed Lydia and wondered why her sister had been in the shop so much lately. Jacqueline had phoned to ask, and Alix had stopped by a couple of times. All Margaret would say was that Lydia was under the weather. Friday's knitting session had been rather unsatisfactory without their teacher and friend, but no one complained openly. Alix just hoped Lydia would be back the following week and so did Jacqueline.

They drove for a good twenty minutes before Jacqueline pulled into the driveway of what looked like a mansion. The house was modern with a big front yard and lots of flowers. The white pillars in front reminded her of pictures she'd once seen in a magazine. Super cool.

No sooner had Jacqueline turned off the engine

than the front door opened and a girl who didn't seem to be any older than Alix stepped outside. Tammie Lee looked like she was ready to pop at any moment and wore shorts, a maternity top and no shoes. She had a smile as big as any Alix had ever seen and her eyes sparkled with welcome.

'You're right on time.' Tammie Lee held open the screen door. 'I've been so eager for you to get here.'

Alix loved listening to her talk. Tammie Lee had the softest, sweetest voice she'd ever heard.

Tammie Lee hugged Jacqueline as if it'd been a year of Sundays since she'd last seen her mother-in-law. 'And you must be Alix. Jacqueline didn't tell me what a beauty you are. Why, this is going to be easier than frying up griddle cakes. You must come in and let me take a good look at you.' Before Alix could object, not that she would have, Tammie Lee had taken her arm and led her into the house.

'Where's Paul?' Jacqueline asked.

'Golfing with his daddy,' Tammie Lee said and sounded surprised that her mother-in-law didn't know.

Alix noticed a flicker of something in the older woman's eyes. For an instant it looked like pain, but Alix was sure she must be wrong.

'I've got everything set up in the spare bedroom,' Tammie Lee said. 'I took out a bunch of my clothes for Alix to try on. That way, when we find something she likes, we'll know where to shop.'

'Good idea,' Alix said, although she couldn't

imagine wearing any style this southern belle would.

True to her word, Tammie Lee had laid an assortment of clothes on the bed in the guest room. At first glance Alix's heart fell. There seemed to be nothing but satin, lace and girly items.

'You sort through what's on the bed and I'll get us all some iced tea.'

'With mint,' Jacqueline added as she sat down.

'Of course,' Tammie Lee said as she rushed from the room.

'She adds mint to everything,' Jaqueline said in a disparaging whisper.

Alix glanced at her quickly – a hint of the old disapproval was back – but didn't comment. Instead she checked out a full-length jean skirt. This was workable but only if she wore a T-shirt with it and a wide leather belt. She set it to one side and reached for a frothy, lacy dress, which she immediately rejected.

Tammie Lee stuck her head inside the door. 'Would either of you prefer a Coke?'

'I would.' Alix wasn't shy. She'd never been a real fan of iced tea.

'With or without peanuts?'

'With.' She hadn't had breakfast and a snack sounded good.

'I'll have the iced tea. Do you need any help?' Jacqueline asked.

'Oh, heavens, no.' Once again Tammie Lee disappeared, but it wasn't long before she returned.

She brought in a tray and placed it on the dresser. Jacqueline stood up to get her glass of iced tea and Alix watched as she removed the mint leaf, using her thumb and index finger as if she were picking out a dead bug.

Tammie Lee served the Coke in an old-fashioned soda glass. She'd apparently forgotten the peanuts, which was fine. Not until Alix reached for her Coke did she notice the peanuts floating on top. She couldn't very well object now and took a sip. The taste was interesting, a blend of salt and sweet. This was probably one of those southern traditions Jacqueline complained about so much.

'I like this,' Alix said and held up the jean skirt.

'I thought you would.'

'You can't wear jeans to a fancy restaurant,' Jacqueline objected.

'It's not the same as regular jeans,' Tammie Lee explained.

While they discussed what could be considered proper attire for a real restaurant, Alix drank her Coke, complete with floating peanuts.

An hour later, after she'd tried on several outfits, the three of them headed to the mall in two separate cars – Alix, still riding with Jacqueline. Inside one of the major department stores, Jacqueline sat and waited, while Tammie Lee carried outfit after outfit into the dressing room. Some of them Alix rejected out of hand, but a few showed real possibility. In the end, she chose a long black skirt and a white silk blouse with a swooping neckline and cuffs that buttoned at the wrist.

It was noon, and by then Alix was starved. She would've been happy with a hamburger, but Jacqueline suggested a sit-down place inside the mall. She insisted they try the delicate finger sandwiches with ultra-thin slices of cucumber. Alix ate her sandwich in two bites and had several more. She could've eaten out for a week on what Jacqueline paid for lunch. No wonder society women were so thin.

'I don't know about anyone else, but I'm exhausted,' Jacqueline said. 'I just might let you two carry on without me.'

'You go home and put your feet up,' Tammie Lee told her. 'I'll take over from here if that's okay with Alix.'

'But I do want to see Alix when you're all finished with her.'

'I'll call you myself,' Tammie Lee promised.

Left to their own devices, Tammie Lee and Alix made fast work of the remainder of their purchases, which included shoes and a silver necklace – all at Jacqueline's expense. Alix would never have guessed how much she'd like Jacqueline's daughter-in-law. Tammie Lee was fun and sweet and the nicest person she'd met in her entire life. Frankly, she didn't know what Jacqueline found so disagreeable about her.

They stopped for a Coke at a fast-food restaurant in the food court. Because she was still hungry, Alix ordered a cheeseburger and fries to go with it.

Tammie Lee took one look at her and burst into giggles. 'Make that two of everything.'

'I'm not going back to the same hairdresser.' Alix wanted that understood in case Jacqueline had forgotten her previous reaction to Ms. Desiree.

'I don't blame you,' Tammie Lee said in a whisper. 'Jacqueline wanted me to make an appointment with Desiree. So I did, shortly after Paul and I were married.'

'Did you come out looking like one of the Brady Bunch?'

'No,' she said with a silly grin, 'I looked more like Don King. Every time Paul saw me, he laughed. I thought I'd die of pure mortification.'

Their order was ready, and they found a table in the middle of the seating area.

'Tell me about you and Paul,' Alix said as she unwrapped her cheeseburger.

'Oh, Alix.' Tammie Lee gave a breathy sigh. 'I don't know where to start. I never thought I'd leave Louisiana, but it's amazing what a woman will do for love.' Her expression was dreamy. 'I discovered it didn't matter where I lived, as long as I could be with Paul. The heart takes on a will of its own, if you know what I mean?'

Alix did understand. The fact that she was in this mall was proof of that.

'If you don't object, I'll do your hair for you,' Tammie Lee offered.

'You will?'

'I might not have all the training Desiree does, but I'm fairly good. All my friends let me do their hair for proms and such.'

'Sure, if you don't mind.'

'It'll be fun.'

When Tammie Lee drove back to the house, Paul had returned from the golf course. He sat in front of the television with an empty plate in his lap and a milk glass on the end table.

'Hi, Tam,' he said and smiled at Alix. He jumped

up from his chair and took the packages from Tammie Lee's hands, kissing his wife on the cheek. 'How'd the shopping go?'

'Great. This is Alix, your mother's friend and now mine.'

'Hello, Alix.' Paul gave her the once-over, as if he wasn't sure she was for real. 'You and my mother are friends?'

'Yeah, we met in the knitting class.'

'Oh, right.' He nodded. 'I remember...'

'I'm going to do Alix's hair. She's got a hot date tonight.'

'Sure, go ahead.' His attention had already drifted back to the baseball game.

Tammie Lee was as good as her word. By the time she'd finished, Alix felt like a candidate for Homecoming Queen. Staring at her reflection in the bathroom mirror, Alix had to blink in order to believe the image was her own.

'What do you think?' Tammie Lee asked.

'I ... you made me pretty.'

Tammie Lee slowly shook her head. 'You're already lovely, Alix, but I have a feeling your Jordan knows that.'

Her heart did a little flip-flop at the way Tammie Lee said *your Jordan,* as if it was understood that the two of them were a couple.

Before long, Jacqueline arrived to give Alix her nod of approval. While Alix suspected she fell far short of the designer dress and fancy hairdo her friend would've preferred, she seemed to pass muster. Tammie Lee hadn't used anything more than a curling iron and mousse, but she'd managed to arrange Alix's plain straight hair in a natural wavy style that suited her better than anything she'd ever imagined.

After a moment, Jacqueline smiled.

'Do you think Jordan will like it?'

Jacqueline laughed delightedly. 'My dear, he's in for a real surprise.'

That evening while she waited for Jordan to pick her up at the apartment, Alix nervously paced the living room.

'Would you stop pacing,' Laurel snapped. She was parked in front of the television with a pint of cookie dough ice cream, which she ate directly from the container.

The knock on the door nearly sent Alix into a panic. She closed her eyes and although she wasn't a person who'd prayed a lot in recent years, she found a prayer on her lips now. More than anything, she wanted Jordan to see her as beautiful.

Holding her breath, she opened the door.

Jordan stood there holding a wrist corsage in a clear plastic box. His eyes widened as he stood staring at her.

'Say something,' she pleaded. 'Anything.'

'Wow,' he breathed. 'Wow, Alix, is that really you?'

'It's me.' Holding back a smile would have been impossible. 'You like it?'

'I like you,' he said and handed her the corsage.

This was the first time in her life anyone had given her flowers and nothing in the world could have pleased her more.

CHAPTER 40

'Whether I am knitting for myself or someone else, my passion for knitting enables me to express my creativity and produces a feeling of accomplishment.'
—Rita E. Greenfeder, Editor, Knit 'N Style Magazine

LYDIA HOFFMAN

Margaret decided to go with me to the meeting with Dr. Wilson at his office. He had all the test results and medical reports back now, and there seemed to be some confusion about the diagnosis.

Notoriously closemouthed, he did mention casually when I was released from the hospital that he'd asked a colleague to review the biopsy. That news, I suspect, was meant to encourage me. But in my heart, I knew the tumor was cancerous.

'Don't be such a pessimist,' Margaret mumbled as we sat in the waiting area. It was the last appointment of the day, another sure sign of my prognosis, but I didn't say any of this to Margaret.

Instead I leaned back and closed my eyes, wanting to block out the world. It was easy for my sister to suggest optimism. This wasn't *her* life, her illness, her impending death. I couldn't help wondering what her thoughts would've been had our situations been reversed. I bit back the words to remind her that she'd come running to me with her own recent scare. I was in that kind of mood right now. I could hardly keep from lashing out at the world and everyone close to me. The person who'd received the brunt of my anger, sadly, was Brad, and he was the last person who deserved it. But I refused to dwell on him or the regrets I felt whenever he crossed my mind. I'd done what I had for his own good. He would never know what it had cost me to send him away; I would carry the weight of that for the rest of my life, however short that might be.

My mother was another one I'd strived to protect. Margaret had, too. So far, we'd kept Mom in the dark. We'd concocted a story about my hospital visit having to do with a routine check-up. My mother had been all too willing to accept the lie.

Long before I was ready to confront the inevitable, Peggy came into the waiting area. This time she wasn't holding that monstrosity of a medical file in her arms. 'Dr. Wilson will see you now,' she announced.

I didn't meet her eyes, although I heard hope and encouragement in her voice. I considered Peggy a friend, but that friendship wasn't exclusive. She was wonderful to all of Dr. Wilson's patients. I realized how difficult this must be for her, too. So often, she had to silently stand by and watch Dr. Wilson's patients lose their battles with cancer. It wasn't a position I envied.

Margaret was on her feet before I'd managed to put my magazine down and pick up my purse. I

331

was certainly in no hurry to have my deepest fears confirmed.

Peggy led us into Dr. Wilson's private office. His framed degrees lined the walls; he displayed a few family photos, which were artfully arranged on a credenza. The mahogany desk was polished and uncluttered, with my file set to one side. I'd been in his private office twice before, and each time I'd been devastated by his news. I didn't expect anything different this go-round.

Dr. Wilson wasn't in the room when we arrived, but he walked in directly behind us. My sister shook hands with him after a murmured introduction.

Dr. Wilson rolled out his big, high-back leather chair and sat down. He reached for my file, which he brought to the center of the table. He paused and then...

'The cancer is back.' I didn't make it a question. The tumor was gone, but I was sure there'd be more, growing in areas not as accessible as this one had been.

'Is it?' Margaret asked and to my surprise her voice quavered slightly.

So often in our lives, I've wanted to prove to Margaret that I was right and she was wrong. Call it sibling rivalry. This time, however, I'd have given anything to be wrong.

As I'd said earlier, there was nothing to be optimistic about. The disease refused to leave my body. I opened my mouth to announce that I'd refuse treatment. I had neither the will nor the strength to face a third battle. Not without my father.

'Because of your history,' Dr. Wilson began, 'I felt it was doubly important to be certain before I made a prognosis. I had the biopsy sent to the top brain cancer specialist in the country.'

I held my breath almost afraid to hope, certain the news would devastate me.

'What did he say?' Margaret asked, slipping closer to the edge of her seat.

'She agrees with me. The tumor was benign.'

'Benign,' I repeated, wanting to be sure I'd heard him correctly. The tumor was benign.

'Yes.' Dr. Wilson smiled at me but I was too shocked to react. 'Everything's going to be all right this time, Lydia. You're cancer-free.' He stood up and walked over to an X-ray display panel on his wall. He removed two X-rays from inside an envelope and clipped them onto the lit panel. Taking out his pen, he pointed to the film. 'This is the first X-ray we took and this is the one following the surgery.'

'Are you saying I won't need radiation or chemotherapy?'

He shook his head. 'No reason for it.'

I sat up straighter.

'It's very good news, don't you think?'

I was too numb to agree with him or even nod. Dr. Wilson's voice faded as the realization slowly came. My life had been given back to me.

I'm not sure when I rose to my feet but suddenly I was standing. I covered my mouth and feared I was about to embarrass myself by bursting into tears. I noticed, to my astonishment, that Margaret was weeping. She rose and hugged me and started sobbing louder.

333

'You're going to be all right,' she kept repeating. 'Oh, Lydia, you're going to be all right.'

Dr. Wilson was explaining a new medication he'd prescribed for me and the side effects, but nothing he said made sense just then. I was too happy to care.

Margaret and I both went from open weeping to ridiculous amusement, and our reactions were almost perfectly synchronized. Our giggles must have sounded hysterical. Margaret placed the tips of her fingers against her lips and refused to look at me. She made an effort to focus on what Dr. Wilson was trying to explain. None of it mattered. All I knew was that I had my life back. My beautiful, wonderful life was my own once again.

Not until we were outside the office did I think about Brad. 'Margaret,' I said, gripping my sister by the arm as the happiness drained out of me. We stood in front of the elevator. Margaret must have heard the distress in my voice because her smile faded.

'What?'

'Brad... I was so cruel to him when all he wanted to do was help.'

Margaret was obviously struggling not to scream *I told you so* at me, but all she said was, 'Talk to him.'

I'd missed Brad dreadfully and I longed to call him, but I couldn't. He'd attempted to visit me twice more while I was hospitalized, but I'd refused to see him. He'd asked the nurse to deliver a letter to me. I knew if I read it he'd change my mind, so I'd asked her to take it away, sight unseen.

Later the nurse returned and told me Brad had been waiting for a reply and she'd been forced to tell him I wouldn't read his letter. Now it all seemed melodramatic and senseless. I might well have ruined the most promising relationship of my life.

'I can try to talk to Brad, but I don't know if he'll listen.' I wouldn't blame him if he never wanted to see me again. My one hope was that he couldn't very well ignore me when he made deliveries to my store.

Bright and early Tuesday morning, I was back in business. I can't even begin to explain the thrill it gave me to walk into my shop and turn the CLOSED sign to read OPEN. Even the noise from the construction across the street couldn't dampen my good mood.

Reality intruded with a list of instructions from Dr. Wilson. I was apparently a good candidate for this new drug treatment to prevent the growth of future tumors.

My morning was constantly busy as customers streamed into the store, all with questions as to why I'd been away for most of a week. It turns out that many of them had learned I was back – one person phoned another who called a third, and so forth. I can't even describe how gratifying that was. Margaret had done her best to be helpful, keeping the store open for part of every day, but my customers were accustomed to dealing with me.

Margaret seemed to have enjoyed working at the store. As little as three months ago, I couldn't have imagined thinking warmly of my older

335

sister. I was deeply appreciative of everything she'd done for me.

At noon, when I had my first lull of the day, I glanced anxiously out the shop windows, hoping for a glimpse of Brad. When the, big brown truck rolled to a stop in front of the floral shop, I nearly raced out the door. But the UPS driver wasn't Brad.

'Where's Brad?' I blurted out.

The replacement glanced over his shoulder at the abruptness of my question. 'Brad is no longer on this route.'

'What do you mean he's no longer on this route?' I demanded. It felt as if the sidewalk had started to buckle beneath my feet. I couldn't believe Brad would do anything as drastic as this.

'Brad's delivering in the downtown area now.'

I knew what had happened. 'He requested a transfer, didn't he?'

The UPS driver shrugged. 'I wouldn't know about that. Sorry.'

'Do you ever see him?' I asked, hoping to use the other man to relay a message.

'Not much.' He was preoccupied, and I was clearly detaining him, so I returned to my store, my steps dragging.

I knew that what I'd done to Brad was wrong. I'd badly hurt the one person who'd proved himself to me over and over. All I could do was hope it wasn't too late to make amends.

CHAPTER 41

JACQUELINE DONOVAN

'Jacqueline.'

Her name seemed to come from far away. 'Jacqueline.' It was louder this time and she recognized Reese's voice. Her eyes flew open and she stared up in the darkness to find her husband standing over her.

'What's wrong?' she asked, rubbing her eyes. Something drastic must have happened for Reese to enter her bedroom in the middle of the night

'Paul just phoned – Tammie Lee's in labor.'

'Now?'

'When did a baby ever decide to arrive at a decent hour?'

He obviously didn't expect a response and she didn't give him one. 'What did Paul say?'

'Just that he's been at the hospital since ten.'

A quick glance at her clock told her it was nearly five.

'She's close to delivery,' her husband finished.

Jacqueline didn't hesitate. She tossed aside the comforter and automatically reached for her robe.

'You actually want to go to the hospital?' Reese sounded surprised.

'Of course.' He could do as he damn well pleased and, as a matter of fact, had for the last twelve years of their marriage. But nothing he said would keep her away from the birth of her grand-daughter. Already Jacqueline had thrust her feet into her slippers and started toward her bathroom.

'I'm coming, too,' Reese announced as if he anticipated an argument.

'Do whatever you want.'

He ignored her petulant remark. 'Don't take long,' he warned. 'From what Paul said, it could be any time now.'

'I'll be ready in ten minutes.' In the best of circumstances, that was a stretch, but Jacqueline was determined to keep her word. Exactly thirteen minutes later, she met Reese who sat in the car waiting. He had the garage door open and the engine running, ready to go.

They were silent on the ride to the hospital and Jacqueline wondered if his thoughts were the same as hers. It'd been on a night such as this that he'd rushed her to the hospital to deliver Paul. Her water had broken in the middle of the night and in a panic, fearing any movement might endanger the baby, she'd clung to Reese. Her one concern was to keep the cord from tangling around the baby's neck.

In true heroic fashion, Reese had swept her into his arms, carried her to the car and driven to the hospital. Fortunately, there was virtually no traffic, since he took the corners at a speed any racecar driver might have envied. Then her hero had carried her into the hospital waiting area. Reese had stayed with her until Paul entered the world. Closing her eyes, she could still hear her son's first high-pitched wail. At the time, it had been the most glorious sound she'd ever heard.

When they arrived at the hospital, they parked quickly. Together, walking side by side, they hurried into the lobby and were directed to the birthing center on the fifth floor.

At the reception desk, Reese gave their names to the nurse, who suggested they take a seat in the waiting room. While Jacqueline sorted through the magazines, Reese went to see if he could round them up a cup of coffee.

He returned five minutes later with two steaming cups. 'It came out of a machine,' he said with a shrug.

At this point, Jacqueline didn't care as long as it was hot and contained caffeine.

They sat two chairs apart in the deserted room and sipped their tasteless coffee. Half an hour and three magazines later, Paul appeared, wearing a light-blue hospital gown. He looked tired, but his eyes smiled when he saw them.

'Tammie Lee's doing just great,' he told them. 'The baby should be here within the hour.'

'Great.'

'Do you want to come in for the actual birth?' he asked.

'Me?' Jacqueline shook her head. This was a private moment between her son and his wife, and she didn't want to intrude. Not to mention that births were messy...

'Of course. If you want,' Paul said, his expression filled with excitement. 'Tammie Lee said you were welcome to be there, Mom.'

Jacqueline couldn't remember the last time she'd seen her son so happy. 'If you don't mind, I'd rather wait here, but you will let me know as soon as the baby's born, won't you?'

'You and Dad will be the first to know.'

Paul returned to Tammie Lee then, and it was just Jacqueline and Reese again. They ignored each other, sipping their coffee and thumbing through old magazines.

'Do you remember the night Paul was born?' Reese asked her unexpectedly.

Jacqueline laughed. 'I remember it like it was yesterday.'

'I was so proud of you that night.'

'For giving you a son, you mean?'

'No ... well, yes, I was happy to have a son, but I would've been equally pleased with a daughter.'

Jacqueline nodded.

'What I meant was, you impressed me with your courage and determination.'

He sounded unaccountably serious, but Jacqueline had difficulty believing he'd ever been 'impressed' with her. It struck her as an odd word to use.

'I remember how the other women in the labor room moaned and carried on and asked for drugs, but not you. Not my Jacquie.'

Dignified even in the face of unyielding labor pains – that was her, all right. Jacqueline knew he intended it as a compliment and sent him a brief smile. 'Despite the pain, it was one of the best nights of my life.'

'Because of Paul.'

Jacqueline lowered her gaze. 'Actually, no. Because of you.'

'Me?' He gave a clipped laugh, as if he didn't quite believe her, either. She wondered when they'd started to doubt each other and then she knew. It had been about the time he'd begun his affair.

'As we were driving here I was remembering the night Paul was born.'

Reese nodded. 'I was thinking about that myself.'

'Do you recall the way you carried me to the car? It was such a ... swashbuckling thing to do. I wasn't exactly a lightweight at the time.'

'Your hero,' Reese teased.

Sadness seemed to weigh her down. 'You *were* my hero,' she whispered and to cover up how wretched she felt, she sipped the last of her coffee.

'But no more,' Reese murmured.

Her lack of response was as clear as agreement would have been. She looked away, struggling with her composure. A part of her wanted to ask why he found her so lacking that he'd turned to another woman, but the pain of it was too great. She feared that whatever he might tell her would hurt even more than knowing he was with someone else.

He didn't say anything or glance in her direction.

It occurred to her then, sitting in this hospital waiting room with Reese, that perhaps this was the very moment *she* should say something. Perhaps she should offer an overture, try to bridge this gap between them. She'd loved Reese so much at one time. Oh damn, she might as well admit it: despite everything, she still loved him. Seeing the love Paul and Tammie Lee shared was almost painful for her because she recognized

341

how much she'd lost. To outward appearances she lived a wonderful life. She didn't need to worry about money, she had a lovely house, her friends were plentiful. Nevertheless, she was miserable and lonely.

'I...' Reese said when the distinct sound of a baby's cry traveled down the hallway.

Startled, they stared at each other.

'Do you think that's her?' Jacqueline asked, surging to her feet.

'I don't know.' Reese was standing now, too.

'Maybe we should ask the nurse?' she suggested.

Reese took her by the elbow and they walked to the nurses' station.

'We just heard an infant cry,' Reese told the woman, giving her their names.

'We were wondering if that could possibly be our granddaughter,' Jacqueline added, keeping her voice hushed so she wouldn't disturb others.

'I'll check for you,' she said, and disappeared into one of the birthing rooms. She was gone only a few moments; when she returned, she carried two light-blue gowns. 'Put these on, and you can join your family.' Jacqueline didn't hesitate and neither did Reese. When they were ready, the woman led them into the birthing room. This was nothing like the room where Jacqueline had delivered Paul all those years ago. Sofa, chairs, television and even a large swirling bathtub. Goodness, if she hadn't known better, Jacqueline would've thought she'd walked into a hotel suite.

Tammie Lee was in bed, smiling over at Paul

who held their baby girl. Her daughter-in-law's face was red, her hair matted with sweat, and tears glistened in her eyes, but she'd never looked lovelier, Jacqueline thought.

'Mom and Dad,' Paul said, gently cradling the bundled infant in his arms. 'This is Amelia Jacqueline Donovan.'

All at once it felt as if Jacqueline's heart had stopped beating. She blinked back unexpected tears. 'You named her after me?'

'Amelia was my grandmother's name and we chose Jacqueline because we both love you,' Tammie Lee said.

The tears rolled unrestrained down Jacqueline's cheeks as she gazed down on this precious child named in her honor.

'Would you like to hold your granddaughter, Mom?' Paul asked.

Jacqueline nodded as silent tears of joy burned her face. Her son placed the baby in her arms. Unusual though it seemed, Jacqueline was sure little Amelia opened her eyes and looked directly up at her. Invisible threads linked their hearts and in that moment, she knew she was going to love this child more than life itself. She smiled at Tammie Lee through her tears. 'Thank you,' she said hoarsely. Then she glanced at Reese and noticed he had tears in his eyes, too.

Very gently, her husband bent down and kissed Amelia's forehead. After a brief pause, he kissed Jacqueline's cheek.

'Now you have the daughter you always wanted,' he whispered.

Not until much later in the day, after Jacqueline

had bought out the baby sections at three department stores, did she realize what her husband had really been saying.

Reese hadn't been talking about Amelia. He'd meant Tammie Lee.

CHAPTER 42

ALIX TOWNSEND

'You like Jordan, don't you?' Laurel asked Alix early Wednesday morning. Alix was getting ready for work.

Like Jordan? That was an understatement if ever there was one. 'Yeah, I guess.'

'You trust him?'

She nodded, and then shrugged. 'Sure.' Quickly her suspicions rose. 'Do you know a reason I shouldn't?'

'No.'

'Then why are you asking?' she demanded.

'I don't know... I guess I'm hoping you learned from my mistake. You tried to tell me John was no good, but I wouldn't listen and now look at me,' she muttered, her bitterness so intense it soured her words.

As for looking at Laurel, all Alix could see was a grossly overweight girl with stringy blond hair who sat on her ass in front of the TV most days. But as long as Laurel made her share of the rent payment, Alix didn't care how she spent her days.

She'd quit two jobs, the video store and the day care center, and was currently working at a dry cleaner. She hadn't lasted a month at the day care center and said she'd hated it.

'When you and Jordan went out on that fancy dinner date, what did you talk about?' her roommate pressed.

Laurel had certainly taken an interest in Jordan all of a sudden. 'I don't know,' she returned flippantly. 'Stuff.'

'What kind of stuff?'

'Why all the interest?' Alix was surprised she was even having a conversation with her roommate, but she wasn't really comfortable with the subject.

'I mean, what do you talk about with a minister?'

'Youth minister,' she corrected. 'I knew him when we were in grade school, you know. He's just like everyone else.' More than once he'd proven he was human – in temperament and in the easy passion that flared between them. So far, everything had been kept under control, but Alix knew she tempted him as much as he tempted her. Jordan might work for the church, but he was very much a man.

'Tell me what you talked about, okay?' Laurel insisted. She seemed close to tears. Alix couldn't imagine why this was so important.

'I told him I wanted to be a chef one day or have my own catering company. We talked about me getting into a good cooking school – not that it's ever likely.' That was only a small part of their conversation. Jordan had a gift for drawing people out and making them feel as if they were the center of the universe.

'You want to be a chef?'

Alix shrugged. This shouldn't be any newsflash to Laurel who'd lived with her for the past year. Any real cooking had been done by her; Laurel had specialized in stocking the kitchen with ice cream, toaster waffles and potato chips. But then Alix realized they'd never taken the time to be more than roommates. Until recently, she'd never really confided her hopes and dreams in Laurel – or in anyone, she supposed. Alix had few friends, although she felt a connection with the women in her knitting class.

Ever since her breakup with the used-car salesman, Laurel had spent most of her time alone. Her self-pity had quickly irritated Alix. She didn't consider the relationship any big loss, but apparently Laurel thought otherwise.

'Does he know about your mother?' Laurel asked next.

The fact that her mother was currently serving time in the Women's Correctional Center at Purdy wasn't a fact Alix willingly broadcast. 'I told him.' There was little Jordan didn't know about her. She didn't want any unpleasant surprises in their relationship. He knew her mother had gone to prison for the attempted murder of Alix's father, too.

'Do you ever think about her?'

'Not much,' Alix found all these questions mildly annoying, but Laurel had been so moody lately that she wanted to encourage her to continue chatting.

'Do you love her?'

'My mother?' That question took some real soul-searching, but she was determined to be honest. If *she* was, then maybe Laurel would be honest with her. 'I suppose I do. I don't have any contact with her because when she writes, all she wants from me is money or cigarettes. She never asks about me or shows any interest in my life. I don't need her.' She said this in a casual way, as if it was well understood that she didn't need anyone. 'My only worry is that one day I'll end up just like her.'

'Not you,' Laurel said with complete confidence. 'You're too strong for that.'

Alix didn't see herself as strong, but it pleased her that Laurel thought so.

'You'd never let anyone hurt you or use you the way John used me,' she whispered.

'Get over him,' Alix said for the thousandth time. She couldn't understand why Laurel had clung to a man who'd treated her so abominably. It didn't make sense, especially when she hadn't seen any sign of him in months.

Laurel looked away.

'You need to get out more,' Alix told her.

Her roommate sighed unhappily. 'I don't like anyone to see me when I'm so fat.'

'Then stop eating.'

'You make it sound easy, but it isn't, you know. It's hard to stop.'

'Then take a walk every day. Walk instead of taking the bus. You'll be surprised at how quickly the fat will melt away with a little exercise.'

'Like *you* know anything about needing to lose

347

weight! You're perfect.'

Alix hadn't realized her roommate had such a high opinion of her figure, but she was far from having a perfect body.

'Do you think you'll marry Jordan?'

Alix brushed aside the question with a short, humorless laugh. 'Yeah, right.' She grabbed her purse on the way to the door, but hesitated after twisting the knob. 'Promise me you'll get out today. It doesn't do any good to sit around here and mope.'

'All right.'

Alix had just stepped out when Laurel stopped her. 'Alix, thank you.'

'For what?'

The question had apparently caught Laurel off guard. 'For being my friend.'

'Sure. No problem.'

It seemed odd for Laurel to thank her, but Alix let the comment slide as she headed for the video store. Without Laurel there to keep her company, the days dragged. She felt guilty now that she hadn't talked to her roommate lately. In her own estimation, Alix hadn't been a good friend, but then Laurel had been pretty unpleasant, so she'd avoided her as much as possible. Any time Alix had tried to talk to her, which wasn't often, Laurel had put her off. Her roommate's one solace seemed to be ice cream. Alix considered her weak-willed, but now she saw how easy it was to judge. That morning's conversation was the first they'd had in weeks, and she was feeling more sympathetic toward her.

During her lunch break, Alix returned to the

apartment, hoping to coax Laurel out. Maybe Laurel would be inclined to exercise if Alix offered to walk with her. To her surprise, Laurel wasn't there. She didn't keep tabs on Laurel's work schedule, and her hours seemed to change from week to week. Either Laurel was at work right now or she'd taken Alix's advice.

On the off-chance that Laurel was out walking, Alix started down Blossom Street, hoping to run into her. When she did find Laurel, however, she wasn't alone.

Jordan was with her.

They sat on a park bench in a shady area of the church grounds. Their heads were close together and they seemed engrossed in conversation.

Alix's initial reaction was anger, followed by a surge of jealousy. All those questions about Jordan had been a way of finding out about him so she could steal him away. Alix was half-tempted to march over and let it be known that she didn't appreciate her roommate butting in on her boyfriend. This was what she got for sympathizing with Laurel, for making an effort to help her.

Then she watched as her roommate broke into tears, buried her face in her hands and hunched forward. Jordan placed his hand on her back, and although Alix was too far away to hear, it looked like he was praying with her.

This was one of the qualities she loved about Jordan. There didn't seem to be anything she couldn't tell him. He genuinely cared for people and longed to comfort them. She had no right to be jealous. Nor did she have a single reason to doubt Jordan. Not once had he misled her or abused their friendship.

They'd talked about the meaning of trust and after the incident with the pastor's daughter, he'd asked her to trust him. It'd been easy to assure him she did – but at the time he wasn't touching her roommate. Determined to put her promise into action, she turned away and went back to work.

Just before closing, Jordan came to the video store. 'How about a coffee when you're through?' he said.

'Sure.' She couldn't help the burst of happiness she felt.

He suggested they meet at Annie's Café and she agreed. He was in a booth, with two cups of coffee waiting by the time Alix joined him.

'How was your day?' he asked.

'Fine. How about yours?' She gave him a sharp look, despite everything she'd promised herself earlier. If he'd been talking to Laurel, she wanted to know why.

Jordan didn't answer right away. 'Do you have something on your mind?'

'Should I?' She tried to make a joke of it, then decided that wasn't fair. Holding her mug with both hands, she stared down at the steaming coffee. 'I saw you and Laurel earlier.'

Jordan didn't offer an explanation. 'That bothers you?'

She shrugged. 'It did at first, but then I thought … well, that's your business, not mine. I don't have any hold on you.'

'You're only partially right.'

'How's that?'

He reached for her hand and raised it to his lips. His mouth gently grazed the inside of her palm. 'You have a very strong hold on my heart.'

'Oh.' From any other man it would have sounded corny, but not Jordan. 'Are you going to tell me what you and Laurel were talking about?'

He hesitated, then shook his head. 'No. Are you going to trust me?'

She stared at him hard and long. Every instinct demanded that she find out what she could. Yet at the same time, she longed to believe him. Finally, with a smile, she nodded.

She hoped it was the right decision. Because a betrayal by Jordan would hurt more than any other betrayal she'd suffered in her whole life.

CHAPTER 43

CAROL GIRARD

Carol stood in the doorway of what would've been the baby's nursery, and her eyes fell on the empty crib with the mobile dangling above it. Tiny zoo animals hung from a small umbrella with a music box attachment. She didn't know why she was torturing herself like this. Nothing was going to change.

Doug came and stood behind her. 'I'll call and arrange for the department store to pick up the furniture.'

'No ... don't. Please.'

'But...'

'I made an appointment with an adoption agency.' She said the words in a rush, as if to convince him that this was the logical next step.

She felt Doug tense.

'We can't give up now,' she implored. She couldn't forget her need for a child. She'd tried. She'd had to accept the fact that there would be no biological child for her, but she couldn't entirely let go of their dream. 'I want so badly to be a mother. I *need* to be a mother. Just like you need to be a father...'

Doug's shoulders sagged and he didn't speak.

'I have to do this,' she pleaded. They'd discussed adoption any number of times, but always as a last resort. Carol had held on to this last thread of hope, and yet she'd feared Doug's reaction. He'd been so quiet lately; she could feel him withdrawing from her emotionally and she couldn't endure it.

'You're sure you want me to go to an adoption agency with you?' he asked.

'Of course! It's important that we prove we're good candidates as adoptive parents.'

Her husband's mouth thinned.

'What's wrong?'

'I don't think having a crib and a change table is going to sway an agency to choose us as potential parents.'

'I know, but it can't hurt. I want the agency to see that we're ready, and that we could take a baby at any time.'

He turned away from her, walked into the

living room, and stood in front of the large picture window that overlooked Puget Sound.

'You don't want to go to the interview?' Carol asked as she joined her husband. They stood side by side without touching. Like Doug, she kept her gaze trained on the waterfront.

'How much is this going to cost?'

Carol didn't have an answer for him. The initial interview required a five-hundred-dollar deposit and as for the actual adoption, she didn't know. 'It costs as much as it costs,' she said. Whatever it was, she didn't care.

He shoved his hands in his pockets. 'Do you have any idea how much we've already invested in this quest for a child?'

She didn't and furthermore it didn't matter. As far as she was concerned, money was of little consequence. 'Not really.'

'There's a limit,' Doug said starkly, 'and frankly I've reached it.'

'All right, then,' she snapped. 'I'll go back to work if that's what you want. The only reason I didn't suggest it earlier is because I thought the adoption agency would prefer a stay-at-home mother, and that might put us closer to the top of the list. But I'll go back to work if you want me to.'

Doug turned to face her. 'This is exactly what I mean,' he shouted. 'We're no longer a couple. Everything we do revolves around a baby. We used to laugh together, go out, have fun.'

'We still do,' she countered, but when she searched her memory, she realized he was right.

'I've been as patient with this whole process as I can stand.' Anger vibrated from him. 'It costs too damn much and I–'

'In other words, money is all you're worried about?'

'If you'd allow me to finish,' he said slowly, enunciating each word, 'you'd have heard me say that the emotional price is too damn high.' He shook his head. 'I can't stand seeing you go through this pain and turmoil when the procedures don't even work – injections five times a day, seeing the doctor every forty-eight hours... It's taken over your life. Our lives.'

She agreed the toll on their emotions, especially in the last few months, had been extreme. One day she was filled with despair and the next, riding a wave of hope and optimism. That was when she'd assumed Rick's baby might be available to them. The only avenue left open to them now was adoption. They *had* to try. Doug couldn't mean they should stop!

'Now you want to drag us through yet another emotional quagmire and, Carol, as much as I love you, I don't think I can do it.'

'You have to,' she cried.

'Why?' he shouted. 'Why is it always about *you* and *your* need for a baby?'

In all the years of their marriage she'd never heard Doug use this tone of voice with her. 'I – it's for us.'

'Not more than five minutes ago, you admitted the baby was for you. It's all about your need to be a mother. You, you, you. What about *me*, Carol? What about my needs? What about my wants?'

'I–'

'For the last ... dear God, how many years has it been? Five, six? The entire focus of our lives has been on getting you pregnant. That apparently isn't going to happen, so fine, let's deal with it and get on with our lives.'

'But...'

'I don't want to adopt.'

The world all but exploded in pain and disbelief. 'You don't mean that.' Was Doug telling the truth? He couldn't be. He was emotionally drained. She understood, because she'd hit bottom herself, but she'd recovered and Doug would, too, given time.

'I do mean it.'

'But ... you just told me we could go to the appointment with the agency.' Carol was counting on that.

'You go. I don't want to.'

'But ... why?'

'Because I can already see what it's doing to you.'

She'd never known Doug to be so unreasonable. 'What exactly is it doing to me?'

'We have to prove to complete strangers that we're worthy of being parents. I feel like a beggar singing and dancing, cap in hand. All so someone I don't even know will like me enough to consider me father material.'

'You'll be a wonderful father!'

'Would have been,' he muttered.

His words scored deep wounds in her heart. *Would have been.*

'I can't do this anymore, Carol. I'm not the man you think I am. I want out.'

355

'Do you want out of the marriage?' she asked through numb lips, hardly able to say the words.

'No. I vowed to love you and I do.'

'You make it sound as if this is some promise you made and regret,' she said bitterly. 'Would you have married me if you'd known I couldn't have children?'

His hesitation was just long enough to supply the answer.

Her pain was so intense that for one unbelievable moment the room went dark and she started to sway.

Doug's arms came around her, and he buried his face in her shoulder. 'I was crazy in love with you when we got married and I'm just as crazy in love with you now. I want us to stay married, but I can't live like this anymore.'

'I ... I can't have a baby.'

'I know and I accept that.'

'No, you don't.' He might be saying it, but deep down he'd always resent the fact that she couldn't give him children.

'I do,' he said sharply, 'but I need you to accept it, too. Let go of this, Carol. Accept the fact that we just weren't meant to be parents.'

'But we could be someday. If we put our name in with the agency, then–'

'Then what? Three, four, five years from now – if we're fortunate – we might be chosen as worthy recipients of an infant? Do you realize I'll be forty-four in five years' time? I'd be sixty-two when our child graduated from high school.'

Carol hid her face against her husband's chest. Her emotions reeled with the impact of what he'd said. Doug was right. It was time to surrender this need. She'd never been a quitter, didn't know how to give up. Everything she'd ever set her mind to, she'd accomplished. Except for this... Her effort to have a child had become the focus of her life; more than that, it had become the purpose of her life. Her clenched-teeth determination was ruining their marriage.

Doug released her and walked away. Carol stood frozen and miserable, shaking with a combination of too many emotions, but mostly defeat.

The front door opened and she whirled around. 'Where are you going?'

'Out. I need to think.'

'When will you be back?' Her eyes begged him not to leave her, but she refused to ask him to stay.

'I ... don't know.'

She nodded and turned back, hands to her mouth.

'We both need to think this through, Carol.'

She nodded silently. The choice was clear. Either she renounced this need or she ruined her marriage and both their lives in the process.

It was nightfall before Doug returned. Carol sat in the darkened living room, curled up tight on the sofa with her arms circling her knees.

Doug came slowly into the room. 'Are you okay?'

She wasn't yet, but in time she'd adjust. 'I cancelled the appointment with the adoption agency.'

He thrust his hands in his pockets. 'You can deal with that?'

She nodded. She had to accept that there

would be no baby.

Doug sat down across from her and leaned forward, bracing his arms against his knees. His shoulders drooped.

'Where did you go?' she asked.

'A walk.'

'For three hours?'

He nodded.

'Do you want anything to eat?'

He shook his head.

'I phoned Bon-Macy's. They're coming to collect the baby furniture next week.'

He stared down at the carpet. 'I'm sorry,' he whispered.

'I am, too.' Sorrier than he'd ever know.

Doug extended his arm to her. 'We'll be all right, just the two of us.'

'Yes,' she whispered as her fingers clasped his. It was true. It would be true.

It *had* to be true.

CHAPTER 44

'Knitting is a haven, a safe place where one can touch history, dance with art and create a peaceful life.'
—Nancy Bush, author of *Folk Socks*

LYDIA HOFFMAN

At first I was angry when I didn't hear from Brad. After all his affirmations about being there for the long haul, he'd walked out on me like every other man in my life, with the exception of my father. A thousand times over, I wished I'd read his letter. Finally I couldn't stand it any longer – I had to know.

I turned to my sister for advice; I'd come to rely on her more and more, especially in emotional matters. So on Monday, I called her.

'Where are you?' Margaret demanded immediately after I'd said hello.

'At the shop.'

'It's Monday. I thought you took Mondays off.'

'I do, but there are always a million things to do here and well, it's where I'm most comfortable.' I did all my best thinking with walls of yarn around me. I'd always looked upon skeins of yarn as unfulfilled promises – the way some people, writers or artists, look at a blank page. The potential is there, and it's up to us to make something with that yarn or write something on that page. It's the sense of possibility I find so exciting.

Actually, I gave a lot of thought to that analogy. My relationship with Brad held promise and because of my fears I'd let him go. I didn't do anything with all those possibilities.

'You're calling about Brad, aren't you?'

Sometimes Margaret seems like a mind-reader. 'If you must know ... yes. Have you heard from him?'

'Me? What makes you think he'd contact me?'

'Wishful thinking, I suppose.' Even over the telephone line, I could tell my sister was amused by my question.

'Are you going to call him?'

The idea had been swirling around inside my head all week. 'I might.'

'Then why are you calling me?' The gruffness I'd experienced so often with her was back in full force.

'I don't know,' I admitted. 'Maybe because I was hoping you'd tell me I was doing the right thing and that I wouldn't make a complete idiot of myself in the process.'

Margaret hesitated for only a moment. 'If I were you, I'd go for it.'

'You would?' Hope sprang to life.

'Call me back once you do, okay?'

'Okay.' I had to pause to be sure the warmth in her voice was directed at me. 'Margaret.' I swallowed, finding it difficult to continue.

'What?'

'I wanted to thank you for being so wonderful these last few months.'

360

My gratitude must have taken her aback, because she didn't say anything for a few seconds. Time seemed to be suspended and then I thought I heard a soft sigh.

'It's very nice to have a sister, you know,' she whispered.

I couldn't have agreed with her more.

Once I'd determined that the only thing to do was call Brad, I was on a mission. I'd rehearsed several approaches before I dialed his home number later that evening.

His son answered on the second ring. 'Hello, Cody,' I said.

'Hi.' He sounded unsure as if he didn't recognize my voice.

'I'm Lydia. Remember? We met a little while ago.'

'I remember! You're the lady who owns the yarn store. You said you were going to knit me a cool sweater with a green-and-yellow dinosaur on it.'

I smiled to myself. 'I've already started it.' I'd put the project aside when I went into the hospital, but with concentrated effort, I could have it finished by the end of the week. 'Is your dad home?'

'Just a minute. I'll get him for you.'

My heart died a hundred deaths in the time it took Brad to pick up the receiver. It must've been less than a minute but it seemed closer to an hour before I heard his familiar voice.

'Hello.'

'Hi.' My mouth was so dry, my tongue refused to cooperate. 'It's Lydia.' His silence was nearly my undoing, but I forged ahead, simultaneously

361

blessing and cursing Margaret for encouraging this.

'What can I do for you?' he finally asked.

'Could we meet and talk?' I asked.

'When?'

'Whenever it's convenient for you.' I wanted to shout *the sooner, the better,* but it depended on his schedule and not mine.

'All right. I'll let you know when I can arrange it.'

I waited for him to say something else and when he didn't, I had no choice but to end the conversation. 'I'll wait to hear from you, then.'

'Goodbye.'

'Goodbye.' The line went dead and I was left standing with the receiver in my hand and the dial tone in my ear.

This was much worse than I'd imagined. I'd secretly hoped that once Brad heard the sound of my voice, he'd be so pleased that whatever pain I'd caused him would evaporate. How foolish I'd been not to consider his feelings.

Over the years Margaret's complaint about me had been that I was self-absorbed. I know she resented the fact that Mom and Dad focused their attention on helping me through my ordeals. I'd always believed that her accusations were unfair, based on her own jealousies and insecurities, but now I began to see things differently.

How cheated she must have felt. Cheated and abandoned. For the first time, I wondered if she could be right about me. I couldn't have done anything about my cancer, but I could've changed my reaction to it. I had the victim mentality down to an art form.

I remained standing in my kitchen, toying with the idea of calling Margaret again, when the phone rang, startling me. I grabbed the receiver. 'Hello.'

'I can meet you in half an hour at The Pour House.'

'Tonight?'

'Yes,' he said as if that should be obvious.

'All right.' The phone clicked as he hung up.

Within five minutes I'd brushed my hair and dabbed my wrists with a lovely French perfume my dad had given me years ago –the one I saved for my most special occasions. On my way out the door, I grabbed a light sweater.

I'd found a corner booth and paid for a pitcher of beer by the time Brad walked into the pub. He glanced around, saw me and then headed toward the booth. He slid in across from me.

Hard as I tried, I couldn't stop watching him. All of a sudden, my eyes started to fill with tears. I would die of mortification if he noticed. I did everything but dive headfirst into my mug of beer in an effort to hide this ridiculous crying jag.

Of course he noticed.

'Lydia, are you crying?'

I nodded and dug frantically in my purse for a tissue. 'I am so sorry,' I sobbed, hiccuping in an effort to hold back the tears.

'For crying?'

I nodded, letting my head bob a time or two more than necessary. 'For everything. I treated you terribly.'

'Yes, you did.'

'I was so afraid and–'

'You didn't read my letter.'

'I know.' I paused long enough to blow my nose. 'I couldn't, because I knew if I did, I wouldn't be able to keep you out of my life. I *had* to let you go, for your protection and for mine.'

Brad lifted the pitcher and refilled my mug. 'I prefer to make my own decisions.'

'I know, but...' All my excuses sounded hollow and insincere now. 'Margaret thinks I'm self-absorbed and she's right. I'm so sorry, Brad, for ... everything.'

'That's what you wanted to tell me? Why you called and asked me to meet you?'

I nodded again. It was what I'd wanted to say, but there were other things, too. My throat seemed to close up, and the silence that fell between us felt utterly unmanageable.

'There's more.'

Brad looked up from his beer expectantly. He wasn't making this easy, but then I didn't deserve that.

'Ever since I met you, since we started seeing each other, I've been ... happy.'

He shrugged. 'You could've fooled me.'

'I know... You see, I've realized I have a hard time handling life when everything's going smoothly. I'm not used to being happy and I don't know how to deal with it. So I do something stupid to mess it up.'

'You figured this out on your own?'

I shook my head. 'Margaret helped.' None too gently, either, but he didn't need to know that. My relationship with my sister was still complicated, but now I knew she cared about me.

'Ah yes, Margaret. Little Ms. Matchmaker.'

'She's all right.' It surprised me how defensive I felt toward her.

'Yes, she is – and so are you.'

I smiled through my tears. 'Thank you.'

He took a deep swallow of beer. 'Okay, now that the apology's out of the way, where does that leave us?'

I didn't know what to tell him. 'Where would you like our relationship to go?' My heart was hammering so loudly, it was nearly impossible to hear my own thoughts.

'In the same direction it was headed until your most recent tests.' His look grew intense as he reached across the table for my hand. 'What about you, Lydia? What do you want?'

'I want the entire month wiped from my memory and I want us to go back to the way things were before and ... and I want us to be close again.' Then, because he should know, I added, 'But it's important that you understand there are no guarantees.'

'Your sister told me everything.'

'Everything?' Then he knew. 'And you still want...'

'I want you more than ever, Lydia, but I don't want you shoving me out of your life because you think I can't deal with your illness. Let me make that decision for myself.'

It was hard to give him that control, but I knew he was right. He was asking more of me than he realized.

'I can't make you any promises,' he continued,

'but I can tell you that I care for you a great deal.'

'I care for you, too.'

'That's a starting point, and where it leads neither of us can know.' He smiled at me with those devilish blue eyes and I understood that Brad Goetz wasn't going to turn tail and run at the first sign of trouble. He was a man I could trust. A man I could lean on. A man who was my father's equal in every way.

CHAPTER 45

JACQUELINE DONOVAN

Jacqueline knew she should give her son and daughter-in-law time alone with Amelia, but she couldn't make herself stay away. The baby had filled a deep emotional void in her, one she'd ignored for years. But the love that blossomed in her heart refused to be ignored. Whenever she held Amelia, the ties that bound her to her granddaughter seemed to grow stronger, more constant and enduring.

Amelia was in her arms now as Jacqueline gently rocked her to sleep. She breathed in the baby's pure scent, and in a rush of nostalgia remembered holding Paul just this way.

'You look so peaceful,' Tammie Lee said, coming into the nursery with a new package of disposable diapers. She set them on the dresser and turned to watch Jacqueline with Amelia.

Jacqueline glanced up. 'Peaceful is how I feel.' She supposed she should apologize for dominating so much of Tammie Lee's time. She'd been over to the house every day since Amelia had come home from the hospital, and some days she visited twice.

'I don't mean to make a pest of myself,' Jacqueline murmured, a bit embarrassed at her own behavior.

'Nonsense.' Tammie Lee dismissed her concern with a wave of her hand. 'I don't think it's possible to give a baby too much love.' She walked to the dresser and pulled out a new infant's outfit. 'Too many clothes, though – that's something else. I'm not sure she'll ever be able to wear everything you bought her.'

Jacqueline tried to hide her amusement. 'I did go a little crazy.'

'Paul says he's never seen you like this.'

'I had no idea I was going to love her so much.' Jacqueline cringed whenever she thought about her long-held resentment of Tammie Lee, and her anger when she'd first learned about the pregnancy. To her horror, she remembered calling Tammie Lee a 'breeder,' certain she was manipulating Paul. Instead, Jacqueline had finally discovered what everyone else had seen about Tammie Lee from the beginning – she was a genuine and compassionate woman.

'You can love her for my mama,' Tammie Lee whispered. 'I so wish she was well enough to travel.'

The idea of sharing Amelia with another grandmother made her feel shockingly possessive, but

367

Jacqueline couldn't begrudge Tammie Lee's mother her precious granddaughter.

'Mama already has five granddaughters, though. And three grandsons.'

'A bounty of riches.'

'That's what my mama says, too. She says she's the luckiest woman in the world to be blessed with such beautiful, talented grandchildren.'

'Amelia's the most incredible baby in the universe,' Jacqueline insisted. Tammie Lee chuckled, and Jacqueline didn't bother to explain that she wasn't joking. This was one special baby to have four sensible adults completely wrapped around her little finger. Denying this child anything was incomprehensible.

Tammie Lee sat on the end of the bed. 'Between you and Paul, I swear Amelia's in someone's arms twenty hours a day.'

Jacqueline smiled as the infant slept contentedly. Her tiny mouth moved in a small sucking motion in her sleep.

'Even Reese wants to hold her.'

'Reese has been over?'

'Almost every day, and he always brings her a gift. It's so sweet the way you two spoil her. Amelia's just a week old.'

Jacqueline pinched her lips together at this news about her husband's visits. She hadn't known that Reese was regularly dropping by, but then she knew very little about his comings and goings. Resolving not to dwell on it, she glanced at her watch. Five-thirty. Paul would be back from work soon and it was time for her to leave.

'I should be heading home,' she said reluctantly. The house had never felt emptier than it had in the last few weeks, nor had she experienced such bitter loneliness. Ever since the night Reese had left her so abruptly, claiming a work emergency when she'd *known* what he was really doing... She refused to imagine Reese with that other woman.

'Is Reese like his son? Does he like to have dinner precisely an hour after he gets home?'

Tammie Lee asked the question in a joking manner, and that was the way Jacqueline should have responded, but at the moment, her granddaughter in her arms, pretense was beyond her. She'd been living a lie for so long, anyone might think it would be second nature. But she discovered, to her dismay, that she couldn't do it. It was as if holding this innocent child made anything other than the truth seem wrong.

'Reese doesn't come home on Tuesday nights,' she said starkly.

'Oh, I didn't know. Does he bowl?'

The question brought a brief smile. Only Tammie Lee would assume that Reese was part of a bowling team. Jacqueline shook her head.

'Mom?'

For a long time Jacqueline had disliked the easy way Tammie Lee had slipped into the habit of calling her 'Mom.' Now it felt like the most natural thing in the world.

'He ... has another commitment,' she said.

Tammie Lee didn't say anything for at least a minute. Then she did something completely unexpected. She sank down on the carpet next to the rocking chair and put her hand on Jacqueline's knee. The gesture was simple and comforting, and it touched her deeply.

'Did I ever tell you about my uncle Bubba and my aunt Frieda?' She didn't wait for Jacqueline to answer. 'It seems that Bubba – well, actually, that's not his name, it's really Othello, but everybody calls him Bubba. It's a southern thing. Anyway, he took a fancy to the waitress over at the Eat, Gas & Go off Pecan Avenue. Started hanging out there at all hours of the day.'

Six months ago, Jacqueline would have stopped her, but after hearing Tammie Lee's stories, she'd grown accustomed to the folksy wisdom her daughter-in-law freely dispensed.

'Anyway, Aunt Frieda got wind of what was happening, and she put up the biggest fuss you can imagine.'

'Did she go after the waitress?'

'Aunt Frieda? No way. She tackled my uncle Bubba. She told him she was all the woman he could handle, and if he didn't believe her, then she'd just have to prove it to him. She told my mama she'd married Bubba and by golly, she wasn't going to let any waitress lure him away. Next thing I knew, Uncle Bubba was walkin' around town with a grin as big as a sink hole. Far as I know, he never went near that Eat, Gas & Go again.'

Jacqueline was amused by the story but she wasn't foolish enough to believe that making a fuss over Reese would change anything. 'More power to your aunt Frieda,' she said.

'No, Mom,' Tammie Lee said, staring up at her intently. 'The power is yours, too. And you can use it as you wish.'

Her daughter-in-law's words still rang in her mind as Jacqueline drove home. She pulled into the garage and entered the dark and silent house. Martha had left a chef's salad in the refrigerator for her dinner; she sat down at the kitchen table and nibbled at it, but she didn't have much appetite. The house seemed full of little sounds. Creaks and moans. They only emphasized the emptiness of the place, and she put on some music to distract herself.

Twenty minutes later, she gave up, deciding to have a bath earlier than usual. After her bath, she generally went to bed to read – and to listen for Reese. Some nights she read until the morning hours without hearing him at all. She'd never acknowledged that she waited for him, but tonight the truth was like an intruder standing in the middle of her bedroom.

Despite all her husband's years of infidelity, the pain was almost overwhelming. At this very moment, he was with another woman and she'd allowed his philandering to continue, accepted it as if it were normal. Jacqueline realized she couldn't pretend any longer. She couldn't and she wouldn't!

Half-undressed, the bathwater running in the tub, she walked into the kitchen, each step filled with righteous indignation. She jerked open a drawer and reached for the country club directory. Tossing it on the kitchen counter, she searched for Allan Anderson's number. They'd been good friends for years, and he was the best divorce attorney in town. Once he got his hands on this case, her husband would pay dearly for what he'd done to her and to their lives.

All at once, the virtuous anger left her and she closed the directory, but her hand lingered there.

Dear God in heaven, what was she thinking? She didn't want a divorce, she wanted her husband. She wanted Reese!

Somehow, some way, she'd have to win him back.

Slowly now, lost in her thoughts, she walked into the bathroom again and turned off the water. Sitting on the edge of the tub, she pressed her fingers to her temples as she considered what to do.

The sound of the garage door closing startled her. Jacqueline stood, her heart pounding at a furious pace. It couldn't possibly be Reese. Not this early. He was rarely home before nine.

'Reese, is that you?' she called out, then silently chastised herself. Who else could it be? A burglar wasn't likely to announce his arrival.

'I'm home,' her husband called back flatly.

Slipping on her robe, Jacqueline came out of the bathroom to see her husband standing at the kitchen counter, sorting through the mail. He seemed surprised to see her.

Where she found the courage, Jacqueline didn't know, but she stepped boldly forward.

Reese casually glanced up. 'Yes?'

'It's over. I want that understood here and now. I won't put up with this any longer.'

He blinked and stared at her. Thankfully he didn't make a pretense of not knowing what she meant.

'I won't,' she repeated.

He continued to stare, his expression incredulous.

'First of all,' she went on, 'it's demeaning to me as your wife. I've looked the other way for the last time. I won't do it again. I tried to pretend it doesn't matter and for a while I managed to convince myself – but it does. It matters very much.'

'What–'

Jacqueline kept talking. If she didn't finish this now, while she had the courage, she might not have another chance. 'I've never been the kind of wife to issue ultimatums or make demands, but I'm doing it now. Whoever she is, get rid of her. I don't care what it costs. I want her out of your life and mine.'

Reese shook his head, apparently speechless.

'I won't allow our grandchildren to grow up seeing me treated with that kind of disrespect.' Here she was, having what was possibly the most important discussion of her marriage, while standing barefoot in the middle of her kitchen dressed only in a robe.

Frowning, Reese went back to sorting the mail.

Tammie Lee's story rolled through her mind and Jacqueline dragged in a fortifying breath. Since she'd come this far, she might as well go for broke. 'There's more,' she announced with as much dignity as she could muster.

'More?'

She nodded and stepped closer. 'As a matter of fact, there's a great deal more. I happen to love you, Reese. I don't know what went wrong between us and ... and whatever it was, I share the blame. But I'm lonely, Reese, and I want you back in my bed.' Her voice caught. For one crazy moment, Jacqueline imagined herself as Tammie Lee's Aunt Frieda. She propped one hand on her hip, jutted out her shoulder and lowered her voice to a husky whisper. 'I promise I'll be all the woman you'll ever need.'

The look in her husband's eyes was beyond description as he dropped the mail. 'Jacquie? Are you serious?'

She laughed in a way she hoped sounded sexy and sensuous. 'Don't take my word for it. Come and find out for yourself.'

Reese's mouth sagged, his face so comically eager that she nearly laughed out loud.

'Jacquie?' He reached for her then, and when his mouth covered hers, it was with the same openmouthed passion they'd experienced in their twenties. In the later years of their marriage, before he'd moved out of her bedroom, their lovemaking had become staid and controlled. Not now. Reese all but ruined her robe in his eagerness to undress her.

When they stumbled into the bedroom and fell onto the bed, they were giggling like teenagers. Their lovemaking was explosive, primal, thrilling. The only sounds to be heard were their moans and deep satisfied sighs.

After they'd finished, Jacqueline lay cradled in her husband's arms, her eyes moist as she listened to the solid, even beat of Reese's heart. There was so much that needed to be said, but in the contentment of the moment, none of it seemed important. What mattered was savoring this time, treasuring each other. If nothing else, Jacqueline would have this one night with her husband to remind her that she was very much alive and every inch a woman.

'I never dreamed,' Reese whispered close to her ear. 'I'd given up hope that we'd ever share a bed again. I love you. I've always loved you, but I didn't know how to make things different.'

She sighed and kissed his bare chest. 'I'm not giving you up.'

'There's no one else who wants me.'

Jacqueline froze. 'What do you mean?'

He gave a resigned sigh. 'We'll speak of this only once and then never again. Agreed?'

'Agreed.'

'I had an affair ten years ago. Which I realize you knew about. It ended quickly and badly. I felt terrible and I still can't believe I was so stupid.'

'But every Tuesday night–'

He didn't let her finish. 'I know. I wanted you to think I was still involved. It was stupid and childish, and I'm embarrassed to admit it, but I was looking for a reaction from you. Something – anything – that showed me you cared.'

'The night I made dinner for you and the phone rang and you left...'

'I know what you thought, but you were wrong. It *was* business. We'd blown a transformer. I swear to you there wasn't another woman that night or any other night in a very long time.'

'All these years...' She had trouble taking it in.

'Once I started this, I didn't know how to stop.'

'We've both been such fools.' Jacqueline wrapped her arms around his neck and wondered how she'd ever survived outside her husband's embrace. All this time, the only thing that had stood between them was pride.

'I don't know what came over you tonight, but I thank God for it,' Reese said.

'You can thank Tammie Lee's Aunt Frieda.'

'Who?'

'It doesn't matter.' She pressed her head against his shoulder and smiled. Every day, she found more reasons to be grateful to her daughter-in-law. Reese had been right about that. She finally did have her daughter, and even if Tammie Lee happened to speak with a southern drawl, she was as precious to her as any daughter could be to a mother.

CHAPTER 46

ALIX TOWNSEND

Alix woke to the sound of smothered groans. Leaning up on one elbow, she stared into the darkness, listening intently. Oddly enough, the muffled agony seemed to be coming from the living room. As her eyes adjusted to the dark she noticed something else out of the ordinary. Laurel's bed, which was across the room from her own, was empty.

Her roommate had been a real jerk lately. After that one brief episode of friendliness, Laurel had started ignoring her again. They were barely speaking but that was Laurel's doing, not Alix's.

She'd done her best, tried to maintain a civil relationship. If Laurel said anything to her at all, it was rude or sarcastic.

Alix hadn't had any news lately about the fate of the apartment complex, but she suspected they'd be losing their place soon. Well, Alix had a plan. Once she had the means, she'd ditch her so-called friend and find a new roommate. The bogus drug bust last spring had been because of Laurel's stash, not hers. Nevertheless, Alix had paid the price.

In the beginning, Laurel had been apologetic and supportive, looking for ways to make it up to her. That had all changed. Most days she avoided Alix and even when she was around, all she did was sit in front of the television and eat. She hadn't even gone to her job at the dry-cleaner's all week.

Lying down again, Alix tugged the sheet up over her shoulders and closed her eyes, determined to go back to sleep. If Laurel was sick, then it was from all the ice cream she'd been eating. She must've gained fifty pounds in the last six months. None of her jeans zipped up and she looked grotesquely fat. Their relationship hadn't been helped by Laurel making a play for Jordan, either. Alix trusted Jordan, but she wasn't so sure about Laurel. She'd obviously gone to him hoping for sympathy – and who knew what else?

Alix never did learn what that was all about. Jordan hadn't volunteered and she hadn't asked. When she'd confronted Laurel, her roommate told her to mind her own freakin' business.

Alix was determined to blot out the muffled

sounds coming from the other room. If Laurel needed her, then she could come and get her. Alix wasn't about to offer her help.

Just when Alix was drifting back to sleep, she heard a loud moan, as if Laurel was in horrible pain. Although she wasn't happy about it, Alix tossed aside her sheet and climbed out of bed.

The living room was dark, and it took her a minute to locate Laurel, who was prone on the sofa with her head braced against the arm. Her knees were bent and she'd draped a blanket over her legs.

'What's wrong?' Alix asked. She wanted it understood that she was none too pleased about having her sleep disturbed.

'Nothing. Go back to bed.'

Alix hesitated, and then decided what the hell. Laurel wasn't willing to ask her for help. Fine, if that was how she wanted it.

'Whatever.' Alix was two steps into the bedroom when for some reason she stopped. Faintly she heard Laurel whimper what sounded like: *oh God, oh God, oh God.*

Walking into the room again, Alix decisively flipped on the light. She stood with her hands on her hips, feet apart. 'You're *not* all right. What's wrong?'

Laurel flung her head back and forth and refused to answer. Eyes shut against the light, she bit down on her lower lip and blood oozed from the sides of her mouth. Alix stared at her aghast.

'Laurel,' she whispered.

Her roommate urgently stretched out her arm and when Alix took her hand, Laurel held it in a

death grip. 'Help me,' she cried. 'I can't do this...
I thought ... oh God, it hurts so much.'

Alix fell to her knees beside the sofa. All at
once, everything added up, and what should've
been obvious suddenly exploded into her awareness. 'You're in labor?'

Laurel nodded. 'I couldn't tell you... I couldn't
tell anyone.'

'Does John know?'

Tears filled Laurel's eyes. 'Why do you think he
dumped me? He said he didn't want the baby. Or
me. He promised he'd pay for an abortion, but he
didn't show up with the money and I couldn't
afford it.'

'Why didn't you say anything?'

'How could I?'

'We're friends.' *Some friends.* Laurel had let her
get arrested and yet she didn't trust Alix with the
fact that she was pregnant.

Laurel closed her eyes and arched her back,
moaning again.

Alix would figure it out later. Right now, she
needed to get Laurel to a hospital. 'I'll go out and
find a phone, call for help.'

'No!' Laurel screamed. Her hand crushed
Alix's fingers. 'Don't leave me. It won't be long
now ... it can't be. I can't take the pain. I can't
deal with this by myself.'

'What should I do?' Alix had never been with
anyone in labor before and had no idea how to
help.

'I don't know,' Laurel gasped, panting and
writhing with pain. 'I think the baby might be
coming,' she cried, all-out panic in her voice.

'What should I do? Oh God, what should I do?'

'Stay calm,' Alix said, forcing confidence into her own voice, although her heart was galloping at frightening speed. She peeled back the blanket and saw that Laurel had placed a stack of towels beneath her hips. 'I'm going to go and wash my hands.'

'No... Don't leave me.'

'I'll just be a minute.'

'All right, all right.' Laurel was rolling her head from side to side once more, her face shiny with sweat.

Alix berated herself for not guessing the truth earlier. But Laurel was overweight, so her pregnancy hadn't been immediately obvious. She still wore her jeans every day and they seemed to be splitting at the seams, but Alix had assumed the weight gain was from depression and her constant eating.

Alix was only away from Laurel for a moment, but her roommate grabbed her hand the instant she was back. Studying Laurel's face, Alix saw that she was in terrible pain.

'Look and see,' Laurel implored. 'Is it ready to come out yet?'

Alix felt completely inadequate to deliver this child. 'Do you have anything for the baby?'

Laurel shook her head. 'I don't want it.'

'Laurel,' she pleaded. 'What were you going to do with the baby?' Talk about living in a dream world! Laurel had to know the infant would need clothes and blankets and bottles.

Her friend sobbed. 'At first I planned to kill it.'

Alix gasped. 'You can't do that!'

'I don't want this baby.' Laurel screamed and arched her back again when the pain overtook her. Her fingers dug into the fabric of the sofa as she slammed her eyes shut and panted. She took in deep gulps of air, her shoulders heaving with the effort.

Sitting on the edge of the sofa, Alix saw that the crown of the baby's head had appeared, thick with matted blond hair. With the next contraction, Alix carefully placed her hands beneath the tiny skull. Laurel drew in a deep breath and tried to look down at the baby but couldn't.

'It won't be much longer now,' Alix promised. She felt frightened and helpless and she hoped she was telling the truth.

No more than a minute later, Laurel grunted and started panting again. Suddenly, the infant slipped free. He seemed to glide directly into Alix's hands. With him came a gush of water and blood.

Tears filled Alix's eyes. 'It's a boy,' she told Laurel. He didn't cry right away and Alix's heart leapt in panic. Acting on instinct, she placed her finger inside his mouth, swabbing it clean. Then she turned him over on his belly and patted his back. Instantly he let out a fierce, belligerent cry. Joy surged through Alix and she stared up at her friend. 'He's beautiful,' she said, awed by the wonder of this moment. A new life had just entered the world.

Laurel refused to look at him and turned her face away. 'Cut the cord,' she instructed without emotion.

'I ... I don't think I should...'

'Do it,' Laurel demanded. 'Or I'll do it myself.'

'All right, all right.' Alix found a knife in the kitchen and, afraid she might infect either her friend or the baby, put it in a pan full of water, which she set on the stove to boil. She dashed back into the living room just in time to deliver the afterbirth.

As soon as she'd cut the cord, Alix took the baby into the bathroom and cleaned him off. Then she wrapped him in the blanket she'd knit in class. Certain Laurel would have a change of heart now that the birth was over, Alix carried the newborn into the living room, hoping to coax her roommate into at least glancing at her son.

'Just look at him once,' Alix pleaded. 'He's perfect, Laurel.'

Laurel refused again with a shake of her head. 'Get rid of it.'

Alix couldn't believe anyone could be so cold-hearted. 'I can't do that.'

'Then give it to me and I will.'

'Will ... what will you do?' Alix protectively cradled the infant.

'I'll take it to some Dumpster and leave it there.'

Laurel didn't even seem to consider this infant a child.

She referred to him as 'it.'

'You really mean that, don't you?' she said in a horrified voice. 'You don't want this baby.'

'How many times do I have to say it?' Laurel shouted. 'Get rid of that thing.'

With one arm around the newborn, Alix controlled her racing thoughts. If Laurel didn't want this baby, she knew someone who did. 'Sign something.'

'What?' Laurel stared up at her blankly.

'I need a statement from you that says you're giving up this baby of your own free will.'

Laurel frowned. 'Who am I giving this baby to?'

'To a couple for adoption.' Alix took a deep breath. 'I know someone who desperately wants and needs a child. I want her and her husband to raise this baby boy. You might not love him, but I know Carol will. I brought him into this world. I feel personally responsible for him now. Like you said, you want me to get rid of him.'

'Do whatever you want. I don't care.'

'You aren't going to change your mind?'

'No.' Then as if to prove her point, she grabbed the knife and raised her arm as if she meant to kill the infant on the spot. 'I want it dead or out of my life, understand? What more do I have to say to prove it? Just get rid of it! I don't care what you do as long as you get it out of here.'

As she held the screaming infant in her arms, Alix grabbed a sheet of paper and a pen, then handed them to her friend. 'Write it down.'

Sitting up, Laurel quickly scribbled a few lines and signed her name. Alix read them over, then returned to the bedroom. She set the baby on her bed and jerked on clothes as fast as her shaking hands would allow. The infant gazed up at her and Alix bent down and kissed his forehead.

'I wish you'd had a warmer welcome to the world, little boy,' she whispered. 'But I know someone who'll love you.'

Without another word to Laurel, Alix threw her

purse over her shoulder and walked out of the apartment. It was early Friday morning and the streets were dark and eerie. Moving as fast as she could with the baby held against her chest, Alix stepped into the foyer of Annie's Café where there was a pay phone. She searched for fifty cents and then pulled out the piece of paper Jordan had given her with his phone number.

She inserted the coins and pressed the receiver to her ear as she punched in the numbers. 'Oh please, be there,' she whispered. 'Please.'

Jordan didn't answer until the fifth ring, just when Alix was about to hang up in frustration and despair.

'This better be good,' he muttered into the phone.

'Jordan, it's me.' She was so glad to hear his voice she nearly wept for joy. 'Remember you said I could phone if I ever needed you?'

'Are you in trouble?'

She wasn't sure how to answer him. 'I'm at Annie's Café... Can you come and get me?'

'Now?'

'Yes, and please hurry.'

'I'll be there in ten minutes.' He didn't hesitate, didn't so much as pause. If ever Alix had doubted her feelings for him, she didn't anymore. She knew with certainty that there was one person in her life she could turn to anytime, night or day, and that was Jordan.

Alix bounced the baby gently in her arms. She cooed and comforted him as she waited inside the lighted foyer of Annie's Café for Jordan's car. When she saw him turn the corner, she pushed through the glass door and walked to the curb.

Jordan eased to a stop and leaned over to throw open the passenger door.

He stared at her. 'Is that ... a baby?' His voice was hoarse with sleep and shock.

'It's Laurel's and that creep John's.... I just delivered him.'

'So that's...' He broke off for a moment. 'She talked to me not long ago, said she was in some kind of trouble, but wouldn't tell me what.'

Alix nodded. She understood it all now.

'Do you need me to take the baby to the hospital?' he asked.

'No.' Because her heart was full and because she knew what had to be done, she bent to kiss him.

'Alix ... you can't keep this baby.'

'I delivered him. I'll be the one to find him a home.'

Jordan's eyes widened. 'What are you thinking?'

'I know someone who needs this baby.'

'Who?'

'It doesn't matter who. Now, either you drive or I'll catch a cab.'

'But it isn't legal–'

'I have a signed statement from Laurel. She doesn't want the baby and there's no damn way I'm turning him over to the state. Is that clear?'

His eyebrows shot up, and a slow grin followed. 'Remind me never to cross you.'

'Don't worry. I have a feeling you're going to get plenty of reminders over the years.'

'Years?'

'We'll discuss that later.'

'Does your friend know you're coming?'

'Not yet.'

'What about Laurel?'

'I'll need you to go back and take her to the hospital.' That would mean involving the authorities, but she'd let Carol and her husband deal with it. 'Take her to Swedish, okay?'

'I'm at your command, Lady Alix, dragon slayer and deliverer of baby boys.'

That had a nice sound to it, Alix decided.

CHAPTER 47

CAROL GIRARD

The piercing ring of the phone woke Carol out of a deep sleep. Doug rolled over and glanced at the clock, and Carol saw that it was barely past four. She didn't know anyone who'd be calling this early unless it was an emergency. Her mind went numb with the possibilities.

On the third ring, her husband reached for the receiver. 'Hello,' he said groggily.

Carol could hear only one end of the conversation and at first she assumed it was a wrong number. To her surprise, Doug said, 'Yes, she's here. Who did you say this is?'

A moment later he placed his hand over the mouthpiece. 'Do you know a girl by the name of Alix Townsend?'

Carol nodded. 'Did she say what she wants?'

'No. Only that she has to see you right away.'

Carol hesitated.

'Should I buzz her up?' Doug asked.

If Alix had come to her in the middle of the night, there had to be a good reason. 'Yes,' she told her husband. 'Let her come up.'

'You're sure?'

'She probably wants to talk,' Carol said.

'At this time of the morning?'

Carol kissed his temple. 'Yes, darling.'

Throwing aside the blankets, Carol reached for her robe at the foot of the bed. 'You don't need to get up.' She supposed that Alix had come to her as one friend to another, presumably to ask for advice about some urgent crisis in her life. In her current frame of mind, Carol wasn't convinced she'd be much help. Then again, maybe she would...

As she walked out of the bedroom, Carol passed the nursery across the hallway. Bon-Macy's was coming that very morning to pick up the furniture. With the crib, changer and chest of drawers would go her dreams of a family. After everything she'd endured, after the frustration and disappointment and heartache, Carol thought it should've been easier to let go. This futile quest for a child was killing their marriage, and Doug was right – this had to end. Still it hurt and the pain would linger.

There was a knock at the door. Barefoot, Carol crossed the tiled entry to unfasten the security lock. She opened the door and gasped when she saw Alix standing there, cradling a baby in her arms.

'Here,' she said, holding the infant out to

Carol. 'This baby boy needs a mother.'

Carol stared down at the newborn thrust into her arms. Speechless, she raised her eyes to meet Alix's, unsure what to think. What to say was even more of a puzzle.

'I delivered him,' Alix explained.

'Whose... ?' She did manage to get out the one word.

'My roommate told me to get rid of him. She said she planned to throw him in a Dumpster if I didn't take him. He needs a mother and a father – he needs someone who'll love him.'

This didn't seem real, didn't seem possible. The only thing Carol could think to do was cry out for her husband, but her voice was hardly a croak. Although she thought he couldn't have heard her, Doug came roaring out of the bedroom, bare-chested, wearing only his pajama bottoms.

'Hi,' Alix said, sounding so unlike herself that Carol glanced at her. 'I'm Alix. You let me up.'

'Alix brought us a baby,' Carol said, tears glistening in her eyes.

Doug looked from one to the other. Like her, he didn't seem to know how to react. But thankfully, he gathered his wits in record time. 'I think we'd better all sit down and talk about this.'

'It's legal,' Alix assured them. 'I got Laurel to write everything out on a piece of paper.' She dug into her pocket and passed the folded sheet to Doug. 'Laurel needs to go to the hospital and once she does the police will be notified, but I figured you could deal with that. Possession is nine-tenths of the law, isn't it? And you've got the baby now.'

'Maybe we should put on a pot of coffee,' Carol suggested. Her mind was spinning and it was difficult to grasp what was going on. All she knew was that she was standing here holding a newborn baby.

'I'll start the coffee,' Doug said. Carol nodded gratefully. She looked down at the sleeping infant and her heart contracted painfully. To think that his mother had been willing to toss him in a Dumpster like a piece of garbage! How anyone could even imagine such a thing was beyond her comprehension.

'He doesn't have any clothes,' Alix said. 'I washed him off and wrapped him in the blanket but I didn't have a diaper.'

'I'll dress him,' Carol said. This seemed more like a dream than reality. She carried him into the nursery, placing him on the dresser and carefully removing the blanket. With one hand on the infant, she reached down for a disposable diaper.

That very morning, in just a few hours, she was supposed to empty these drawers so the department store could take everything away. Thank God that hadn't happened yet! She gently cleaned his bottom and secured the diaper. The tiny T-shirt came next. When she'd finished, she bundled him in the thick, soft folds of a flannel receiving blanket.

He made a small mewling sound and she picked up a baby bottle, clean and sterilized, ready for formula. She dared not allow herself to think this was her child, her son. Alix had come to her for help and Carol was the logical person to contact.

'Exactly how old is he?' she asked when she returned to the living room.

Alix glanced at her wrist, but apparently hadn't remembered to put on her watch. 'About an hour.'

'How'd you get here?'

'Jordan. He dropped me off, and now he's on his way back to the apartment to take Laurel to the hospital.'

With Alix following her, Carol joined Doug in the kitchen, and they waited for the coffee to drip into the pot. 'He needs to be fed,' Carol announced as though she were an authority on the subject of newborns. Without asking, she handed the baby to Doug, then found a can of formula in one of the cupboards.

She filled the four-ounce bottle and set it inside the microwave just long enough to warm it. After shaking the formula on her wrist to test the temperature, she picked up the baby. He took immediately to the nipple, nestling in her arms as if ... as if she was his mother.

'Okay. Time to talk,' Doug said. He gestured Carol and Alix into the living room and carried in the coffee tray. Carol sat in the recliner, touching the baby's tiny wisps of hair. She almost burst into tears when the infant wrapped his hand around her little finger. He's *mine*, she wanted to cry out. She felt both a profound, soul-deep satisfaction – and greater fear than she'd ever experienced.

'I brought him into the world,' Alix said proudly. 'Laurel doesn't want him and I told her I knew someone who'd love him.' She paused, clearly waiting for Carol to respond.

'This *can't* be legal,' Doug said, answering for her, sounding uncertain and confused. 'I've never heard of anything like this...'

'You have the baby, don't you?' Alix said. 'He's yours now.'

'I know, but...'

'She signed a paper saying she didn't want him.' For the first time, Alix looked unsure of what she'd done. 'I thought *you'd* want him.'

'I do,' Carol cried. Doug had concerns and so did she, but this baby filled her arms, filled the emptiness inside her. God help her, she wasn't letting him go! She refused to give in to the fear that she might lose this child, too. 'Doug?' She turned to her husband, her eyes entreating him to do whatever was necessary.

Doug leaned forward, resting his elbows on his knees and his chin on his hands.

'Do you want this baby or not?' Carol demanded. 'Because I do. I'll take him, no questions asked. I'll love him, I'll raise him, but I need to know that you will, too.'

Her husband met her eyes, and Carol saw his apprehension. 'I don't know if we'll be able to keep him, Carol. Like I said, this *can't* be legal. A woman can't just give her baby to complete strangers.'

Carol didn't care what it cost, what sacrifices were required, she was willing to fight to make this child her own. Just when she'd given up all hope, a miracle had happened. She was going to accept that miracle, whatever it took.

'First thing we do is talk to an attorney.' It was

clear that Doug had reached a decision. 'As Alix said, with Laurel in the hospital, the police will be notified. We have to make it look like she intended for us to adopt him from the very beginning.'

Carol saw in him a resolve that made her want to weep with joy. 'We have a son,' she whispered through her tears.

'Not yet, we don't,' Doug said, 'but we will soon enough.' Taking charge now, he stood. 'Give me a few minutes to dress and make a couple of phone calls. Then, Alix, you're coming with me.'

He disappeared into the bedroom.

Carol put the baby bottle aside and held the infant against her shoulder. 'How can I thank you?' she said as she patted his back.

Alix pointed at the tray, which held the coffeepot and three mugs. 'I could really use a cup of that coffee. Do you mind if I help myself?'

'Of course ... sorry.'

'Do you want one?'

Carol shook her head as Alix poured a mug of coffee and added cream. 'I can't believe I didn't know,' she murmured. She took a sip of her coffee. 'About Laurel,' she said, obviously caught up in her own thoughts. 'It just never occurred to me that she could be pregnant.'

Carol's hand rubbed the infant's back protectively. With her he would be secure and loved and very much wanted.

'Laurel was overweight before, and then she just seemed to be getting fatter.'

'What about the father?'

'A used-car salesman. He rented XXX-rated

videos. I was never keen on him, but he was kind of good-looking, I guess.'

'And Laurel?'

Alix shrugged. 'She's all right, I guess. Just mixed up and angry at the world. I thought that once the baby was born she'd change her mind, but she didn't.'

Doug appeared then. 'To which hospital did your friend take the mother?'

'Swedish,' Alix told him. 'Do you still want me to come with you?'

Doug nodded. 'I called Larry,' he said, mentioning the name of a good family friend. Larry was an attorney who worked for the insurance company that employed Doug. 'He said I should go to the mother and call him from the hospital.'

'What should I do?' Carol wanted to know.

'For now, stay here. Look after the baby. I'll be back as soon as I can.'

'All right.' Carol didn't know how long she'd have the opportunity to nurture and guard this child, but she intended to treasure each moment.

Minutes later, Doug and Alix hurried out the door. Carol moved into the nursery, this room she'd decorated with such anticipation and care. Each item, each piece of furniture, had been an affirmation of hope and joy ... and had become a symbol of her pain.

Sinking down in the cushioned rocker, she cradled the sleeping infant and sang him a lullaby. His entry into the world had been abrupt and frightening, but he was safe now. And he'd always be safe if she and Doug could possibly arrange it.

Carol lost all track of time as she cradled the

baby, rocking gently back and forth. She might've been there an hour, possibly two. It didn't matter. The happiness that stole over her was complete.

The baby woke, cried huskily and after Carol had changed his diaper, she fed him a second bottle. He returned to sleep and she settled him in the crib, then stood over him, one hand pressed to his tiny back.

Doug came home shortly after eight but without Alix. When he found Carol in the nursery – the first place he looked – he stood beside her, his gaze on the sleeping baby. Then he drew Carol into his arms, and hugged her so close she could hardly breathe.

'What happened?' she asked.

His eyes were bright with unshed tears and his voice trembled. 'We have to take him to the hospital and have him checked out, but it looks like we have a son. Laurel was more than agreeable to letting us adopt him. She insisted to the authorities that it'd been her plan all along.'

Tears flooded her eyes as they clung to each other, weeping with happiness. *A baby.* A miracle of life, a gift that had come from the most unlikely of places at the most unbelievable of times.

She'd known from the first day she'd walked into the yarn store. The fact that they were knitting baby blankets had been a sign from God – and He had kept His promise.

CHAPTER 48

JACQUELINE DONOVAN
The Next Year

Jacqueline could hardly contain her excitement as she drove toward Paul and Tammie Lee's house. She'd been on a cruise with Reese for the last three weeks and was badly in need of what she called a 'grandbaby fix.' Little Amelia was almost walking now and Jacqueline considered her granddaughter the cutest, smartest baby in the entire universe. Not that she was biased or anything...

First she'd collect the requisite hugs and kisses from Amelia, and then her next stop would be Lydia's store. She'd found the loveliest yarn in a tiny shop in one of the Greek islands during their Mediterranean cruise, and she was eager to show it to her.

Tammie Lee was watering the flower beds and Amelia, balanced against her hip, waved her chubby arms at a passing butterfly when Jacqueline pulled into the driveway. The back seat was loaded with gifts she and Reese had purchased on their trip, but none of that was important just now. The sooner she held her granddaughter, the better.

'Amelia, Amelia, Grandma's home.' Jacqueline slid out of her car and held her arms open to her baby girl.

Amelia squealed with delight and reached for Jacqueline. It didn't matter that the child was teething and slobber ran freely down her chin and onto her designer bib. All Jacqueline cared about was holding this beautiful baby once again.

'Welcome home,' Tammie Lee said with a wide smile. She bent down to turn off the water and dragged the hose back to the side of the house. 'What time did you and Dad get in last night?'

'Late.' Had it been a decent hour, Jacqueline would've raced over to kiss Amelia goodnight, but Reese had convinced her everyone would be asleep.

'I'm still adjusting to the time change,' she said, hugging her daughter-in-law. The love she felt for Tammie Lee was genuine now. Jacqueline had gradually grown close to her. Tammie Lee's natural, unforced kindness, her generosity and willingness to assume the best, had transformed Jacqueline's rigid view of life, and in the process brought the entire family together. Her practical wisdom had opened Jacqueline's eyes to what she was doing to Reese and to herself. Without Tammie Lee, Jacqueline wondered how long her marriage could possibly have lasted.

'We missed you both something fierce,' Tammie Lee said, taking Amelia from Jacqueline as she led the way into the house. The nine-month-old was on a mission to explore every cupboard and corner she could find.

Tammie Lee headed into the kitchen, where she settled Amelia in her high chair and brought out a pitcher of iced tea and two glasses.

Amelia banged her fists against the tray and gurgled in apparent approval. From the beginning she'd been a happy, cheerful child, just like her mother. Jacqueline walked over to the cookie jar for a graham cracker and broke it into manageable chunks. Amelia immediately grabbed one, gleefully shoving it into her mouth and gumming it with such an expression of delight, it might have been the world's finest delicacy.

'It's so good to be home.' Jacqueline sighed as she accepted the glass of tea, complete with a sprig of mint.

'Sit down, and tell me all about exploring the Greek Isles,' Tammie Lee insisted. 'I declare, this is the most romantic trip I've ever heard of. I just hope Paul and I are as much in love thirty-three years down the road as you and Dad. It sounded just like a honeymoon.'

Her daughter-in-law was closer to the truth than she'd ever know. Jacqueline's marriage was vastly different since the night she'd confronted Reese about his Tuesday-night-mistress-who-wasn't. From that moment on, everything had changed for the better. The very next day he'd moved back into the master bedroom with her. Together they explored the delights of married love and gradually, over the next few months, they'd worked on rebuilding what they'd been so ready to destroy.

'I just hope Paul's as romantic as his father,' Jacqueline murmured, playing with Amelia. 'Oh, I swear she's grown so much these last three weeks.'

Accepting her right to be the center of attention, Amelia Jacqueline Donovan grinned a toothy radiant smile, her cheeks smeared with mushed-up graham cracker.

'You're such a cutie pie,' Jacqueline cooed. The love she felt for this child was unlike anything she'd ever experienced. Amelia and her mother had changed Jacqueline's life in ways she could never have predicted.

Thirty minutes later, Jacqueline had emptied the back seat of her car. She hugged Tammie Lee goodbye and covered Amelia's now-clean face with grandma kisses, then reluctantly drove off.

She went to A Good Yarn next. Luck was with her, and she slid into a vacant parking spot directly in front of the store. The Blossom Street renovation project was completed now. The brick apartment building where Alix had once lived had been turned into swanky, updated condominiums; they sold for prices that shocked even Jacqueline. Alix, however, liked her new home better, as well she should, seeing that she was living in the guest house formerly occupied by Martha, who had retired. Who would've believed when they first met that Alix would become as close as family?

'Jacqueline,' Lydia cried as the bell chimed above the door. 'Welcome back! How was the cruise?'

'Fabulous. Reese and I loved every minute of it.' She opened the shopping bag and pulled out a skein of the Greek yarn, a wool-cashmere blend in a soft shade of mauve with flecks of white. 'Look what I found.'

Lydia examined the yarn, weaving it between her fingers, then letting it run through her fingers. She handed it to Margaret. 'Feel this,' she said. 'It's incredible.'

'I bought enough to knit a sweater. I didn't have a clue how much I'd need, so I bought everything they had. You can have whatever I've got left over.'

After Margaret had exclaimed over the yarn, Lydia handled it again. 'Where did you ever find this?'

'On an island. I can't remember the name right now. Reese went with me from store to store in my search for yarn. His memory's better than mine – I'll ask him.'

'Reese helped you search for yarn?' Lydia shook her head laughingly. 'Most husbands would consider that above and beyond the call of duty.'

'We do everything together these days,' Jacqueline confessed and although she would've objected had anyone pointed it out, she blushed. This trip with Reese was the second honeymoon every couple should have at least once in their marriage.

'I don't think I've ever seen you–'

'Happier,' Jacqueline finished for her. She'd heard that over and over again from family and friends. She had no intention of denying it; she *was* happy.

'Actually, I was going to say you're looking tanned,' Lydia said with a mischievous smile.

Jacqueline extended both her arms. 'Oh, that. Reese had me out on every golf course in the Mediterranean.' She grinned. 'I've got a wicked slice if I do say so myself, and I'm a formidable putter.' She glanced at her watch. 'I've got to scoot. I'm meeting Reese at the country club in an hour –we're having drinks with some old friends. I need to run over to the house first.'

'It's so good to have you back,' Lydia said, hugging her. 'Will you be here on Friday?'

'Of course!' Jacqueline waved away her question as if the answer should be understood. 'I wouldn't miss it for the world.'

With that she was off, eager to join her husband – the man she loved.

CHAPTER 49

CAROL GIRARD

'Cameron Douglas Girard, what are you *doing?*'

Cameron gazed up from the carpet where he sat sorting through his daddy's sock drawer. The nine-month-old grinned up at her guilelessly as Carol stood with her hands on her hips, trying hard to look stern while struggling not to laugh. 'Come here,' she said, lifting her baby boy into her arms. Raising him high, she pressed her mouth against his bare belly and made a loud smooching noise. Cameron let out a squeal of pleasure. When she lowered him, he buried his face in her shoulder, gripping her hair with both hands, gurgling and chattering.

In this past year, Carol had learned about a whole new facet of love – about how much one person could love another and how much a mother could love her child. Cameron might not have come from her womb, but he was her son in every way that counted.

'It's time for our walk,' she told him.

Cameron knew what that meant and squirmed, wanting her to put him down. She did, quickly returning Doug's socks to the bottom drawer of their chest of drawers. Then she carried Cam to his room, where she dressed him in tiny jeans and a hand-knit sweater. The pants were a gift from her brother, who'd sent them, plus a matching jacket, shortly after the adoption was completed. Released again, Cameron crawled rapidly toward the stroller. Once he reached it, he pulled himself into a standing position, then looked over his shoulder to be sure she'd noticed his feat and appreciated his skill. Cameron loved their walks.

'We're visiting the yarn store this afternoon,' Carol told him as she buckled him in. 'We're going to see Miss Lydia.'

Draping her purse over her shoulder, Carol left the condo and pushed the stroller into the hallway and then into the waiting elevator. They took the same route almost every afternoon, stopping at a park two blocks from their building to chat with other young mothers.

Carol's circle of friends had broadened dramatically since she'd left work and Cameron had come into their lives. The other mothers she'd met at the park had formed a casual group, meeting once a week for coffee. They shared advice and experiences, traded parenting books and magazines, passed on toys and clothing their own children no longer needed. Carol was the oldest member of the group, but that had never bothered her.

After their park visit, Carol steered Cameron

into the yarn store. 'Carol,' Lydia called out cheerfully. 'Hello.' She squatted down so she was eye level with Cameron. 'You, too, Cam.'

The baby grabbed for a skein of bright purple yarn but Carol was too quick for him and automatically rolled the stroller backward and away from the tempting yarn.

'I need another ball of that Paton worsted.'

'The olive-green, right?' Lydia had an uncanny ability to remember who'd bought what yarn for which project. Carol had so many projects going now, it was hard to keep track of them all. Lydia, however, had no such difficulty.

'Jacqueline was by earlier this afternoon,' Lydia said.

'She's back?'

'With a gorgeous tan, too. She looks so happy,' Lydia said with a contented smile.

'That's great.'

'She'll be here Friday.'

'What about Alix?' The fourth member of their knitting group wasn't always available on Fridays. It had been hit-and-miss with her because of culinary school commitments.

Lydia shook her head. 'I don't think she'll be able to make it.'

Carol sighed. 'I miss her when she can't be here.'

'Me, too,' Lydia admitted. 'I remember what we thought when she first signed up for the class?'

'I was convinced Jacqueline and Alix would go for each other's throats within the first five minutes.' Carol laughed. 'They were impossible, always sniping at each other.'

'It was like third grade all over again.'

'You're telling me.' Carol marveled anew at how the relationship between those two had turned out.

'Jacqueline was ready to drop out more than once,' Lydia said, reminiscing.

Carol nodded. 'I understood why she wanted to, but I'm so grateful she didn't.'

'I am, too. And if Alix hadn't stayed...'

They could never have guessed how one defiant, angry young woman would influence all their lives.

'Do you ever hear from Laurel?' Lydia asked.

'Not a word. Not since the day Cameron was born. She went into court on her own, signed the paperwork and walked out the door without a word to either Doug or me.'

'What about Alix? They used to be roommates.'

'If she's heard from Laurel, she's never mentioned it to us.'

'What about Jordan?'

Carol sighed. 'I understand he hooked her up with a counselor and got her housing when the apartment building was sold.' The urge to take Cameron in her arms and hold him protectively against her was nearly overwhelming, but Carol resisted. 'She was a sad, confused young woman with a lot of problems.'

'But she did one thing right in her life, and that was to give you and Doug her son.'

'I wish her well,' Carol murmured, and she meant it.

At some point, years from now, Cameron might be curious about his birth parents; he might even want to search for them. That decision would be his, but for now, during these formative years, this baby boy was hers and Doug's. It was their love and their values that would shape him.

Lydia brought the yarn to the counter and rang it up. After Carol had paid for it, she tucked the plastic bag in the basket behind the stroller and headed for the door. 'I'll see you Friday afternoon.'

Lydia gave her a final wave and Carol wheeled the stroller down the sidewalk, past the florist and the café and toward the hill to the waterfront area and the condo.

She'd only been home a few minutes when Doug arrived. He kissed Carol, then reached down for Cameron, lifting him up and hugging him close. Carol was always profoundly moved when she saw her husband with his son. Cameron's face lit with joy at the sight of his daddy and he squealed and clapped his hands.

The moment was poignant and real. They'd waited so long for this. They'd suffered and sacrificed but none of that seemed important now. They had their son. They had their family. Carol closed her eyes, holding on to this moment, experiencing it as fully as possible.

Doug sat on the floor and played with Cameron and together father and son stacked blocks while Carol looked on, tears moistening her eyes. She knew that in the years to come, everything might not be as perfect as it was today. It didn't matter. She felt content and happy, and the emptiness that had nearly destroyed her was gone.

She was complete.

CHAPTER 50

ALIX TOWNSEND

Alix put the finishing touches on her crème brûlée and stepped back to give her instructor a chance to grade her work. Mr. Diamont moved forward and studied it with a discerning eye, then tapped the burnt sugar crust. He tasted the creamy custard beneath and nodded approvingly. He turned in her direction. 'Nice job, Alix. You may go.'

Alix stared at her teacher, certain that she hadn't heard him correctly. She didn't wait long, however, but removed her hat and apron and hurried out of the class. Praise from Diamont was as rare as discretionary cash.

Her budget was tight and would be for the next year of the two-year program. Alix had lived on far less. The lack of money didn't bother her because she was doing something she loved. Cooking. For years she'd dreamed of attending cooking school, but the tuition costs were as high as a college education. It would've continued to be far beyond her means if not for her friends Jacqueline and Reese Donovan.

Alix had met Reese shortly after Carol and Doug adopted Laurel's baby. Reese had lots of prominent friends; through his connections he was able to steer her toward a scholarship program offered by a local service club. And if that wasn't enough, Jacqueline had insisted Alix live in their guest house while she attended school. Their housekeeper had recently retired and now Alix had a house-cleaning job that supplied her with enough money to pay for her basic needs.

All of this seemed too good to believe. Every now and then, Alix had to pinch herself to prove this was real. To make sure it was happening to *her*, Alix Townsend.

Once she'd changed out of her uniform, Alix called Jordan's cell from the pay phone in the locker room.

'Hi,' she said when he answered.

'Finished for the day?' He seemed to have been waiting for her call.

'Mr. Diamont said I could go.'

'Already? You must've done all right.'

'I must have,' she said, biting her lip to keep from bragging. There'd be plenty of time for that when she was out of earshot of the other students.

'I wonder what it would take to bribe you into making crème brûlée for me,' he said playfully. 'It *is* my favorite dessert.'

'Oh, I don't know, but I'll bet I could think of something.'

'I'll bet you could, too. Should I pick you up?'

'If you want.' His days were busy, and it was a lot to ask of him. Normally she wouldn't phone but she'd been worried about this test and he'd asked her to let him know how she'd done. 'I can always take the bus,' she said now.

'I'm on my way.'

She waited outside the Seattle Cooking Academy for about ten minutes before Jordan's car approached. They'd been dating nearly a year now, and she'd grown accustomed to having him in her life – accustomed to a lot of things. He'd even managed to talk her into attending church on a regular basis. For the first time she felt like a normal person who lived a normal life with people around her who cared and wanted her to succeed. She figured Jordan was right. God hadn't given up on her.

Jordan parked at the curb, and leaned across the seat to open the passenger door. Alix slid inside and they kissed briefly. Jordan checked his rearview mirror, then merged with the traffic.

'I don't suppose you remember what today is?' he asked nonchalantly.

Alix wracked her brain but could think of nothing. 'Is May sixth supposed to have some significance?'

'It doesn't to you?' He tossed her a hurt-little-boy look.

'Apparently not.'

Jordan grinned and pretended to be absorbed by the flow of downtown Seattle traffic. 'That was the first day you flashed your baby blues at me at the video store.'

'My eyes are brown!'

'Whatever,' he said in the same flippant voice she'd so often used with him. 'You honestly don't remember? It was May sixth when I saw you standing outside the video store, smoking. I was minding my own business, going in to rent a video, when you interrupted me with some weak excuse.'

'I set aside a video for you.'

'You were making eyes at me.'

'Making eyes at you?' she snorted. 'You're dreaming.' She looked at him with mock scorn, but it pleased her beyond measure that he'd recalled such a minute detail of their relationship.

'So I figure today is something of an anniversary for us.'

'Us, is it?' she asked, loving every second of this banter between them.

'You are my girlfriend, aren't you?'

'And your chef.'

'That, too.'

She shrugged as if it was of little consequence. 'I guess.'

'In that case, you might want to check out the little box in my glove compartment.'

All at once it felt as if they were flying instead of driving. 'A box in the glove compartment for me?'

'Take a look.'

Her hand trembled as she opened the compartment. Sure enough, a small black jeweler's case with a bright red bow was nestled in among the owner's manual and the car registration papers. She pulled it out and held it in the palm of her hand.

'What's inside?' she asked. She couldn't help it; she sounded breathless.

'Go ahead and see,' Jordan said.

The banter was gone, and the car seemed to grow suddenly warm and airless.

When she didn't immediately comply, he prodded her. 'Well? What's holding you back?

Open the box!'

'It's a very pretty box.'

'Thank you, but what's inside is even prettier.' Alix removed the bow and then with exaggerated care lifted the lid. Inside was a lovely ring with a ruby and two small diamonds, one on either side.

'Jordan.' She said his name on a single lengthy breath. 'It's beautiful.'

'I thought so, too.'

'But ... why?'

'Didn't I just remind you it's been a year since we linked up?'

'Yes, I know, but...' If he made her cry Alix didn't think she'd forgive him.

'Try it on.'

She slipped it out and placed it on her finger. The fit was perfect.

'It's official now,' Jordan said.

'What is?'

'You and me.'

She wanted to tell him she didn't need a ring – however lovely – to prove that. But she only smiled.

'Next year for our anniversary,' he continued, 'after you've graduated from cooking school, I'd like to replace that with a diamond engagement ring. What would you think?'

The tears did come then. 'I think that'd be just fine,' she whispered. 'Now would you stop this car so I can show you how damn much I love you?'

'That,' said Jordan, 'can be arranged.'

CHAPTER 51

'To learn to knit you need beginner's hands and a beginner's mind. Knitting is a hobby. Breathe, relax and have fun.'
  –Donna Druchunas, SheeptoShawl.com

LYDIA HOFFMAN

It's hard to believe that A Good Yarn's been open for a year. I've decided to hold my first – and, I hope, annual – yarn sale. Margaret, who works part-time for me now, created the flyers and the signs. My sister has an artistic bent, although she's quick to deny it.

This has certainly been an eventful year. My business has prospered and I've achieved every goal I set for my first year, plus some. My class list has grown. My original three class members are still with me and we share a deep bond. We're friends. Our Friday afternoon sessions are an ongoing social event – with knitting. I'm holding other classes, too. My inventory doubled in the last twelve months and continues to grow, although space is becoming a problem. Brad has been wonderful and together with Matt, my brother-in-law, has constructed shelves to hold the newer yarns I've made available to my customers.

One morning this week, I was sitting at my desk, dealing with long-overdue paperwork. I glanced into the shop where Margaret was busy tending an early customer; just seeing her made me treasure my business all the more. I'm so grateful I took this giant step in faith. A Good Yarn is everything I dreamed it would be. I hardly think of it as coming to work because it's such a joy to do what I love and to be able to share my passion for knitting with others.

My father is the one I thank for giving me the courage to move forward with my life. His death taught me such valuable lessons. I suppose the irony is that his death taught me about life. I'd come to depend on him, but in this last year I've learned to draw upon the inner strength he instilled in me. I suppose it's fanciful to think he's smiling down on me, but I do.

That smile of my father's would include Margaret. My sister and I have come a long way in repairing our relationship. We've grown steadily closer, first as sisters and then as friends. A year ago, if anyone had told me that my sister and I would be working side by side in my yarn store, I would've keeled over in a dead faint. Margaret and me – oh, hardly. And yet that's exactly what we're doing.

Margaret started filling in for me while I was going through my most recent scare with cancer last year. Dr. Wilson wasn't giving the cancer a chance to recur, and while the treatment wasn't as aggressive as the chemotherapy and radiation I'd endured in the past, it was aggressive enough. It was often necessary for me to take a day off, so Margaret, with her limited experience, helped me out. How grateful I am to my sister. She was more familiar with crocheting than knitting when she started, but in recent months, she's mastered knitting, too. Now she's as much a part of the store as I am, and the customers have warmed to her. Margaret will never be a spontaneous sort of person, but she's excellent at sales and I'm proud to have her as an employee. Mom is pleased with our new relationship, too.

Perhaps the biggest change in my life, however, is Brad and Cody. We're together as much as our schedules will allow, and I've fallen deeply in love with this special man and with his son.

'The flyers are back from the printer,' Margaret said, stepping into my tiny office and interrupting my thoughts. 'When would you like me to get them to the mailing service?'

I looked up from my desk. 'Today if possible.'

She nodded. 'I can do that.'

'Thanks.' I wanted her to know how much I appreciated everything she did for me. 'I owe you so much, Margaret.'

She shook off my praise, as I knew she would. My gratitude seemed to embarrass her. 'Are you sure you're up to the Mariners game tonight?' At times, although they were increasingly rare, Margaret fell into that protective older-sister mode.

'I'm perfectly fine,' I said, letting her know I was capable of judging my own limits. In any case, I had no intention of disappointing Brad and Cody. We'd had tickets for this game against the San Diego Padres for weeks.

'Good.'

'What about you, Matt, Mom and the girls? You'll be there, too, won't you?'

'Of course!' Margaret's eyes widened. 'We wouldn't miss it for anything.'

'As long as you're up to it,' I teased.

She ignored that and craned her neck to look out the front windows. 'Our favorite UPS delivery man just pulled up.'

Five minutes later, Brad entered the shop, whistling as he rolled in the stack of boxes, filled with my latest shipment of yarn.

'Mornin', Margaret,' he said as he handed her the clipboard.

My sister signed her name and Brad came to the back to see me.

'Hey, beautiful.'

I always blush when Brad talks to me like that. I don't think I'll ever get used to his love. I'm the luckiest woman alive. Brad and I have talked about marriage, but I'm the one dragging my feet. I had to be sure first – not about loving him, because I do. No, I had to be sure about the cancer. I'm safe for now, and the future's like a blank page waiting for a story to be written on it. Or a ball of yarn waiting to be knit...

I love Brad and Cody. I've worked hard to establish a good relationship with Brad's son. His mother and I have talked a number of times; she loves her son, but she's concentrating on her own needs just now. The funny part is, she seems grateful to me for stepping in.

Still, life doesn't hold any guarantees. Brad and I have talked about this often, and I'm ready to accept his proposal. I know that's what I want.

Brad tucked his arms around my waist. 'You're looking mighty kissable this morning.'

I smiled and kissed him, letting my mouth linger on his. I didn't often let our kisses get this involved, especially during business hours. Yet there are moments when it's easy to forget where we are.

'To what do I owe this?' he asked in a husky whisper close to my ear.

'It's just because I love you,' I told him.

'I love you, too.'

I gave his backside a friendly pat. 'See you tonight – and don't forget, you're buying the hot dogs and peanuts.'

'You got it, sweetheart.'

He left the shop and I stood next to Margaret as I watched him walk away. 'He's one of the good guys,' my sister said.

'Yes, I know.'

'Are you going to marry him?'

I eyed Margaret, wondering what she'd say when she learned I'd made my decision. 'Yes.'

She gave me a wide smile. 'It's about time.'

'Yup, I figure it is. I love him. And you know what the real bonus is? Brad and I can laugh together.'

My sister was still grinning. 'Life sure has a way of keeping you in stitches.'

I don't think she meant the pun, but I couldn't help agreeing.

This Large Print Book for the partially sighted, who cannot read normal print, is published under the auspices of

THE ULVERSCROFT FOUNDATION